TENTION BOOKS

Possessed by Death

John Dolan hails from a small town in the North-East of England. Before turning to writing, his career encompassed law and finance. He has run businesses in Europe, South and Central America, Africa and Asia. John is the author of the *Time, Blood and Karma* and *Children of Karma* series.

He and his wife Fiona divide their time between Thailand and the UK.

CU00684665

Also by John Dolan

The *Time Blood and Karma* series

Everyone Burns

Hungry Ghosts

A Poison Tree

Running on Emptiness

The *Children of Karma* trilogy

Restless Earth

Two Rivers, One Stream

Everyone Dies

Fun with Dick

Adventures in Mythopoeia

Land of Red Mist

The Otford English Dictionary

POSSESSED BY DEATH

by

John Dolan

TENTION BOOKS

POSSESSED BY DEATH published by Tention Publishing Limited

Paperback Edition

Copyright John David Dolan 2023

John David Dolan has asserted his right under the Copyright, Designs and Patents Act 1988 to be identified as the author of this work

Tention Publishing Limited Reg. No. 8098036
Unit 45 St Andrews Wharf, 12 Shad Thames,
London SE1 2YN,
United Kingdom

ISBN 978-1-912361-19-9

"Death is a very dull, dreary affair, and my advice to you is to have nothing whatsoever to do with it."

—William Somerset Maugham

I

A Jigsaw Puzzle with Two Pieces

Devesh Banerjee could easily be mistaken for Marilyn Monroe if Marilyn had been male, in her late sixties, bald, brown-skinned, morbidly obese and missing the lower half of her body.

As it is, the torso on the mortuary slab is that of a Bengali dentist of grumpy temperament and solitary habits. In life, among his less-endearing features was a predilection for verbally abusing the homeless and an ironic intolerance of immigrants; but perhaps in death he is somewhat more forgiving. Though that seems unlikely.

"Where's the rest of him?" I ask.

DCI Zachary shrugs her shoulders.

"We haven't found the pelvis and legs yet. The pathologist thinks they were cut off by a chain-saw. This is definitely Mr. Banerjee, though, Mr. Braddock, isn't it?"

"Yes, that's him. But if his other half turns up, I won't be able to identify it from the feet and genitalia. He was a neighbour but we weren't *that* close."

The expression on her face tells me that she doesn't appreciate my flippancy.

"It would be helpful if you would sign a statement that the body you have seen is that of Mr. Banerjee," she says through clenched teeth.

"Of course," I reply. "Provided the wording says I've only seen *some* of the body. You know how nit-picking lawyers can be about that sort of thing. And maybe you could rustle me up a cup of tea while that's getting sorted?"

"I'll be happy to."

She doesn't look happy.

* * * * *

Zachary and I go back a long way. Or so it feels. She was only a DI the first time I met her, but since then the Metropolitan Police have seen fit to promote her despite their legendary misogyny and the resultant systemic bias against officers without testicles. On that basis, she must either be doing something right or have some serious dirt on the Commissioner.

It's fair to say that the Braddock family has been something of a thorn in Zachary's side over the years. Me most of all. I imagine her heart sinking when one of her juniors told her that Banerjee's next-door neighbour, a certain David Braddock, was the only person who could be dredged up for formal corpse identification.

It transpires that our partially-chilled orthodontist has no living relatives and no close friends – unsurprising given his personality. Why anyone would have been willing to let him loose in their mouth with a drill is beyond me, but I digress. His tax accountant and lawyer declared themselves 'unqualified' (whatever that means) to view the body. His business partner at the surgery is away in the Philippines attending an extended family funeral, and his young, newly-hired receptionist had baulked at the notion of setting foot in a morgue. Moreover, her predecessor has inconveniently emigrated to Canada.

So, short of issuing extradition papers or ringing up some of the clinic's customers to try and lure them in with promises of having their speeding tickets cancelled, that left the Met with me: the guy who exchanged bland words with Devesh Banerjee when we put our bins out.

Zachary and I are sitting at a plastic table in a bare, whitewashed room drinking stewed tea from Styrofoam cups. I've signed the statement and she is waiting impatiently for me to leave. It is uncommon for someone as senior as her to attend an identification, but I assume she is there because she knows my history of causing trouble and doesn't want her murder investigation messed up.

"So, I understand from one of your colleagues that our friend's body was the one discovered outside Highgate Cemetery. I saw the news report on TV," I say cheerily to break the silence.

"Yes. Though he had no business telling you that," Zachary replies tersely. "I suppose you prised that out of him in return for your cooperation."

"Something like that. I'm the curious type as you know."

She doesn't comment on this.

"Highgate is where his dental practice is," I continue. "He used to drive there and back every day in his shiny black BMW. I remember his rants about the traffic."

"Uh-huh."

"I gather that his office and surgery were ransacked."

"My officer seems to have been very accommodating in supplying you with information. I shall have a quiet word with him about that."

"But neither your officer nor any of the news reports mentioned that the corpse had been dismembered. Though they did say that the body was found inside a rubbish bag."

"The media can be discreet sometimes when we ask them to be. And I should be grateful if you wouldn't mention it to anyone either. It might hinder our investigation."

"All right."

"Thank you," she says coldly.

"Was it a black rubbish sack or a green one?"

Zachary raises her eyebrows.

"What difference does that make?"

I wrinkle my nose.

"Well, it might indicate whether the killer had a conscience about environmental matters. Perhaps he wanted Banerjee to be recycled."

The DCI sighs and looks at her watch.

"Do you have a suspect yet?" I persist.

"I can't discuss that."

"Not even with an old friend?"

"Not with anyone outside my team."

"And I suppose there's no point in my asking you – as a concerned citizen – exactly *when* you think he was killed."

"No, there isn't. Have you finished your tea?"

"Almost. Hey, you should give me one of your business cards."

"Why? You've already spoken to my talkative colleague and he told me you were unable to give him any information that might be useful to the case. You've got *his* card if you remember anything relevant."

"So, you don't want me to have one of your cards?"

Zachary reaches into her bag and puts a card on the table. She can't be bothered to argue.

"Don't call me unless it's something really urgent," she warns.

I pick it up and read the details.

"You know, I haven't congratulated you on your promotion."

"Thanks."

"And no wedding ring on your finger yet, I notice."

She points at my cup.

"Are you done?"

"We should maybe get together sometime for a glass of wine when you're off-duty. Just the two of us. We could catch up on old times."

"No," she says.

* * * * *

I am duly turfed out onto the London streets.

It's cloudy and cold, but dry. It's also Monday, my least favourite day of the week. Monday the seventh of November, to be precise.

Bonfire Night, with its usual flashes, whooshes, bangs, over-enthusiastic idiocies and multiple burns victims, has come and gone. The effigies of Guy Fawkes have all been consigned to the flames. This seems to me a harsh judgement on the last honest man to set foot on the grounds of Parliament, but hey ho.

And a week before that, we'd again suffered that most appalling of US imports: Halloween. Now celebrated by feral, scrounging children all over the United Kingdom. Except, one presumes, in Slough where every day is the Day of the Dead and therefore no specific festivities are required on the thirty-first of October.

Capitalism, however, doesn't sleep.

The West End streets and shops are aglow with Christmas decorations, and have been for weeks. Santa Claus' elves are busy working their little fingers to the bone on minimum wages to provide the brats of the planet with more things they don't need and will have broken within hours.

Then there'll be the Boxing Day hangover to look forward to, and the anticlimactic arrival of 2017... The roll-call of pleasure goes on and on.

And every day the city appears to me to grow darker.

It's not just that the winter nights are drawing in. It's more that, since I returned to live permanently in the land of my ancestors, I miss the brightness of Thailand with its endless merry-go-round of sun, sand, sex, corruption, murder and Chang beer. And having a Thai wife doesn't do enough to insulate me from the gloom, shabbiness and class obsession of Little Britain. Especially as Da prefers Western food these days and, like my (also Thai) stepmother Nang, likes to read the *Daily Fail*.

Those who have never left the UK for any length of time tend to see the country of their birth through rose-tinted spectacles. "It's still the best place in the world to live," they announce proudly.

This attitude is most toxically entrenched in London taxi drivers; though they are happy to follow up this declaration of loyalty with a litany of all the things that are wrong with the country. They will then go on about how it was better 'in their day' when you could buy a property in Mayfair for a tenner. This is one of the reasons that I usually travel on the Underground. The other reasons being the hideous traffic and the extortionate cost of a ride in a black cab.

I take stock of my whereabouts and wonder whether I should do some early Christmas shopping. But the thought that I have nothing more important or entertaining to do than wander around the stores a full six-and-a-half weeks before Jesus' birthday depresses me. As does the sight of London's walking dead who move around me.

Coated and muffled against the cold, their eyes down, their lips fixed in a thin line of customary grimness, they clutch mobile phones and briefcases or designer bags; striding confidently or gliding gingerly over the capital's pavements, while some looping internal dialogue plays in their heads. I'm generalising, but not much. The ostracised beggars asking for change and waving their Starbucks cups seem jolly by comparison. Plus, most of them are indefatigably polite – even the ones without shoes.

I hand over a couple of quid to a bearded man with a dog and a cardboard sign which says he is trying to raise the money to stay in a hostel tonight. He wears a red hat and blesses me. The dog doesn't say anything.

The satisfying high that I achieved by winding-up DCI Zachary has faded. It appears I must go home and peel some vegetables for dinner.

I make my way to the nearest Tube station, and descend into the Underworld.

II

The Pull of History
and the Happily-Ever-After

Tuesday morning finds me in my study which doubles as my consulting room whenever I have a hypnotherapy client. As I do today.

My practice can best be described as a part-time hobby which I do my utmost to conduct in a thoroughly unprofessional manner.

It is a throwback to my Thailand years on Koh Samui running the *David Braddock Agency*, where I used to do a spot of therapy on the side to supplement my earnings as a private investigator. My PI work I left behind when I sold the business to an annoyingly cheerful Austrian by the name of Braun (who, incidentally, is a *proper* psychiatrist with certificates and so on). But my therapy practice somehow followed me back to England like a stray dog. And this despite the fact that I have no vocational qualifications whatsoever and an eye-watering lack of empathy for the suffering of humanity.

Perhaps that's what gives my practice its unique competitive edge: people don't want to be understood. They simply want the experience of being in a room with a complete stranger who won't either judge them or stab them; and who will reassure them that they're not insane or afflicted with demonic possession.

While my business cards describe me as a hypnotherapist, in fact hypnosis per se plays no part in the majority of my sessions. That is just as well, as I'm not good at putting folks into a trance state without getting them to first swallow recreational drugs. My typical chargeable hour, therefore, consists mostly of either trying to persuade the punter to talk or of telling them to shut up.

Sometimes I have plenty of clients and sometimes I have only a few. I am currently experiencing one of my fallow periods – though it is remarkable that anyone comes through my door at all given that I do hardly any advertising. The business generally arrives via a word-of-mouth recommendation.

I guess on that basis I must be doing something right.

The odds are around 50-50 (I estimate) as to whether the client I'm seeing today will count among my successes. The difficulty is that he wants *sympathy*, which is not one of my key skills. And anyway, that's not what he needs. He needs a solution. Therefore, I need to persuade him that he requires something else. And I also have to work out what that something else is. But slowly, and believably, and in an ethical way. Because I rather like the chap.

The man sitting facing me is Ben Quinlan. He is forty-three years old and heads up a successful company which specialises in the decorating and fitting-out of retail spaces. He also owns a pizza franchise and four buy-to-let apartments. He is not, therefore, short of a bob or two.

What he is short of, is a wife. He and his good lady separated about fifteen months ago. She insists she is not in any kind of romantic or sexual relationship with another man, and that she simply needs time to herself. They have no children, and Quinlan has told me repeatedly that she makes no demands on him for cash as she has money of her own. She does not want a divorce, but there has been no indication that she wants to go back to him either.

This unresolved situation is causing him such a degree of anxiety, that his GP has prescribed him medication. To date, this has been only partially effective. Being the boss of multiple businesses, Quinlan doesn't want any of his employees or associates to be aware of his mental distress, and therefore he is obliged to conceal his condition while he is at work. He also doesn't want to burden his friends with his concerns.

All of which means that in recent months he has been like a pressure-cooker holding everything in.

He's been seeing me once a week for the last four weeks. The talking helps him, he says, though any alleviation of his condition is temporary.

Thus far I've been – for me – uncharacteristically restrained. For instance, I haven't put on the table the possibility that his wife might be engaged in a romantic *lesbian* relationship but doesn't know how to break it to him. Or that she is fed up with hearing about shop-fittings and pizza, and feels the need for conversation on more spiritual matters. Or that she is a sadist who gets an erotic frisson from his stress.

My candid view is that what he requires is not a therapist but rather the services of a private detective to find out what's really going on with Mrs. Quinlan. Never mind about his or her mental processes, what's she up to? And I know just the PI who could do the job for him: me.

But that's not going to happen.

I've quit sniffing around in rubbish bins, snapping photos from dark doorways, and sitting in a car all night on stakeouts. Plus, almost getting killed on occasion. I promised Da that we would leave our *Agency* days behind us when we relocated to England; and thus far I've made good on that promise – although I have noticed that I do have a tendency to conduct some of my therapy sessions as if I'm questioning a suspect.

I become aware that my client has stopped talking, and conscious of the fact that I haven't been listening to what he has been saying for the last few minutes. Once he starts rabbiting, Quinlan does go over and over the same old ground, so I've found I can usually switch off for a while and think about other things. Like today, for instance, I've been musing on the subject of Devesh Banerjee's murder and what I would do if I were DCI Zachary.

"Please continue, Ben," I say.

"But I've finished," he replies.

I tilt my head.

"Are you sure of that? Because I don't think you have."

(This is my stock-response, by the way, for any occasion when I haven't been paying attention. It usually works. Except it's ineffective on Da and my stepmother: they've known me too long.)

Quinlan pinches his nose and squeezes his eyes closed. When he opens them again, I notice how blood-shot they are.

"I'm hardly sleeping, David. When I do drift off, I wake up after an hour or two. Then the whole cycle restarts. I do have some sleeping pills, but I've been reluctant to take them."

"But you're still keeping up with your anxiety medication?"

"Yes. As I said, at first it helped me to sleep as it used to make me drowsy, but that effect seems to have worn off. I tend to alternate between manic highs – when I can keep a perspective on things – and zombie-like lows. It's becoming harder to appear 'normal' at work."

"Ben, have you considered taking a holiday? Even a mini-break. Surely your businesses can spare you for a few days? If you're not having even a minimal amount of rest, you'll pretty soon become unable to cope."

"Mnnn."

"You need to get this situation with Kirsten into perspective. Nobody's died. Nobody's shouting at anybody. Nobody's killing anybody. You're dealing with a period of uncertainty, but that's all. I'm not trying to trivialise your pain in any way, but worse things happen at sea, Ben."

I have a momentary dread that he will break down and tell me how much he loves his wife, how he can't live without her, how she is his soul mate… and all the rest of that stuff. He did that in our second session and it was hard to listen to. I almost had to slap him; which would probably have made both of us feel better.

Fortunately, today he's being more stoic. I don't have to go into my speech about how much worse life is for a starving African child caught in a civil war.

"You know, David," he says, "what I like about you is that you're a good listener. But also, you don't mollycoddle me."

I'm tempted to tell him that he's wrong on both counts. But I don't. As I said before, I rather like the guy.

"I will think about what you've said."

Which is basically the same thing as I've said in all his previous sessions. But it is taking a while to register.

"That's our time up, I'm afraid," I announce. "Same time next week?"

"Same time next week. And thank you."

For what? I am tempted to ask, but don't.

He at least manages to fill up some of my Tuesdays. And if I wasn't spending time with him and my other crazies (to use a medical term), I'd likely be seeing a shrink myself.

* * * * *

I've barely got Quinlan out of the front door when my phone rings.

The number on the display is not one I recognise, so I answer with caution.

The caller is one Kenneth Reid, and he asks if he might drop by to see me as he is in the area.

"Are you looking for a therapist?" I ask.

He says he is, though not for himself, but he'd rather discuss that in person. I confirm my address, and he says he'll be straight over.

My intended saxophone practice is put on hold.

* * * * *

Kenneth Reid is an elderly gentleman with a weather-beaten complexion and slicked back silver-grey hair. His attire is rather old-fashioned with a vaguely colonial air to it. He carries a cane, although that appears to be an affectation as there is nothing wrong with his gait.

I invite him into our living room and we sit down.

He pulls out a handkerchief and blows his nose robustly.

"When I was researching therapists around here, I came across your name and it jumped off the screen at me," he says.

"Oh?"

"I don't suppose by any chance that you're related to the Edward Braddock who used to be a rubber planter in Malaya? I assume he must be long-retired by now."

"I'm his son. And he's very much retired. So much so that he's been dead for seven years."

Reid looks discomfited.

"Ah, my commiserations, Mr. Braddock. You see, my father was also a rubber planter. Our estate was purchased by your great-uncle Sebastian; and I had the pleasure of meeting your father on a few occasions. I don't suppose he mentioned me?"

"I don't recall us ever having a conversation about you, but he did mention a Ken Reid in his memoir on Malaya."

"Yes, that would have been me. I don't suppose he gave a terribly flattering view of my personality."

Reid flashes me a wry smile, but I make no comment.

"Well, I was a bit of a rogue and a spendthrift in those days. After I left Malaya, I went off to Indonesia and got into some bother in Bali which taught me a few hard lessons, I can tell you. But we won't go into all that.

"Anyway, your father and I bumped into each other in a London gentleman's club years later, and we re-kindled our acquaintance. I'd like to think he regarded me more favourably thereafter. I'd grown up a lot in the meantime, you see. Accepted my responsibilities and so on. Then we lost touch again – as often happens – but I'm sorry to hear of his passing. He was a good man."

"He was certainly a character," I respond noncommittally.

"So, when the name 'Braddock' came up on my search, it felt like an aspect of my past reaching out to me again. Serendipitous, one might say: a happy coincidence. Or Fate, if you're of a religious persuasion. Which, I hasten to add, I'm not."

"You picked me off a list of therapists because of my surname?"

"Yes. Call it an old man's fancy."

I don't want to be drawn into a discussion about the merits and demerits of my late father, so I decide to move the conversation along.

I ask him why he considers he needs the services of a therapist.

"As I mentioned on the phone, it's not for me. It's for my granddaughter Anneke. Anneke Reid. She's my son's girl."

"Then, why isn't your son here?"

The old boy wriggles uneasily.

"Anneke and her parents aren't getting along at the moment. But she and I have a connection, and it's possible that I might be able to persuade her to come and see you. Particularly if I explain that your planter father was a friend of mine. She always enjoyed my stories of Malaya when she was little."

"And what age is she now?"

"Seventeen."

I hold up a hand.

"Mr. Reid," I say, "I'm sorry, but I make it a policy of not seeing children in my practice. I'm not trained in pediatrics, and the teenage girl is a species that I prefer to avoid. Plus, my treatment methods might be a bit too maverick for a young, impressionable mind. So, my cut-off is eighteen. Minimum."

"*Maverick*, eh?" Reid muses. "That sounds like just the thing for Anneke. She finds most adults uptight and sanctimonious. At least you'd give it to her straight."

"Is she as foul as most teenage girls?"

"Absolutely."

"You're not exactly selling her as an appealing prospect."

"She'll be eighteen in a few months."

"Well, maybe I could see her after that."

Reid shakes his head.

"That could be too late. She might have burned down her parents' house by then."

"Why? Is she into arson?"

"No, she hasn't moved onto that yet. At present, it's primarily heavy metal music, shoplifting and boys. Well, men, actually."

"Ah. Then, a female therapist will definitely be more suitable for her. Frankly, Mr. Reid, I have quite enough problems in my life without having a schoolgirl come onto me in my own house."

The old man studies me for a moment or two before saying, "I read in your advertising material that you used to be a private detective, Mr. Braddock."

"Yes. My wife thought it might make me sound like I had a suitably broad range of life experiences. She said that my CV sounded boring otherwise. But I don't do that anymore."

"Do you miss it? The investigative work, I mean."

"On occasion."

"Because it strikes me that my granddaughter is more of a project for a detective than a therapist. The Mystery of Anneke Reid. Why she does what she does. Why she thinks the way she thinks. You could treat the assignment as if it were a case."

I can't help but laugh at this. The old boy has some charm and a certain way in the art of persuasion.

"Are you throwing out some different bait to see if the fish bites on it, Mr. Reid?"

"Possibly," he grins.

"And do you believe that – regardless of my policy on teenagers – you've found a weak spot in my professional armour? That I might prefer being a PI to being a therapist?"

"I don't know. Do you?"

I sense the quicksand of my past sucking at my feet.

First, Reid mentions his association with my estranged and no-longer-living father, then he raises the spectre of Braddock the Sleuthhound. It is almost as if the old bugger can sense the ripples of ennui and nostalgia rippling around in my brain. Ripples, I might add, that have gathered in strength since seeing half of Devesh Banerjee on a mortuary slab.

It all feels like some dastardly karmic trap.

What's next? Am I going to start seeing the ghost of my dead first wife again?

But this is one of those situations where I have to be sensible and grown-up, and set all jesting aside. I might have a lot of time on my hands at present, but am I so desperate for something interesting to do that I need to spend my hours in the company of a delinquent teenager with raging hormones? And a female to boot? The answer is obviously *no*. I must therefore reject Reid's lure.

Plus, if I don't, Da will tell me that I am an idiot.

* * * * *

"You are an idiot, David," says Da.

It's evening, and we're preparing dinner.

My stepson Pratcha is in his room playing video games, and my daughter Jenny is in her room doing her homework. That pretty much summarises the difference between them. Pratcha is eleven and Jenny is sixteen, though she has the thought processes and maturity of a forty-year-old.

"Whatever possessed you to accept a disturbed seventeen-year-old girl as a client? Especially one who sounds like she has Daddy issues. I suppose I shall have to book time off work and stay home while you're seeing her. Otherwise, who knows what chaos she'll cause."

"Ken Reid is an old friend of my father," I say sheepishly. "And he was very persuasive."

"When is this – what's her name? Anneke?"

"Yes."

"When is she booked in for?"

"Tomorrow. Two o'clock."

"Shouldn't she be at school at that time?"

"Apparently, she's currently suspended from school. Something about daubing messages on her classroom walls."

"What sort of messages?"

"Her grandfather didn't say."

"Then, I'd better take a couple of hours off. I'll reschedule some of my appointments."

"That's not necessary, Da. I'll ask Ken Reid to stay around. I'll rig up the sound system so that he can listen in on us from the living room."

"All right, if you're sure," she says reluctantly. "Tomorrow *is* rather busy for me. I have an important showing in Kensington. Now, you check on Pratcha. Make sure he *really* doesn't have any more homework. I'll finish making dinner and call you all when it's ready."

Da, I should explain, has a senior role in a local estate agency which specialises in selling expensive homes to well-heeled foreigners, mainly Asian. The fact that she is efficient, personable (when she wants to be), Thai, and speaks excellent English and passable Chinese and Japanese, makes her a valuable asset to the company.

My wife also defies the stereotype of the Thai woman looking for a Western husband to supply all her needs. She is fiercely independent and likes earning her own money. Furthermore, she resists our dipping unnecessarily into the substantial savings and investments we have courtesy of legacies from my Aunt Jeanne and Braddock Senior; and insists that we say nothing to the children of our financial status. *It will make them lazy if they think money will fall from the trees for them*, she has declared on numerous occasions.

And because we live in an expensive part of Notting Hill, she has told both Pratcha and Jenny that we have an enormous mortgage and that is the only reason we can afford to live in this house. Which is a bare-faced lie. And so that the kids don't take me for a slacker, she has informed them that I spend my weekdays trading stocks and shares on the Internet; and that my hypnotherapy practice is my way of 'giving back' to the community. Which is another bare-faced lie. But it does demonstrate a certain creativity and attention to detail on her part.

I believe Da has become more assertive in recent years. She was always forthright in her opinions when we worked together at the *David Braddock Agency*, and moving to England hasn't made her any more bending. Quite the opposite. Though that doesn't stop me from thinking the world of her.

It is therefore a source of considerable frustration to my wife that she is finding it increasingly difficult to stamp her authority on young Pratcha. There are signs that an early rebellion against parental control might be brewing, and his mother is concerned that he might be *lazy*. Which to someone with Da's work ethic is more shameful than having a serial killer for a son.

I trudge upstairs to Pratcha's bedroom and knock on his door. There is no reply, but that usually means he is wearing his headphones and not that he is being unduly stroppy.

I open the door and sure enough there he is, cross-legged on the floor, his fingers and thumbs punching away on the buttons of his controller, his eyes fixed on the flashes and darting figures on the screen in front of him.

He spots me hovering, puts his game on hold, and pulls off his headphones.

"Hello, Papa David," he says.

"What are you up to?"

"It's kind of like a history lesson."

"Playing a video game is like a history lesson?"

"It is when it's a *classic* game like this one."

I squint at Pratcha's screen. Muscly, shabbily-dressed men with hateful expressions on their faces are caught in freeze-frame hacking and stabbing innocent passers-by with a variety of nasty weapons. In the background, some of their colleagues appear to be dragging away their bloodstained victims for purposes I can only guess at.

"Is that Piccadilly Circus?" I ask.

"Yes. The LOLs have just emerged from the Tube station. They can come up from several Tubes all over the city. They spend most of their time underground, you see."

"I bet they do. What did you call them? 'LOLs'?"

"Short for 'Members of the League of Loki.'"

He passes me a small booklet. On the front of it is a large red circle with a white centre, and burned on the white are the letters LOL in black. They have been designed to look a bit like a swastika.

"And what's the purpose of the game?"

"You take on the role of a LOL avatar and try to kill as many surface dwellers as you can in a limited time. Depending how well you do in the killing tables, you can move up the chain of command until you control multiple groups of LOLs. The game is not restricted to London, either. There's New York and Tokyo as well…"

"I get the picture. You destabilise the planet one city at a time, and end up with a body count which rivals that of Hitler, Stalin and Mao Zedong."

Pratcha beams.

"See, I told you it was like having a history lesson. The great genocides of the twentieth-century in one package. And, by the way, Papa David, you forgot to mention Pol Pot."

I read the blurb on the back of the booklet. It purports to describe a game which will "educate people on the forthcoming worldwide uprisings of the downtrodden underclasses." All of which sounds praiseworthy (if a trifle grandiose), until you consider what actually goes on in the game. Carnage, basically. LOL seems a highly inappropriate title for what is a teaching aid for mass slaughter. A hazy memory stirs.

"I think I recall some fuss around this game coming out. It's fairly old, isn't it? Wasn't that about ten or more years ago? And I thought it had been banned because of its ultra-violent content."

"Not *banned*," my stepson tells me patiently. "It was withdrawn by the company that made it, *Cali-X Dreaming*. They were game-making legends, those guys. But they went bust. So, it's hard to find a decent copy these days. I figured I'd have to go on the dark web, but I was lucky enough to get a copy off eBay."

"And what do you know about the dark web, may I ask?"

Pratcha sighs.

"I know it's mainly used for criminal communications, pornography and conspiracy theories. But it can be useful sometimes."

"So, you can get on there?"

"Of course. Everybody can."

"Well, your mother and I can't. And she wants to know if you've got any homework to do."

"I've done it."

"Honestly?"

"Honestly. Mama seems to think that I should have the same amount of homework as Jenny. But she forgets that Jenny's five years older than me."

"Exactly. You're way too young to be playing a video game like *The League of Loki*, especially on a school-night. Now switch it off. Dinner will be ready soon."

"Oh, all right," he replies.

"And, don't worry, I'm not going to confiscate it. Not unless you start carrying a sharpened knife around. Just – be discreet. And don't let your mother see that booklet."

I leave him to mull over the causes of violence in today's society. Which he won't.

I knock on Jenny's door.

"Enter," she says, sounding like a headmistress greeting a recalcitrant child who has been summoned to her office.

As expected, my daughter is seated at her desk, working. A pile of papers sits by her left hand. Her flame-red hair is tied back and her pale skin appears even more delicate in the screen-glow of her laptop. She is the image of her mother, whom I met when she was not much older than Jenny is now.

Jenny is not the daughter of my now-deceased first wife Claire. She is the daughter of her sister Anna. And me. A family scandal was averted by Anna keeping this fact secret – even from me – until shortly before her own death.

When Da and I relocated to England, we adopted Jenny, but my second wife advised that the child not be informed of who her real father was until she attained the age of sixteen.

That birthday was a few months ago, and after a few difficult weeks the close relationship we had enjoyed up to that point was restored. This is largely thanks to Jenny's maturity, and the fact that for the last two years she has anyway been calling me *Dad* rather than *Uncle David*.

Katie, my other (and somewhat older) daughter by Claire was informed of my more personal role in Jenny's existence while I was still living in Thailand. Her reaction to the news was understandably emotional, but she has come to terms with it. Fortunately, she has always held Jenny in great affection; and when I told her, Claire had already been dead for nearly ten years. Time softens such blows.

"Need any help with your homework, sweetheart?" I ask.

"No, I'm good, Dad," she replies. "I'll be done in about ten minutes or so. Easy stuff. Jane Austen."

"Excellent. Dinner will be ready in about quarter-of-an-hour."

"OK."

Pratcha and Jenny are both good kids. Neither of them is really any trouble. And, in their different ways, old for their ages.

Da worries too much.

Whereas I don't worry enough.

* * * * *

Later, after Jenny and Pratcha have turned in, Da and I sit on the sofa with half a bottle of wine, and I raise the topic of Devesh Banerjee.

"I'm a little concerned about some aspects of his murder," I offer as an opener.

"Well, I'm more concerned about who will buy his house," says my wife. "Not some party-giving champagne socialist, I hope. At least Mr. Banerjee was quiet and kept himself to himself."

"It's this business of his being cut in half by a chainsaw –"

Da stops me.

"David, let it go. You're done with detecting. This is not *your* case, even if he was our neighbour. You've already irritated DCI Zachary enough by your own account. Leave the poor woman alone and let the police do their job."

"It's just that –"

Da consults her watch.

"All right, then. I'll give you five minutes on this, but then we're going upstairs to bed. I want to have sex this evening, and this is not the sort of discussion that's going to put me in the mood. I've had a tiresome day, and I need to work off some stress."

"Would it be better if I talked about it after we've had sex?"

"Yes, much better," she says grabbing my wrist. "That way, hopefully I'll drop off to sleep while you're talking. Bring the wine."

* * * * *

The two of us are lying in bed, and our desire has been sated. The wine bottle is empty. And I mean that both literally and metaphorically.

Da is in a more accommodating mood.

"Go on, then," she says, stroking my chest and running her fingers over the scar of my old bullet wound. "Let's hear what you want to say about Mr. Banerjee. Now that you've done your duty."

I consider where to start.

"The police didn't tell me when or where he was murdered. But I know from the news that his torso was found early last Friday morning by Highgate cemetery. He would have been at his surgery until at least five o'clock on Thursday afternoon."

"Because you've checked his opening times?"

"Yes. So that means he was killed either on Thursday evening or sometime between midnight and, say, six o'clock on Friday morning. And his business was smashed up. So, he was probably murdered there or near there. Are you with me so far?"

"I was an investigator myself once, you might remember," Da replies drily. "I'll tell you if I have trouble keeping up."

She yanks a hair out of my chest.

"Go on," she says.

"The body I saw had multiple stab-wounds to the neck and upper chest. Likely on his hands and arms too if he was trying to fend off his assailant. But I didn't see them: they were under the sheet. A frenzied attack, I'd say. Those stabbings would have been the cause of death, not the severing of the lower half of his body. That must have been done afterwards."

"That makes sense. It would be rather difficult to get someone to hold still while you cut them in half. Messy and noisy too. Though he could have been restrained and gagged, I suppose. But then, why the knife wounds too?"

"And why cut him in half anyway? Perhaps to make the body easier to transport. But if that was why it was done, why haven't the legs turned up? And why leave the torso in a place where it would be found quickly? It's like someone has left a deliberate trail. *Here's half of the puzzle: now see if you can find the other half.*"

"All of which leaves you where, exactly, David?"

"I'm not sure. The multiple stabbings suggest hatred. Maybe the chainsaw business indicates contempt. Or something else entirely. Something… cold and calculated.

"Although this looks like straightforward butchery by a disturbed mind, I doubt it was a spur-of-the-moment thing. Highgate is a pretty busy place. To avoid discovery would have required planning. Or a damn huge slice of luck."

Da eyes her bedside clock.

"It's getting late, David, and I have a full day tomorrow. Have you done?"

"Sure. You can put the light out."

"No, I mean have you done *with the case*?"

"Ah."

"Because part of the reason you gave up being a private detective was the effect it was having on your mental health. Plus, you nearly died on several occasions, if you recall. And once stress starts, it goes on building up. Do you want to take the risk of all sorts of bad memories resurfacing? You can become rather fixated with death when you're left to your own devices, my darling. I realise you're feeling bored, but there must be healthier ways to fill up your time."

"Like my giving Anneke Reid therapy, you mean?"

"Don't try to be smart, David Braddock. It doesn't suit you."

* * * * *

I can't sleep.

I'm tempted to get up but I don't want to disturb Da.

Having resolved nothing on the Banerjee conundrum, I'm mulling over my situation.

My wife is right. I am bored.

I think about the old myth of the Hero's Journey, which in some ways is not dissimilar to my own story – not that I regard myself as a hero, you understand. Man leaves home, travels, has adventures and returns home bringing his learning and enlightenment with him. Cue the Happily-Ever-After ending.

But what happens after *that*? When all the great deeds have been done, the battles won, the temptations resisted and the monsters slain?

What became of Odysseus after the Trojan War and his ten-year journey back to his patiently-waiting wife?

Homer doesn't say.

But I doubt somehow that he spent his time thereafter dabbling in therapy, putting out the bins and peeling vegetables for dinner.

Was he a dissatisfied, aimless and spent man after his Happy Ending?

III

Talking Heads

My 10.00am client is a spotty nineteen-year-old by the name of Jamie Sykes, and he's already five minutes late.

I was supposed to see him on Friday morning, but he pulled out at the last minute, claiming he couldn't get the time off work, so this is a rescheduled appointment.

Our last session ended on a fiery note, so it's surprising in a way that he bothered to rebook at all. He stomped out of my front door with a seething resentment in his eyes as a consequence of my challenging some of his 'truths.'

Sykes lives with his parents in Islington, and he was only prepared to be on my client list because his parents threatened to throw him out of the house if he didn't agree to psychological help. Come to think of it, they're probably the reason he's coming back: he doesn't fancy trading his room for a cardboard box just yet.

He describes himself as a casual labourer. This seems entirely plausible as his IQ is about that of a moth. I expect he has to be kept away from naked flames.

Our Jamie has had some brushes with the police, and received a caution a few months ago following a fight outside a pub. He doesn't *look* like a brawler, being weedy in build; and therefore, I'd have thought he's more likely to get beaten-up than to be the one doing the beating-up.

He's been prescribed some meds to help him control his anger; and he does seem to be on a permanently short fuse. Though the three previous times I've seen him, it's never crossed my mind that he's likely to be physical with me. He's always been more focused on sulking and answering my questions with as few words as possible. It is a struggle for him to achieve both of these things at the same time.

Sykes is on an NHS waiting list to see a competent psychiatrist. But given the current state of funding for mental health services, that's going to be a long wait. In the meantime, he has to put up with me, and his folks have to pay for that privilege.

Despite his surface bluster, he strikes me as the type who could be easily led by the right sort of person. Or *wrong* sort of person, I should say. The peer-pressure of his mates would carry a lot of sway with him, I figure, and he'd be mesmerised by the authority of a working-class alpha male. But, let's not be too technical here.

So, to summarise Jamie Sykes in everyday language, I am inclined to the opinion that he is an ignorant, miserable little shit.

He makes me wish that I'd set my age limitation policy at a minimum of twenty years, not eighteen.

My doorbell rings. He's arrived.

* * * * *

We've only got a few minutes of Mr. Sykes' session left, and I have a headache.

I don't know who he's been talking to in the last week-and-a-half, but he's gone from being almost totally uncommunicative (unless you count grunts) to wanting to express his views on the world. Or somebody's views on the world.

It appears that every government on the planet wants to oppress young people, and they are supported in this endeavour by the middle classes. The Brexit vote that we had here in the summer was a complicated conspiracy perpetrated by the ruling elite and old people, and saturated fat isn't actually bad for you.

Of course, Sykes didn't use any long words during this diatribe, and when I asked him why he was so down on the *bourgeoisie*, he replied that he'd always hated the French.

Apparently, people like me are the problem. I/we have betrayed his generation and undermined his self-respect, and that is the reason why he is so angry most of the time.

"So, it was nothing to do with you, then?" I interrupt.

"What wasn't?" he asks with his habitual eloquence.

"That fight outside the pub that got you the police caution."

"He was askin' for it."

"And was the man you attacked a member of the entitled classes that you hold responsible for your current situation?"

"He was a Spurs fan."

"I see."

He has nothing further to add.

"You seem unusually agitated today, Jamie," I say in my most patronising voice. "Are you still taking your medications?"

"No. I'm not puttin' any more of that shit in my body. It's rubbish anyway."

"And how do your parents feel about that?"

The courage he has stoked up suddenly fails him and he looks away.

"I presume you haven't told them, then?"

He scratches the side of his face.

"Well, let me be clear, Jamie. Unless you resume taking your meds immediately, we will not be having any more sessions. And I will phone your father and tell him why."

"You can't do that," he exclaims. "Whatever I say to you is supposed to be private."

"This is not a confessional and I'm not a priest. And unless you are prepared to start taking responsibility for yourself, there is no value in my continuing to see you. It's as simple as that."

I glance at my watch.

"Right, that's it for today. I'll pencil in another session for us at this same time next week. But whether that will happen depends on you. No medication, no therapy. Think about what I've said. And when you've made your decision, call me."

He shuffles out of the house exuding hurt and resentment. Another satisfied customer.

I sincerely hope he chooses not to take his meds.

* * * * *

Following Sykes' departure, I down a couple of headache tablets and make a sandwich.

I plough through the first three chapters of *Mobi-Dick*, a project I've been meaning to tackle for a while, but the nineteenth-century prose rapidly exhausts my powers of concentration. I decide life is too brief for Herman Melville, and I consign the book to the bin. This gives me a strange feeling of elation, and in this positive mood I phone my elder daughter.

Dubai – where Katie's law firm is based – is currently four hours ahead of London, and I'm fortunate that I catch her between meetings.

Neither of us has any particular news to report.

Her second husband Lucien Croft is a partner in a different law firm (*Croft Daniels*) and he heads up their branch office in the UAE. He's also on his second marriage.

Lucien was formerly Katie's boss in the UK and he was instrumental in getting Katie her current position. He is a good egg, even if he is a lawyer, and he always had a soft spot for his protégée. He and his first wife divorced a few years back and he and Katie – or *the marriage wrecker* as Lucien's first wife calls her – have recently celebrated their second wedding anniversary. No kids, and no plans for any.

Katie tells me good-naturedly that I sound like a fed-up house-husband and I tell her good-naturedly to sod off.

After our conversation has ended, I retrieve *Mobi-Dick* from the bin, wipe the cover and inspect it, before dropping it back in the bin.

* * * * *

Around two, for want of anything better to do, I find myself gazing out of our living room window to see what's going on in our street. Nothing much by the looks of it.

The Scottish widow from number twenty-two is out walking her Chihuahua which she has dressed in tartan against the cold. My neighbour across the road is presumably having some work done as there is a white Transit van parked outside the house. Number sixteen's hedge needs a trim, and number fourteen hasn't yet taken his bin in after this morning's collection.

I have become a curtain-twitcher, I reflect ruefully.

At the stroke of two, a Merc comes to a halt outside. A girl climbs out of the passenger side, speaks a few words with the driver, then shuts her door. The car pulls away. She walks up to my front door and rings the bell which utters a sound of imminent expiry.

I give it a few seconds – so as not to appear too keen for human company – before opening the door.

"Mr. Braddock?"

"Yes. You must be Anneke."

A nod.

"Your bell's dying, by the way."

"Ah, right."

She's slim and of average height, with raven-black hair cut short, kohl on her eyes, dark lipstick, and a stud through her tongue. Her skin is very white. She wears a *keffiyeh* around her neck, a leather jacket, ripped jeans, and a pair of Doc Martens. No handbag. She's either a Goth or an Emo. I've never understood the difference, but neither is particularly fashionable these days.

"Isn't your grandfather joining us?" I ask, craning my neck to see if Ken Reid is trying a find a place to park. There is no sign of the Merc.

"No, he isn't. He wanted to, but I told him it wasn't appropriate. I'll catch up with him later."

"Then, you'd better come in."

When we are in the study, she hands me an envelope.

"Grandpa said to give you this."

She hands me an envelope. It's cash for my hourly fee.

"Aren't you going to count it?"

"No."

She stares at me.

Confident. Unfazed. Ready to test me.

"You realise this is going to be a waste of time, don't you?"

"My sessions usually are, Anneke. But we'll give it a go regardless. If you only last thirty minutes or less, your grandfather can have half his money back, OK? Now, please, sit down."

We take our places in the two armchairs.

"What have you been told about me?" she asks.

"Only the basics. You've done a bit of shoplifting, like to skive off from school now and again, and don't get on with your parents. And in your spare time you play bass guitar with a local death metal band and call yourself 'Needle.' Whether that's because you sometimes shoot up on heroin or because you like to irritate people, your grandfather didn't say. But my guess would be the latter."

"Correction: I *used* to be with a band, but I'm not now. We've split up."

"Artistic differences?"

"No money to buy better sound equipment, and the venues think we should play for free."

"I shouldn't have thought sound quality was that important for death metal."

"Well, it is. And I don't do drugs."

She studies me for a while.

"Did my grandpa tell you that I like to screw older men?"

"No, he didn't. He was more concerned with the fact that you and your parents aren't speaking."

"Well, I do like to screw older men. Much older men. Ones about your age."

"Right."

"Grandpa should have told you about that, really, shouldn't he?" she says.

"Maybe he knew that you'd tell me yourself. In which case, he was right."

She smiles, then opens her mouth so that I can have a good look at her tongue piercing. She waggles her tongue, then closes her mouth and sits back in her chair.

"You might as well know, *Anneke*, that I'm not easily shocked. I've seen and heard it all before. I spent ten years living in Thailand."

"Then, you can teach me a few things, *David*."

"I doubt it. You don't appear to be bendy enough. So, if you've had your fun, can we start the session proper now?"

I watch her regroup her thoughts.

"I suppose it must make you feel vulnerable, being alone in your house with a young girl. Does it?"

"Not especially. Why should it?"

She puts on a face of mock-concern.

"Well, there's so much in the news these days about pedophiles. About middle-aged men grooming schoolgirls for sex. And someone's reputation can so easily be destroyed, can't it? Even when an accusation is false."

"And where's this going, may I ask? You're seventeen and past the age of consent. Anyway, you're not my type."

"Not old enough or not young enough?"

"Not Asian enough."

She waggles her foot.

"But I wonder what your neighbours would make of it if I were to run out into the street, all distressed, and say you tried to force yourself on me."

"I doubt they'd bat an eyelid. We have lots of sex offenders living in this street. It's one of the problems with Notting Hill. I'm amazed the property prices are so high."

Anneke laughs. It's a genuine, connecting laugh.

"OK," she says. "I'll stop playing games with you. I'm not going to freak you out, am I?"

"I'm afraid you weren't ever going to." I remove my cell phone from my pocket. "Not so long as I was recording our conversation."

"Oooh. Sneaky. But clever," my client adds grudgingly.

"So, shall we begin again?"

A wave of seriousness passes across her face. As she removes her scarf and jacket, she frowns.

"Would you turn off the recorder first?"

I search her eyes.

"You want me to trust you? After all that… talk?"

"Yes. Please."

I switch off the recorder.

Anneke lets out a long breath.

"Thank you. And I'm sorry about earlier."

"It's OK."

She reaches into an inner pocket of her jacket and takes out a pouch.

"I need a smoke," she declares. "Would you mind?"

"Let's go out into the garden," I reply. "Put your jacket back on. That Iron Maiden T-shirt isn't going to keep you warm in this weather."

We sit down on the patio chairs. The sky is clouding over, but further rain today seems unlikely.

"I have some weed," Anneke announces. "As we're outside, would it be all right if… I mean, it helps me to relax. If not, I'll roll tobacco…"

"You said you didn't do drugs."

"Weed isn't exactly a hard drug, David. Everybody does it. By the way, is it OK for me to call you 'David'?"

"It is. Go on then, roll a joint. I'll have a puff with you."

"You smoke?"

"I quit smoking cigarettes a few years ago. But this isn't really a *cigarette*, is it?"

Anneke starts talking. It's not about anything profound, but I want her to feel comfortable with me, so I don't interrupt. Sooner or later, she'll get to the point. We smoke the whole joint.

After a while, she breaks off.

"Grandpa said that he'd met your father in Malaya. And that you used to be a private detective."

"Yes. But we're supposed to be talking about you, not me."

"We can talk about me next time."

"You want there to be a next time, do you?"

"I do, yes."

"Go on, then. What do you want to know?"

"Did you do investigations into people who were being unfaithful to their husband or wife?"

"Yes. Lots of times. It got wearing after a while. And it can make you rather cynical about relationships. Why do you ask?"

She hesitates.

"Next time," she says.

* * * * *

The hour is up.

I am still giddy from the weed, but decidedly more chilled than I was earlier.

"What are you doing now?" Anneke asks me.

"Taking a trip into town on the Underground. I need to collect some shirts from my tailor in Jermyn Street."

"You have a tailor?"

"I certainly do."

"Would it be OK if I come with you? I don't want to go home yet."

"Isn't your grandfather picking you up?"

"No. He doesn't need to. I only live ten minutes' walk away from here. Grandpa only brought me in his car this first time so that he could be sure I'd turned up for the appointment."

"Sure. Come with me if you like. But let your folks or Ken know what you're doing."

She rings her grandfather, then passes her phone over to me to confirm her story.

"Make sure she calls me when she leaves you," he says. "So that I know where she is and when we should expect her home."

Anneke and I don't talk much while we undertake the short stroll to Notting Hill Gate. The contrast in our dress and ages attracts a few curious glances along the way.

We descend to the Central Line eastbound platform together. The display tells us that the next train is due in two minutes.

My young companion is lost in thought, staring down at the tracks.

"I wonder how many people have committed suicide here," she says.

"I've no idea how many jumpers there have been here specifically, but I believe on the whole network they can have up to a hundred a year. But here's a practical tip if you're thinking of doing it yourself.

"You see the four rails?

"The furthest one is the positive power rail, then you have a running rail, then the return power rail, and the one closest to us is the second running rail. So, if you *dive* over as the train is coming in, and can reach all four rails, the electric current will kill you even if the wheels severing your head and feet don't."

"I'll bear that in mind."

It occurs to me that the marijuana might be affecting my mental filters and better judgement, so I resolve to shut up until I have something more life-affirming to say.

The train rattles into the station, and we ride it to Oxford Circus.

As Anneke isn't in any hurry to forsake my company, I buy us each a cappuccino in a franchise coffee shop. It's not terribly hot and tastes disgusting, but my new companion doesn't seem bothered.

"So, when can I see you again, David?" she asks.

The question earns me a disapproving look from a middle-aged lady at the next table.

"Well, next time it won't be on a weekday afternoon, when you should be at school," I reply.

The woman tuts and shakes her head.

"Well, how about the same day next week, at about six o'clock? I can easily walk round to your house. I won't need a lift like I did today."

"Fine."

"But won't your wife be home then?"

The female at the next table has heard enough.

"You should be ashamed," she tells me before picking up her shopping and making for the door.

"Do you think she's gone to find a policeman?" Anneke says.

"Very probably."

I phone Ken Reid and tell him where we are, and that his granddaughter wants another therapy session. He's pleased about that.

"Your grandfather is asking what time you'll be home."

"I suppose you want to go to your tailor's now?"

"Yes."

"And it might be embarrassing for you if I tag along?"

"If the reaction of that woman who just left is anything to go by, that might well be the case."

"Then, I'll be home in an hour or so."

I convey this information to Ken and ring off.

Anneke shows no inclination to move. She's either lonely or she loves shitty, lukewarm coffee.

"Is your wife really from Thailand?" she asks.

"She is."

"I'll bet she's pretty."

"She is. Now finish your coffee."

"I want you to know that I'm happy we connected this afternoon, David."

And I'm happy that the lady on the next table has already gone.

* * * * *

Having collected my shirts – black ones for when I'm performing at the jazz club – I buy a couple of reeds for my saxophone from a shop on Tottenham Court Road, then take the Tube home.

The curtains are drawn at Devesh Banerjee's house, and there is no sign of his BMW. I expect it's in a police compound being crawled over by a forensics team.

My own vehicle remains on our drive looking neglected. It is rarely used, and it needs a wash.

Nobody's home yet.

I phone Da and suggest I order a Chinese takeaway for dinner.

She says yes, and asks me how the session with my new client went.

"I'll tell you later," I say.

* * * * *

Both the kids are doing homework, and the Chinese takeaway has been eaten.

Da insists on my giving her a full account of my time with Anneke Reid, which I do.

My wife summarises the salient points of my narrative in her own distinctive style.

"So, she has a Father Complex."

"Possibly."

"But you didn't record all the session."

"No."

"And you both smoked weed in our garden."

"Yes."

"Then you took her into London and bought her a coffee."

"Yes."

"And the woman in the coffee shop thought you were a dirty old man."

"Probably."

"And you've agreed to see her again next week."

"Yes. But not during school hours."

"Ha. Well, that's something I suppose."

"Are you annoyed with me? I'm only –"

Da cuts me off. She musters all of her patience.

"David, I am perfectly aware that you are acting from the best of motives. And I'm sure you're only trying to help this girl. But your behaviour has become increasingly reckless of late. You need to be more careful. For all our sakes."

"All right. Understood. But there is one more thing I need to do which you will also consider to be reckless."

She sighs.

"Go on, then."

"The Devesh Banerjee murder –"

"Oh, my Buddha. Not this again."

"Tomorrow, I want to go up to Highgate, have a mooch around and ask some questions."

"Why?"

"Because I'm not going to be able to get this out of my brain until I do."

My wife purses her lips in reproach.

"I wasn't joking the other day. Sometimes you *do* have an unwholesome fascination with death. Either that or you can't stop looking for trouble."

I make no reply.

She sighs again.

"David, I want you to be aware that I'm becoming concerned about your mental health. You're showing all the signs of someone who is suffering from depression."

"Thank you for the medical labelling, Doctor Da."

"Be serious. I'm no psychologist, but I think you have all sorts of issues that you haven't properly dealt with. And that's not surprising given some of the awful things you've been through. But perhaps it's time that, instead of practising as a therapist, you went to see one."

"Really?"

"Yes, really."

I want to remind her that the last time I talked to a psychiatrist on Samui it was a disaster. However, I do need to address her worries.

"Then, I'll tell you what. Once I run up against a wall on the Banerjee killing, I'll stop. And I'll go and talk to a shrink. You can even choose the shrink yourself. Is that fair?"

Da is relieved.

"That's fair," she says.

Following this exchange, I spend a while practising on my saxophone until my family decides they can't stand any more of it.

The TV news reports that there has been a tram derailment in Croydon and some people have been killed.

I don't mention this to Da lest she think I'm indulging my death obsession.

IV

A Lack of Faith in Modern Policing

I leave home while the commuters are making their unenthusiastic way to work. Consequently, the Central Line is awash with humanity, a few of whom smell like they have not washed. It's a relief to change onto the Northern Line, but even more of a relief when I get off at Archway.

I begin the long walk up Highgate Hill which will take me past Devesh Banerjee's dental surgery.

This morning, everything is bathed in the typically dull light of an English November. But at least it's dry. I turn up my coat collar and wonder what the weather is like in Thailand.

I quickly locate my ex-neighbour's premises.

The surgery windows are boarded up and the front door is locked. There are no lights on inside so far as I can tell. A slight smell of burning lingers despite there being no external signs of a fire. On the pavement lies a sliver of police 'do not cross' tape, the rest presumably torn off by some wag for the fun of it. There is not even a letter-flap to peep through as the surgery has a mailbox fixed to the wall. And while there is a buzzer for the flats above, it's too early in the day to be attempting fraudulent access.

I briefly contemplate going around the back of the property and seeing if I can break in through a window, but it's also a bad time for that: too many people about.

After this inauspicious start, I continue my steep climb up the hill towards Highgate Cemetery; and I'm a bit out-of-breath by the time I arrive.

I pause for a minute. If I still smoked, now would be the time for a cigarette. But I don't, so I can't, and instead of taking in nicotine I absorb my surroundings.

If you chopped down all its trees, the cemetery would have a great view of the city in the distance, though its occupants are not going to care much about that. It has – the Internet informs me – over fifty-thousand graves, and is in fact two cemeteries: West and East. There are many famous stiffs interred here, such as Michael Faraday, Henry Moore and George Eliot (or Mary Ann Evans, to give the novelist her proper name). Plus, its most famous occupant: Karl Marx. His communist plot attracts frequent visitors, some of whom are believers in the cause and some of whom are vandals.

The whole business is a veritable necropolis of vaults and tombs. It was one of seven cemeteries consecrated in the nineteenth century within a six-mile radius of the city, when all the burial grounds of the centre were overflowing with corpses.

And the place serves as a reminder, if one were needed, that London is one gigantic grave; sitting, as it does, atop the plague pits of the Black Death and the later Great Plague. The Victorians, taking their lead from Queen Victoria's pathological mourning, raised the glorification of human demise to a whole new level in their architecture and celebration of morbidity. They were, it has been said, half in love with death. Hence the construction of elaborate granite and marble shrines like Highgate.

Da's right. I'm way too interested in this subject.

Enough of the ruminations. I need to focus my attention on one specific passing: that of a singularly unpleasant dentist. That's the reason I'm *supposed* to be here.

I find the location by the perimeter wall where the dear departed's remains were discovered. I recognise it from the TV footage. And even if I wasn't sure, the presence of inexpertly-erased bloodstains on the concrete confirms it.

As I had surmised, it's a public area. The cemetery doesn't allow admittance until ten o'clock, but even so there are people around. An early finding of the corpse would have been pretty much guaranteed.

So, why was it left *here?*

And where are his legs?

"I'm afraid you're too early," says a voice from behind me. "They don't open for another half-an-hour."

It's an elderly lady with a blue rinse. She's wearing what appears to be a rug made out of multicoloured patches and she is holding a lead. On the end of the lead is one of those pampered small-breed dogs that yaps a lot.

"I'm not looking to go in," I reply. "I'm here to pay my respects. My neighbour's body was found here a few days ago. Mr. Banerjee."

"Oh, yes, the poor man. He was my dentist, and a good dentist he was too. Shocking business. Shocking. So, you live next door to him? In Notting Hill, isn't it?"

"Yes. My name is Braddock. David Braddock."

She's interested. She strikes me as the type who is interested in everything, always.

"Oh, Mr. Braddock, how sad for you. I'm Doris, by the way. Doris Trent. Like the river."

We shake hands awkwardly. The dog tics nervously.

"Were you a very good friend of Mr. Banerjee?" she asks.

"Well, let me put it this way: I was the one who had to identify his body."

"Oh, my goodness! That must have been a terrible ordeal for you."

"I've spent better hours."

"I'm so glad the police have arrested the man who did it."

"The police –"

This revelation stops me in my tracks, and I have to gather my wits.

"But there's been nothing about that on the news."

She hesitates a moment or two, then plunges in.

"No, well it only happened this morning. Early. My friend Elsie told me all about it. Though I'm not sure we're supposed to say anything until there's been an official announcement," Doris says doubtfully. "But as you're Mr. Banerjee's neighbour and friend, I suppose it's all right to tell you, Mr. Braddock."

"Please, call me David. And how does your friend Elsie know this?"

"She lives only two houses up from the killer," she lets this last word roll around her palate, savouring it. "So, she was on the phone to me straightaway. We're school friends you see, and we've both spent our whole lives in Highgate."

"Elsie lives nearby?"

"She does, yes."

I think fast. Then I kneel down and stroke her dog which, to my surprise, doesn't bite me.

"What a lovely dog. What's her name?"

"Cherry. Like the brandy. She likes you, David. And she's usually a good judge of people."

I make a few goo-goo noises at the quivering oversized rat before gazing up at her patchwork-quilted owner.

"Doris, you're going to think this a terrible imposition, and I realise you've only just met me, but might it be possible for me to meet your friend? I'm keen to learn whatever I can about what happened to poor, dear Devesh. And my wife, you see, was fond of him too. She and he used to exchange curry recipes."

I'm worried this might be pushing it, but Doris proves understanding and takes out her mobile phone.

* * * * *

Three-quarters-of-an-hour later, I am in a local teashop that smells of lavender and decline. Sitting opposite me are Doris and her best buddy Elsie Schilling.

They could pass for sisters, except that I know they're not since Doris told me most of her life story – including a blow-by-blow account of her husband's long and grisly terminal illness – while we awaited the appearance of her friend.

I, in turn, felt obliged to tell Doris some of my own history. The fact that I am a retired private investigator has energised her even more to satisfy my curiosity, and she was quick to put Elsie in the picture on my former profession.

Our second pot of tea arrives, and it has a knitted cosy on it. It's brought to our table by an ancient waitress who has a crooked nose and wobbles as she walks. She sets down scones, jam and cream: my treat.

Doris' rodent is under the table eating dog chews and emitting the occasional fart.

"Schilling," I observe, making small-talk. "That sounds like a German name."

"My late husband was Swiss. From Zurich. After the War, his family had had enough of Europe. It's a shame he didn't live to see the result of the Brexit vote this year. He'd definitely have approved."

"Yes, my stepmother was happy about that too." Neither of these ladies voted 'Remain' I guess, so I add, "And, of course, so was I."

They smile. Good call.

I let them tuck into the scones before I ask Elsie about the morning's events.

"Well," she says, wiping cream from her lips, "the man the police arrested is called Lee Vance. He's a tree surgeon-cum-gardener. Has one of those white Transit vans, but he doesn't advertise his business on it, which is rather peculiar. Though it might be like that because he can argue it's not a commercial vehicle, and leave it in one of the residents' parking spaces. He lives at number twenty in my street. I'm at number sixteen."

"And which street is this?"

"Stewart Road."

"I see. Please, continue."

"He's a horrible man. Looks like a gangster, and I imagine his house is filthy inside. Drinks and likes to shout. Nobody in the street has a good word to say for him. Goodness knows how he gets any work. And as for that so-called 'friend' of his —"

I steer her gently back on course.

"Before we move onto that, Elsie, can you tell me what happened?"

She frowns to gather her concentration.

"It all started a couple of weeks ago with Vance's dog."

"His dog?"

"Yes, Mr. Banerjee accidentally ran over Vance's Rottweiler on Highgate Hill. It was a disgusting animal, just like its owner, and nobody is sorry it's dead. He shouldn't have let it roam around in the street without a lead. But that's Lee Vance for you. He's one of those people who believes the rules don't apply to them.

"Anyway, there was quite a public scene with Vance threatening Mr. Banerjee with all sorts of things that he was going to do to him. The ruckus even made the local community newspaper. I'm surprised he didn't mention it to you, David, with your being such a good friend of his."

They scrutinise me for a reaction, so I improvise.

"I expect Devesh was too embarrassed to talk about it. He was a private man. If something upset him, he'd be inclined to keep it to himself."

"He was Elsie's dentist too," pipes in Doris apropos of nothing.

Elsie gives a sagacious nod.

"And an excellent dentist he was. I don't believe this woman that's taking over his practice is in the same league. She's from the Philippines, I understand."

She wants to add something more, but thinks better of it.

"Anyway, I noticed that Vance's white van hadn't been around for a day or two. It's usually parked inconveniently in the road, so it's obvious when it's not there. The next thing is, a police car has turned up this morning and carted him off."

"So, he murdered Devesh because of the dog?"

"Yes. And I think the police took his van away first and found forensic evidence in it, and then they came back and nabbed him."

"It seems a bit of an extreme reaction to losing a pet," I suggest.

"He loved that animal. And he had a terrible temper. Plus, he could have used the chainsaw he has for his tree-surgery business to cut poor Mr. Banerjee in half. It all adds up for me."

I suppress a gasp.

"How did you know about his being cut in two? The police haven't released that information, and I was sworn to secrecy about it."

"Oh, David," Doris responds. "This is *Highgate*. We might be part of London, but we're more of a village here. Everyone knows everything about everyone. And it was another of our friends who discovered the body."

The ladies exchange a smug glance.

"A right couple of Miss Marples you two, aren't you? You should consider setting up a detective agency."

They like this.

I order us a plateful of biscuits and give one to the dog. She doesn't want it.

"All right, then," I say, "what's your theory about where Devesh's pelvis and legs are? I presume you have one."

"We don't know *where* they are," replies Elsie, "but we know *who* the police should be asking – aside from Vance, that is."

"Oh, and who's that?"

"His pedophile friend, Edwin Jessop. He lives in the first-floor flat at Number 2, Rockingham Road, here in Highgate; and he sometimes helps Vance out with the gardening side of his business. We've both seen him going in and out of Vance's house."

"It's the only work he can get as he's a convicted – what's the term, Elsie?"

"*Kiddie-fiddler.*"

"Yes, that's right."

"And how would you know that?" I ask, before raising a hand. "No, don't tell me. This is Highgate and everyone knows everything about everyone, right?"

"Right," the two widows say in unison.

"But why would this man Jessop be involved?"

"It stands to reason," chirps Doris. "For a start, he's the only friend that Vance has."

"And secondly, it would have required more than one man to move Mr. Banerjee's body. So, he must also know where the legs are," continues Elsie.

"Plus, with his record, the police might find him easier to crack than Vance," concludes Doris.

I raise my teacup in a salute.

"Here's to you, ladies," I say. "You've got it all figured out. Congratulations."

* * * * *

But they haven't got it all figured out.

Even assuming the police are working exactly along these lines, and that the widows' theory about the police examining Vance's van is correct, there are some things about this narrative that strike me as unsatisfactory.

It's time to agitate DCI Zachary's tree.

I take out my phone and call her.

She is not in the mood for niceties.

"What is it, Mr. Braddock? I'm busy today, and I told you not to call me unless it was an emergency."

"We never did agree on a full definition of that, but if it's mainly to do with urgency –"

"What do you want?"

"It's about Lee Vance, the man you picked up this morning for Devesh Banerjee's murder."

There is a short choking noise on the other end of the line.

"What?"

"And his friend Edwin Jessop, the convicted pedophile."

"How did you obtain all this information?" she asks angrily.

"Oh, I have my sources," I reply airily. "Remember I am a detective too, *detective*."

"You're a bloody nuisance, that's what you are," she says. "Too much time on your hands to make mischief."

"Temper, temper, DCI Zachary. Remember your training. And, incidentally, you have the same opinion of me as my wife. If I didn't know better, I'd say you were related."

"In case you're not aware, *Mister Braddock*, I am leading a murder investigation here. Now, unless you want me to charge you with wasting police time, get to the point."

"I have some info that might be pertinent to your investigation. So, I'd like to meet you. When and where would be convenient?"

There is a brief silence while her professionalism wrestles with her deep desire to tell me to fuck off.

"Where are you now?" she says finally.

"In Highgate."

A beat while she takes this in.

"Are you familiar with the *Tout Mangé* sandwich shop near Bank Tube, opposite the London Mithraeum, and towards Cannon Street?"

"No, but I'll find it."

"Meet me there at one o'clock sharp. I'll be buying my takeaway lunch, and I won't hang around."

"You don't want me to come into the police station for an official session?"

"I do not. Frankly, I doubt you have anything relevant to say, and I don't want to inflict your presence on my team. They have enough to do."

"Well, this is all rather irregular."

"I'll give you five minutes to say what you have to say, and that's your lot. Do we understand one another?"

"We do."

She cuts the line.

* * * * *

I arrive early at *Tout Mangé*, buy a black coffee and hang around outside.

DCI Zachary appears at the stroke of one, marching purposefully along the street. She looks pissed off.

She walks straight past me into the shop and emerges after a minute clutching a brown bag.

"Follow me," she barks in a not-entirely-friendly fashion.

She leads me down the empty cul-de-sac beside the shop, and when she's content that we're far enough away from passing pedestrians, she stops and removes a bottle of orange juice from her bag.

"Well?" she says, before adding, "Five minutes only."

"You don't buy this idea that Vance killed Banerjee because he ran over his dog, do you?"

"Humour me, and tell me why we shouldn't."

"It doesn't make sense."

"Why not?"

"Because it's understandable that in those circumstances someone might act in the heat of the moment and do something violent and stupid. That's basic psychology. But that's not what happened, is it? Banerjee was killed some time after that event, so Vance had time for his anger to cool down. Only a psychopath would risk doing time for murder because somebody accidentally ran over his dog."

"And what makes you think that Vance isn't a psychopath? Have you met him?"

"No, but –"

"You saw all the stab wounds on Banerjee's neck, didn't you? That was the work of someone with a score to settle."

"We could argue that either way. Maybe it was just meant to look like a frenzied murder."

"To *look* like one?" she scoffs. "By whom?"

"That I can't say."

"And this psychology crap is all very well, Braddock, but we found traces of Banerjee's blood on Vance's chain-saw and in his van. How do you explain that?"

"How does *he* explain that?"

"He says – through his lawyer – that his van was broken into, and he knows nothing about any blood stains. And he also has no real alibi for the time of Devesh Banerjee's murder."

She shouldn't be telling me any of this, but her annoyance with me is making her uncharacteristically loose-tongued. I decide to keep prodding.

"Then there's the matter of the transportation of the body. You and I both know that Vance couldn't have done that on his own. He must have had help – *if* he did it. Have you questioned his unsavoury convicted friend Jessop?"

"We have. And, for your information, Jessop *does* have an alibi. A watertight one. He was in hospital overnight having had his gallbladder removed. So, he couldn't have had anything to do with it. He might be a pervert, but that doesn't mean we're going to fit him up."

"You've checked that with the hospital concerned."

"*Yes,*" she says crossly. "We in the Metropolitan Police are methodical. We're not amateurs like you, Braddock."

Zachary has now completely dropped the *Mr.*

"You haven't yet found Banerjee's legs, though, have you?"

"Not yet, but we will."

"And you do understand that Vance couldn't have done the murder and moved Banerjee's body if he were acting alone."

"Your five minutes are up," the officer announces.

I am more than a little crestfallen at her dismissal of my arguments.

"Now, I have a question for *you*," she says brusquely. "Where did you get all this information about Vance and Jessop?"

"No magic there," I reply. "It's common knowledge among the good folk of Highgate. If you still believed in community policing, you could have spoken to pretty much any of them. I got my info from two old biddies in a teashop."

"Now, you listen to me," she says with a touch of menace in her voice. "You are not to utter so much as a word of anything you have heard in Highgate or anything you have heard from me today. I'm not having your game-playing and police-baiting getting in the way of having a murderer put behind bars.

"We will make a public announcement on the Banerjee case at the right and proper time, and not before.

"And if I hear of you shouting your mouth off to anyone, I might be tempted to forget my principles about fitting someone up for a crime they didn't commit.

"Do I make myself clear?"

"Yes. But may I –"

"No, you may not. Just shut up for once. And don't you ever dare to phone me again unless it is a matter of imminent danger to human life. There's my definition of 'emergency' for you."

"Right. Got it."

* * * * *

Home again, and feeling both restless and discouraged.

I remain of the view that Zachary is missing something, although the hard evidence against Vance sounds compelling.

My teasing of the DCI has been counter-productive. There remain lots of questions I would like to ask her and which she will definitely not answer now. I've placed myself firmly on the outside of the investigation, and therefore I'm lacking data for developing a cogent theory of my own.

What put Zachary's team onto Vance in the first place? Do they have any relevant CCTV footage of Vance and/or his van? Is the police case against the suspect so strong that I should quit my cogitations and move on?

I pull a Booker Prize-winning novel off my bookshelves and read the blurb. It sounds worthy but dull. I replace it and pick out a volume of Sherlock Holmes stories to give me some inspiration.

This keeps me amused for about an hour.

Then I switch on my laptop to see what I can discover on the Internet about Lee Vance and Edwin Jessop. It's not much, and after some tedious browsing, I squander more time perusing an online bookseller where I make two purchases: a book on Jane Austen to help Jenny in her English Literature class, and a used *Gamer's Guide to The League of Loki* for Pratcha (for the which I'll probably cop hell from Da).

What next?

Some saxophone practice until the kids get home?

Yes. Why not?

* * * * *

Thursday evenings would normally find me at *Blue Rhythms*, a small jazz club in Soho. Thursday is amateur night, so four of us retirees make a laid-back racket together and are given free drinks for our pains. But tonight, the club has been rented out for a corporate bash so our services are not required.

Instead, I take the family out to a local Italian restaurant for dinner. So that Da is satisfied that Jenny and Pratcha have completed their homework to her satisfaction, I book a table for eight o'clock.

We travel by taxi there and back.

Our car continues to gather dust.

* * * * *

The BBC News reports that a fifty-two-year-old man has been arrested in connection with the murder of Devesh Banerjee. They hold back from mentioning that some of the victim's body remains missing.

Da takes this as an appropriate opportunity to request an account of my day's sleuthing.

"So, DCI Zachary actually called you an 'amateur'?" my wife asks with evident glee. "That must have hurt."

"I've been called worse things. By you, for one."

"Well, if the police are confident enough to charge this Vance person, then I suppose your investigation is done. It *is* done, isn't it, David?" she adds suspiciously.

"Yes. Almost. But I've decided I need to go back to Highgate tomorrow. To tidy up a few things in my mind."

"David –"

"And maybe see if I can find Banerjee's legs."

Da pours herself another glass of wine, then tops up my glass.

"Did you do anything *normal* today?" she asks.

"I bought Jenny and Pratcha each a book from the Internet."

"I hope the book you bought for Pratcha was on algebra," she warns.

V

The Other Half

To demonstrate that my role in the Braddock household is not solely that of ballast, I make breakfast for the family before washing up and waving them off.

"Behave yourself today," are Da's parting words.

Before I leave the house, I search the Internet for the exact location of Elsie Schilling's address in Highgate. I don't have her phone number, and she's unlisted, so I'll have to hope she's home. My tech-smart stepson could have found the number for me, but Pratcha is already on a warning from his mother about the time he spends in front of a screen, and I don't want to make further trouble for the beleaguered soul.

It's another cold, dry day as I emerge from the bowels of Archway. I could have saved my legs by getting off at Highgate, but I want another look at Devesh's surgery. Plus, I need the exercise as I haven't been to the gym since I renewed my annual membership two weeks ago.

The dentist's place is as I last saw it except for the fact that the final piece of police tape has gone. No joy to be had there.

I make my way to the top of Highgate Hill, cross the road and turn right. A few minutes later, I'm ringing Elsie's bell.

Luckily, she's in.

"Hello, David," she says. "This is an unexpected surprise."

"I'm sorry to turn up on your doorstep like this, but I wonder if you can spare me a few minutes."

"Yes, of course. Come in and I'll put the kettle on."

Elsie's lounge is exactly like I'd expect an elderly widow's lounge to be. Framed photographs everywhere, embroidered cushions and a lingering smell of lavender. On her coffee table is a Jeffrey Archer novel, and on the mantelpiece is an urn which I imagine contains her late husband's ashes.

Elsie sets down the tea tray and offers me a Jaffa cake.

"I hope you like Earl Grey."

"I do. Milk but no sugar for me."

She pours our teas.

"I suppose this is about Lee Vance and Mr. Banerjee, is it?" she asks.

"Yes. I need to pick your brains on a couple of things if that's all right."

"I assume, then, that you have some concerns about how the police are handling things."

I bite into the Jaffa cake.

"I managed to speak to the Senior Investigating Officer and… Well, let's say that what she told me didn't exactly fill me with confidence that they're tying up all the loose ends."

"Why, what did she say, David? You did say *she*, didn't you?"

Elsie is keen to have all the lurid specifics, but I'm going to have to disappoint her.

"I did. But I'm afraid I can't share that with you, Elsie, or DCI Zachary will have my guts for garters."

"A hard-nosed type, eh?"

"The hardest. And, by the way, I might be going off on completely the wrong track with my concerns. The police do seem to have quite a lot of evidence against Vance, but…"

"You're not satisfied?"

"Not entirely, no."

"Well," she says briskly, "how can I help?"

I take a moment to consider how to proceed.

"When we spoke the other day, we talked about the murder likely needing the participation of at least two people."

She nods.

"We did. Vance and his disgusting friend Jessop. He's the –"

I stop her.

"It can't have been Jessop. The police have already checked him out, and we're going to have to trust them on that."

"Oh, that *is* a surprise. Well."

"So, do you know of anyone other than Jessop who has been visiting Vance's house? Someone that one of your neighbours might have seen him with in a pub, for instance? I should imagine that you good people of Stewart Road keep tabs on our tree surgeon, and compare notes."

"We do. And no, there's nobody I can think of. And I'm sure I'd remember. As you say, David, we all keep a close eye on Lee Vance's activities. When he wasn't working, apart from

Jessop's visits and walking his Rottweiler, he lived a bit like a hermit. Curtains always closed, that sort of thing. That's probably why he took the death of his dog so badly."

"And he didn't get on with any of his neighbours?"

"Absolutely not."

"Relatives?"

"No. He only has a nephew, and they haven't spoken in years, I understand. Hardly surprising," she adds.

"I see."

I decide to try another tack.

"Tell me, does Vance have any enemies? People he's got into a local pub fight with, for instance?"

"No. And the Highgate grapevine is efficient at reporting that sort of thing."

"Has he perhaps upset any of his customers?"

"Well, he doesn't do work for anyone around here," she snorts, "and as for his client-base, I wouldn't know."

"And is there *anyone around here* who has a particularly deep dislike of Vance?"

"Only all of us," she replies. "Though he's had the most shouting matches with Mr. Solomons at number sixteen on account of Vance blocking his drive with his van now and again. Mr. Solomons might be in his late seventies, but he's more than happy to stand up to a bully. Ex-services, you see."

"Right."

"But how is any of that relevant to someone helping Vance kill Mr. Banerjee?"

"It might not be, Elsie. I'm just trying to get a picture of life on Stewart Road. It's probably not relevant," I say evasively.

"Do you want another cup of tea? There's enough left in the pot."

"Sure. Thanks."

I can see the cogs going round in the old lady's head.

"I presume the best way to find Lee Vance's accomplice would be for you to find Mr. Banerjee's legs. Where there might be forensic evidence and so on."

"My thoughts precisely."

"Unless Vance decides to give the police the name of his helper."

"That's not going to happen so long as he protests his innocence to the crime."

"And is that his position?" she asks craftily.

I wag a finger at her.

"Now, Elsie," I say.

"Well, the legs are not buried in Vance's back yard," she announces confidently. "That's all just slabs and a lean-to shed. Mr. Solomons had a peek over the wall to make sure nothing had been disturbed recently, and it hadn't. Besides, that would have been the first place the police would have searched."

"True."

"Don't you have a theory, David?"

"I don't. I'm thrashing around in the dark here."

"So, what's next?"

"I'm going to try and speak to Edwin Jessop."

"But you said –"

"Yes, I did. But I'm running out of people to talk to. Devesh's surgery is still boarded up. And so far as I'm aware, his dentist partner is still abroad."

Elsie purses her lips.

"You know, the police might have missed something at Vance's house," she says thoughtfully. "Something that might help identify his accomplice. It wouldn't be too difficult for you to force open one of his back windows and climb in. Mr. Solomons could lend you a ladder –"

"No, Elsie," I say. "We're *not* going to go there."

* * * * *

So, what now?

A bottle of imported beer and a ham and cheese ciabatta at a local café give me time to ponder my next move.

My embryonic (and possibly moronic) theory that someone other than Vance might be responsible for Banerjee's murder is crumbling under the weight of common sense, the police forensic evidence, and the lack of another suspect. Moreover, any information emanating from Elsie's Highgate gossip mill is unlikely to impress a jury.

Such brainpower as is left to me, therefore, needs to be concentrated on identifying Vance's accomplice(s). And that route doesn't seem too promising either. Because despite my chat with Elsie, I'm no further forward.

Zachary's team will be pumping Vance for information about this, and they are in a much better position to do so than I am. Plus, I'd guess that a key part of any 'not guilty' plea would depend on his lawyer highlighting that this couldn't have been a one-man job. So, any considerations of loyalty towards his helper aside, Vance's best bet is to keep his mouth shut.

And provided the police have indeed done their job properly in checking the hospital records about Edwin Jessop's gallbladder surgery, then Vance's pedophile friend couldn't have assisted him. I suppose I have to trust Zachary's boys on this matter.

My investigation – which, to be blunt, hardly warrants such an impressive label – has hit a wall.

I told Elsie that I would talk to Jessop. But is there really any point?

If there is no way he could have been actively involved in the crime, what exactly can I expect to get out of him? It would be a purely speculative encounter, and one in which he would be unlikely to cooperate.

I order a chocolate muffin. Maybe the sugar hit will provide me with inspiration.

It doesn't.

I check my watch.

I have hours to kill before any of my family will be home. So, I figure, as I'm already in Highgate and Jessop's place is only a few minutes' walk away, I might as well pay him a visit.

Even if it's a wasted one.

* * * * *

Gentrification has evidently not spread to every corner of Highgate.

Rockingham Road comprises old terraced properties which I guess were nice enough in their day, but that day has long passed. The street has an unloved feel to it, and the majority of houses appear to have been converted into upstairs and downstairs flats for low-rent tenants.

Number Two's front garden is full of weeds and bins, and the paint is peeling on the front door. Grubby net curtains obstruct the outside view through the windows.

The card-slots on the entrance control give no information on the occupants, merely stating 'Flat A' and 'Flat B' respectively. The system has a camera lens to show who is standing on the doorstep.

I press the buzzer for the first-floor apartment.

There is no response, so I press it again.

Still nothing.

I press the 'Speak' button and talk into the grille.

"Mr. Jessop, I know you are home. I saw your curtains twitch."

Silence.

I put my finger on the buzzer again for longer than would be considered polite.

A crackle, then a guarded male voice.

"Who is it?"

"My name is Braddock. I'm a private investigator. I need a few minutes of your time, Mr. Jessop."

A brief pause.

"Go away. I have nothing to say."

"My investigation has nothing to do with you. I promise you. But I believe you may be able to help me with some information."

"Go away or I'll call the police."

"I promise you I am not a journalist or some stupid vigilante. I am investigating the recent death of my neighbour. It's important or I wouldn't be bothering you."

A beat.

I add, "You don't need to let me in, if that's what's worrying you. I am happy to have a conversation on your doorstep. You can even leave the chain on if you want."

Another beat.

"Show me some ID. Hold it up to the camera."

At this juncture, I wish I'd had some business cards printed, dammit.

I improvise, and hope the image on Jessop's camera is low-quality.

"That's a library card," he says.

"I also have an Oyster Card, if that helps."

"That's not any kind of official identification either. You must think I was born yesterday."

"I *am* a private investigator, I assure you."

"Pull the other one."

"How about if I come back later with my passport? Will you see me then?"

"No. Now, leave me alone."

I try a few "Mr. Jessop" addresses and press the buzzer a couple of times more, but there's no response.

Another dead end.

"So, pedo-boy's not playing, eh?" says a voice from behind me. "Well, that's not surprising. He's been beaten up too many times to fall for that one. I suppose you're aware of his history?"

I nod.

The speaker is a tweed-clad gentleman of advanced years. He sports a grey, bushy moustache and even bushier eyebrows, and looks like he's just returned from a walk in the English countryside. The beagle on a lead further reinforces this impression.

I don't know how long he's been standing there, but long enough to deduce that I'm not one of Jessop's fellow child-abusers. Otherwise, I expect his tone would be less friendly.

"No. I'm not having a terribly successful day so far," I reply.

He cocks his head to one side and the dog mimics him.

"Did I hear you say you're an investigator?"

"You did. The name's Braddock. *David*."

"George Cooper-Clark."

We shake hands and the beagle relaxes.

"So, what are you investigating?"

"The death of Devesh Banerjee."

"The Highgate Hill dentist? The one who was chopped in half?"

"The same."

"But haven't the police arrested somebody for that?"

"They have, but… well, it's complicated. I was rather hoping that Mr. Jessop might be able to assist in tying up a few loose ends. But obviously not."

George makes a face like he's chewed a wasp.

"He's unlikely to be of much use to you anyway, that one. And anything he does tell you will be a lie.

"We residents have been trying to have him moved out of the area, but that's not so easy to do – even with some of the local teenage boys giving him hell at every opportunity. We can't even persuade Haringey Council to make him give up his allotment, and it's not like he even uses it. And that in spite of there being a seven-year waiting list for a plot. Bureaucracy and do-gooders: the curse of modern Britain."

"Jessop has an allotment? Here in Highgate?"

"Yes. He sort-of had it transferred to him from his father when the old man died. Henry Jessop was a decent bloke, by the way. I knew him. And I reckon it was the shame of what his son did that killed him."

I take this in, then say, "Do you know where his allotment is, George? And would you mind taking me there?"

My new companion is somewhat mystified by this request, but assents, explaining it is only a short walk away and that Jessop's plot is a *ten-pole* affair (two hundred and fifty square metres in plain English).

We chat amiably during our stroll to the site. George, it transpires, is an elected member of the Highgate Allotments Committee: hence his enthusiasm for Jessop's plot being reallocated.

"This is it," he announces, indicating an overgrown area.

We wander around on it and spot in its centre what looks like a recently-disturbed zone of piled, loose earth.

My companion scratches his head.

"George," I say, "can you lend me a spade?"

* * * * *

Fifteen minutes later, I'm on my phone to a testy DCI Zachary.

"I realise that, technically, this is not a matter of imminent danger to human life," I explain, "but you might want to send some of your boys over to the central allotments in Highgate post-haste. There's already a crowd gathering, and I'm worried that they'll destroy evidence, or that some journalists and photographers will turn up before you get here."

"What's going on *now*, Braddock?" she asks wearily.

"I've found Devesh Banerjee's legs."

* * * * *

Da, Jenny, Pratcha and I are sitting around the dinner table.

DCI Zachary has just been on the evening news reading out a hastily-prepared statement that human remains have been discovered on an allotment in Highgate, but that she is not in a position to comment further until a forensic examination has been completed. She appeared nervous and rattled, and when she said she would not be taking questions the journalists ignored her and started yelling about whether the police thought the body parts were those of the murdered Indian dentist. Zachary ignored them and walked away, and the report promptly cut back to the studio newsreader who asked, "And who is the mystery detective who found this hidden grave when the Metropolitan Police could not?" Cue a blurry photograph of yours truly snapped on a camera-phone. "The police are keeping silent on the matter," the tanned newsreader continued, "but it seems that we have a new Sherlock Holmes in our midst."

"A new Sherlock Holmes? *Really*?" Da had remarked, rolling her eyes. "The BBC has gone down even further in my opinion."

Now, the TV has been turned off and three sets of eyes are on me. The Braddock family is waiting impatiently for the grisly details, and for once my wife is uncharacteristically indifferent to protecting our children from the darker truths of life.

I run through the entire narrative of my investigation up to the time when the police arrived at the allotments. But before I can continue, Pratcha has a few queries.

How deep were the legs buried? Were they in a sack like the torso? Was there a lot of dried blood? Was he still wearing his trousers? And what was the smell like?

To which, my replies were: about a foot, yes, yes, yes, and not so good.

"How do you know the parts belonged to Mr. Banerjee?" Jenny pipes in.

"Good question. And the honest answer is that I don't. We'll have to wait for the police lab boys to determine whose they are. But I'll be surprised if there's another spare set of legs lying around in Highgate."

"But were the feet brown?" my daughter persists.

"He had his shoes on," I reply. "And I didn't want to disturb the evidence unduly. Plus, there was rather a lot of..." I reach for a term acceptable to the ears of children.

"Viscera?" Pratcha suggests helpfully.

"Yes."

Da decides that's enough anatomy talk.

"What did DCI Zachary have to say when the police turned up?" she asks.

"After cordoning off the area and complaining loudly that her crime scene resembled a public circus, she took me off to one side for some not-so-subtle questioning."

"And?"

"It's fair to say that she was somewhat bemused by my investigative reasoning, and insisted that Edwin Jessop's alibi had been thoroughly checked out. They will have to take him in for further questioning, but she remains adamant that he could have had no part in the murder."

"Even though the missing dentist parts were found on his allotment plot?" Da asks.

"Yep."

"It's interesting though," says Jenny as if she were referring to an encyclopaedia article rather than a dismemberment. "My dad's an ace sleuth, even if your identity has to remain secret."

"Well, as to that, it's not going to require a genius to find out it was me," I reply. "The guy who accompanied me to the allotment knows my name, and the two elderly ladies I mentioned earlier – Doris and Elsie – are rather gossipy individuals. Then there is the matter of all the impromptu photos that were taken by curious members of the public. It's not going to be long before the paparazzi show up. Frankly, I'm surprised they're not here already."

"I take it that DCI Zachary was suitably grateful for your contribution?" This from Da.

"Hardly. I suppose that fact that I found the other half of Banerjee makes her and her team look incompetent, and she won't have appreciated having her hand forced to make a public statement. In fact, she warned me off any further involvement in her case and told me to keep my mouth shut about the events that had led me to the allotment."

"And what did you say to that?"

"*You're welcome.*"

* * * * *

Once the kids have gone to bed, Da approaches me on the sofa and hands me a glass of wine. Her expression is ominous, and I brace myself for something bad.

"I'm glad you managed to wrap-up your investigation, darling, even though I'm not exactly looking forward to having the press camped on our doorstep."

"As to me wrapping-up my investigation, there are one or two aspects of it that I find troubling and inconsistent," I reply unwisely.

She closes me down immediately.

"You have to drop all this now, David. Zachary has warned you off and you should take note. You've had your fun so I want you to promise me you'll let it go."

"But –"

Da raises a warning eyebrow.

"All right. If you insist."

"I do insist."

I raise my hands in surrender.

"I shan't mention Devesh Banerjee again unless it's in connection with his untimely death affecting property prices."

"Good. Now, you remember that discussion we had about your seeing a psychiatrist?"

I nod cautiously.

"Well, I've booked an appointment for you to see a professional psychologist by the name of Rufus Ogilvy."

"And who is this paragon of the Talking Cure, may I ask?"

"He comes highly recommended by one of my regular clients who has been seeing him for years. She said I could mention her name, which I did when I phoned him today."

I sigh.

"And when am I seeing him?"

"At two o'clock tomorrow afternoon."

"Tomorrow? But tomorrow's Saturday. Isn't his practice closed at weekends?"

"It is, yes. But as I explained it's an emergency situation, he's agreed to see you at his house in Islington."

"An *emergency* situation? What exactly have you told him?"

"That recently you've been entertaining suicidal thoughts."

"Da, I've not been having any such thoughts," I say indignantly.

"It was the only way to get you a quick appointment. If I'd said you could wait, you would have gone to the back of the queue. Just act a bit depressed at the start of the session, and everything will be fine."

I should be annoyed at her, but I'm not.

"Are you really that worried about me?"

"Yes, David, I am."

"Then, I'll keep the appointment."

"Thank you. We won't mention it to the children."

"No, we certainly won't."

"We'll tell them you're doing early Christmas shopping."

"Whatever."

Before we turn in, I leave voicemail messages for Nang and Katie warning them of my impending celebrity status and say I'll call them tomorrow and fill them in on what's going on.

* * * * *

Later, I lie in bed wide awake while Da lies beside me sleeping the innocent slumber of the lying estate agent.

I realise I've promised her that I won't pursue the Banerjee matter further − and I won't − but there's one fundamental aspect of the case that will go on bugging me. And it is this.

By all that is logical, I should not have found his legs buried on that allotment.

It simply does not make any sense.

VI

Not Lying on the Couch

As a general rule, I dislike English rain.

But this morning, seeing the damp, shivering posse of newshounds and photographers on the pavement outside our house, it fills me with a satisfying glow.

It's only just turned eight o'clock and one of group has already had the temerity to knock on our front door and ask to talk to me. My usual reply would be to tell them to piss off, but as the kids are up and about, instead I open the door a little and inform the soggy reporter that I have no comments to make and won't be giving interviews or making any statement.

This strategy fails to remove them – which is unfortunate as Da and Jenny are going out shortly and will have to run the gauntlet of their unwanted attention – but it can't be helped. I am reluctant to incur DCI Zachary's further displeasure, so I can only hope that the rain gets heavier and the temperature drops a few more degrees.

As we're finishing breakfast, Katie phones in response to my cryptic message of the previous evening.

"I didn't want to wait for your call," she says. "I wanted to find out straightaway what trouble you've got yourself into this time."

"Oh, nothing too serious. I just happened upon half a corpse yesterday in Highgate, and that's what passes for headline news here these days. So we have a load of journos hanging around outside this morning."

"Are you doing detective work again, then?" my elder daughter asks with a hint of disapproval in her voice. "I thought you'd promised Da you'd give all that up. And what do you mean by *half* a corpse?"

I fill her in on the Devesh Banerjee happenings, and explain that this was a one-off investigation. I'm not sure she believes me.

"We had a *whole* dead body turn up in Dubai yesterday," Katie announces. "Found buried out in the desert. Apparently been there a few years. But no information yet about who it might be."

"Well, please be sure not to keep me informed of developments. I need to keep a low profile with Da on the whole digging-up-murder-victims thing because she thinks it's not healthy for me."

"She does have a point, Dad."

"She does indeed. From now on, I'm going to spend all my spare time lighting scented candles, doing Buddhist chanting, and watching Disney cartoons."

As soon as that conversation ends, I phone my stepmother to pre-empt a call from her.

Nang is feeling grumpy, but that's nothing to do with my lapse into private dicking or my disinterring of the dead. Rather that, as a rabid supporter of Brexit and one-nation Toryism, she is concerned that under the current Conservative leadership of Theresa May there may be backsliding on the 'purity' of our withdrawal from the evil European Union.

I receive an unasked-for tirade on this, and she only pauses to pour herself a second cup of Darjeeling tea. I intersperse her rant with occasional *hmmns* so that she realises I'm still listening.

For a Thai-born lady of advancing years, these days she is more resolutely British than Winston Churchill. Were she ever to be put in charge of UK immigration, I suspect that we would see the rapid establishment of concentration camps as a precursor to something considerably worse.

None of which stops me from loving her dearly. Provided she can be kept off the subject of politics, she has a heart of gold and is as sweet a lady as anyone could wish for.

Nang has a word with Da before the call finally ends. She and my wife are of similar minds and personalities, and occasionally I worry that I might have inadvertently married someone who, as the years go by, will mutate into my stepmother.

Da is taking Jenny clothes-shopping in town today, and they wait for their taxi to pull up before pushing their way through the media throng. My wife says something to one of the crowd which causes them to give her room, but I don't catch what it is.

Pratcha helps me clear up the breakfast things before disappearing upstairs to his room to play video games.

I wonder briefly about the identity of the corpse uncovered beneath the sands of the United Arab Emirates.

Some years back, I had occasion to befriend – but stop short of sleeping with – an attractive Japanese-American woman by the name of Hitomi Tanaka, whose husband Akira disappeared while on a trip to Dubai. Hitomi and I have lost touch since, but I half-hope that the body is that of her husband since it will give her closure.

This thought gives me a shudder inside. My encountering Ken Reid the other day has awakened the notion that unwelcome aspects of my past continue to cling to me despite my best efforts to shake them off.

It is, of course, impossible to rid oneself completely of one's history, however desirable that might be.

Da and I periodically stay in touch with Ross Gallagher (a retired Scottish hit-man) and his Balinese wife Wayan (my housekeeper on Koh Samui), who now live a life of quiet seclusion outside Chiang Mai in northern Thailand. Gallagher currently goes under the name of Ralph Gibson, so at least his initials are the same.

I exchange Christmas cards every year with Bill Munks – a former Chief Superintendent of the South Yorkshire Police – who has done me some good turns over the years. He and his wife Hazel live in the Algarve, keep themselves to themselves, and remain in good health.

My continuing contact with Katie, Nang and these individuals therefore comprises the only present interactions of the old David Braddock, although memories of my first wife do stray into my head whenever I let my guard down.

Da and Nang, on the other hand, remain committed to preserving their relationships with their friends and family in

Thailand; and this despite the fact that Nang's relatives are all gangsters.

These ruminations are interrupted by a knock on my front door.

Expecting it to be a reporter – and now geared-up for some seriously righteous anger – I pull it open.

But it's not one of the news-pack. It's Anneke Reid.

Some cameras go off and I usher her inside.

"Sorry," she says with a shy smile. "I'm rather wet."

"Don't you own an umbrella?"

"I didn't realise the rain was going to be this heavy."

I recall Da's warning words on the subject of seventeen-year-old girls, and that uncomfortable episode with Anneke in the coffee shop. But I'm not exactly *alone* with her. Pratcha's upstairs, and I suppose I can always scream if she tries anything funny.

Which is not funny. But I can't kick her out. Not with all those people outside.

"Go through into the living room and I'll get you a towel," I say. "You look like you've just swum the Channel fully dressed. And give me that."

I take her rucksack, leather jacket and scarf, and hang them up.

She has traded her Iron Maiden T-shirt for one that reads *Teenage Cannon Fodder*, but otherwise she's wearing the same clothes she had on at our first meeting.

I retrieve a towel, and she sits on the edge of the sofa and starts drying her hair. I go off to the kitchen to boil the kettle and wonder what the hell she's doing here.

"So, what the hell are you doing here?" I ask when I return with two mugs of tea.

"Is it an inconvenient time?" she says innocently.

"Well —" I gesture to the window.

"Yes. A lot of photographers out there. I knew it was you in the picture on last night's news. You're quite the detective."

"I'd rather not discuss it."

"OK."

I hand her a mug of tea.

"There's no sugar in it. Do you want some?"

She declines.

"You're not supposed to be seeing me till Wednesday."

"Yes. Sorry."

The cockiness she showed at our first meeting has gone. She seems lost.

"Is your wife here?" she says.

"No. She's gone shopping with my daughter. But my stepson's upstairs. Why do you ask?"

"I hoped she'd be here. Because last time, I put you in an awkward position, and I don't want to do that again. Because I really like you, David."

This last remark makes me want to run out of the house, but I control my flight response long enough to realise that this is a person in pain.

"What's happened, Anneke?"

"I had a blazing row with my parents last night, and I've hardly slept a wink. This morning was even worse. There was lots of shouting and my dad said things that I'm not sure I'll ever be able to forgive. I was so angry with them both that I stormed out of the house."

"What was the argument about?"

Her bottom lip trembles and she stares into her mug as if the answer to my question lies there.

"My dad's fucking another woman. He has been for months. My mum won't do anything about it. Everything's falling apart."

She looks up at me. Her eyes are wet and it's not rainwater.

"I'm sorry I said *fucking*."

"It's all right."

"I didn't have anywhere else to go, you see, so I came here."

"Drink your tea and calm down."

I give her a few moments to recover her composure, then say, "Have you considered staying with your grandfather for a while? Give things a chance to settle. He loves you, you know."

"I couldn't. His wife's more or less housebound. An invalid. He has enough to do taking care of her. Didn't he tell you?"

"No."

"Ah. Well, he's a very private person."

"And is your dad's affair the cause of your difficult relationship with your parents?"

Anneke snorts.

"Sometimes. But it's not the only thing we row about. It just – makes things worse."

"What else, then?"

She glances at me miserably and shakes her head.

"Half-an-hour ago I wanted to talk to you about – stuff. But now I don't feel up to it. I'd rather just sit here for a bit if that's OK."

"Yes, that's OK."

The teenager relaxes and sips her tea.

Then she says, "There is something else I'd like to mention though, if it's all right with you. Not a family thing."

"What?"

She hesitates.

"I don't want you to think I'm paranoid and overwrought."

"I won't. I'm not one to confuse paranoia and anxiety."

"And I don't want you to think I'm some stupid girl."

"Stop playing for time and spit it out."

A breath from Anneke before she plunges in.

"Well… for the last few days, I've had the sense that I'm being followed."

"How do you mean?"

"Young women always have blokes eyeing them up on the street. I'm used to that. But this feels different."

"Have you noticed the same man around you at different times?"

"No. But I've noticed two or three young men walking at a distance behind me at different times, and they look shifty."

"But different men?"

"Yes, different ones."

Perhaps there's a stalkers' convention in town, I don't say.

She laughs suddenly. It's not a joyous laugh.

"I sound ridiculous."

"Not at all."

A tear runs down her cheek as her frustration bubbles over.

"I'm probably imagining it, though, aren't I? With everything else that's going on? It sounds idiotic when I say it out loud. My head's all screwed up, David. Why would anyone want to follow me anyway? I'm a mess. I'm not even sure why I've mentioned it. Attention-seeking behaviour on my part. Trying to justify to myself – and to you – why I've turned up on your doorstep."

A deep sigh.

"God, I could do with a joint. But don't worry, I'm not going to light up in your living room."

"Have you got some weed?"

"I've always got weed."

For a second, I'm tempted to grab an umbrella and go upstairs to tell Pratcha I'm going into the garden for a cigarette with a distressed client. But then good sense reasserts itself.

"Well, it's lucky it's raining or I'd be inclined to light up with you out the back. And that wouldn't be good for either of us."

She scrutinises me and makes a decision.

"I shouldn't have come."

She starts to rise.

"Finish your tea."

"I'm fine."

"At least go and wash your face. I can't have the paparazzi taking photos of a teenage girl leaving my house with ruined mascara. Especially as they saw my wife go out earlier."

"Oh, I... I didn't think."

She hurries into the downstairs cloakroom and reappears with her makeup repaired and a determined expression on her face. She doesn't meet my eyes.

"We can have a good talk on Wednesday, yes?" I offer.

Anneke puts on her jacket and scarf, slings her rucksack over her shoulder, and says, "This is really not your problem, David. It's something I have to sort out for myself."

"Anneke, I —"

"Thanks for the tea. I'm sorry to have troubled you."

"I'll see you on Wednesday."

But she has already gone.

The front door slams behind her.

I peep out of the window and see her hurry through the crowd and the drizzling rain.

She keeps her head down.

* * * * *

This little life.

I go to the kitchen, rinse our mugs, and experience a sensation of defeat.

I feel like I've failed Anneke. Da was right when she gave me a talking-to. What possible use can I be to a distressed seventeen-year-old girl? What relevant training and life experience do I have that could be helpful to her? None. I've spoken to her twice and still have no idea what's at the bottom of her anxieties other than the superficial information that her father is having an affair. And I can't even take that at face value because I haven't dug deep enough.

So, she's out there now, pounding the pavements in the rain, her head full of goodness-knows-what. And I don't even have the number of her phone, damn it.

However, there is one thing I can do: I can ring Ken Reid and inform him that she's been here and the sort of state she's in.

I use my mobile and call his number. It goes to voicemail, so I leave a brief message.

It's something. Not much, but something.

To take my mind off things, I switch on my laptop. My inbox is full of messages from journalists and other people I've never met. I turn the laptop off and check on Pratcha. He's fine;

playing League of Loki zombies (or whatever they are). He is oblivious to the fact that I've even had a visitor.

I've barely got back downstairs when my phone buzzes. I anticipate that it's Anneke's grandfather responding to my message. But it's not. It's Ben Quinlan.

I take his call reluctantly.

He sounds breathless and over-excited. He's just had a bad anxiety attack, isn't sleeping, and asks if he can come and see me on Monday morning. I tell him yes, even though I feel like throwing in my hand on the therapy game.

My wife's insistence that I talk to a psychiatrist this afternoon now seems like an excellent idea.

* * * * *

When I leave the house at twelve-thirty, the rain has stopped, and the crowd outside has thinned somewhat.

Microphones and cameras are pushed in my face but I restrict my comments to a declaration that it is not appropriate for me to say anything as I don't want to prejudice the police investigation.

This doesn't deter the questions and I struggle not to lash out with my rolled-up umbrella.

"How did you manage to find the body, Mr. Braddock?"

"Did you know Mr. Banerjee well?"

"Is it true that you practiced as a private detective in Thailand?"

"Would you be open to an exclusive interview?"

"What do you think of the Metropolitan Police?"

"Any theories about the murderer?"

"Are you investigating any other cases?"

"How does it feel to be labelled the new Sherlock Holmes?"

The pack follows me down the street for a hundred yards or so before they give up.

I'm in a decidedly grim mood by the time I descend into Notting Hill Gate.

There are (unspecified) delays on the Central Line and I am reminded of the conversation I had with Anneke here after our first meeting. I hope the interruption to services has not been caused by someone throwing themselves onto the track.

While I'm standing on the platform a young man whom I don't recognise seems to be staring at me, but looks away when I meet his eyes. He's probably wondering where he has seen me before.

On last night's news, I want to tell him. *Would you like an autograph?*

A Braddock tip: if you're depressed, the London Underground is the worst way of travelling across the capital. It might be convenient – at least usually – but the claustrophobia and knowledge that you are *below the earth* can create the unsettling feeling that you're dying, if not actually dead.

Eventually, a packed train arrives and I squeeze onto it. I change at Oxford Circus onto the Victoria Line and get off at Highbury and Islington.

The rain is still holding off as I make my way on foot to Rufus Ogilvy's address. It's one of those gentrified houses much beloved by the Friends of Tony Blair.

Because of the Tube delay, I'm a few minutes late for my appointment. On the plus side, I'm not going to have to do too much acting to appear like I'm a suicide risk.

Rufus Ogilvy answers the door promptly as if he had been lurking in the hallway eagerly awaiting his latest victim/client.

He's of average build with black-rimmed glasses and neatly-trimmed ginger hair. No caricaturish beard, although he is dressed in the uniform of the customer-friendly shrink: smart-casual with the mandatory brown cord trousers and loafers. A liberal lefty, if ever I saw one; and not yet over the existential shock of the affirmative Brexit vote. I'd put him down as a vegan as well. In other words, the sort of character my stepmother would enjoy torturing.

"David, is it?"

"Yes."

"Please come in."

He takes my coat and brolly and leads me through to the rear of the house.

Even though Ogilvy has a separate practice premises, his study looks like a consulting room: walls lined with books, an old desk, comfortable armchairs and a chaise longue.

"Would you like me to lie on the couch?" I ask.

"I'd rather you told the truth in a chair," he replies, pleased at his witticism.

I sit and he plonks himself down opposite me.

"Will it bother you if I take notes?" he says, reaching for a pad and pen.

"Not if you can keep up."

"Why? Do you have a lot to tell me?"

"No point in my sitting here silent, is there? Not at your hourly rate. No offense."

"None taken. And please call me Rufus."

I've decided that – rather than have him extract information from me step by step (a technique I used with Braun, the shrink on Samui) – I'm going to let him have the David Braddock story with both barrels. See what he makes of that.

He opens his note pad.

"I understand that you've been depressed lately, but you start wherever you like, David."

I sit up straight and begin my recitation.

"Right. Well, I was born in Malaysia where my mother was murdered by communist bandits when I was only a few weeks old. My father and I have never got along. He remarried – a Thai woman – and we moved to England while I was a kid.

"My first wife Claire and I had a stillborn baby boy, but our daughter Katie survived. Which was more than Claire did. She contracted cancer and died in 2001.

"Meanwhile, I'd got her sister Anna pregnant, although I didn't find out that I was Jenny's father until much later; after Anna was murdered in my house by a gangster.

"Following my wife's death, I spent about ten years in Thailand practising as a private detective and counsellor. There

I had frequent conversations with my dead wife, indulged in numerous affairs and narrowly avoided being murdered on several occasions. Towards the end of my time in the Land of Smiles, I was shot in the chest by a bodyguard working for a Russian oligarch who had tried to have my daughter Katie killed after she was acquitted of the murder of his son.

"After that, I married Da, my Thai business partner, and together we returned to the UK along with her son, where we adopted Anna's child Jenny. I only told Jenny that I was her biological father recently, by the way, when she turned sixteen.

"The four of us now live in Notting Hill. Da is a property management agent and I run a part-time hypnotherapy practice. The kids are both at school, and my elder daughter is practising law in Dubai.

"I no longer do any private detective work, though I did track down a corpse's legs yesterday. But that was a special case as they belonged to my next-door neighbour."

I pause while Ogilvy desperately tries to record my stream-of-consciousness narrative.

He peers at me. Judging from the expression on his face, he is struggling to decide whether or not I am bullshitting him.

"I'm not bullshitting you," I say reassuringly.

"Right."

"Oh, and I forgot to mention that after I was shot, I was dead for a couple of minutes. So, technically, you're looking at a resurrected man."

Ogilvy consults his notes. He doesn't know where to start. His brain searches for some safe ground.

Finally, he comes out with, "You've certainly led an eventful life so far, David."

"I guess so."

He plays for time.

"And your wife suggested that you might now be suffering from depression. Is that correct? Though, based on what you've told me, there might be some PTSD too."

"I might have whatever it was that Lazarus had."

Ogilvy frowns.

"*Lazarus?*"

"Haven't you heard about the myth that grew up surrounding the miracle of Lazarus?"

"I don't believe I have."

"It's said that after he was brought back from the dead, he didn't ever smile again. Maybe that's what I've got."

He clears his throat, and consults his notes.

"You said that you and your father have never got along."

Ah, we're going for the Freudian angle, are we?

"That's right."

"Do you feel you might have some unresolved issues there?"

"Possibly."

Ogilvy is encouraged by this.

"Are you and your father in touch?"

"No. We haven't spoken for quite a while."

"And why is that?"

"Because he's been dead for seven years."

"Oh."

"I do get on well with my stepmother Nang, though. She's a formidable lady, not unlike my current wife."

I must say, I'm enjoying this session much more than I thought I would. There is something immensely entertaining about watching a psychiatrist who is overloaded with data trying to find a way through it.

Ogilvy is not a complete dolt, however. He hones in on a weak spot.

"David, you said you had discussions with your dead wife Claire."

"That's correct."

"Why don't you talk about that?"

So, I do.

I reassure him that I know there are no such things as ghosts, and that it was my mind's way of dealing with losing her – even if the phantom conversations were accompanied by aural and sometimes visual hallucinations.

"And have these conversations with Claire now stopped?"

"Not entirely. But I don't obsess about her, if that's where this is leading."

Ogilvy steeples his fingers.

"It does strike me, David, that over the course of your life you have had many brushes with death. You've lost a number of people near to you. Almost died yourself. Perhaps you've not found proper closure yet."

"I suppose that's possible," I concede grudgingly.

He consults his notes again.

"There are too many threads here to pick up in a single session. But what do you consider is weighing most heavily on you right now?"

At this stage, I feel that I've already disclosed much more than I had intended, but what the hell. In for a penny, in for a pound.

"This will sound banal."

"No matter."

"I think my main problem is that I'm deeply and profoundly bored."

"*Bored?* But given all the things that have happened to you –"

"Yes, yes," I say impatiently. "But that's just it. My nervous system must have grown accustomed to stress, and now I don't really have any. I have a happy marriage, and my relationships with my children and stepmother are fine. We have no financial concerns. I literally have nothing to worry about. And that's what I'm worried about.

"After all my years of turmoil and dangerous living, I've achieved my Happy Ending. And the plain fact is that I don't know what to do with it."

Ogilvy appears unconvinced by this and decides to try another tack.

"I believe you said you're practising as a hypnotherapist?"

"Yes. Though I have no qualifications that would impress you."

"I'm less concerned about your qualifications than whether you are in the right mental state to be seeing clients."

"Ah."

He waits for me to continue while I fidget uncomfortably.

"As to that," I say, "you may have a point. The other day, I smoked a joint with a seventeen-year-old female client, and my wife was not too pleased about it."

"I should think not," he replies trying to keep the disapproval out of his voice. "What would your professional body make of that? You *do* belong to some association, I presume? Even if it's not one that most medical professionals would recognise," he adds snootily.

"My association doesn't give a toss so long as I pay my annual subscription and carry insurance," I respond in a devil-may-care manner, "but I have been thinking about knocking my practice on the head – for a while, at least."

"I'd say that's wise in the circumstances, David."

We wrap up shortly afterwards.

* * * * *

On my way home, I am a bit disturbed by my melodramatic summary of my life thus far. It was, after all, intended to shock my psychologist, not me. Plus, some of Ogilvy's words prey on my mind; especially his statements and inferences about death, and the space that mortality occupies in my head.

It's not something I've especially dwelt on, but like my former shrink's observation (*"Women die around you, Braddock"*), Ogilvy's suggestion that I might have as-yet unfinished business with the Grim Reaper strikes a chord.

Is that why I was so drawn to the idea of investigating Devesh Banerjee's killing? Because of the pull that the notion of death has on me?

Accordingly, my return Tube journey is like a transit through the netherworld, and my brain becomes skittish as melancholic notions assail me.

I unhelpfully – and indeed uncontrollably – remind myself that when the deep tunnels of the Underground were being dug out for use by the slack-jawed, bleary-eyed multitudes of London, horrors were discovered which had to be accommodated.

The kink in the Piccadilly line between Knightsbridge and South Kensington is only there because the remains of innumerable interlocked skeletons proved too hard to drill through.

Only last year, during the Crossrail diggings around the western end of Liverpool Street, the tunnellers came upon the mass grave of the Bedlam burial ground containing an estimated thirty-thousand bodies.

I could go on.

Suffice to say that London's underground train system curves around, burrows through and sits above myriad plague pits and cemeteries. The Tube literally exists inside a multiplicity of charnel houses; as all across the city, the old dead press unceasingly against its tunnel walls.

These are not reassuring contemplations for a man who has been told that he might be suffering from a death obsession.

Perhaps I should consider travelling by taxi for a while.

* * * * *

When I arrive home, the journalists have gone, their attention span exhausted. Good.

I have an acknowledging *OK* message of response from Ken Reid on my phone; and several more emails in my inbox which I don't have the resolve to tackle right now.

Da, Jenny and Pratcha are all back (my stepson having been at a friend's house while I saw Ogilvy).

I am treated to a modelling session by Jenny of the clothes that Da has bought her, and I withhold my opinion that these could have been bought at half the price once the Christmas sales start.

I have another long phone conversation with Nang who has now caught up with my bloodhound activities relating to the murdered dentist, and also wants my opinion on how well the government is managing illegal immigration.

"And did you see the news today about the Birmingham police arresting a group of men trafficking underage girls?" she continues.

"I didn't, no."

"Most of those swine were dark-skinned. Probably illegals."

"Nang, *you* are dark-skinned."

"That's not the same thing at all."

Once we've turned in, Da wants a full account of my session with the headshrinker.

"He believes I'm fixated on death," I conclude.

"Well, I could have told you that," she replies. "And you *will* see him again, David, won't you?"

"It's already arranged."

"Good boy," she says, switching off the light, "now let's have sex. Would it turn you on if I lie still like a corpse for you?"

"No, it would not."

VII

Lost Soul

The fickle press corps hasn't returned to my front gate. I guess they've smelled blood elsewhere and moved on. I've had my fifteen minutes of fame.

I slept fitfully last night, and after my session with Ogilvy yesterday, I half-expected to be visited by three spirits during the hours of darkness, and to be shown the site of my grave while I cry my heart out to a hooded spectre and promise to change my ways. Well, we are drawing close to that Dickensian time of year.

So, since I was wide awake at six o'clock this morning, I took the opportunity to amble to our local newsagent and buy a copy of one of the better Sunday papers. Reading the news somehow feels more palatable than watching it on a wide-screen television.

"I see the police have formally charged Lee Vance with the murder of our neighbour," I casually inform Da over breakfast. "But there's no mention of anyone else being involved. I guess Jessop's off the hook."

"*David*," she says in a warning voice. "You're not involved with that business any more."

"And he's being done for possessing indecent photographs of kids. They likely found pornographic images on his laptop. I can imagine him and his pedo friend drooling over them, the sick bastards."

"David, not in front of the children."

Jenny and Pratcha appear unconcerned, but I have to agree that this is indeed an unsuitable topic for the breakfast table.

But before I set the paper aside, I examine the article's headshot photograph of Vance. He has tattoos on his neck (and, I'd guess, elsewhere on his body too), untidy grey hair, a slight stubble on his chin, and is coarse-featured. The eyes are cold and they certainly look like the eyes of a killer; or at the very least those of a jailbird.

The journalist who wrote the piece has managed to get hold of Vance's only living relative – his twentysomething nephew William Ackerman, a builder from Walthamstow – who doesn't have a good word to say for his uncle, whom he describes as 'having a violent temper.' So much for families sticking together in difficult times.

Perhaps Vance *is* strong enough to have heaved Banerjee's body about on his own, and perhaps I should drop all my other concerns about the apparent inconsistencies of the case. There is really nothing more I can do. Except follow from afar how matters progress.

I put the newspaper away and tuck into my bacon and eggs.

* * * * *

Lunchtime approaches.

I've had a productive few hours.

Taking advantage of the dry and intermittently sunny weather, I've given my back lawn what I hope will be its final cut of the year. Plus, I've tackled the plethora of emails in my inbox. Some were from folks (including journo scum) curious about my role in the Banerjee investigation while others were from potential therapy clients – no doubt alerted to my existence by the news media, and eager to have their phobias treated by a celebrated gumshoe.

I send two standard replies: one, I am unable to discuss *sub judice* matters and, two, I am not taking any new therapy clients.

I am committed to a session with Ben Quinlan tomorrow morning, but at the end of it I will tell him that I'm having a break from therapy for personal reasons, and recommend a replacement to him. And I'll give the same speech to Jamie Sykes and Anneke Reid when I next see them. That will clear my counselling calendar completely.

Though goodness knows how I will fill up that extra spare time.

More saxophone practice, maybe? Read a few of the books that have been sitting on my shelves for a while? Take up darts? Conduct a line-by-line review of each and every homework assignment the kids have, and make helpful adult suggestions? Find a job stacking shelves in Sainsbury's? Protest about climate change and homelessness? Start smoking again? Paw through *Daily Fail* articles on scumbag criminals until I am outraged enough to become a vigilante? Talk to the dead?

My phone rings before I can come up with any more ideas for improving the planet while making my own life more fulfilling.

It's Ken Reid.

"Hi, Ken."

"David, I'm sorry for this intrusion into your weekend, but I thought I should call you."

The anxiety in his voice is all-too-evident.

"Don't worry about it. What's the problem?"

"Well, it's Anneke. She and my son had a heated argument yesterday morning, and we haven't seen her since. She didn't come home last night and her rucksack is gone along with some of her clothes."

"She came to see me."

"Yes, I got your message, and that's what I'm phoning you about."

"Go on."

"We checked with all her friends that we have contact numbers for, but they couldn't tell us anything. So, we rang the police this morning to report her missing.

"They normally wouldn't act immediately, but in view of Anneke's age a couple of officers arrived at the house a short while ago. They were given photographs of her and other information."

"I'm sorry to hear that, Ken. You guys must be beside yourselves."

This sounds rather too pat, so I add; "She did seem distressed when she dropped by, but I believe I managed to calm her down a bit before she left. Though I must confess, I didn't think through the significance of her having a rucksack with her."

"It's just…"

His voice falters.

"What?"

"Well, as far as we know, David, you're the last person to see her, so I felt we should give the police your name and address. I feel bad about that but —"

"Don't worry, Ken. It's fine. I'd have done the same if I were in your position."

"That's very understanding of you. I expect you'll get a knock on your door today. The officers were keen to talk to you."

"I'll be here."

He sighs.

"If I hadn't browbeaten you into seeing my granddaughter in the first place, you wouldn't have this hassle. I feel horribly guilty."

"Don't. And I'm sure Anneke will turn up. She strikes me as a competent and resourceful young woman."

"I certainly hope so."

We end the call.

My brain is now a jumble of thoughts, and none of them are cheery ones.

* * * * *

Both Jenny and Pratcha have friends over this afternoon.

This is somewhat embarrassing given the presence of two police officers in our living room, but it's not to be helped. A girl has gone missing, after all.

I've brought Da up to speed with what's going on, and she is adamant about sitting with me through the interview, even though I've told her it's not necessary. Given her experience of corruption in the Thai police force, she wants to make sure that the British bobbies are not similarly inclined to fit up an innocent person for the sake of getting a case 'solved.'

The more assertive of the two officers is female, while her male colleague has an *I've-seen-it-all-before* air about him. His role is to take notes while policewoman Taylor asks the questions.

"I understand that you are a therapist, Mr. Braddock," she says, "and that Miss Reid has been seeing you in connection with her anxiety problems."

"We've only had one session so far," I reply, taking an instant dislike to the sound of her voice. "That was last Wednesday, and it was more by way of introduction, so I'm not able to give you any information about what her problems are. And because of client confidentiality, I'm not sure I'd be able to discuss them with you anyway."

The male policeman raises an eyebrow at this but makes no comment. Ms. Taylor is not amused either.

"This is a seventeen-year-old girl who has gone missing, sir. It's hardly appropriate for you to hide behind professional discretion at such a time."

"I'm not hiding behind anything. I'm simply telling you that I am unable to shed any significant light on what is troubling her

– other than to say she appears to be going through a difficult time at home."

The policewoman controls her annoyance and says, "Can't you give me any more than that?"

"Not really. She'd had a row with her father, and – so far as I could see – just wanted to let off steam. I gave her some tea, she stayed for a few minutes, then left. She did, however, mention that she'd had the feeling recently that she was being followed. But she couldn't say by whom, and she quickly dropped the subject."

A note goes into the book.

"And this was at what time?"

"Around nine o'clock."

"Was anyone else here when she arrived?"

"My stepson Pratcha was upstairs playing computer games, but my wife and daughter were out."

"Did your stepson see her?"

"No. But there was a crowd of journalists outside. Some of them might well have photographs of her coming and going."

"From which newspapers?"

"I have no idea. I refused to talk to them."

"And why were they around?"

"Because I discovered the missing half of a murder victim's corpse on Friday, and they wanted an interview. Don't you watch the news?"

This takes her aback, but she recovers quickly.

"And how did a hypnotherapist come to find a body? That would seem to be outside the scope of your usual professional activities."

"If you must know, I used to be a private detective," I say impatiently, "and the victim was my next-door neighbour. And if you want to know more, I suggest you talk to DCI Zachary who is leading the investigation. She's fully up-to-speed on it. Now can we go back to talking about Anneke Reid?"

Another raised eyebrow from the male officer.

Da places a hand on my thigh and gives me a small warning squeeze.

She says, "You will have to excuse my husband's belligerence, Sergeant Taylor, but this girl's disappearance has upset him. We have a daughter who is only a year younger than Miss Reid, and David has been brooding that this could have been Jenny going missing. It's a nightmare for parents having a child at a vulnerable age. I'm sure you understand."

"I understand," replies the policewoman unconvincingly.

Da's grasp of English never ceases to amaze me. Where did she dredge up the word *belligerence* from? Sometimes she puts my own vocabulary to shame.

My interrogator is talking again.

"Can you describe in a little more detail Anneke's frame of mind during her visit, Mr. Braddock?" Taylor asks sweetly. "And maybe give me more of a flavour of what you talked about – provided it's not breaching any client confidentiality."

This last phrase sounds distinctly sarcastic, but I tell her what I can: repeating (using a different form of words) that the girl was agitated about her relationship with her parents. I don't mention Anneke's disclosure about her father's affair. No doubt this doggedly persistent officer will winkle out of Anneke's folks anything pertinent relating to family rows; if she hasn't done so already.

The other plod keeps writing.

"She didn't indicate where she might be going when she left your house?"

"No."

"Weren't you alerted to the risk of her running away by the fact that she had a rucksack with her?"

"No, I wasn't. And what makes you assume that she's run away?"

"We don't assume anything," she replies stiffly. "It's just an expression."

"I see."

"Did she strike you as being potentially suicidal?"

"Absolutely not."

"You sound definite about that, Mr. Braddock. You did say she was very agitated," the officer presses.

"I didn't use the word *very*."

Taylor's colleague flips back through his notes and nods.

"She's a troubled teenager, for sure," I continue, "but she is also an intelligent and confident young lady. And she didn't even hint at the possibility of taking her own life."

"Though you haven't had time to get to know her particularly well, have you, Mr. Braddock?"

"I still know her better than you do," I reply.

Another warning squeeze from Da, which I ignore.

"Now, are we done?" I say.

* * * * *

"Well, that went well," my wife remarks acidly after we've seen the officers off the premises. "If your smoking weed with Anneke had come up during the conversation, you'd find yourself in handcuffs being dragged off to the police station now."

"That Taylor woman could do with some sensitivity training," I grumble.

"Antagonising the police is never a good idea, David. I'd have thought that you of all people would understand that. I'll be surprised if they don't come back with a warrant to search our basement. Your behaviour was highly suspicious. Like you had something to hide."

"It's not like we have a teenage girl chained up downstairs, Da. The worst they'll discover is those unwanted Christmas presents from last year that we've been hoping to palm off on somebody, and whatever it is you've confiscated from Pratcha this week."

"Calm down."

I make an effort to do just that.

"I feel like I've failed her," I say, deflated. "Anneke."

"What could you have done? You've only just met her."

"I know, but... something. Maybe I should have taken her through to the study and had a *proper* discussion with her yesterday morning. Given her some of my time instead of worrying about the journalists outside and my appointment with Ogilvy.

"And then there's the rucksack. I completely missed that. But I don't believe she's run away from home – not for any length of time anyway. I think the rucksack was her making a point. Teaching her parents a lesson. But perhaps she hoped I'd at least *ask* her about it. Which I didn't."

My wife gives me a sympathetic hug.

"Then why don't you use the sergeant's business card that she left with you? Give her a call and tell her what you just told me. And maybe apologise to her for being so..."

"Belligerent?"

"Exactly."

I weigh this up.

"OK," I say.

"And has this reinforced your resolve to stop practicing therapy for a while?"

"Absolutely. Ogilvy's right about that. My head's not in the right place at all. Once I've seen Ben Quinlan tomorrow, I'm putting my practice on ice. And right after I've phoned Sergeant Taylor, I'll ring Jamie Sykes' parents and tell them I'm taking a break for family reasons and recommend someone else."

"Good. Even though I can't imagine what you're going to do with yourself if you have no therapy clients and aren't doing private detective work. Get under my feet, I expect."

"Yes, probably. But we'll figure something out."

"Right. In that case, I'll go and let Anneke out of her cage. She must need to stretch her legs by now."

"You and I are well suited, Da. Worryingly so."

"I know, darling."

* * * * *

Yet it's not really a laughing matter, and gallows humour can't shield you from the world's happenings indefinitely. You can only keep reality at a distance for so long.

Later, after our kids' friends have left, Da and I explain what's going on to Jenny and Pratcha; and my wife uses the opportunity to give out stern warnings about the dangers facing children in big cities.

Jenny is concerned about her dad's demeanour, and she gives me a cuddle.

And, for once – my habitual swagger stripped away – I feel like I need one.

Anneke Reid: lost soul.

David Braddock: lost arsehole.

VIII

The Past Comes Calling

Monday morning: the start of a new week for those who have a working routine.

These days, for me it feels like the arrival of an old school friend whose presence has become irksome because we no longer have anything in common.

Once Da and the children have departed for the day, I clear out my email in-box which has accumulated more dross since I last logged on. There's a brief, enigmatic message of congratulations from Katie who has been familiarising herself with the Devesh Banerjee affair. Apparently, she has a busy couple of weeks ahead of her which includes flying to Seoul to have a meeting with a new South Korean client.

I flip through the news websites to see if there is anything on Anneke Reid. There isn't. I consider phoning her grandfather, but decide that's a bad idea. The poor man needs intrusive phone calls from well-wishers and nosey parkers about as much as I need them from journalists. Happily, there are none of *those* outside our house this morning.

And despite my promise to Da of non-interference in criminal matters, I can't resist checking the London court listings. Lee Vance will be making an appearance in the

Magistrates Court tomorrow. Doubtless the police will oppose bail.

At ten, there is a rat-tat-tat on the front door.

It is not, however, the expected Ben Quinlan, but a hopeful freelance writer who wants to put together a piece on me for one of the Sunday papers. I decline politely, and when he insists on continuing his sales pitch, I decline less politely and escort him off my property.

One of our neighbours is out for a stroll and he shakes his head sympathetically, expresses his views on the gutter press, and gives me a *well done* for solving the Banerjee murder case.

"Just doing my bit for the community," I reply.

"Good man, David," he says, and I wish I could remember his name.

Our postman joins the party, gives me a pat on the back, and hands me our mail.

This comprises the books I ordered for Jenny and Pratcha, various flyers, an electricity bill and an envelope postmarked in the USA.

This last item turns out to be an early Christmas card from Jedediah Reichenbach, an ailing, retired officer of the NYPD who lives in North Carolina.

The message inside reads:

All the best for the Festive Season and the New Year.

I'm hoping that in 2017 we will finally nail You-Know-Who.

Despite the fact that I never contact him – and indeed cut off communication from him some years ago – the American stubbornly insists on leaving the door ajar.

Reichenbach is a man with an obsession: to bring to justice a certain Jim Fosse, the individual he believes was responsible for the death of his half-sister. Jim is the *You-Know-Who* that Reichenbach refers to; and although Jim and I have crossed swords viciously on several occasions over the years, I do not share the former policeman's passionate desire to see Fosse incarcerated.

No, the whole Fosse thing is yet another part of my history that I'd prefer to forget, and I refuse to have Reichenbach draw me into his futile worldwide manhunt. Sometimes, it's best to let sleeping dogs lie; especially when the dog in question is as rabid as Jim Fosse.

Ten-thirty comes and goes with still no sign of Quinlan; and I am about to ring him when the rapping of our brass door knocker announces a visitor.

But once again, it's not my therapy client.

The individual standing on my doorstep has deep furrows etched into his face, and there is something familiar about him, but no name straightaway presents itself.

"Your bell isn't working," he says.

"I know."

He notices my puzzlement and smiles.

"You don't remember me, do you?" he says. "Well, I've got a few more miles on the clock and a few more pounds on the waist since we last met. Though I must say, you don't look much different, Mr. Braddock."

I squint at him and he extends a hand.

"Martin Banks," the visitor announces. "Our last conversation was that time when your daughter Katie went missing. A few years back."

"*Banks?* Christ, you've got old. Life in the police force has certainly taken its toll on you."

He gives me a lopsided grin.

"As charming and diplomatic as ever, I see. Mind if I come in?"

I scan the street hoping to spot Quinlan, but there is no sign of him.

"Well, I'm expecting a therapy client, but I'm free until he shows up, I suppose," I say reluctantly.

We go through to the living room. He removes his coat and I offer him tea.

"I don't suppose you have anything stronger, do you?" Banks replies. "It's nippy outside."

I pour us both a whisky and we sit down.

"I guess you're wondering what brings me to your doorstep out of the blue."

"The thought had occurred."

"Don't worry, I'm not going to tell you that I've morphed from copper to journalist and that I want an exclusive interview with London's latest superstar sleuth."

I wince at this.

"So, you follow the news, do you?"

Banks relaxes into his chair.

"I still keep my ear to the ground, even though I retired from police work a while ago. Plus, I've stayed in touch with DCI Zachary."

"Ah, yes, dear DCI Zachary."

"She sends her regards, by the way."

"I rather doubt that."

Banks laughs.

I am tempted to tell him to drink up and go.

It's not like I owe this man any of my time or attention. The first time we met, he tried to fit me up for the murder of Jim Fosse's second wife Monique, and the next time we crossed paths was during the search for an international hit-man known as *Captain Nemo*: an individual whom I subsequently learned was called Ross Gallagher, and who later married my housekeeper Wayan.

I need to tread carefully. Banks may no longer be a serving plod – if I believe what he says – but there are skeletons in my closet which I would rather remain undisturbed. In my view, Ross and Wayan deserve to live out their days in obscurity in Chiang Mai without the past tugging at them.

As indeed I feel my past pulling at me. Right now.

A message from Reichenbach on Fosse, and a visit from one of the police officers who was hunting Fosse – all in the same morning? Something is afoot in the universe. And, if my experience of the workings of providence is anything to go by, it will not be anything pleasant.

Banks deduces that I am not about to speak, so he breaks the silence.

"So, anyway, here I am again. Showing up unannounced like the proverbial bad penny, eh?"

"You could say that."

He finishes his whisky and wiggles his glass.

I top him up.

"I was in the area and felt that I should say hello," he says.

"Pull the other one, Banks."

"Well, there is a *bit* more to it than that."

"I'll bet there is."

"It's to do with DCI Zachary."

"Oh?"

"I went to see her about the Devesh Banerjee murder. And, even though we're old colleagues, she was less than forthcoming about the case. She pointed me in your direction. Rather sarcastically, I thought."

"And why would you be interested in the death of a Highgate dentist, may I ask? Unless you've gone into the private detective business. You haven't said what you're doing since you left the police force."

"Oh, haven't I?" he replies shiftily. "I'm a security consultant these days."

He takes out his wallet and hands me a business card.

I glance at it and wait for him to enlighten me further.

"It's my wife," he says with a sigh. "That's why I'm here."

"*Your wife?* I don't understand."

"My wife Estela is – or *was* – Banerjee's business partner. In the Highgate dentist surgery. She was buying the old boy out."

"Your wife is a dentist?"

Banks nods.

"Estela already owns three dental practices in London."

I process this.

"I'm rather surprised to hear that you're married, Banks. You didn't strike me as the marrying sort. And, *Estela?* Is she Spanish?"

"No, she's from the Philippines. We met… oh, that's a long story. I won't bore you with it."

A memory rouses.

"Ah, of course. The *Philippines.* Zachary said Banerjee's business partner was attending a family funeral there. That's how I ended up identifying the body. I imagine our good DCI mentioned that."

"She did, yes. Apologies for the inconvenience. I suppose we owe you for that."

"Not at all. But you do owe me an explanation for why you're here. The police have already charged a suspect for the dentist's murder. What more do you expect me to tell you?"

Banks scratches his chin.

"I'm not really sure, to tell you the truth. You heard that the surgery was ransacked and some of it was torched?"

"I did. And? Are you concerned that the killing was not simply a personal affair between Banerjee and the suspect Lee Vance? That your wife Estela also has reason to be concerned for her safety?"

A worried expression crosses Banks' face briefly but he makes no reply.

"Do you think this is part of some wider vendetta? That somebody has a grudge against all Highgate dentists?"

He gives an amused snort.

"Your sarcasm is well-placed," he says evenly. "I should have retired from policing much sooner. It's made me overly suspicious. The policeman's lot is not a happy one, as the song goes. But when a crime is committed as near home as Banerjee's murder was... well, it was a shock for Estela, as you can imagine. It's made her rather jittery coming so soon after her brother's death."

I don't find this convincing, but as Banks shows no inclination to expound further, I close off the subject by telling him there's nothing I can add and that he already knows as much as I do.

The ex-policeman plays with his whisky glass for a while, then brightens up.

"Changing the subject," he says, "did you ever meet up with our old American friend Jim Fosse when you were in the Far East? You realise the case file on his wife Monique's murder was never closed? And I recall you telling me before you left England that you – what were your words? – *owed him a reckoning*."

"That was a long time ago. Over fifteen years, in fact. I figured that at the end of the day, sorting out that mess was the job of the police."

"Ah."

"Anyway, I heard that Fosse had died in Bangkok."

My visitor leans forward.

"Did you, now? And who did you hear that from?" he says, interested.

I shrug.

"Someone or other."

He is scrutinising my face, but I am giving nothing away.

As I'm in no way indebted to Banks, and since he is not being forthcoming with me, I am not inclined to be helpful to him.

The only people who know the full story about Jim Fosse are me, Ross Gallagher and Jedediah Reichenbach, the sender of this morning's Christmas card. And it's going to stay that way: that can of worms is not going to be re-opened. Certainly not by me.

Whatever it is that Banks suspects – and I doubt his mention of the sociopathic Yank is based on casual curiosity – I am not going to participate in his fishing expedition.

He understands that our conversation is over, thanks me for the whisky, and leaves.

I am none-the-wiser as to why he came, but at least I have managed – for now – to fend off the resurgent spectres of my disreputable past.

Will I ever finally be able to lay these memories to rest, Claire? I ask my dead wife.

Not if you are going to start talking to me again, she replies.

"You're right," I say out loud. "That's a terrible idea. Forget that I spoke."

* * * * *

I contemplate phoning Quinlan to moan at him for missing his therapy appointment, but then remember that I didn't really want to see him; so instead, I apply myself to a few neglected household chores.

I do some vigorous dusting and hoovering, change the battery in the door-bell, and rehang a hall picture whose crooked angle has been bugging me lately. Now the picture next to it looks crooked.

Enough domestic matters. I take out my saxophone to make sure I'm not rusty for this Thursday (though our band will be playing the same stuff as usual, which I can now pretty much do on auto-pilot).

Mid-afternoon, Da rings to tell me that she's had a call from Pratcha's school. My stepson has not reported back for lessons after lunch; and my wife speculates he is playing video games somewhere with his mates. He is going to be in hot water later, and I don't think I'm going to be giving him the *Gamer's Guide to The League of Loki* that arrived this morning.

* * * * *

Once we're all home, Pratcha receives the expected dressing-down from Da (who confiscates his consoles for a week); and I lecture the children on the importance of always keeping us informed of where they are.

This topic is much in the forefront of my mind as Anneke Reid's parents have been on the TV news giving a tearful plea for their daughter to come home and asking for any information on her whereabouts.

I give Jenny her book and inform my stepson that he will only receive his *Gamer's Guide* once his mother is satisfied that he has learned his lesson. The little chap is suitably apologetic and goes off to his room with his tail between his legs to apply himself to his homework. Jenny is happy that her dad is back to his former self.

When we're alone, I give Da an account of my day's happenings.

"I'm glad that you're being transparent," she says. "I believe that weekend session with Ogilvy has done you good. And you *will* see him again, won't you."

This is not a question, but I reply in the affirmative anyway.

"I've been mulling things over today, David. And I've come to a decision."

This sort of declaration usually presages a reprimand about the inappropriateness of my behaviour, so I'm instantly on tenterhooks.

"Oh?"

"You were full of energy and enthusiasm when the Devesh Banerjee thing happened. But now that's over, I feel I was a bit harsh on you. Plus, you *are* having therapy, and I don't want you to dwell on this Anneke Reid business."

"Go on. I'm liking this so far. Provided there's not a *but* coming."

"Well… you need something to do. I know you miss being in the detective business, and if I'm being honest, I miss it too. So…"

She hesitates.

"So?" I prompt.

"So, I have a case for you to investigate."

I'm not sure I've heard her correctly.

"You have… What?"

"A case. Oh, don't worry. Nobody's going to be shooting a gun at you, and it won't involve gangsters, or drug-smuggling, or human trafficking. Indeed, it might be rather mundane. But you need something to occupy you. Plus, it might remind you of how tedious most detective work is; and make you take off your rose-tinted glasses about the Good Old Days. Walking the streets, doing boring stakeouts, laboriously digging out information…"

"Never mind about all that, Da. What is this case and how did you come to find out about it?"

I pour us both a large glass of wine.

"This morning I was nattering with a female client – Rebecca Oliphant, a medical assistant – who has recently come into an inheritance and wants to buy an apartment in Kensington. She was in a chatty and upbeat mood. Apparently, she was named as her maiden aunt's sole beneficiary and had no idea that the old lady was worth so much money –"

"Da, I don't need this woman's life story. Get to the meat, please."

"I'm getting there. You're so impatient."

It's best if I don't reply to this, so I don't.

"Anyway, Mrs. Oliphant currently lives in Battersea. And she was telling me about her next-door neighbour, a married lady in her early fifties by the name of Pearl Webster. Are you with me so far?" my wife asks mischievously.

"Mrs. Oliphant lives in Battersea, next door to Mrs. Webster. Yep, I think I've got it."

"Good."

"Now, let me guess the rest. Mrs. Webster has a second-cousin whose blind friend's guide dog has gone missing."

"You're on the right lines," Da replies. "But it's Mrs. Webster's husband who has gone missing. He's a train driver for the London Underground, and he vanished completely a couple of weeks ago."

"Ah, now you begin to intrigue me. Continue."

"Unsurprisingly, the police have been no help, and Mrs. Oliphant says that the poor woman is at her wit's end. She'd like to engage a private detective, but I gather that the Websters don't have much money, so that's out of the question for her.

"So, I told my client that I have a husband who is a private investigator, and that you sometimes do *pro boner* work –"

"Da, my darling, your English is excellent, but your Latin perhaps not so much. I believe you mean pro *bono*. Pro *boner* work sounds like the sort of thing a prostitute would do."

"Yes, well, I didn't have the benefit of your public school education," she says stiffly.

"No matter. What happened next?"

"Mrs. Oliphant phoned Mrs. Webster, and to cut a long story short, she was most grateful for the offer of help, and is expecting you to call on her tomorrow."

Da waits for my reaction.

"What do you think? Have I done well? Am I a considerate and understanding wife?"

I down a mouthful of wine. Maybe tonight's full moon is exerting an influence on her neural pathways in some way that a mere man cannot comprehend.

"This is all very sudden. I'm rather taken aback by your change of heart, my love. It's not that I'm not grateful, you understand, it's just that… And you told Mrs. Webster that I *am* a private detective, not that I *was* one?"

"You can have some business cards printed tomorrow morning, and Pratcha can produce you a website tomorrow evening as part of his penance for playing truant. Then you'll be set up again."

"As simple as that?"

"As simple as that."

She digs in her handbag and hands me a piece of paper with Pearl Webster's address and phone number on it.

"I told her you'd ring her in the morning and fix a mutually-convenient time to meet," she says.

I am stunned by this rapid sequence of revelations. But having an investigation of my own might be just the ticket for driving away the gloom of my sticky past, my exclusion from the Banerjee business, and my guilt over Anneke Reid.

Hmmn.

The labyrinthine process of Da's reasoning always amazes me.

It seems my dear wife has invented an alternative version of the popular game Rock-Paper-Scissors.

I'm going to call it Man-Woman-Logic.

Man beats Woman.

Logic beats Man.

Woman beats Logic.

IX

A Missing Railwayman

Weather-wise, the day starts miserably with an overcast sky. It's not raining, but the gloomy light is enough to dampen my spirits without the need for any assistance from dihydrogen monoxide.

It requires an effort to propel myself out to a local shop to get business cards printed.

Since it's a rush job, I am ridiculously overcharged for the one-hundred rectangles of cardboard which carry my mobile phone number and the words:

David Braddock

Confidential Investigations

There is no mention of a website (since I won't have one until Pratcha sorts that out this evening), and certainly no address.

It's enough. Especially as there is a good chance that I'll only use one of these pricey bits of felled tree.

When I'm back home, I clear out more junk emails then phone Mrs. Webster and arrange to call on her at three o'clock. She sounds guarded but not unfriendly.

I follow this up by ringing Quinlan's number.

There is no reply, so I try his office only to be told by some sniffy secretary that he is not in today. I don't leave a message, since if Quinlan has decided he doesn't need a session after all, then that's fine by me.

I make a sandwich for lunch and dig out my passport so that I have some official ID for Mrs. Webster. I don't want a repeat of the fiasco of when I turned up at Jessop's place. As an afterthought, I stuff an electricity bill in my pocket to corroborate my address in case my new client is of a nervous persuasion.

Before leaving the house, I give in to the temptation to ring Ken Reid only to be told that there is no news of his missing granddaughter. Unsurprisingly, it's a brief conversation since neither of us knows what the hell to say.

By the time I step out into the street for a second time, London appears a tad less dismal, and I remind myself that I'm about to embark on a new project and should be full of enthusiasm and seasonal cheer.

This fails, however, to have the desired effect.

As I stand on the Circle Line platform at Notting Hill Gate – which subterranean lair is starting to feel like my second home – I find that dispelling thoughts of Anneke Reid is not at all easy. Although I know I have to concentrate on presenting myself as a consummate professional investigator for my meeting with Pearl Webster, my discussion with Anneke's grandfather has done little to set my mind at rest; or indeed to put Anneke out of it.

I stare at the train tracks and remember my chat with the girl about suicide and my helpful tips on how to go about it. Plus, her mention of having a feeling of being followed seems to have infected me too.

I peer around the platform. It's not busy, but it's not exactly deserted either. To my right, a young man is looking at me, and on my left side a middle-aged man is also looking at me. But that's probably because I am looking at them. The older man is dressed smart-casual and carries a newspaper while the younger one appears as if he's either just come off a building site or escaped from the gorilla enclosure at London Zoo: his eyes jitter around in small saccades as if he's suffering from some visual impairment.

I offer each of them a stern glare, and they both find something else to occupy their attention.

It seems that I will have some new neurosis to confess to Ogilvy at our next session: *a sense of being stared at.*

Great.

The screeching arrival of a train sets my nerves further on edge.

* * * * *

I change at Victoria onto the Victoria Line for the two stops to Vauxhall during which we pass under the murky flow of the Thames: a reassuring notion.

South of the river is not well-served by the Underground system due to a combination of geology, economics and historical legal restrictions. So, getting to the Websters' house in Battersea requires my climbing into a cab, educating myself on the eccentricities of local buses, or taking a walk.

This last option strikes me as the least problematic. Also, it gives me time to cheer up: a process assisted by my acquiring a can of cider from a general shop (along with a packet of mints to remove the smell of alcohol from my breath).

Cold lungfuls of filthy South London air, supplemented by the sight of the decaying chimneys of Battersea Power Station, restore me to a less-troglodytic and more-surface-dweller outlook.

By the time I ring the doorbell of the Websters' modest mid-terrace house, I am almost ready to don traditional Cockney regalia and do the Lambeth Walk.

Almost, but not quite.

Pearl Webster opens the door, grants me a fleeting smile and compliments me on my punctuality.

I show her my passport, offer the opinion that one can't be too careful these days, and hand her a business card.

"It's all right, Mr. Braddock" she says. "I recognise you from the telly. That awful business with poor Mr. Banerjee. He was Ronald's dentist, actually. And my dentist too. So, when Mrs. Oliphant said that your wife had offered me your services, it seemed like our meeting was destined to be. Karma, one might say. The Universe sending one of its messages. Unless you're one of those people who believe everything is coincidence."

I put on my 'no comment' face.

She ushers me through to her lounge and we sit down.

While we indulge in small-talk, I surreptitiously study my pro bono client, while she does the same to me.

Pearl Webster is one of those women who could be anywhere between her early forties and her mid-sixties. I doubt she was ever young, even when she was. She wears no makeup; her hair is permed and she is dressed 'sensibly.' There is no jewellery in evidence apart from her wedding ring and a silver Eye of Horus charm on a necklace. She has, however, kept her figure – either through working-out or careful diet. Not the classic yoga-hag type, in my estimation, despite some of the esoteric articles in the room. Her voice is soft, though I detect a certain hardness behind the eyes.

Inevitably, she offers me tea, and while she goes off to make it, I scan my surroundings.

The room is old-fashioned: antimacassars on the furniture, every flat surface covered in knick-knacks and figurines, and on a small side-table is a crystal ball and a pack of tarot cards. The smell of rosewood emanates from an oil burner, and there are a few unlit candles around – doubtless scented ones. It is the lair of someone of a witchy temperament.

When she returns, she catches me examining the crystal ball.

"Are you interested in the spirit world, Mr. Braddock?" she asks as she sets down the tea tray.

"Well, I –"

"Because I couldn't help noticing that you have a striking aura," she continues.

"Do I?"

139

She gives a decisive nod.

"Purple. The colour of the third-eye chakra. It indicates intuition and possible psychic abilities."

"Does it?" I reply unenthusiastically.

"It does indeed. And I can tell you that it gives me a good deal of confidence that you are the right man to find Ronald. Especially given the shared connection with Mr. Banerjee, and the fact that you managed to find him."

I don't know how to respond to this, and technically speaking I only found half of Banerjee, so I say nothing.

She strokes the crystal ball fondly.

"My late mother was a medium," she continues. "I was fortunate enough to inherit her gift, and I use it to bring comfort from the ethereal world to the physical world. Yes, I've held many successful séances in this very room."

She sits and begins to pour the tea, some herbal concoction which I am sure will taste of grass cuttings and potpourri.

"Do you believe in an afterlife, Mr. Braddock?" she asks. "Or does my talk make you feel you are dealing with a charlatan or a crank? Because I can assure you that I am neither."

I don't think you want to get into this conversation, David, my dead wife whispers to me.

It's a bit late for that, Claire, I reply.

Just steer her off the subject. And do not under any circumstances tell her to ask the spirits if Ronald is already on the other side. I know what you're like.

It might save me a lot of time.

It would be rude.

All right.

"As to the afterlife," I say as sincerely as I can, "I'm on the fence about it. Although I did have a near-death experience some years ago when I was shot in the chest."

"My goodness!" Pearl Webster exclaims. "And did you bring anything back with you from the other side? Any visions or memories or impressions?"

"Only the impression that I preferred to be alive."

"Oh."

She appears disappointed, but then a practical thought strikes her and she changes tack abruptly.

"Mr. Braddock, before we begin… Mrs. Oliphant said that you wouldn't be charging any fee for your services. Is that correct, because if not –"

I raise a hand.

"There will be no bills or expenses or costs of any kind, Mrs. Webster. Occasionally, I take a case because I like to put something back, if you follow me."

She is both reassured and impressed by my philanthropy.

I venture a sip of tea. As expected, it's as bitter as a jilted bride.

To business.

"Tell me what the police had to say when you reported that Mr. Webster had gone missing."

She frowns.

"The two officers who came to see me didn't inspire me with a lot of confidence, I must say. It felt like they were simply going through the motions so they could keep their paperwork tidy. And they asked me some rather impertinent questions."

She shows me the investigating officer's card, and I note the details.

"I'm afraid I might be asking some impertinent questions too. Plus, I'll likely be going over the same ground, so apologies in advance."

"I understand."

At this point, I need to manage her expectations so I say, "Did they share with you any numbers on missing persons?"

"Not really. They did say it happens a lot, but that most people turn up again."

"Well, the official statistics place it at around one-hundred-and-eighty thousand a year for the whole country, but according to the UK Missing Persons Bureau that's a big underestimate. Their most recent figures say that over three hundred thousand missing person reports are filed in the UK each year. Many of those are for children and over eighty per cent of them are found within twenty-four hours."

"And how many missing adults are found?"

"It depends whose numbers you believe, but a significant proportion don't reappear. Whether that is by choice or not, there is no way of knowing."

Unless a body turns up, says my dead wife unhelpfully.

"Over three hundred thousand a year," muses Pearl Webster. "That's getting on for a thousand people a day."

"Yes."

"I see."

I take out my notebook and she eyes it warily.

"When did you last see your husband?"

She swallows some of the revolting tea.

"Two weeks ago today. On the evening of Monday, the thirty-first of October. He'd been working that day, and he went out on his own about nine o'clock and didn't come back."

"Did he say where he was going?"

Mrs. Webster purses her lips.

"Research," she replies.

"Research for what?"

"For his book on the history of the London Underground. Whenever he went out it was usually for that," she says with a trace of rancour.

"What research can be done at that time of night?"

"I have no idea. I'm afraid that I stopped talking to him about his damned book some time ago. There is only so much I can absorb on the subject before my eyes glaze over. The topic is not one that interests me, Mr. Braddock. And Ronald is a man who is very, very keen on details."

"So far as you know, no-one else has seen him since then?"

"No-one. And I've phoned everyone I can think of. His parents are dead, and he has no siblings and few friends.

Ronald is rather a solitary person, you see. He prefers trains to people."

"Have you checked to see whether any of his clothes are missing?"

"They aren't."

"How about his passport?"

"Still in the drawer."

"Any large withdrawals from his bank account either immediately before or since the thirty-first of October?"

"Not according to his October bank statement, and at the end of each month when his salary goes in, he transfers almost all of it to our joint account so there wouldn't have been much in there to take out. He does have a credit card, but rarely uses it. I can show you his last statement for that as well if you want."

"Is there anywhere he might have gone, Mrs. Webster? If not abroad, then in this country?"

Sad eyes from the woman.

"Ronald doesn't like *abroad*, Mr. Braddock. I've only been able to drag him out of the UK on two occasions: to Greece in the late nineties, and then to Spain three years ago. He hated both trips and couldn't wait to get back. As to where he might be in England, we usually holiday in Scarborough, Brighton or Cornwall – but I can't see him being in any of those places. He never wants to be anywhere but London, although he has done some railway outings with the Clapham Junction Locomotive Club."

I make a note of this and tell her I'll come back to it.

"Mrs. Webster, I need to be a little personal now."

"Go ahead. Ask me whatever you want."

"Can you think of any reason why your husband might want to disappear? Does he, for instance, gamble? Does he drink a lot or have a drug habit?"

"None of those things. Our three decades together might have been a lot more interesting, Mr. Braddock, if he did indulge in any of them."

I glance up from my notebook.

"I'm being flippant," she says, abashed.

I continue.

"No mental health or other health issues?"

"No. Not unless you count an obsession with trains as a mental health issue."

"He hasn't seemed depressed to you recently?"

"No."

"I'm sorry to ask this, but is there any possibility that your husband has a mistress? It's just that if he's been vanishing regularly in the evenings, we have to consider that."

She shakes her head.

"Ronald is not much interested in sex. He hasn't been for years. Whatever he needs in that department he can get on the Internet."

She bites her lip, and adds, "Perhaps I'm being unkind to him."

"Not at all. You must be under a lot of strain at the moment."

She pats my hand.

"Thank you. You're most kind."

She tops up my tea cup and I give her a weak grin.

"I have a couple of photographs of Ronald for you," she says, rises and takes them from a drawer in the sideboard.

The first is a passport-style head-and-shoulders shot.

In it, Ronald Webster looks like a startled cadaver. Flaky skin – presumably a consequence of spending his days underground – and the tuberous nose of someone who likes a drink (even though his wife says he doesn't). Spectacles, comb-over thinning hair, and watery eyes.

The second picture is a full-length one of him standing against brickwork with wood beams on either side of him. Possibly he's in an old-fashioned pub. His posture is awkward, and the overall effect is one of a corpse who has been jiggled about in his coffin then propped up against a wall. He has a pot belly and is wearing cheap, unfashionable clothes and dirty trainers. I doubt he's been anywhere near a gym or sports field since he was at school. If Mrs. W had showed me this photograph at the start of our discussion, I wouldn't have bothered with the question about a mistress. His face is frozen in a ghastly smile, and he has a missing left incisor.

"Yes," says his wife, as if reading my thoughts. "He isn't at his best. I've written his mobile number on the back because, well, just in case."

"I should have asked before, but how old is he?"

"Fifty-four."

He looks a lot older, Claire suggests.

"Are these recent pictures?"

"In the last two years. Reluctantly, I might add. Ronald doesn't like having his photo taken."

Claire tells me that's hardly surprising, and I tell her to shut up.

"How tall is he? It's hard to tell from this."

"He's five-foot-eight."

"Does Ronald have any other distinguishing features that might help in identifying him?"

"Like what?"

"Does he, say, walk with a limp? Have a lisp or a stammer? Any scars or tattoos? Anything like that?"

"No. Sorry. He's just an ordinary middle-aged man."

"Can I hang onto these pictures?"

"Yes."

I set the photographs aside and ask her to describe what sort of a man he is.

In the next few minutes, a portrait emerges of a charmless, nondescript individual, socially awkward and inarticulate about everything except railways and the London Underground. He likes crosswords, the History Channel and quiz shows. His one redeeming feature – if I can call it that – is his driving ambition to write a history of the Underground. The rest of his life appears to have been subservient to that overarching goal; even his thirty-year marriage.

"We rubbed along though," Mrs. Webster concludes. "Maybe if we'd had children, our life together might have gone in a different direction. But Ronald never wanted them. And I never wanted them enough to argue about it."

"You said that your husband is not much given to attending social functions, but that he does have a *few* friends. Can you give me their names and contact details?"

I consult my notes.

"You mentioned the Clapham Junction Locomotive Club."

"Yes, Ronald does attend their meetings whenever his shift rota allows. They get together on a Saturday evening, mid-month, and talk about trains."

"Have you ever been to one of their meetings?"

She curls her upper lip.

"Once, a couple of years back I allowed Ronald to badger me into attending as he was giving a talk. But that was sufficient for me."

"Did he see any of the members outside of these meetings?"

"There is a young man who belongs to the Club whom Ronald used to take with him sometimes on his research outings. I did meet him that one time. Gustaw Belka is his name. I believe his family is of Polish origin. He also works for Transport for London or at least he did then."

She rises from her chair and starts rummaging in the sideboard.

"I took a photograph of the group, and I might still have it somewhere."

She pulls out an album and flips through it.

"Yes, here it is."

She points at a gawky-looking individual.

"That's him. That's Goose."

I squint at the image. The face is somewhat familiar. A dim lightbulb flickers.

"*Goose*, did you say? That's his nickname?"

"Yes."

"I think I might have met him. Here in London. But that must have been – let's see – about seven or eight years ago. If it is the same person, he was working as a barista then. He has the sort of face you don't forget and he hasn't changed much. Plus, I recall he was obsessed with numbers and a bit of a conspiracy nut…?"

"That sounds like him."

"Do you have a phone number or an address for him?"

"I don't, but they might have at the Club."

She flips through her contacts on her mobile phone.

"The Chairman is a gentleman by the name of Fred Eggers. Here's his number."

I jot it down.

"Thanks. Maybe I'll go along to their next meeting."

"I'm sure you'll be made welcome. They don't have many members."

I consult my notes again.

"Ronald's manuscript on the history of the Underground. Would it be possible for me to see a copy?"

"He keeps it along with everything else on his laptop. Come with me and I'll show you his man-cave. He converted our second bedroom into a shrine for the railways."

She leads me upstairs into a room whose interior largely comprises a model train set on a large trestle table. A small desk has been squeezed into the corner, and one wall is covered in shelves which contain books and the ephemera of the model railway enthusiast: paint, brushes, tweezers, screwdrivers, spare track, miniature people, trees, hedgerows, rolling stock, signage and sundry modelling materials. The layout is impressive: years of work and devotion must have gone into it.

Pearl Webster unplugs the laptop, lifts it off the desk and deposits it into a carry-bag.

"Here," she says. "Keep it as long as you need to. There's no access password. But I'd like it back when you've done."

I am still staring at the trainset.

"Now, perhaps, you see what I'm up against, Mr. Braddock."

"Your husband certainly loves trains," I reply. "Does he, by any chance, keep a diary?"

"Not to my knowledge."

She opens a drawer of the desk.

"Only these notebooks for his train-spotting."

I flick through them and hand them back to her.

"OK. We're done here."

We return to her front room and I put the photographs into the laptop bag.

"Is there anything else you need from me?"

"I'd like to talk to Ronald's employer."

"All right."

"Would you mind contacting Transport for London and fixing up a meeting for me? If you explain that I'm acting for you on the matter of your husband's disappearance, they'll be more likely to agree to see me than if I ring them out of the blue."

"Yes, I'll do that today."

"Message me on my mobile with the meeting details."

"Should I come with you?"

"I don't need to put you through that, Mrs. Webster. But I may want to see you again once I've been through Ronald's laptop files."

"I work part-time at the Battersea Candle Emporium – usually three mornings a week – and I sometimes help out at a local charity shop. But other than that, I'm around. I only ever hold séances in the evening at weekends."

"I'll remember."

She shows me to the front door, but then pauses.

"There is one thing I should maybe mention before you go."

"Oh?"

"About a fortnight before he disappeared, Ronald came back late from one of his research excursions in an excitable state. He didn't discuss with me exactly what he had found out, but he did mention that he might have discovered a new angle for his book."

"Is that all he said?"

She gives me a rueful grin.

"When you're married to a train fanatic, Mr. Braddock, you tend to develop selective hearing. I hope it wasn't anything important."

On my walk back to Vauxhall, I go into the general shop and buy a bottle of water to wash away the taste of Pearl Webster's herbal tea.

I mull over our conversation. At this stage, I rate my chances of finding this unmemorable railwayman as slim to zero.

I try his mobile phone number anyway. Nothing. That would have been too easy.

* * * * *

After dinner, while Pratcha is working (post-homework) on getting my website up, Da is keen for a report of how I got on today.

I give her a summary, omitting the brief discussion of Banerjee which will make Da suspicious that I haven't let that case go.

"Did she seem upset?"

"Not unduly so. There was certainly no crying."

"So, what does your gut tell you, Sherlock?" she asks.

"Well, there are one or two things that stick in my mind."

"Such as?"

"The first is, that although we were both careful to refer to Mr. Webster in the present tense, Pearl Webster stated at one point that they 'rubbed along together.' Past tense."

"That could be a simple slip of the tongue and you shouldn't read too much into it."

"I know. But you did ask."

"What's the other thing?"

"I'm not sure I want to tell you now. Especially after that 'Sherlock' remark."

"Go on."

"The other thing is – considering she had only ever attended one meeting of the Clapham Junction Locomotive Club (and even then, on sufferance) – why would she have the Chairman's phone number readily available on her mobile?"

Da looks impatient with me, so I continue.

"You do realise that, statistically speaking, if Ronald Webster has been murdered, there's about a ninety-per-cent probability that his wife did it?"

"Just as if, were something to happen to you, my darling, there would be about a ninety-per-cent probability that I did it."

"Now, there's a comforting thought."

X

Home Alone

Once breakfast is done and everyone has cleared off, I make a list of things to do, starting with the easy task of approving the website that Pratcha threw together for me yesterday evening.

It's a simple affair comprising two pages, each of which has a corny cartoon magnifying glass at the top and *DAVID BRADDOCK CONFIDENTIAL INVESTIGATIONS* in a bold modern typeface. I suppose I should be grateful there's no silhouette of a man smoking a pipe and wearing a deerstalker hat.

The *Home* page describes my confidential services offered, and details on how to get in contact. There is no mention of prices: seemingly we celebrity detectives don't talk about anything so vulgar as money.

The *About Us* page comprises a catalogue of my investigating exploits and experience. The wording for this was definitely put together by my dear wife, and contains an overblown account of my ten years in Thailand. It goes on to mention that my professional practice has continued since returning to England and that I was instrumental in resolving the recent Devesh Banerjee case ('as seen on national television') working alongside the Metropolitan Police. I can only hope that DCI

Zachary doesn't see this as it will not be good for her blood pressure. Or for my liberty.

Oh, well. It will do for now.

I tackle my inbox, either deleting or politely declining pretty much everything in it; and can't resist doing a quick online trawl to see if there is any news on Vance or Anneka. There isn't. I suppose Ken Reid will be in touch if his granddaughter shows up. The poor sod.

Right. On to our disappearing railwayman.

If I weren't so unpopular with the police and didn't want to bring myself further to their attention, I could call the officer handling the Ronald Webster disappearance for a chat and to compare notes. But I am, so I don't. And besides, I understand only too well that his case will not be getting priority, so there won't be much to discuss anyway. The overstretched Met Police will be more concerned with missing youngsters, traffic violations and the odd terrorist to do anything but the minimum for RW. And that won't be enough.

If Webster is voluntarily missing, where would he go? Based on the character portrait that his wife gave me, it seems unlikely that he would have left London. But if he doesn't want to be discovered, he's not going to be anywhere near Battersea or Clapham Junction: he might run into his missus or one of his fellow train enthusiasts. However, that still leaves a big swathe of city for me to cover. Somehow, I have to narrow that down, or my legs will be worn down to stumps in no time.

If Webster did indeed have little money on him when he walked out of the house, that would limit his options on where he could stay and for how long. And he's already been gone for a fortnight. Two weeks in London, even in some cheap rathole of a hotel, would eat up his cash fast.

By now, unless someone has secretly taken him in, he may already be living among the homeless of the capital.

An Internet search on a few salient websites throws up some alarming and dispiriting findings.

According to official figures, the number of homeless people in London has risen from about four thousand in 2010-11 to an estimated seven thousand now. A disturbingly large proportion of those sleeping rough are young people, and something like a fifth of them are female. There are homeless hostels, but not anything like enough, and many of those on the streets are suspicious of using them anyway.

And these are the official figures which, if my experience of such matters is anything to go by, will be an understatement.

Living my comfortable, privileged existence, I had no idea that the scale of London's homeless problem was so large. And this in one of the world's richest cities. Pause for the counting of blessings. It's going to make me think twice from now on before walking past a street beggar with his cardboard sign and cup of change.

I open Webster's laptop and start mooching around his hard disk.

He's a tidy chap, I'll give him that. Perhaps too tidy. His files are all saved under suitably descriptive folders, but there is zilch that could be described as 'personal' or insightful on the missing man. There's certainly nothing that equates to a diary or the recording of thoughts or emotions. A huge chunk of his disk drive appears to be taken up with photographs of trains and railway stations, of both the underground and overground variety. And, boy, does he love spreadsheets. He would have made a good actuary, assuming there is such a thing.

The folder *Schedule* contains only a planning spreadsheet giving a timeline for each draft chapter of his book. It's as meticulous as a railway timetable, and stops in September of this year, fully completed. But the columns indicating whether each chapter has been edited have no dates, either 'target 'or 'achieved.' It is as if he ran out of steam or, maybe on reading it back to himself, he was discouraged by the dry factual garbage before his eyes.

The folder labelled *My History of the London Underground* has four-dozen files in it, and all but one of them – tagged *Draft Manuscript* – read as detailed notes on specific aspects of his magnum opus, arranged by chapter title.

I flick through a few of them. The one called *The Complexities of the Northern Line* runs to over sixty pages, and I start to wonder where Da has hidden our headache tablets. The file named *Short Biography of Frank Pick* (the man – I learn – who was behind the iconic Underground roundel image) is about thirty pages in length. And though the documents entitled *Ghost Stations* and *London's Dead and Suicide Pits* promise more interesting reading, I decide to set Webster's research material aside and concentrate on his draft manuscript, otherwise I'll likely end up sifting through all this tedious crap twice.

I note with horror that his unedited *History* runs to over fifteen-hundred pages; and this in a blindness-inducing small font. The first thing I do is expand the font to a readable size. This puts the revised page count at over two thousand. Shit.

A stiff whisky is required, plus two Paracetamols.

Webster's Introduction is prefaced by a quote from *Punch* dating from a mid-nineteenth century edition of the magazine: 'Man is everywhere born free and is everywhere in trains.' And the style of the opening paragraph gives me some hope that the experience of reading the railwayman's work might be less depressing than I have assumed.

The London Underground is the oldest Metro system in the world. The story of its development is one of grand vision, compromise, human eccentricity, greed and death. And it all began with a single line laid by Metropolitan Railways in 1863 in what was to all intents and purposes a shallow grave, running between modern-day Paddington and Farringdon Stations.

Unfortunately, after this appetising start, the writing style deteriorates rapidly into a tedious catalogue of dates, names and the sort of information that would cure the worst insomniac. It is as if someone had told Webster that a gripping beginning was needed to hook the reader, but neglected to mention that boredom sets in rapidly if there is no suitable follow-through. I imagine the author must have agonised over and re-written his preamble, then decided that literary style was not his forte and that what his readership wanted was facts, facts and more facts.

Do I care that the nickname for Charles Pearson – the system's first entrepreneur – was 'the gadfly'? No. Am I enthralled by the commercial rivalry between the Metropolitan and the Great Western Companies? Not so much. Am I bothered about the quality of the subterranean air in the days when all the trains were powered by coal? Not really. Does it interest me that over half of the current Underground is actually above-ground? Well, maybe a bit, to be honest.

However, after some skim-reading, when I reach a chapter entitled *Engineering Challenges of Deep-level Tubes*, I decide it's time for a break.

Resisting the urge to pour a scotch, I make a mug of tea, and wander out onto the street to see what's going on. The answer is, nothing much. I perch on our front wall and wave at passers-by, but after five minutes of this I start to wish I'd put on a jacket, or at least a sweater, as it's nippy and the sky is an unwelcoming grey.

I wonder if, as part of Pratcha's penance, I should ask him to read Webster's manuscript for me and to highlight anything odd or suggestive of any mental anguish on the author's part. But I quickly dismiss the notion. Given the monotony of the railwayman's writing, I am concerned that this might constitute child abuse.

I go back inside, close the laptop, take out my notebook and a pen, and revert to analogue mode.

Musings are scribbled down as they come to me.

Do some legwork around places where homeless people hang out, I write, and make a list of the spots highlighted by my research. It's a long list. And although I am doubtful that I will locate Webster this way, I have to start somewhere.

But perhaps I'll run across Anneke.

My thoughts dart around this possibility, even though I should set aside the matter of her disappearance and leave it to the Old Bill to sort out. But that's hard to do. Ever since I tripped over the loathsome world of pedophilia with my abortive visit to Jessop's premises, the subject of kidnapped children has been playing on my mind. It seems like I've been seeing white, windowless vans everywhere – and though I know it's a cliché that the unmarked Transit is the sole modus operandi of the child abuser, I'm finding it difficult to dislodge the concept from my head. Just as I can't entirely dismiss my disquiet about the whole Banerjee/Vance thing, and how aspects of it still don't make sense to me.

Find Webster, I tell myself firmly. If only to convince him not to continue writing his Baedeker of all things mechanical and electrical situated beneath the streets of London. Because that is the last thing humanity needs.

My mug of tea has gone cold but I finish it anyway.

Could Webster have literally *gone underground?* And by this, I don't mean that he's lying dead in some unmarked plot, but rather that he's in some bolt-hole that would only be known to a Transport for London train driver.

I reopen RW's laptop, go to the chapter in his manuscript that deals with abandoned stations and write down their names. There are a lot of these now-redundant locations; each made obsolete by the restless, never-ending march of economic imperative. And pasted into Webster's notes, there is a map showing them all, put together by some other train fanatic. Transport for London (or 'TfL' to use their corporate branding) even give tours around some of them. These ones, I cross off my list as possible hideouts. If our railwayman doesn't want to be found, he's not going to pick a place where the inquisitive, goggling public will be trooping through.

My phone pings.

It's a message from Pearl Webster.

She's arranged a meeting for me at TfL's headquarters with one of their HR people, a lady who goes by the exotic name of Ursula d'Ambrosi.

That's progress anyway. And while I'm at it, I'll use the opportunity to see what I can also squeeze out of Ms. d'Ambrosi about RW's friend and co-worker Gustaw Belka. And if she's uncooperative, I'll see what the Clapham Junction Locomotive Club can tell me.

Presumably the police have already checked out Goose, so I'm likely to be going over old ground. But maybe I'll find something they've missed. Maybe.

I rack my memory for details of that strange individual.

The only times I came across him was when I visited that coffee shop in Shad Thames during the time of Katie's legal troubles in late 2009. *Tower Bridge Beanz*, I believe it was called.

The place always seemed to be a magnet for eccentrics. There was that wide-boy trader with the loud voice, whose name escapes me. The manager was some painfully introverted individual; and then there was that barista who always came on to me whenever I set foot in the place. What was she called? Jane? Janine? No, *Janice*. Yes, that's it. Janice. She was protective of Goose, as I recall. I wonder what's happened to her in the last seven years. Hopefully, she's snared a man by now.

Goose.

I dig out the photograph of him that Pearl Webster gave me.

Hmmn. His hair is sticking up and he doesn't look like he's all there. The eyes are blank, his attention turned inwards towards some mental puzzle. An ADHD sufferer, forever restless.

Didn't understand the concept of humour, so consequently wasn't able to recognise when people were ripping the piss out of him. And wasn't he fascinated by the number 23? One of *those* types. Plus, at the time there had been a few unsolved murders around Angel and Goose thought he could find the killer using some insane technique of triangulation. Probably the phases of the moon or something equally weird. If I hadn't been so wrapped up in my daughter's court case, I'd likely have paid more attention.

And what of Pearl Webster? Has she really told me everything? She wasn't exactly a blubbering wreck when we spoke. If anything, she appeared to me to be *too* controlled about her husband's disappearance. It's early days for her to be resigned to his never coming home, surely? If Da were to go missing, the uncertainty of where she might be, and of what might have happened to her, would drive me frantic. Unless, of course, there is no uncertainty for Mrs. Webster because she knows for sure that she won't see her husband again...

But if she is in some way responsible for RW's absence, then why engage a private detective? For appearances' sake? To demonstrate that she has pursued every avenue?

Something smells; though as yet I am unable to recognise the odour.

I make a few notes then reluctantly return to Webster's manuscript. Over the course of the next few hours, I'm resolved to skim-read the lot. If there is some kind of coded message in its wearisome chapters, I won't spot it. I just have to hope that something leaps off the page at me.

* * * * *

The kids are due home shortly, and not a moment too soon.

Apart from the temporary relief of a bowl of soup and two mugs of strong tea, my brain has been so assailed by bad writing, dates and lists, that there's barely any space left in it for anything practical or optimistic.

I find myself wishing that I was back on Samui dealing with bent cops, gangsters and unfaithful girlfriends. At least the sun would be shining. Being home alone doesn't suit me.

The sound of a miniature whirlwind announces the arrival of Pratcha, and I happily close Webster's laptop.

"How's the investigation going, Papa David?" he asks, throwing down his rucksack.

"Badly," I reply.

"Well," my stepson says, "I reckon he's either run away because he was sick of his wife or he's been murdered."

"Thank you for your wisdom and input. But they're not the only possibilities. He could have committed suicide. Writing his book about the London Underground might have tipped him over the edge. Reading it today made me feel like topping myself."

Pratcha shakes his head.

"It's not a suicide," he states confidently.

"Oh? And why is that?"

"Because his body would already have turned up. You can't kill yourself then bury your own body in an unmarked grave afterwards. And if he'd drowned himself in the Thames, the corpse would have washed up in the estuary by now. Plus, someone would have seen it floating once the gases in it had brought it back to the surface. Putrefaction," he adds. "Methane and ammonia."

"You know a lot about this for one so young."

"Google, video games and YouTube," he says. "It's all there if you look."

"I'll bear that in mind in future. Do you want something to eat?"

"Naw. I'll get on with my homework. I need to be back in Mum's good books."

While he stomps off upstairs, I stare out of the front window.

Jenny is usually home before Pratcha, but there is no sign of her. I keep my eyes fixed on the street for a good quarter-of-an-hour, but she doesn't show.

Images of white vans and predatory pedophiles start to insinuate their way into my thoughts, and I begin to worry. Anneke Reid's name pops into my head. This is what comes of occupying one's attention with mortal matters and wicked characters. The world takes on a permanently dangerous aspect.

I ring Jenny's phone, but it's switched off.

Another ten minutes tick by, and I am on the point of slipping on my jacket to go out and search for her, when Pratcha comes downstairs for a soft drink.

He notes my anxiety.

"Is something wrong, Papa David?"

"Jenny's late," I say. "And she's not answering her phone."

"Music Club," he responds blithely.

"What?"

"After school. Don't you remember? Mum's picking her up later. We discussed this at breakfast. They have to switch off their phones."

"Did we? Do they?"

"Are you sure you want to go back to private detective work?" he asks with a sigh.

I am so relieved that I give him the *Gamer's Guide to the League of Loki* that I'd bought for him, say it's a 'thank you' for setting up my website, and pat him on the head.

And I don't even care if Da chews me out for it later.

XI

Out of Sight, Out of Mind

This morning I was up and out at five o'clock, while my family were still sleeping.

The reason? To get around as many homeless hostels as I could before their guests were once more disgorged onto the London streets.

I set out into the cold blackness of the capital armed with my notebook (containing a list of places to visit), my two photographs of Ronald Webster, and a picture on my phone of Anneke Reid sent to me yesterday evening by her grandfather. I figured that, while I was asking about RW, I might as well ask if anyone had seen her too – though most of the places I'd be visiting specialised in older homeless men.

Noon has now come and gone, and I haven't even covered half the hostels I'd hoped to visit today. In fact, I've only managed to have conversations, of sorts, at five facilities in Camden, Hackney and Whitechapel. And none of those were in the least enlightening. Unless you count my becoming better acquainted with the misery of those who have fallen through society's support nets. The folks running the hostels were highly suspicious of me, and their night guests – for the most part – didn't want to talk to me either. Add to that the unwelcome discovery that the hostels had personnel changes between night and morning shifts, and the whole process had the feeling of futility.

If I'd thought the matter through rather more, I'd have realised that most homeless people are not only out of sight and out of mind, but many of them wish to remain so. I may only be a humble private detective, yet I represent 'authority' to some degree. So, cooperation is not going to be high on any of their agendas. I'm not part of the solution, I'm part of the problem.

Accordingly, I am now sitting in a grotty pub not far from Brick Lane having a greasy lunch and a pint while I reconsider my strategy.

I look down the long list of shelters in central London and try to figure out how long it would take me to visit them all and – even if Webster or Anneke were staying there – whether I'd even find them then. After all, it's not as if I'll ever be given unrestricted access to the sleeping areas. Plus, they wouldn't necessarily always be sleeping at the *same* shelter each night. Short of engaging a small army of foot-soldiers to help me in my search, it's worse than trying to discover a needle in a haystack: because I don't know whether the haystack even *has* a needle in it.

So, my itinerary of dormitories is done for the day. They will now all be closed up until the evening. And can I even in conscience cross off the shelters I've been to as having been 'covered'? Hardly.

I consult my second list which shows the most common places where the homeless doss down for the night when they're sleeping rough. Those locations are likely to be pretty much empty too at this time of day unless I want to pore over dirty sleeping bags and lumps of cardboard which have been left behind as place holders. Which I don't.

And this list, I might add, is not comprehensive. Nothing like comprehensive.

I push away my plate of half-eaten food and order another beer from the heavily-tattooed barman who looks like he might be stoned. The whiff of weed that hangs in the air reinforces my suspicion.

It's all rather depressing.

* * * * *

Several hours later, I'm still down-in-the dumps.

I've been to the bank, drawn out a load of one-pound coins, and walked along Oxford Street staring at the beggars and giving each of the polite ones a couple of quid. At one point I got excited when I thought I'd spotted Anneke, but it turned out to be a different kohl-eyed waif: one who spoke with a broad Glaswegian accent.

* * * * *

I managed to obtain a last-minute booking for a tour of the disused Aldwych Underground Station: seventy-five minutes of plodding around a frozen moment in time, as if the past has been preserved in aspic. Which it has. Film companies reportedly love using it.

However, for me the experience was disturbing and vaguely claustrophobic: the decaying structure, and decommissioned train parked within it, echoed with foreboding and death.

After I got home, I opened my laptop and did some searches for further self-mortification.

The UK comprises around ninety-five thousand square miles, Mr. Google tells me. Of that about a quarter is urban space. So, assuming Webster is *not* alive, and hasn't been shoved down a London drain or some other, less-seemly Underworld orifice, or that he isn't hanging in an attic or a cupboard; the chances are that he's lying in a three-square yard plot under soil somewhere in the (roughly) seventy-five thousand square miles of our country's farmland, moorland or woodland.

Well, I said I wanted a challenge.

I'd better buy a new spade. Or sign a long-term hire agreement on a mechanical digger.

Nope. I'm not going to find RW using a scatter-gun approach.

Success is more likely if I wield a pragmatic scalpel. And that means assuming that he's unwillingly dead, and that what I need are *suspects*.

* * * * *

Now that the family has had dinner, the youngers are upstairs on homework duty, and Da is settling on the sofa to binge-watch some soap opera while I'm out at the jazz club.

We'll discuss my latest detecting failure when I return. If she's still awake.

I pick up my saxophone case and go.

* * * * *

Our jazz quartet (unimaginatively named *The Four Guys*) comprises me on saxophone, and three other reprobates: Chalky on keyboards and vocals, Noel on double bass, and Keith on drums. We all have wrinkles, and we all prefer to play rather than talk; so that makes for a soothing evening.

Noel and Keith are both divorced and borderline alcoholics while Chalky is happily-married, smokes two packets of cigarettes a day and consequently has a voice like a crow with a sore throat. This makes his rendition of Louis Armstrong's *What a Wonderful World* particularly affecting and authentic. Plus, it keeps the audience guessing as to whether or not he'll survive the evening.

Our set today is our usual stuff – classic Duke Ellington, Thelonious Monk, et al – with a couple of new old numbers thrown in to see if our regulars in the audience are paying attention.

Attendance is sparse tonight. When Chalky announces we're taking a twenty-minute break, there is polite if unenthusiastic clapping from the *Blue Rhythms* punters.

However, I can happily say that I haven't ruminated once about detecting matters or white vans since leaving the house. So, there is that.

While we catch our breath, and Chalky goes outside for a few cigarettes, I am approached by a young audience member who queries whether we do requests.

When I tell him yes, and ask him what he'd like, he replies, "I don't actually know any jazz music. Play anything you want, but say it's for my girlfriend."

Later, I mutter into the microphone, "This is a John Coltrane number for somebody's girlfriend whose name I don't know, and who knows nothing about jazz. I don't know her boyfriend's name either. But I hope you both enjoy it. Or that somebody does. If not, we don't give refunds. Because that's how capitalism works. Get used to it."

Chalky has a good cough and we launch into our streamlined version of *Blue Train*.

* * * * *

Da is in bed when I arrive home. She's reading a book entitled *Getting into Property*, but the fact that she's naked under our duvet suggests that her focus is on a different type of penetration. Nonetheless, my wife is prepared to give me a few minutes of her time on the Webster case before we descend into a rather less cerebral activity. Moreover, she has done some preparation for the discussion, as evidenced by the fact that she has made notes which she proceeds to go through with me.

"You're going to have to organise your time better, David," she informs me. "You can't go wandering around London staring at homeless people all day."

"I am aware of that. I do have a plan."

Da is unimpressed by this statement, and continues as if I hadn't spoken.

"When we were at the *Agency* together, your specialist areas were investigating illicit affairs and dead people. You're not exactly an expert on missing persons, my darling."

"Neither are you, my love. But apparently that's not going to stop you from telling me how to do my job."

"These are only suggestions," she responds coolly waving her paper at me. "I wouldn't dream of telling you how to do your job."

She then proceeds to do just that.

"To narrow things down, I think you should concentrate on Route One: assume Webster is dead as a result of foul play, and work out who might want to kill him."

"Thanks, Da, but I'd already decided that was the way to go."

She smiles.

"Good boy. See? We're both on the same page."

"Although I doubt Mrs. Webster would be happy with my taking that approach."

Da dismisses this objection.

"She's not paying you, so she's hardly in a position to complain. Anyway, you don't need to tell her."

"Right."

"So, assuming the railwayman has been murdered, how many suspects do you have at present?"

"One. His missus."

"Try harder, David. You're going to need at least half-a-dozen suspects to make this interesting."

"You're ignoring the possibility that Webster might have committed suicide. Nobody else might have been involved."

Da rolls her eyes.

"I thought Pratcha had already put you straight on that. It's not a suicide."

"Have you and Pratcha been talking about this behind my back?" I ask.

"Obviously. And Jenny's been chipping in too. She has some sound psychological observations on Webster's personality traits, by the way."

"Does she indeed?" I huff.

"In any event, the three of us concluded that if he hasn't been murdered – and has instead gone missing deliberately – you'll never find him. Not unless he runs out of money and *has* to go back home. Or he gets hit by a car. Or an Underground train. Or whatever."

Da hands me her notes and tells me to switch off the light and remove my boxer shorts.

"Am I to take it that this lecture you've given me was *foreplay*?" I enquire. "Because, if so, it's hardly left me in the mood for lovemaking."

"Who's talking about lovemaking?" she replies. "I'm thinking about something much less romantic than that. Now put the light out."

My wife disappears under the duvet, and I stop cogitating about missing persons.

XII

A Restless Spirit

Jenny nonchalantly informs us over breakfast that yesterday her school had given all the students a talk on personal safety after a man was seen earlier in the week outside the school gates with a camera.

"What sort of camera was it?" Pratcha asks.

"That's not the point of the story, son," Da informs him sternly. "Remember you're in England now. There are lots of perverts here."

I am somewhat affronted by this remark, so I declare that most English perverts are in fact living in Cambodia and Thailand where the pickings are easier and there are hardly any CCTV cameras.

My wife promptly changes the subject, responding with some passive aggression by asking me what time my appointment is with Ogilvy.

"Eleven. I'm taking Webster's laptop with me into town, so I can bore myself silly afterwards in some coffee shop."

"Don't forget to take my notes with you too," she instructs. "They'll keep you focused."

I spoon cereal into my mouth to stop me from saying something I might regret.

Being married to someone who is the font of all wisdom – as well as being mighty talented in the bedroom – is, however, a great boon. I fleetingly consider having alternative business cards printed for her while I'm out today. I can give them to her as a Christmas present.

Da Braddock knows everything.

Don't bother searching the Internet.

Just call her on this number.

Premium rates apply.

* * * * *

My meeting with Ogilvy is at his business premises on Harley Street, the hang-out of choice for most of the overpriced quacks in London.

I take the Central Line to Bond Street and walk the ten minutes to his place, lugging Webster's laptop with me. Oxford Street is bustling with shoppers, many of whom seem to be agonising over what Yuletide gifts to buy their nearest and dearest to best demonstrate the depth of their affection. But maybe I'm mistaken. They could be fretting over the damage being done to their credit cards, and cursing silently the fact that they have a family at all.

Ogilvy's practice operates out of the ground floor of a four-storey, eighteenth-century townhouse. His reception area is understated, and his carefully-made-up receptionist is dressed in a fashion that is not too clinical. I'm a few minutes early, so I am offered a choice of coffee (decaffeinated or regular), tea (herbal, or regular) or water (presumably all regular). I plump for the water.

While I wait for the Psyche God to finish whatever he's doing, I muse on what we're going to talk about and sip my glass of Evian.

I haven't experienced the sensation of being followed for a few days, so I put that down to intermittent paranoia. Perhaps, if we can't think of anything else, we should chat about my conversations with my dead wife and hopefully lay that subject to rest. Though, I have discussed this topic with Da from time-to-time, and it's not something that concerns her. Indeed, she has confessed to me that she still talks to her dead husband on occasion – usually while doing some aggressive hoovering to work off her frustration after a bad day at work. Knowing Da as I do, I suspect she talks *at* him rather than *to* him. I doubt the poor bugger gets a right of reply. She doesn't consider that unusual, by the way. But then she is Thai. In the Land of Smiles, chatting with the dead is a natural part of everyday existence. Or non-existence, if you're one of the deceased.

Ogilvy appears and beckons me into his inner sanctum, which I note is furnished much like his study, but with less books.

Having satisfied himself that I feel less depressed than during our last encounter, and that I am no longer entertaining hypnotherapy clients, he settles back in his chair.

"What would you like to talk about today, David?" he asks affably, his pen at the ready.

"Death," I say.

"Death?"

"Yes. You see, I went to Battersea to visit a medium recently," I tell him.

Ogilvy tightens up slightly.

"A medium? For a consultation?"

"You could say that. Though she was consulting *me*, as it happens. In my capacity as a private investigator. Her husband's gone missing."

"Ah. And you think he might no longer be with us?"

"Possibly not, but I'm staying open-minded. But in various ways, I seem to be crossing paths fairly regularly with the Grim Reaper and his acolytes. I reckon we might give that subject a go today. Unless you have a better suggestion?"

"It's your choice, David. Are these – *mortal coincidences*, let's call them – bringing back Claire into your thoughts?"

"Sometimes, yes."

"And does it bother you?"

"It doesn't bother me, but I figure I should air it while I'm here."

He gives a sagacious nod.

"Is it intrusive?"

"Not at all. Claire stops talking to me when I tell her to, and I do realise I'm really talking to myself."

"Does it happen when you're stressed?"

"No. It's usually when I'm relaxed or in the zone."

"When you don't have enough to occupy you?"

"I guess so."

"Well, considering the life you've led, David, it's not surprising that your brain finds it hard to switch off. Perhaps it's keeping busy and part of it is impersonating your former wife as an easy way to stay engaged. A lazy way, one might say."

I weigh this up.

"You could be right. Claire has talked to me a lot more since my life became settled. Domesticated."

"And does she still sound like the Claire you knew?"

I weigh this up too.

"No, now you come to mention it. She sounds like a female version of me. Which is to say, she sounds like Da, my current wife. And she never speaks when Da is around either. Perchance I'm being unfaithful to Da with a mental construct of herself. Christ, I can't tell her that. She'll be unbearably smug."

"So, you do accept that Claire is dead?" he probes.

"As a doornail."

Ogilvy relaxes back in his chair while I continue.

"Maybe I can get rid of Claire completely from my thoughts by replacing her with a different ghost. One who's more helpful and less demanding. One who's quirkier or tells better jokes."

"Well —"

"Like my deceased sister-in-law, Anna, for instance. I'm sure she and I could have some interesting chats if we put our minds to it."

"David, I —"

"Or I could make sure that I'm constantly anxious or in a life-threatening situation. That would do the trick too."

"I'm not sure –"

"Cheers, Rufus, that's very helpful. Worth your fee all on its own."

Ogilvy stares at me worriedly.

"I wasn't suggesting that at all, David," he stammers.

"It's OK, doc, I know you weren't. I'm yanking your chain. Your sarcasm detector doesn't work too well, does it?"

* * * * *

Once our session has ended, I'm pretty confident that I've transferred all my tension and uncertainty to Ogilvy. Which is exactly as it should be at his hourly fee.

I have the sensation that my tread is lighter, and even the bleak November sky seems to hold promise.

"Claire?" I say.

Nothing.

I say it again.

Still nothing, apart from a curious glance from a passer-by.

I dredge up the one question which I have not been able to bring myself to ask since Claire's passing.

"Why did you want to be cremated and not buried in the churchyard beside our son Daniel?"

Silence.

Rien.

I let out a deep sigh.

Damn that shrink Ogilvy, but he's good. Regardless of the doubts I've managed to plant in *his* head.

It really feels like Claire has gone. Just like that. Even when I thought I'd let her go before – years ago – there was always a tiny part of me that wasn't convinced. But this is different. It's like adamantine bonds have been severed. But it can't simply be a couple of sessions with Ogilvy that did it, surely? Two sixty-minute exposures to corduroy and pomposity couldn't have done that on its own unless the chains were already weakened.

I try again to connect. Nothing.

I stop walking and lean against a lamppost.

Could it be that those recent conversations with the first Mrs. Braddock were the final throes of delusion? That the neural network in my cerebellum has been quietly, plastically rearranging itself? Maybe that is why Claire's voice sounded like my own, or like Da's. And now that channel has closed up. It can no longer be accessed. The wire's been snipped. Would that my other baneful memories could be so comprehensively sealed off.

Wait. Perhaps I'm being premature. After all, Claire has come back before. But somehow, I don't think so. Something has definitely shifted.

I should probably feel sad, but I don't. I feel *relieved.*

I'm cured? Jeez.

This must be what sanity is like.

* * * * *

My euphoria lasts until I've spent ten minutes on Webster's laptop.

I've ordered a double-shot espresso at the coffee shop, and I'm going to need it as the noisy comings-and-goings of other customers barely make a dent in the mist of silent depression emanating from the computer screen.

I grit my teeth and attempt a second skim-read of RW's manuscript. Skimming even more shallowly than the first time, I might add.

For a few minutes, I am actually interested in the section on the Necropolis Railway. This was a dedicated line which used to ferry corpses to an out-of-town cemetery. There is also stuff on the pestiferous overcrowding of Victorian burial grounds, and the *danse macabre* of skeletons at the intersection of Bank and the crypt of the church of St. Mary Woolnoth. I quickly conclude, however, that my temporary fascination with these morsels has more to do with my morbid conversation with Ogilvy than with anything pertinent to the Webster case.

I jot down a few more notes on the abandoned Underground stations, and one or two other bits and bobs which might serve to give me credibility with the members of the Clapham Junction Locomotive Club when I attend their meeting tomorrow evening.

I order a second double espresso and a vegetable panini, then close the laptop. Once that additional caffeine hits my system, I will be incapable of any further absorption of Webster's ramblings about underground rumblings.

Praise the Lord.

* * * * *

The Braddock family is nestled on the sofa watching the evening news on TV.

Today seems to be a politics day as the headline report is on some London MP who has been spouting off about the 'whining youth' of the country, and how it's about time they accepted the result of the Brexit Referendum and got used to not being pawns of the EU's authoritarian empire. Needless to say, the Honourable Member in question – one Giles Feathercroft – is of a right-wing persuasion and a rabid Brexiteer. He sports an anachronistic handlebar moustache which makes him both instantly recognisable and instantly detestable. I expect his idea of compassion comprises serving warm porridge to the inmates of detention centres while playing them *Land of Hope and Glory* until their ears bleed. Which point of view would doubtless be applauded by my stepmother who harbours a deep distrust of 'the masses' though is inclined towards selfless kindness for unfortunate individuals.

When Feathercroft starts citing the sacrifices of those courageous Brits who fought in World War II, I decide I've heard enough and click the off button on our remote control.

"He doesn't have a clue, does he?" asks the sagacious Jenny.

"He has the same voice as one of my teachers," chips in Pratcha. "He's a Fascist too."

Da now decides the children have heard enough of current affairs for the day and sends them off to their rooms.

Pratcha is back in favour, so he's allowed to do some more slaughtering on his League of Loki game, and Jenny uses the time to do some extra-curricular reading on the life of Jane Austen after she's checked out some makeup tips on YouTube.

"How was your session with Ogilvy?" my wife inquires once the kids have left the living room.

"It went OK. Though he did express some concern about your occasional conversations with your dead husband. He thinks you might be a bad influence on my mental health."

"Huh. When are you seeing him again?"

"In four weeks. We'll stay with monthly consultations unless I start cutting myself or spending time on high ledges."

"Good. Any progress on the Webster investigation?"

"Not much."

"Well, it was always going to be more of a marathon than a sprint, David. Unless you get lucky. So, take this weekend off and we can do something nice together. All of us."

"As to that –"

"And next weekend we're going to drive up to the Midlands to stay with Nang for a couple of nights. It's been a while since we've seen her. She's long overdue a visit."

"Next weekend is fine. But tomorrow evening, I have to go to a meeting of the Clapham Junction Locomotive Club."

"That sounds thrilling."

"Doesn't it? But for the rest of this weekend, I'm all yours. Starting immediately. Consider my diary already blocked out."

"Sacrosanct and inviolate?"

"Yes, and stop showing off your knowledge of English adjectives. I'll book us a table at an obscenely expensive restaurant for Sunday. Somewhere that isn't near an Underground station."

"And you won't talk about trains?"

"*That* I can promise you."

XIII

Playing with Trains

I decided not to call Alfred Eggers on the number that Pearl Webster had given me. Instead, I figured I'd turn up unannounced at the latest meeting of the Clapham Junction Locomotive Club. That way, the Chairman and other members of this august body won't have the opportunity to prepare their responses in advance. Though, if Mrs. W has tipped off Eggers that I want to talk to him, that strategy is already in tatters.

The train anoraks meet in a room above a spit-and-sawdust pub off Clapham High Street called *The Frog and Signalman*. A poster on the wall says that the room is available for hire and that it is the venue for an amateur stand-up comedy show every other Thursday. I don't expect there will be any laughs tonight.

Equipped with a pint of Belter Bitter, I make my way up the narrow stairs which are lit by two bulbs dangling from a peeling ceiling. The smell of stale ale hangs heavy in the air.

I've arrived about fifteen minutes before the meeting's official start time so that I can introduce myself and maybe have a chat with Eggers before the boredom proper kicks off.

Once upstairs, I count eight people: all male, all dressed badly and all supping beer. There are bowls of crisps, crudités and pickled onions on a side table, along with some dubious dips. A dozen or so non-matching chairs have been laid out theatre-style. My heart sinks when I spot the white screen and projector. That means there is going to be an illustrated talk.

There is no sign of Goose – at least, not the Goose that I remember.

I am buttonholed by a wild-haired, acned youth who introduces himself as Sammy. The other club members stare at me, presumably because it's the first time they've seen anybody at one of their meetings with an expensive coat and a decent haircut.

"My name is Braddock," I tell him. "I'm here to see Mr. Eggers. Which one is he?"

"Fred isn't here yet," Sammy says, eyeing me suspiciously.

"Are you a policeman?" asks one of the others.

Everybody has stopped talking. A man with a grey, unkempt beard has frozen mid-action while stuffing a handful of crisps into his mouth.

"Private investigator," I reply. "I'm working for Pearl Webster, looking into the disappearance of her husband Ronald."

"Yeah, Fred phoned round to tell us all that Ron had gone AWOL. Terrible business," someone says.

There is a tangible lessening of tension in the room, and suddenly I'm the subject of interest rather than apprehension.

"Wait a minute," Sammy exclaims. "Aren't you that bloke that helped the police on the Highgate murder? I think I saw you on the telly. I thought you seemed familiar."

My stock rises among the group.

"Yes, that was me. But I can't discuss it, I'm afraid. It might prejudice the case coming up in court."

"Ah."

"So, if we can get back to Ronald Webster –"

"Poor Ron," interrupts the man with the mouthful of crisps.

"A good guy," says another.

"Any leads?" queries Sammy.

"Some," I respond noncommittally. "But it's early days. Have the police talked to any of you yet?"

There is a general shaking of heads.

"Typical," I remark, and there is a general nodding of heads.

As I have their attention, I decide to make the most of it.

"Do any of you have any theories as to where Ronald might have gone?"

Much shuffling.

"We don't know much about each other's private lives," Sammy offers. "We only come together to talk about trains, not personal stuff."

"I see. I'm also looking for a man named Gustaw Belka, usually called Goose. I gather he comes to these meetings, and he's friendly with Ronald. Any idea where I might find him?"

The guy with the grey beard has now swallowed his crisps, and he chips in, "Yeah, Goose has been to some of our meetings, but not for a while. Strange guy," he adds.

"Even among our group," Sammy says, showing some understanding of irony.

"But none of you knows where he lives?" I press.

All heads shake again.

"You can always ask Chairman Fred. When he arrives," suggests the crisp-eater.

"*If* he arrives," says Sammy.

"He'd better arrive. He's giving tonight's talk," somebody grumbles.

"Oh, he'll be here all right," declares a sallow man with a comb-over. "He just likes to make an entrance. That's Fred."

And indeed, at that moment, the speaker duly appears, full of apologies for his tardiness. He carries a laptop which he proceeds to plug in and connect to the projector.

"This is Mr. Braddock, Fred," says Sammy as the Chairman bustles around the equipment. "He's a private detective, and he's looking for Ronald. Mr. Braddock – Alfred Eggers."

"Call me Fred. Everyone does. Alfred Penhaligon Eggers is too much of a mouthful for most people. Pleased to meet you."

He offers me his hand. He has a firm grip.

"That sounds like a West Country accent."

"It is indeed. I'm originally from North Devon. And though I've lived in London for more years than I care to count, it's never really left me."

I size him up. Medium height. In his fifties. A good head of hair. Florid complexion. Confident manner. A cut above his fellow anoraks. Smart blazer with an obscure railway crest on the pocket. A dickie-bow tie. White shirt. Creases in his trousers you could cut yourself on. Shiny black shoes.

"I wonder if I might have a chat with you about Ronald Webster."

"Of course, anything to help. But unless it's going to be a brief chat, can it wait until after my presentation? I've kept these gentlemen waiting long enough."

Politeness dictates that I'm going to have to sit through his talk, so I agree reluctantly.

"Besides," he says with a twinkle in his eye, "you might enjoy it. It's on the Kent and East Sussex Railway. And I have lots of slides."

* * * * *

"Did you like my presentation?" Eggers asks.

The anoraks meeting is over, the room has been cleared, and the Chairman and I are sitting downstairs in the bar. I'm having a double whisky. Because I need one.

"No," I say. "For me, railways are just a way of getting from A to B."

He laughs.

"I thought not."

"Are you in the railways business, Mr. Eggers?"

"Please, call me *Fred*."

"*Fred*, are you in the railways business?"

"I'm wedded to the railways, I'm afraid. That's why I've never married a woman. It's the only place I've ever worked. I started post-education life in the British Railways Planning Department, then when privatisation came under Mrs. Thatcher, I transferred to British Rail Engineering Limited. I'm still a part-time consultant/historian with them now, though I also have my own consulting business which I run from home. Far too expensive to rent an office in London these days."

"Tell me about it."

He hands me a card, and I give him one of mine in exchange.

Enough chit-chat.

"So, what can you tell me about Ronald Webster?"

"Well, I suppose you could say that he and I are rivals. *Friendly* rivals, I would add."

"In what way?"

"We are both writing a book on the history of the London Underground. Didn't Pearl tell you?"

"No, she didn't."

He dismisses this.

"That's not surprising. She has a lot on her mind, the poor lady. It's such a shame."

"So, you know Mrs. Webster as well as Ronald?"

He pulls me up short.

"I'd hardly say I know her *well*. Ron dragged her along to one of our meetings. But she didn't come again. And nobody can blame her for that."

"I see. Let's go back to your and Ronald's books on the Underground. Has that been a cause of tension between the two of you?"

He shrugs.

"A little authorial jealousy, perhaps. On both sides."

"I guess it's a race to see who can get their book to an agent or publisher first, is it?"

"Not really. It doesn't work that way. And neither of us is under any illusion that we're writing a best-seller. Most likely no publisher will want to pick up either of our manuscripts. It's more a labour of love."

"The first draft of Ronald's book is almost finished, I understand. How is yours coming along?"

He squirms slightly.

"About the same."

I let the matter drop.

"Assuming that Mr. Webster has voluntarily gone missing, do you have any idea where he might have gone? Or why?"

"Ron and I were not bosom buddies, Mr. Braddock. But I doubt he's left London. I don't think he *knows* anywhere else. Or nowhere else he'd like to live. And, frankly, I thought he was settled and content with his life here. He has a lovely wife and a job he enjoys. So, I can't help you with your *why* question either."

"I see."

"And if Ron had money worries or had upset the wrong person, I have no insight into that. He's always struck me as a painfully private individual. Uncomplicated. But I guess you've already spoken to Pearl about those issues anyway."

"When did you last see him?"

"Two months ago, at our meeting here."

"And there was nothing out-of-the-ordinary about his behaviour or mood?"

"No, nothing."

"What about his friend Gustaw – Goose? What can you tell me about him?"

Eggers reflects.

"An unusual young man. Very knowledgeable about the Underground, but socially awkward to an extreme degree. Even by the standards of our Club. Didn't seem quite all there to me, if I'm being frank."

"When did you last see him?"

"A few meetings ago."

"He wasn't at Ronald's last gathering at the Club?"

"I don't think so. But I can't be entirely sure. One meeting tends to merge into another."

"And you don't have an address for him? Or maybe an idea where he lives?"

"Sorry, no. But I remember he works for TfL. You could check with them."

I finish my whisky.

"Then, that's that. Thank you for your time, Fred. If anything does occur to you, don't hesitate to call me."

"I wish I could have been more help. It's the first time anything like this has happened to a member. It's upsetting for everyone."

"I imagine it is."

* * * * *

Da greets me on my return home with, "You look worn out. How did your railway enthusiasts' meeting go?"

"I thought we weren't supposed to be discussing my investigation this weekend."

"Well, if you're tossing and turning stuff over in your head, it means you'll be tossing and turning in bed all night. And when your sleep's disturbed, you tend to snore. Better that you get it off your chest. So that I can tell you where you're going wrong."

"I do *not* snore."

"I'll record you sometime," Da says evenly. "Now, did you make any progress? What was Eggers like?"

She pours me a glass of wine.

"Smart. Slick. He seemed rather out-of-place among the train nuts. But perhaps he likes being a big fish in a small pond – and there was certainly some pond life on show at the Locomotive Club. Eggers' talk on the Kent steam railway had them eating out of the palm of his hand.

"But I detected something rascally about our good Chairman. Struck me as the sort of guy who would rope you into a financial pyramid scheme, then leg it with all your money. He was probably one for the girls when he was younger. Indeed, he might still be chasing skirt. He's never married, and he's a smooth talker. You ladies like all that guff."

"Let's not get sidetracked, David," my wife warns. "Did Eggers have any guesses as to why Webster might have vanished or where he might be?"

"No. None of them did. The unwashed members were all on the spectrum – zero insight into the minds of others. And nobody could tell me anything useful about Goose either."

"So, you wasted your evening?"

"Not entirely."

"Ah, so this story is going somewhere after all. Continue."

"Eggers is writing a book on the London Underground. Same as Webster."

Da appears disappointed.

"Is that it? Your hypothesis is that Eggers might have murdered Webster over *that*? Some dull contest over manuscripts which nobody is going to be interested in publishing?"

"These *are* railway obsessives we're talking about," I respond tartly. "Their brains don't work like those of normal people. Both of them have lived unmemorable existences. Maybe they each see this as their one chance to do something special with their lives."

My wife is patently unconvinced by this argument.

"Anyway," I plough on. "Eggers and Webster might not only be rivals in writing."

"Ah, this sounds more promising. Go on."

"Mr. Engineering Consultant says he and Pearl Webster have only ever met once –"

"Which is the same as she told you."

"Yet she has his number on her phone, and Eggers referred to her fondly as 'Pearl.' Also, he didn't seem surprised to see me, and didn't ask to see any ID; which suggests he knew I'd be pitching up at some stage. And only Mrs. W could have told him that I was investigating her husband's disappearance."

"You suspect something's going on between Eggers and Pearl Webster? An affair?"

"It's possible."

"You said she was plain. Something of a home bod. Not the sort to lure men into bed."

"There's no accounting for taste. Ugly people have sex too, I expect. And Eggers is a notch above her husband. Plus, attraction is not all about physical appearance, is it? We're a case in point, my darling. I only took up with you because of your neat handwriting and your ability to organise my diary."

"Well, I will say this. If Fred Eggers has bumped off Webster – with or without his wife's help – lust is a more likely motive than some feud over a book on railways."

"It could be a combination of both. Anyway, I've increased my number of suspects for Webster's murder from one to two."

"*If* he's been murdered," Da sighs. "It's all a bit thin, David. You're still in the area of supposition and conjecture."

"True. Though I might be adding Gustaw Belka as suspect number three on Monday once I've spoken to the TfL HR

Department. I'm hoping they can give me some dirt on him and an address, or at least a phone number."

"And what would Belka's motive be for doing away with Webster?"

"I haven't a clue. If things get desperate, I might have to make something up."

"I love your professionalism," says my wife. "It's what first drew me to you."

* * * * *

Sunday passes without incident.

The Sunday Times carries an interview with the MP Giles Feathercroft in which he spouts off about young people having it too good. His outlook is so uncaring and extreme that I catch myself sympathising with Jamie Sykes' view: that society's cards are stacked in favour of élites and older people.

While Da is distracted by a long phone conversation with Nang, I do a surreptitious online search to see if there is any news on Anneke Reid or Lee Vance. There isn't. And a quick call to Ben Quinlan reveals that he still isn't answering his mobile.

I put out the rubbish. Next door, Banerjee's house remains closed-up.

We have a ruinously-expensive family dinner at *Roi des Escargots*, an exclusive French restaurant in Notting Hill. Da orders a bottle of champagne, and I note with alarm that the kids are displaying signs of enjoying the experience of fine dining.

What the hell is wrong with burgers all of a sudden?

I don't ask.

XIV

Human Resources and Weaknesses

Monday starts foggy, but by the time Da and the offspring have left the house, the mist has transformed into light November rain.

I've just settled down with a mug of tea to review my notes on Webster and draw up a list of things to discuss later with his employer, when the doorbell rings.

It's the two police officers who had previously called on me to talk about Anneke Reid.

"Mr. Braddock, I wonder if you can spare us a few minutes," says policewoman Taylor.

I show them into the living room and offer them a drink. They decline.

"Is there any news on Anneke?" I ask.

"We're not here to talk about Miss Reid," Taylor answers curtly.

Her colleague opens his notebook.

"Fire away then," I say.

"We understand that Benjamin Quinlan is a therapy client of yours. Is that correct?"

"Yes. Well, not entirely. He was a client of mine."

"*Was?* How do you mean?"

Taylor and her colleague lean forward eagerly.

"Since you were last here, I've stopped giving hypnotherapy sessions."

"Oh, and why is that?"

"It's on the advice of my psychiatrist. He thinks I should be taking things easier and not becoming involved in other people's problems."

The policeman makes a note.

"And did you tell Mr. Quinlan that you would no longer be seeing him?"

"I've tried to. But I'm having no luck contacting him. I must have phoned him two or three times."

Another note goes in the book.

Taylor smiles insincerely.

"Can you tell us when you last saw Mr. Quinlan?"

"A couple of weeks ago."

"I mean *exactly* when you last saw him."

"Give me a moment."

I fetch my diary from the study and open it.

"Tuesday the eighth of November. 10-11am. That's – what? – thirteen days ago."

The two officers confer and check their previous notes.

"That would have been the day before you saw Anneke Reid for the first time. Is that correct, Mr. Braddock?"

"Yes, but I don't see the relevance –"

Taylor holds up a hand to forestall me, but it doesn't work.

"Has something happened to Ben Quinlan?"

"We'll get to that shortly," she says. "But can you confirm that you haven't seen or spoken to Mr. Quinlan since the eighth?"

"That's right. He was supposed to see me on Monday the fourteenth of November, but he didn't show up."

"He didn't ring you to cancel the appointment?"

"No. As I said, I've tried calling him a few times, but without any luck. I also telephoned his office, but they couldn't give me any information."

"When did you last try to get hold of Mr. Quinlan?"

"Yesterday."

"What can you tell me about Mr. Quinlan's mood and behaviour during your last meeting? I presume your professional standards will not allow you to tell me what he was seeing you about?" she adds acidly, in reference to my last interaction with her.

"Look," I say, "Ben was seeing me for anxiety about his separation from his wife. The last time I saw him, he was on one of his better days. Even so, I advised him that he should consider taking a holiday. Now will you tell me what this is about?"

The policewoman stares at me coldly for a few seconds before replying.

"Mr. Quinlan has been reported missing."

"When?"

"Nobody seems to have seen him since Friday the eleventh of November – three days after your last appointment."

* * * * *

As soon as the plods have left, I ring Da at her office to report the morning's bombshell.

"You're losing people faster than you're finding them, David," she remarks drily. "Are you sure you're in the right business?"

"I'm beginning to wonder."

"Perhaps you should move into the spare room for a while. Until I decide whether I want to sleep with a possible serial killer."

"I'm glad this amuses you."

"Lighten up, Braddock," she snaps. "We'll talk about this tonight when I don't have a client with me."

"Oops. Sorry."

* * * * *

When I step outside later, the afternoon has already forgotten the morning's rain. A cold, dry wind is whipping through the capital. Rays of weak sunlight occasionally pierce the cloud cover, but not in sufficient quantities to dispel my mental gloom. It's not the sort of day you'd want to be a homeless beggar.

But then, what day is?

I take the Circle Line to St. James' Park, and emerge onto Broadway, where Transport for London has its headquarters.

Designed by Charles Holten and completed in 1929 (I learn from Webster's manuscript), this imposing, irregularly-shaped edifice is faced with Portland stone, and was originally built as a HQ for the Underground Electric Railways Company of London. It was eventually acquired by TfL at the turn of the century.

I consult my notes one last time, then head inside.

I am escorted through the internal 3D labyrinth to the office of Mrs. Ursula d'Ambrosi, Human Resources Manager.

And while the office itself is bland and anonymous, Mrs. d'Ambrosi is anything but.

I'd put her in her mid-thirties. She is carefully made-up, has a pretty face, and wears a black business jacket with a cream-coloured chemise open at the neck. I can't see what she's wearing from the waist down. Her dark-brown hair is pulled back into a bun. She is every inch the corporate executive, although her eyes lack the self-serving coldness that I detect in many business people.

That may, of course, simply be the image she chooses to present. We'll see.

I am offered tea, which I accept. Business cards are exchanged.

We make small talk while we're waiting for the tea, during which I sense a certain chemistry in the room. But that may just be on my side. I mustn't get cocky. Not in any sense of the word. This is an HR Manager I'm dealing with, after all, not some siren from a Thai bar. Though she's the only human resources representative I've met with such a soft, low voice.

Having removed an imaginary stray lock of hair from her face, Mrs. d'Ambrosi suddenly remembers why I'm here.

"Mrs. Webster explained to one of my assistants that she has engaged you to help find her husband. Is that right?"

"It is," I reply.

"I must tell you, Mr. Braddock, that this is the first time I've ever met a private detective. In my position, as you can imagine, I have sometimes had to deal with the police on various items. But you are my first –"

"Sam Spade lookalike? Character from a noir crime novel?"

She sees I'm joking, and smiles. It's rather a nice smile.

"I was going to say *celebrity*. You are the David Braddock who was involved in solving that murder in Highgate, aren't you?"

"I'm afraid so. But using the term 'solving' is overstating my expertise. I got lucky, that's all."

"A private detective with modesty too? Is that a common thing in your business?"

"I don't think it's a common thing anywhere."

"Ah, a cynic. How refreshing."

"I consider myself a cynic with a heart."

"Ah. My favourite type, as it happens."

We are making an inordinate amount of eye contact, so I decide to continue in the same vein.

"Then, I'll try not to let down my profession, Mrs. d'Ambrosi. I'll make our conversation as memorable for you as I can, to preserve the illusion for as long as possible that we investigators don't spend all our time being nosey and objectionable. And please call me 'David.' I'm not a policeman, and I haven't come here to grill you. But I do need your assistance."

A flicker passes across her features.

"To be candid with you, Mr. Braddock –"

"David, please."

"I am not sure how much information I am able to give you. At TfL, we have to respect our employees' confidentiality, unless we're talking to the *official* police and some crime is involved. Although, I do realise that you are acting for Mrs. Webster and that the current situation must be very uncomfortable for her," she adds apologetically.

"Anything you can tell me will be helpful," I reassure her. "Mrs. Webster wanted to come along with me today, but I told her no. The nature of investigative work means that sometimes unexpected things turn up which a person's nearest and dearest might find unpleasant. So, anything you say to me will be strictly off-the-record and unattributable. And I don't want to put you in a difficult position. But I do need to pursue any leads I can to find Ronald Webster. His wife, as you can imagine, is in a state of some distress."

This last statement is rather a stretch, but I do need to leverage the HR Manager's compassion. Assuming she has any.

A flunkey brings in our tea on a tray, and we halt our conversation while Ursula d'Ambrosi plays mother.

"Milk?"

"Please."

"Sugar?"

"No thanks. I'm sweet enough."

A grin, and her professional façade melts further.

"I'm sure you are, David," she says. "No doubt that's how you get people to talk. Women, especially, I should imagine."

Encouraged by this *David*, I answer with, "Well, if it makes any difference, I should maybe mention that you are the first female HR Manager that I've ever talked to, so I'm not sure whether a charm offensive on my part would be either welcome or effective. You'll have to guide me on that, Mrs. d'Ambrosi. I wouldn't want to cross any lines that your husband wouldn't like."

She wants to say something, but stops herself. After a beat, she says, "Well, I suppose you can call me 'Ursula' as 'Mrs. d'Ambrosi' *is* a bit of a mouthful. And I have to leave for my next meeting in about forty minutes, so it will save us time. How's the tea?"

"Perfect."

"What do you want to ask me?"

"Well, I'd like to start by asking you whether you got those lovely hazel eyes from your mother or from your father."

"Really, David, you'll have to be much less obvious than that."

As she raises her cup, she catches me staring at her left hand. The tip of her index finger is missing, and she sets down her cup and self-consciously moves her hand under the desk.

"I'm sorry, Ursula. I didn't mean to gawp."

She gives a shrug.

"I grew up on a farm. An accident with machinery when I was eleven. It could have been worse. Let's talk about Mr. Webster."

"Actually, I wonder if we might first have a chat about a gentleman by the name of Gustaw Belka who also works for your company. He's a friend of Ronald Webster."

"Belka?" she appears taken aback, but quickly recovers her composure. A corporate tone creeps into her voice.

"Are you familiar with how many people work for TfL, David? I don't know all of them. In fact, I had to check the files on Mr. Webster before you arrived. I'd need advance warning of questions like that. And even then... well, I can't discuss just *anybody* with you. I thought you were here about Mr. Webster?"

"Gustaw Belka is a friend of Ronald's, and that's why I'm trying to track him down. All I need is his address. I've spoken to various people who know him, and none of them could shed any light on where he lives. Or even give me a phone number for him."

"Mrs. Webster doesn't have his address?"

"No. All she could tell me was that he worked for TfL. And nobody seems to have seen hide nor hair of him recently. Belka does work here, though? You can at least check that out for me."

A worried look has crept into Ursula's eyes.

There is a danger she is going to go 'official' on me, so before she can reply, I say, "Listen, I don't want to make things difficult for you, and I respect the fact that you have your position to think of. So, let me lay my cards on the table.

"There are only three questions I need answered. One: what kind of worker is Ronald Webster? Two: has he come to management's attention for anything he has done or not done? And three: where does Gustaw Belka live? All the other stuff that I need, I can get from Mrs. Webster."

I see the human being in Ursula wrestle with the HR Manager.

"A man *is* missing," I say.

She reaches a decision. Sort of.

"Ask me some boring, safe questions while I reflect on how you can find out the information you need."

I ask her some boring, safe questions which she answers while looking at files on her computer screen. I make notes which I am sure I will never refer to again. Whenever she glances at me, I smile reassuringly.

Once this charade is over, there are a few seconds of silence while she studies my face.

"As to your three important questions, I have a friend who might be able to help you, David. But I will have to be assured of your discretion."

"I'll promise you whatever you want, Ursula."

"Will you?" she replies, continuing to hold eye contact. "*Whatever* I want?"

"Yes."

This appears to satisfy her.

"My friend finishes work at five o'clock. There is a tasteful wine bar about ten minutes' walk from here, called *The Grapes of Ralph*. Do you know it?"

"No, but I'll find it."

"I'll tell my friend to meet you there around, say, five-fifteen with the information you require. You can buy her a couple of glasses of red wine in return. Decent stuff, mind. Then the pair of you can talk about Webster and Belkaw. Though you might need to treat her to dinner some time as well because she'd be taking a big risk for you. Would you be up for that? I notice you're wearing a wedding ring."

"*Her*, you said?"

"Yes."

"Yes, I'm up for that."

"Good."

"How will I recognise her?"

"Oh, you'll recognise her easily. She looks a lot like me."

"*The Grapes of Ralph*. Five-fifteen. Got it. Does your friend prefer red wine or white wine?"

"Red. The colour of danger."

* * * * *

I send Da a message that I will be late home as I'm following up a lead, and that I'll have dinner while I'm out.

The rest of what I have to tell her is not suitable material for a text message, and I'll have to convey it to her face-to-face. After which, I'll have to weather her fury as best I can. Then clear up any broken crockery.

I know what she'll say: *I've warned you before, David, that your flirting would land you into deep trouble one of these days.*

And I'll say, *I wasn't flirting.*

And she'll reply, *The trouble with you is, you don't even recognise that you're flirting.*

I locate *The Grapes of Ralph.*

But I go and have a pint somewhere else.

To offer some temporary distraction, I phone Pearl Webster to request if I can drop by to see her tomorrow. She says yes, and asks whether I got from Mrs. d'Ambrosi everything I wanted.

"Up to a point," I tell her, and ring off before she starts pressing me for details.

Who'd have thought that an HR Manager could be so devious and brazen? Especially a married one. An attractive married one. With hazel eyes that a man could fall into.

Enough.

* * * * *

It's five o'clock and I'm installed at a table in the wine bar after two hours of conscience-searching and strategising. It's early for business. Only two other people are drinking: a couple in their thirties. From their furtive demeanour, I deduce they are having an affair. Perchance *The Grapes of Ralph* is renowned for such liaisons. If so, that's worrying.

Regardless, I've managed to convince myself that meeting Ursula here will not be a complete marriage-threatening disaster. We'll have a conversation and a couple of glasses of wine, and that will be it.

I'm sure – as a level-headed, married professional woman – she will have cooled down and realised that we both got over-enthusiastic; and that her demeanour will have morphed into one of a woman being unofficially accommodating on a missing person case. She'll remember that she has a husband, and that she has too much to lose on a casual dalliance with a private dick. And perhaps all she wants anyway is a little attention. A frisson of forbidden pleasantry.

Yeah, that's probably it. Don't blow this out of proportion, David.

I can't help wondering, however, whether my behaviour towards her wasn't utterly inappropriate. Maybe even predacious. Is it possible to groom a thirty-odd-year-old woman? Or was she coming onto me? I delicately pick through the bones of our discussion, and the exercise fails to set my mind at rest.

Damn it, Braddock. Damn, damn, damn. You're not in Thailand now. You're a married man with two kids and living in England. You're respectable. You've left all that nonsense behind you. You're not supposed to be having *adventures*.

Focus. This is all about finding Ronald Webster, and nothing else.

At exactly fifteen minutes past five, the door to the wine bar opens and TfL's HR Manager enters. The mystery as to what she was wearing from the waist down is solved: a black skirt which stops above the knee and killer high-heels. She has long, athletic legs that I mustn't look at.

I rise as she approaches the table, and I can sense something else rising as well. I can already feel my saintly intention and moral rectitude disintegrating like half-baked New Year's resolutions, and she hasn't even opened her mouth yet.

"You must be Ursula's friend," I say. "You know, you could easily pass for her twin sister."

"Yes, I get that a lot," she replies. "Though she's more strait-laced than me."

We shake hands for longer than is necessary before sitting down.

"So, what shall I call you?" I ask continuing to play along.

"Just 'Ursula' would be fine. And it will keep things simple."

She reaches behind her head to undo the bun, and lets loose her shoulder-length brown hair.

"Better? Does it make you more comfortable that you're not talking to a strait-laced HR Manager?"

She gives me a flirtatious grin.

"I'm not sure that *comfortable* is the right word."

Ursula removes her jacket and hangs it on a chair. As an apparent afterthought, she unfastens a button on her blouse.

"There. Does that help?"

"Yes and no."

"Life's too short for wasting time, David, don't you think?"

I feel the last of my angelic resolve depart unmourned.

"I like your candour," I say.

"Are there any other bits of me you like?"

"Pretty much everything I can see. And your mind, naturally."

She holds eye contact.

"I'm divorced, by the way," she announces. "Two years ago. An Italian who's now gone back to Rome. I've kept my married name because I prefer it to my own surname. Also wearing a wedding ring at work gives me more *gravitas*, and keeps unwanted male attention away. Well, usually."

"Not today, though."

"I said *unwanted* male attention. And you wear a wedding ring too, David."

"Yes."

"Is that going to be a problem? For *you*, I mean?"

Before I can reply, she continues smoothly with, "Forget I asked. We'll find out soon enough. You haven't ordered yet?"

I indicate my glass of water and tell her that I've been waiting for her in case I select the wrong wine.

Ursula picks up the menu and points at a Cabernet Sauvignon.

"Shall we have a bottle of this?"

"Whatever the lady desires."

"That's the second time you've said that today."

"Do you want anything to eat?"

"No. That's for the next time we see each other. Or is that too forward of me? Too soon, David?" she queries.

"Well, you did tell me you don't like wasting time."

"Exactly. I'm glad we're on the same page."

And – disturbingly – I suspect we *are* on the same page.

I catch the waiter's attention and give him our order.

"Oh, I suppose I should let you have this."

Ursula rummages in her shoulder-bag and pulls out a folded sheet of paper, which she holds out to me.

As I reach for it, she pulls it away.

"Or perhaps you shouldn't have this until we've finished the wine. After all, I don't want you running out on me straightaway."

"We both know I won't do that, Ursula," I reply evenly.

Satisfied, she hands over the paper.

I unfold it. It's Gustaw Belka's address and cell phone number printed on an A4 sheet.

"No handwriting," I muse. "Unattributable information. Smart of you."

"It's a trust thing," she responds. "And I don't know how much I can trust you – yet. I don't want to see my job come to an end any more than you want to see your marriage come to an end. But don't worry, David. Neither of those things is going to happen."

"You're not planning on re-enacting the plot of *Fatal Attraction*, then?"

"Only the good scenes. And there's something else you should be aware of. Mr. Belka hasn't reported for work for the last three weeks. Nobody at TfL has seen him since the same day that anyone last saw Ronald Webster. Quite a coincidence, eh? And we haven't been able to contact Belka either. I hope you have better luck tracking him down."

"Now that *is* interesting. Thank you."

Our bottle of wine arrives. I wave away the waiter and pour us two full glasses.

"What shall we drink to, then, divorced Ursula d'Ambrosi?"

"Well, married David Braddock, how about pleasurable meetings with an attractive stranger?"

"That sounds good."

She nods her approval of the grape.

"So, tell me a little about yourself, David. But skip the happy family stuff, OK? I'm not interested in that, and it would be a definite turn-off."

I give her a brief summary of the Braddock history to date.

"Your life has been more exotic than mine," she says ruefully.

"What happened to Mr. d'Ambrosi?"

"He screwed around too much," Ursula answers grimly. "End of. Let's talk about something else."

"Like what?"

"Like where you're taking me to dinner this Saturday."

"Saturday?"

"Yes."

"I'm supposed to be driving up to the Midlands with my wife and family this weekend."

"Ah, so you're dumping me already?"

"I didn't say that."

"So, what are you saying?"

Ursula studies my eyes carefully. Then she undoes another button on her blouse.

"I'm saying that my family will have to make do without me this weekend. In the interests of my investigation."

She likes this reply.

"You'll be in London alone, then?"

"I will."

She refills our glasses. The bottle is empty.

"Good. Because by then I should have some more information for you."

"Which you're now dangling for me as bait, right?"

This touches a nerve.

"My ex-husband was a control freak," she replies quietly. "I promised myself when our marriage ended that I wouldn't ever let a man control me again. And that I would be the one to set the terms for any relationship."

"I see."

"If you want to see me again, that's fine. In fact, it's more than fine. You don't have any obligation to me, and nobody will ever know that we drank a bottle of wine together. You can walk away today without any guilt or regret if you want to."

"But then I won't get this other information that you mentioned."

Ursula strokes the back of my hand thoughtfully, and a jolt of electricity runs through me. She gives me a sly, seducing look.

"I suppose that's true."

"In that case, when and where are we having dinner?"

"There's a French restaurant on Bermondsey Street in SE1. I can't recall the name, but it's the only French restaurant there. It's small and discreet. I'll book us a table for eight o'clock."

"Why Bermondsey Street, may I ask?"

"Because it's only a short walk from my house."

"Ah."

She produces a slip of paper and hands it to me.

"Here's my private mobile number. You can call me on it if you're going to be late. Or if you have to cancel. Or if you change your mind about seeing me again."

"You know that's not going to happen, though, Ursula, don't you?"

"I hope not, David. And if *I* have to cancel for whatever reason, I'll send you a message to your business phone number. Something dull like, *Apologies but I have to postpone our business meeting this weekend. Please call me next week to rearrange.*"

"Right."

"Something that won't arouse your wife's suspicions," she adds.

* * * * *

During my walk back to the Tube, I call Goose's number.

As expected, there is no answer.

* * * * *

When I get home, I decide to come clean and tell Da everything that's gone on today. Minus the sexual innuendo stuff and the hand-touching, obviously, which would be like a red rag to a bull. And it's not as if anything untoward is going to happen on Saturday evening. It isn't. It really isn't.

Nevertheless, I check there's nothing sharp within Da's reach before I begin.

I open by giving her a full account of my morning police visit before moving onto TfL matters. I relate that Mrs. d'Ambrosi has helpfully given me contact information for Goose and that he has also gone missing, and that this was done unofficially over a drink in a wine bar after she finished work.

This raises Da's antennae.

"How old is this woman and what does she look like?"

"Mid-thirties. She has the tip of one of her fingers missing."

This fails to deflect her.

"What does she *look* like, David?"

"Slim, moderately attractive. Smartly-dressed, as you'd expect a corporate manager to be."

"And you had a drink with her?"

"Yes. She was sympathetic about Webster's disappearance, but felt she couldn't talk freely while she was in the office. Hence our meeting at the wine bar."

"Did you flirt with her?"

"Maybe a bit. She struck me as being a lonely sort of person."

"Even though she's married?"

"Well, she's divorced, if you want full disclosure."

"So, you used your charm to get a vulnerable woman to meet you in a wine bar, and convinced her to risk losing her job for the sake of your investigation?"

"That's putting it rather strongly."

"But basically, *yes.*"

"Yes."

"And how did you find out that *Mrs.* d'Ambrosi was divorced?"

"She told me."

"You seem to have had rather a cosy tête-a-tête with this woman."

"She wanted to talk, so I listened."

My wife shrugs.

"Oh, well. I suppose there's no real harm been done. And it's not as if you'll be seeing her again, is it?"

"Well, as to that –"

"You *are* seeing her again?"

There is a sudden dangerous edge to Da's voice.

"She's digging out more information for me this week on Webster and Belka. More confidential stuff. I promised I'd meet her for dinner on Saturday. It was the only evening she could make."

"Saturday?"

"Yes."

"When you're supposed to be coming up to Nang's with me and the children?"

"Yes."

I await the explosion. But it doesn't come. Instead, my wife gives a long-suffering sigh.

"Well," she says, "I suppose I got you involved in this Webster investigation, so I only have myself to blame. You were bound to end up talking to an attractive woman at some stage.

"I am annoyed, however, that you're not coming with us to the Midlands, and that you'll be spending some of the time that I'm away wining and dining an unattached female. What are her breasts like, by the way? And don't tell me you didn't notice."

"They're not as nice as yours. From what I could see," I add. "She was wearing a suit jacket," I further elaborate.

"You shouldn't flirt, David. You're too good at it."

"Sorry. It seemed the best way to get a result."

"Just make sure you don't get a result that you don't intend. And whatever hole you dig for yourself on Saturday, you'll have to get yourself out of it."

I don't comment on this.

"Make sure things don't get out of hand."

"I must say, my love, that you're being remarkably understanding."

"Yes, well, it's lucky for you that we Thai women are renowned for being passive and submissive."

I risk a smile at this. And, fortunately it doesn't result in my wife engaging in any act of violence.

"*Some* Thai women," I say.

"But remember that we also have a reputation for being unforgiving and for exacting revenge when appropriate."

"I assure you that thought will be uppermost in my mind for the whole of Saturday evening."

"Good. Now you can pour *me* a glass of wine."

XV

In Training for Widowhood

I'm having what one might call a reflective few hours before I see Pearl Webster. Taking stock.

Da was uncommunicative over breakfast. Not unfriendly exactly, but not her usual energetic self either. I think the kids suspected that we'd had words because they kept their heads down and left for school without a murmur. I guess my wife was still processing our frank chat of the previous evening. There may be ructions yet to come once she has thought things through, but for now it's all quiet on the family front.

Now, I'm pounding the chilly pavements of old Londinium with my hands thrust deep into the pockets of my trench coat, and longing for a cigarette. Which I won't have because the lingering smell of smoke on my clothes would definitely set Da off on one, and I don't want to give her any further reason for outrage at my behaviour.

So, where are you, Braddock? Let's recap, shall we?

Well, for starters, two of my therapy clients have gone missing. This was not the first thing on my mind yesterday evening, when I was more concerned with whether my wife was going to murder me. But now that that crisis has passed (at least temporarily), the implications of these two disappearances are weighing on me.

I've had a brace of unnerving visits from the Metropolitan Police. Having to account for my movements to them was humiliating enough, but David Braddock Esquire is now firmly on the police radar. I can imagine the discussions taking place and the sort of questions the police must be asking themselves. At some point, the coppers will doubtless be knocking on my door again to make a few 'clarifications' about the nature of my therapy business and my relationship with Anneke Reid and Ben Quinlan. It's too juicy a coincidence for the Met that I appear to be the only obvious link in these two disappearances – especially if DCI Zachary is stirring the pot in the background.

My imagination goes into overdrive.

I can see Zachary standing in front of a whiteboard, and hear her saying, "We know these things for sure: Braddock discovered the missing half of his next-door neighbour's torso at the same time that two of his clients were vanishing. These events were all within a few days of each other. That has to be more than a coincidence. I've known this man for several years, and I've long suspected he might be a head case: that arrogance of his concealing a dark criminal core." Then, as an afterthought, "I wonder if he's on any form of medication or whether he's having any psychiatric treatment. We should check up on that."

Which would lead them to Rufus Ogilvy.

How much can I trust my shrink's professional discretion, I wonder?

"Two of Braddock's clients have gone missing," policewoman Taylor will inform him. "And one of them is a seventeen-year-old girl."

Ogilvy will blanch and say, "He told me that he'd been doing drugs with an underage client. Perhaps that was her. Plus, Mr. Braddock's wife was worried that lately he'd been feeling depressed, maybe even suicidal. That's why I saw him initially on an emergency appointment. And then, there's the matter of his having conversations with his dead first wife…"

"Does he strike you as being the violent, unstable type, Mr. Ogilvy?"

"Not especially, but…"

"But what?"

"Well, he had a number of brutal life experiences during his time in Thailand. They could easily result in a person developing PTSD. And, yes, it's entirely credible that some recent event could have triggered a psychotic episode."

I note that I'm wandering through Hyde Park, and I decide to sit down on a bench and have a moment. A watery sun is peeking through the clouds, but it's not doing nearly enough to dispel the day's chill.

However, this breather fails to provide any respite from the narrative playing in my head.

I see myself in a police interview room sitting opposite DCI Zachary.

"Where have you buried the bodies, Braddock?" she asks. "And did you sexually assault Anneke Reid before or after you murdered her? Did you drug her?"

"What?"

"Don't play me for a fool. You're involved in that pedophile ring with Lee Vance and Edwin Jessop, aren't you? That's why you were so happy to take on Anneke Reid as a client."

"That's ridiculous."

"And then there's Devesh Banerjee."

"What about him?"

"You were so insistent that Banerjee's mutilated body couldn't have been moved by a single person — and that's because you knew how difficult it had been for you and Vance to move it. That's how you knew where to find the dentist's legs. A double bluff on your part to deflect attention away from yourself."

"And why would I want to kill Banerjee?"

"Who can say?" she coos. "A dispute with your neighbour that escalated out of control? As a favour to your pedo friend Vance who hated the dentist? You tell me, Braddock."

Finally, I succeed in clicking the 'pause' button on this fictitious drama.

I gaze around me.

In the real world, it is a tranquil November day. I can see ducks on the Serpentine, mothers wheeling push-chairs, young couples with their arms around each other, kids who should be in school kicking a football, and a dog chasing a thrown rubber toy. *Normality.*

Clearly, I'm overwrought, and my brain is being too creative for its own good. For *my* own good.

It is, though, slightly alarming at how the Metropolitan Police could put two and two together and make five, should they choose to do so.

But they can deliberate, cogitate and mentally masturbate as much as they like, because they have no hard evidence to link me to either Anneke's disappearance or Ben's. And as for that Banerjee stuff... where did *that* come from? From my fixation that Vance's case has not being properly looked into, that's where.

I really should let the Vance thing drop. *Properly* drop. I have more than enough on my plate.

And what about the state of my own missing person investigation?

I check my watch.

I've faffed around too long on my own worries this morning; and none of that is going to help me with my Ronald Webster investigation.

I try ringing RW's and Gustaw Belka's mobiles again. No joy.

Bollocks.

I inhale a deep, cough-inducing breath of wintry air.

It's time to move.

* * * * *

I'm in a calm state when I arrive in the Websters' street.

But as I'm passing her neighbour's house, I am accosted by a squat, middle-aged female who gives all the appearance of having been lying in wait for me.

"Mr. Braddock, is it?" she says in a slightly squeaky voice.

"Yes."

"Pearl said you were dropping by today. I'm Rebecca Oliphant. I spoke to your wife, who's helping me buy a flat in Kensington. I suppose you could say it's because of me that you're on Ronald's case."

"Ah, I see. Well, thank you, Mrs. Oliphant," I add for want of a better reply.

"You look taller than you do on television."

"I'm shorter when I'm on the radio."

She laughs politely and asks how my investigation is going. The nosey cow should be buying an apartment in Highgate, not Kensington. She'd likely rub along well with Doris and Elsie, as she seems the gossipy type too.

I mutter something about it being early days, and she nods understandingly.

"How do you think Mrs. Webster is bearing up?"

"Pearl is a trooper," she replies.

"So, she's managing all right, is she?"

"It's a hard thing that's happened to her, but she's carrying on with her life. As she should, in my opinion. It's not her fault that her husband has walked out on her."

"Indeed."

She glances around furtively before dropping her voice.

"And, although I shouldn't be telling you this, Mr. Braddock, but I half-hope that you don't find Ronald."

"Oh, and why is that?"

"Because in my opinion, she's better off without him. He's a selfish man who never paid her enough attention. And perhaps now she can do all the things she's always wanted to do, but couldn't. Like travelling, for instance. Taking holidays abroad. Running her séances without her husband belittling her about it. She helps a lot of people."

"I'm sure she does. And I'm sure they're all suitably grateful. Even the dead ones," I add.

Fortunately, Mrs. O doesn't pick up on my sarcasm.

She continues with, "Pearl told me that you have a powerful aura."

"Purple, if my memory serves, yes."

"It gives her a lot of confidence in you, she said."

"That's reassuring."

Though she might have a good deal less confidence in me if she knew that she is my number one suspect for her husband's murder. Assuming that he's dead, that is. Like many of the other people Pearl has 'helped.'

Mrs. W's neighbour squints at me.

"I suppose you're not a believer? In the afterlife, I mean. I guess you have to be hard-nosed and logical in your line of work."

I answer this with an equivocal gesture.

A voice that is not from beyond the grave interrupts our chat.

"Rebecca, are you monopolising my private detective?"

Pearl Webster has materialised (probably not the best word) at her front door.

"Oh, sorry, my dear. I'm rabbiting away. But it's not every day a girl gets to meet Sherlock Holmes. Good to talk to you, Mr. Braddock."

"And you, Mrs. Oliphant."

I follow my client into her house. She shows me into the lounge, I remove my coat, and we sit down. Her crystal ball is still positioned prominently in the room, and some of her tarot cards are spread out on the side table. I wonder whether she's been talking to any amusing dead people today.

"Would you like some tea?"

I remember the last tea she made me, and politely decline.

"So." She lets out a sigh. "Do you have any news for me?"

"Not much as yet, Mrs. Webster. I've visited a number of homeless hostels without any luck, and I didn't learn anything useful from the members of the Locomotive Club. The HR Manager at Ronald's employer was as helpful as she could be, but she didn't have any information that struck me as significant."

"Oh. And what about Ronald's laptop? Anything there?"

"Not so far. But I'm still going through his files. There's rather a lot of data."

"But nothing useful…?" She pauses. "Or unusual?"

"No. Not that I've found."

"I see."

"However, it's not all doom and gloom. One interesting thing has come up. It's to do with Ronald's friend Goose."

"Goose?"

"Yes. It seems that he also has gone missing. Around about the same time as your husband."

She appears to be genuinely shocked by this information.

"That's a strange coincidence. If it *is* a coincidence."

"My thoughts exactly. I have managed to obtain Goose's address through a source of mine, and I plan to go there in the next couple of days. It might be a dead end, and I don't want to get your hopes up, but we'll see."

Mrs. W reflects on this before saying brightly, "Then what do you need from me today, Mr. Braddock?"

"If it's all right, I'd like to go through Ronald's wardrobe. Check his pockets and so on. Then, I'd like to spend some time examining his den in rather more detail than I did on my last visit."

"That's perfectly in order. Though I did a search in Ronald's clothing in the days following his disappearance. But there is always the possibility that I might have missed something."

She shows me up to their bedroom and leaves me to it. Which is good, as I don't plan on rifling only through her husband's private things, but through hers as well.

I spend several minutes in his wardrobe and turn up nothing but old railway tickets and some loose change. It's the same story in Pearl Webster's wardrobe (except for the railway tickets and loose change, naturally). I check both bedside cabinets and see only the usual sort of stuff that ends up there. Finally, I rummage in their chest drawers. The only item of note is in one of Mrs. W's drawers: a diaphanous black negligée from Anne Summers which still has the price tag on it.

I move across the landing to Ronald Webster's man-cave.

Mrs. W calls up the stairs, "Are you sure you don't want anything to drink, Mr. Braddock? I have ordinary tea if you don't like herbal."

"Then, a cup of English Breakfast tea would be most welcome. Black, please," I yell back.

"Coming right up."

I examine Webster's train set.

It's a N gauge – which is to say that the rails are 9 mm. The detailed landscape, stations, buildings, vehicles and miniature people must have taken many, many hours to make, paint and deploy. There are only two trains on the tracks, a steam locomotive with two carriages parked at a replica of Abbey Wood station, and a modern engine at Fenchurch Street. Other carriages from different eras sit in various sidings. There is a big chunk of Webster's life right here on this table. But the work shows signs of not being completed.

In the centre of the display is what one might describe as a cardboard hillock cut through end-to-end by two tunnels, and which has not yet been grassed or fixed in place. No track connects these tunnels to the rest of the model's rail system, and beside them is a partially-decorated platform and building, two crudely-made brown crates that are oversized in comparison with the rest of the models, and a cluster of station signs. Unlike the other stations on Webster's railway set, these signs are for Underground stations and carry the familiar TfL roundel. They read: *Lords, Bull & Bush, South Kentish Town, British Museum* and *Highgate.*

I take some pictures on my mobile phone camera of the layout (even though I'm doubtful they will be of any use), and am relooking at RW's shelves of modelling materials when Pearl Webster appears carrying a tea tray which she places on the small desk.

"I shan't interrupt you," she says, and goes back downstairs.

I pour myself a cuppa and peruse the railwayman's book collection. The titles alone are enough to put me off opening them, but I do flick through a few, noting that – while Webster has likely read the whole lot of them for his research – they are in pristine condition. There are no underlined sections or scribbled notes in margins, and he's not one of those uncivilised animals who fold over the corners of pages instead of using a bookmark.

But then my eye falls on a book with a bright red spine, and which has a large number of different coloured Post It Notes sticking out. It doesn't belong in the library of an anal retentive like Webster.

The book is titled *The League of Loki*. But it's not about the video game that my stepson is so keen on. As its subtitle declares, this is a study of the roots and development of the anarchic movement that took its cue from the game. The mock-Nazi iconography of 'LOL' is displayed prominently on the cover – presumably in an attempt to drum up sales for what promises to be a dry read. The back cover tells me that the author is one Felicity Fennimore, Professor of Political Philosophy at one of the US East Coast Universities, and there is a head-and-shoulders photo of her looking suitably prim and academic.

And in stark contrast to Webster's other books, a swift perusal of it reveals many scribblings, particularly on those pages where there are paper insertions.

Meanwhile, someone has turned up at the Websters' front door, and Pearl isn't too happy about it.

"I wasn't expecting you for another hour," she says crossly.

"My apologies, Mrs. Webster, but I had a couple of appointments cancel on me, so I thought I'd see if you were free as I was already in the area…"

The voice – a man's – stutters to an apologetic silence.

"Well, I suppose you'd better come in," Mrs. W says resignedly.

I use this as the cue to move my arse, the tea tray and Professor Fennimore's book downstairs.

My client and her visitor are sitting in the lounge. He wears a cheap grey suit, and has slicked-down hair and the face of a solicitous undertaker. He looks like the sort who still uses the term 'omnibus' and enjoys test cricket because it's not too exciting. When I enter the room, he is busy taking papers out of a briefcase.

I hold out the tea tray and ask, "What would you like me to, er...?"

Pearl Webster takes it from me and heads for the kitchen. I follow.

"I didn't want to talk in front of your visitor," I say, "but I'm done for now. And you were right: there's nothing in Ronald's pockets. You've been thorough in your search."

"What about in his man-cave?"

"The only thing of any interest was this book."

I show her *The League of Loki* tome.

"It doesn't seem to be his usual reading material. I wonder if you can tell me anything about it. Like, did he buy it recently?"

"I couldn't say," she says. "I don't recall his ever mentioning it. Does it matter?"

"Probably not. But do you mind if I borrow it?"

"Help yourself."

"Thank you. Well, I'll be going. I'll be in touch when I have any news."

We move back to the lounge so that I can collect my coat.

Pearl Webster reluctantly introduces me to her visitor.

"Mr. Kettle, this is Mr. Braddock. He's the famous private detective I mentioned to you previously."

"Ah, right."

Kettle rises and we shake hands. I give him a business card.

"In case you ever need a PI," I say.

He fumbles in his pocket and hands me his card.

"In case you ever need life insurance," he replies with a grin.

A flash of alarm crosses Mrs. W's face. I pretend not to notice.

"I'll be off, then, Mrs. Webster. We'll speak soon."

She shows me to the door and closes it quickly behind me.

* * * * *

I walk to Vauxhall, and reflect on Pearl Webster.

I've watched her reactions more closely today than at our first meeting. They confirmed that she's a cool customer, and not easy to read. Was she relieved or disappointed by my lack of progress? Hard to tell. Her manner was very controlled, and the only time she was thrown off-balance was when I met Kettle – who, fortunately for me, had showed up early for his appointment. Otherwise, I wouldn't have known he existed. But at least I've been spared any fake displays of emotion. If

Mrs. W was a doormat for her husband – as Rebecca Oliphant believes – then she's certainly put that behind her. She's every inch a widow-in-training. An advanced stage of training, I might add.

Too much, however, must not be read into her serenity. She is, after all, a medium. And if one is not afraid of death, what else is there to be afraid of? Only the monstrousness of eternity itself.

I take out the card I've just been given.

Titus Kettle

Independent Insurance Agent

Available for Personal Consultations

What sort of sadist would call their son 'Titus'? Perhaps he was an unwanted accident, or his parents were Shakespeare buffs.

I'll give him a ring later.

* * * * *

By the time I'm standing on the platform at Vauxhall, I've stopped worrying about Pearl Webster and started stewing over Ursula d'Ambrosi instead.

Now, to employ a railway metaphor, there's a potential train wreck waiting for me.

Claire remains silent. She is probably as disgusted with me about that messy situation as my living wife is. Either that or she really has gone for good.

Maybe I should discuss Ursula with Ogilvy at our next session. He can add *hypersexuality* to my long list of mental issues. Assuming that I'm still able to talk and Da hasn't removed my head by then.

This causes me to remember my other mania about being followed, and I look around the platform for likely stalkers. The only candidate is a young woman with cropped hair, and she doesn't seem *that* likely. Not unless – like Ursula d'Ambrosi – she has poor taste in men.

How simple and uncomplicated my life was only two weeks ago. I will never complain of being bored again. A chasm is opening up between where I want to be and where I am now.

The train arrives to whisk me off into the noisy, rattling dark.

"Mind the gap," says the recorded announcement.

XVI

Things Concealed

I wait until I get home before calling Titus Kettle to be absolutely sure he's finished his business with Pearl Webster.

To hook him in, I explain that I've been considering taking out life insurance for a while so our brief encounter was timely. He says he has a gap in his schedule tomorrow, so we make an appointment for him to come to my house in the morning.

"You're being exceptionally wise, Mr. Braddock," Kettle tells me. "Not enough people think about how their loved ones would manage financially in the event that something happened to them."

"Yeah," I reply. "Celebration parties can be expensive."

He gives a nervous titter and we end the conversation on that note.

Da is having an evening out with a few of her girlfriends this evening, so I'm babysitting Pratcha. Jenny also won't be at home as she's going to the cinema with a couple of mates from school. I hope none of them are boys, because she's at the age now where I'll have to endure all those teenage crushes – and eventually the loss of my younger daughter's virginity. The thought of this makes me insist that she's home by nine-thirty.

"And don't go near any white Ford Transit vans or walk through any unlit areas on your own," I warn her. "In fact," I add, "forget using the Tube. There are too many weirdos around. Take a taxi there and back. Here's some money. And don't get into conversation with the driver unless it's a female."

"Dad," she sighs, giving me an old-fashioned look. "I'm not stupid."

"Unlike your father," Da comments on her way out of the door.

She's gone before I can come up with a suitable retort.

I show Pratcha the LOL book I've borrowed from the Webster household.

"Wow," he says. "I might read that after you, Papa David. For more insight into the video game. That guide you bought me is excellent, by the way. It gives short-cuts and weapons hints, and I've used a couple of them already."

"Good."

"Is this book anything to do with your investigation?"

"Perhaps, but it's a long-shot. I've not found anything much in the files on Webster's laptop and I'm starting to run out of ideas."

"Have you checked his hidden files?" asks my precocious stepson.

"What do you mean by *hidden files*?"

Pratcha and my daughter exchange a glance. They roll their eyes.

"You're not terribly tech-savvy, Dad, are you?" says Jenny.

"They're the files you keep on your computer that you don't want anyone to see," the little gamer explains patiently. "If you fire up this guy's laptop, I'll show you how to access them."

"I'll be off," says the other one following Da out of the door. "I'll leave you two to the porn."

"Porn?"

"Yeah, it's usually porn," states Pratcha.

"Usually? And exactly how much experience do you have of this, young man?"

"What other stuff would somebody want to keep secret. Unless he keeps a black file of mistresses and prostitutes on there too. Or he's a drug-dealer, or…"

"Yes, I get it," I interrupt quickly.

Once Webster's laptop is running, Pratcha starts typing.

After a couple of minutes, he presents me with the machine.

"There you go. I'll write you some notes so you can access it yourself next time."

"Thanks. Now go to your room and find something else to do."

"But, can't I –?"

"No, you can't. If there *is* inappropriate stuff on here, you're not going to look at it. Are we clear?"

"Clear," he says resignedly, and leaves me to it.

Everything on the hidden area of Webster's hard drive appears to be either video files or photographs. He has organised these under two folders named *VIDS* and *PICS*.

I gird myself for what might be coming, and decide to start with the still images. There's a couple of hundred of them, and as I go through them one-by-one, I see that they are all pictures of girls from (I guess) around five years old to mid-teens. None of the photos are pornographic in nature, and the kids are not dressed provocatively – unless you consider school uniforms arousing – but one has to be concerned about the mindset of anyone who would want to assemble a collection like this. Most give the impression that the children were unaware that someone was photographing them, as they are not posing for the camera. Some are blurry and of poor quality as if they had been taken on a cheap camera-phone.

I remember Jenny telling us a few days ago that some man had been spotted hanging around the school gates, and it makes me shudder. None of the photos are of *her*, thank God.

I pour a whisky, check that Pratcha is indeed upstairs, and return to Webster's laptop.

The *VIDS* folder comprises two sub-folders: *CLASSICS* and *HARDCORE*. I'm not ready to look at the second one, so I open *CLASSICS*.

The videos are sorted alphabetically by title, and I recognise some of them as being soft porn films that were available on general cinema/video release.

They include such fleshy offerings as *Deep Throat*, *I Spit on Your Grave*, *In the Realm of the Senses* (a Japanese Pink Film, I recall), and *Emmanuelle*, as well as others that I am not familiar with. Some of them might even be snuff movies.

The title which follows *Violating Monica Part II* – the deviants made a sequel? Jesus! – is *Rock Bottom*.

This rings a bell with me for some reason, and I'm sure it's not because I've watched it. I down my whisky, pour another generous one and rack my brains.

The connection comes to me. It's *Janice*, the barista from Tower Bridge Beanz: the place where Gustaw Belka, aka Goose, used to work. I remember Dagenham Dave, or Brixton Bert, or Canary Wharf Charlie, or whatever that wide-boy's name was, trying to tell me about it. I told him to sling his hook, but not before he'd informed me that Janice had been in it. In some minor role, I believe, and not one that had involved her stripping off. But it was enough to cement Janice's celebrity status in that idiot's head.

It's a curious coincidence, though. And a potential hitherto-undisclosed link between Webster and Goose.

I take a deep breath, and set the *Rock Bottom* video to play.

It opens with what looks like a younger version of the barista I remember, chatting in the street with some attractive, busty friend whose clothes are too tight for her (and are therefore likely to be jettisoned soon). The Janice doppelgänger, having served her introductory plot function, disappears from the story shortly after; while the well-endowed friend goes on to be sexually tortured by some mad medic. This eventually culminates in her being murdered and having a large stone inserted into her bottom.

I fast forward. Several other young women meet the same fate – the rocks seemingly increasing in size with each victim. I continue to fast-forward until the baddie comes to a suitably violent end and the credits roll.

Another whisky is required after that cinematic ordeal.

I gather my wits and endeavour to put rock formations out of my thoughts.

So what if Janice was in a porn movie? Where does that get me? And what might it have to do with Webster and Goose?

There's only one thing for it. I have to review the *HARDCORE* videos and hope they don't make me throw up.

A skim through a dozen of them almost makes me do just that.

They all show sex with kids – and a couple that I peruse are particularly nasty and violent. Who gets off on this kind of stuff? And what sort of pervert thinks it's OK to make money out of this suffering?

I switch off the laptop and throw it on the sofa. I feel like I should wash my hands and scrub myself down in the shower.

The only thing that I can be certain about after seeing Ronald Webster's secret files, is that he is a pedophile. Whether or not he is a practicing one has yet to be established, but either way, he's definitely a sicko.

Does his wife know? Or suspect?

I replay my conversations with her.

"Ronald is not much interested in sex. He hasn't been for years. Whatever he needs in that department he can get on the Internet."

Plus, didn't she ask me whether I'd found anything 'unusual' on her husband's laptop? Or am I misremembering?

Does she know?

And – more to the point – do I want to keep searching for the twisted git or should I hand his laptop over to the police, tell them what I've found, and have done with it?

But I'm not ready to throw in the towel. Not yet. However, after Webster's videos, I don't have the stomach for doing anything more on his case this evening either. And those horrible images have spooked me about Jenny's safety. I'll be glad when she's back home; though that won't be for another hour-and-a-half, and her phone will be switched off while she's at the cinema.

I make a pot of tea and take Pratcha a cup of hot chocolate.

Unsurprisingly, he's on his console, but pauses the game when I enter his bedroom.

"Did you find any porn on the laptop, Papa David?" he asks, skipping the small-talk.

"Sadly, yes."

"Thought you would."

"Have you done all your homework?"

"I have. I need to make sure I stay in Mum's good books."

"Yeah. Maybe you can give me some tips on that too."

I return to our living room and switch on the TV.

An anchorwoman is relating the news that a fourth English footballer has come forward with child abuse allegations.

I click the channel change button, and up pops a political debate programme where the panel is discussing the latest outrageous remarks by *persona non grata* politician Giles

Feathercroft. An outraged young person is grandstanding, hogging the camera.

Click.

Now it's a reality TV show where a has-been celebrity is told that for his 'trial' he has to eat a pig's anus to earn his team their dinner. The team's evening meal does not appear to be the thing that's at the forefront of his mind.

I continue changing channels until I come across a Guy Ritchie film. I've seen it before, and it's already halfway through, but the sounds of overamplified punches, squealing car tyres, and gunshots keep me on an even keel until I hear Jenny's key in the front door.

It's twenty-nine minutes past nine. She's cut it fine.

Two hours later, when Da finally arrives home, she's tipsy, and declares that she doesn't want sex. That's a sure sign I'm still in the doghouse, even though she's smiling when she tells me.

XVII

Claims and Causes

"Pratcha tells me that there is pornography on Webster's laptop," my wife remarks after the kids have left for school the following morning.

"That's right."

"Is it any good?" she asks in an effort at civility.

"Definitely not. It's disgusting stuff involving children."

Da wrinkles her nose.

"Are you going to hand it over to the police?"

"Well, let's put it this way. I don't want it in our house a second longer than is necessary. If I'm caught with that in my possession, I'll be the one ending up on a sex offender's register."

She mulls this over, then says, "I suppose if I hadn't suggested you take on this missing person case, you wouldn't have that dilemma. And you wouldn't be meeting this d'Ambrosi woman on Saturday either."

"You weren't to know. And the weekend dinner appointment is my own fault."

Da switches from guilty wife to attack dog in a nanosecond.

"Yes, that's absolutely true. It *is* your own fault."

However, faced with my glum appearance and lack of self-justification, she cannot maintain her glare for long, and her voice becomes softer.

"So, what's on your agenda for today?"

"I have an agent coming to see me this morning about life insurance. I met him at Pearl Webster's yesterday, and I want to find out why he was there."

"Sounds like a lead. What else?"

"I was going to go to Gustaw Belka's place since I now have his address. But I've decided to postpone that for a day to do more research on Webster's laptop and read through a book I found in his den. And before you ask – no, I won't be looking through his collection of video nasties again. I need to cross-reference some material from his manuscript. That's why I still need his laptop, for now."

"Well, don't leave it lying around. Pratcha might get curious. You know what boys are like, and I don't want him exposed to that sort of thing."

"Don't worry. I don't even want *me* exposed to that sort of thing."

I study Da while she absent-mindedly drinks her coffee.

"So, are we good?" I query.

"Good-*ish*," she says.

* * * * *

Titus Kettle arrives a few minutes early at the *Maison Braddock*. He's hoping, no doubt, for a fat commission to help pay off his inevitable post-Christmas overdraft.

I have already determined that my strategy with him will be to hint that I am privy to more about Pearl Webster's financial arrangements than I actually am, and see what that brings.

After we've seated ourselves, he produces some papers and starts going into his patter about the various insurance products on offer.

I stop him abruptly.

"Mr. Kettle," I say, "I already know what sort of insurance I'm after. I want the same policy that Pearl and Ronald took out. So, if you can run through the terms of that with me – to make sure I've understood it correctly – that would be great."

"Ah, the pure insurance cover with *Manchester and Edinburgh Assurance* which only pays out on death. Excellent choice, Mr. Braddock. And this would be for yourself, would it?"

"Just like Ronald's," I say, taking a punt.

The gamble pays off, and Kettle is unfazed.

"I see. And what *level* of cover do you want?"

I pretend to consider this, before asking, "Do you think the same level as Mr. Webster has would be suitable for me?"

"Well, that depends on your personal circumstances, but I should have thought that five hundred thousand – the same as Mr. Webster's – would be more than ample for most people. Unless you have a particularly large mortgage."

Half a million quid. Now it's my turn to appear unfazed.

"Sounds good. Let's start doing some paperwork," I say to encourage the agent to feel comfortable and loose-tongued.

He's happy to fill in the boxes on the forms for me while he peppers me with questions about my age, state of health and so on.

While he's into this routine, I offer the comment that it must be a difficult situation for Pearl making a claim, and ask him how the insurance company handles such a matter in the event that the insured person has disappeared and there is no proof of death.

Kettle becomes visibly alarmed at this, so I go on to say, "I was thinking what my wife might have to go through if she were in the same position as Pearl is now."

This soothes him, and he becomes almost apologetic.

"As I'm sure you'll appreciate, Mr. Braddock, it's rather challenging for any insurance company to make a payout unless they can be sure the insured hasn't simply gone missing on a temporary basis."

"Especially when he's only been missing for three weeks," I offer sympathetically.

"Precisely."

"Then, maybe Pearl should have waited longer before contacting you?"

"Ideally, yes," Kettle replies passing a hand across his forehead. "Particularly as it's only recently that the policy was taken out. And the fact that it's only eighteen months since we paid out a claim on Mrs. Webster's mother's life policy... well, that doesn't help either. Though, of course, the two events are not related," he adds hastily.

I nod sagely as if this information is not new to me.

"Yes," I say, "It's been a trying time for her these last two years, poor lady. Having to go through the same depressing process twice – and not even knowing for sure what has become of Ronald. But Pearl's mother *had* reached that age where things happen to a person's body."

This is a safe observation given Mrs. W's vintage.

"Indeed. And a heart attack *is* the most common cause of death, as those of us in this business are only too well aware. At least it's a quick way to go."

We have a moment's silence before I say, "But now that I'm on Ronald's case, hopefully we'll have a speedy resolution to *that* one way or the other. And, with luck, you won't have to pay out on his policy. One must be optimistic."

"That's what insurance is all about: optimism. Hoping for the best, but planning for the worst, as it were."

"Right. Well, let's get this form finished so we can talk about how much my premiums are going to cost me. And I do have the right to cancel within fourteen days if I decide it's not for me. Is that right?"

"Absolutely. In fact, the cooling-off period for the *Manchester and Edinburgh* is thirty days. Though I'm sure you'll be pleasantly surprised at how reasonably priced it will be."

And who knows? Perhaps I won't cancel it.

* * * * *

Kettle has left, confident of another sale.

I process what I've learned.

Two claims by Pearl Webster (née Thompson) on life insurance policies in short order of each other. Curious and worthy of note, I'd say. I wish I could have asked our morose, exsanguinous agent how much Mrs. W collected on her mother's policy – but that would have been pushing things too far, given that he's already told me more than he should have.

I wonder how thorough the autopsy was on Mrs. Thompson. There are many ways to bring on a heart attack, and if the pathologist wasn't being too diligent in his work, he could have missed something important. It's happened before.

Might Pearl have done away with her mother and her husband for the proceeds of their life insurance policies? That's a motive with a decent pedigree too.

But now I think of it, we could be dealing with an insurance scam rather than murder. Mrs. Thompson could have died entirely innocently of natural causes: but it might have been that financial windfall that gave her daughter the idea of making a bundle on Ronald's death too.

Maybe Mr. W isn't dead at all. There was that case of insurance fraud in the North of England about ten years back of a prison officer faking his own death while out canoeing. That was an instance where both the husband and wife were in on the deception. And, if memory serves, he actually had the gall to live next door to his wife for quite some time before the fraud came to light.

Perhaps the Websters have cooked up some similar plan. But, if so, where would they go once Pearl has her hands on the readies? They certainly couldn't stay in Battersea. Panama? Argentina? The Outer Hebrides? That would be a tall order given that RW had to be dragged kicking and screaming each time his wife wanted him to set foot outside the capital. Even the members at the Locomotive Club hinted that our Ronald got dizzy whenever he had to cross the Greater London boundary.

Then Pearl engages a private detective to give credence to her assertion that her husband has disappeared, all the while knowing that the chance of anyone tracking down a missing person is virtually zero...

None of this, though, helps me find our elusive, railway-mad pervert. However, it's food for thought, even if I still have nothing even approaching objective evidence of wrongdoing on anybody's part. But before one can go about testing a hypothesis, one has to have a hypothesis to test.

Let's hold onto that happy notion. It might comfort me during today's hard grind.

I take out my mobile phone and switch on Webster's laptop. And although I have Pratcha's notes on how to access Mr. W's hidden files, I don't expect – or want – to have to use them.

For the next couple of hours, I look at the photographs that I took of Webster's train set, and try to make sense of the things about the model that puzzled me by searching through sections of his monotonous manuscript.

Maybe there is a coded message here waiting to be deciphered. Or perhaps I too have been infected by Dear Ronald's mental disorder about railways, and I'm going to waste yet more of my time chasing down blind alleys or unlit tunnels.

But let's proceed with optimism, regardless, shall we? As the cheerful, ever-hopeful Mr. Kettle would do.

I examine my pictures of the miniature station signs in the uncompleted part of Webster's layout.

The first one is Lord's, which I'm sure is no longer operational. I check the manuscript's index and follow the link to the text reference.

There it is: *Lord's was previously called St. John's Wood, and was closed in 1939. Cricket fans now have to use the new St. John's Wood station; and though there is still occasional lobbying for the old place to be reopened, this would appear to be unlikely to happen as a hotel has been built over it.*

The next one up is Bull & Bush. I learn that this station, between Hampstead Heath and Golders Green, was never opened owing to restrictions on above-ground building, although the platform level work was completed – some 220 feet below Hampstead Heath.

I read through what Webster had to say about South Kentish Town (closed in 1924) and British Museum (closed in 1933). They both became victims of competition and shifting economics and, while their below-ground voids remain to this day, like Lord's and Bull & Bush, you won't see their names on any modern Tube map.

Unlike Highgate, the last of the miniature signs. But I remember from my earlier reading that there are *two* Highgate stations. One underground (the working one) and the derelict Highgate London and North Eastern Railway Station above: designed as an over-ambitious hub of electrification, and which was killed off in the 1950s.

Consequently, they all appear under Webster's chapter on 'ghost stations' – a list of which I'd made previously – along with Aldwych where I went on the TfL tour, and various other relics of the past.

So, my research hangs together. But where does that get me?

Answer: nowhere.

It could simply be that our railway enthusiast wanted to add some historic flavour to his model, and considered these locations notable or somehow special as they are no longer functioning entities. Hell, he might even have been planning building a lower level to his train set so that he could take young girls under the trestle table when his wife was out.

That's enough of that.

I close the laptop, percolate a coffee and pick up *The League of Loki* book. If nothing else it will provide a distraction after my futile efforts to uncover the logic of Webster's model. Assuming there is any logic, or that it 'means' anything.

The learned Professor Felicity Fennimore opens her introduction with the following spiel.

The League of Loki began life as a popular video game of the shoot-'em-up variety, but the game's extreme and gratuitous violence soon brought it to the attention of various concerned groups, and its makers were eventually compelled to withdraw it from the market.

Since then, the game has achieved cult status and, despite its official unavailability, it can still be downloaded from a number of pirate sites today.

This book, however, is not about the video game, but rather about the anarchic and nihilistic movements that it sparked in the real world.

I resist the temptation to skip to the pages marked by Ronald Webster, and instead let Ms. Fennimore whisk me off on her narrative journey.

I note that the author hails from New York, and as I progress through the book, it becomes apparent that most of the research she has done is US-based; although she does cover LOL activities in Japan and South Korea – those hardy outposts of American economic colonialism. There isn't much on Europe; presumably because we Europeans are already world-weary and pessimistic, and therefore don't require a video game to introduce us to cynicism about the human race and its murderous tendencies.

Fennimore goes on to describe instances during the period 2002-14 when LOL 'cells' were active. The book, I note, was published in 2015, so there are no examples of incidents in the last two years. I have vague recollections of one or two of the US events she covers, but the Yankee media seems to have collectively decided after the first few years that school shootings were what their audiences really wanted to read about; and LOL outrages therefore tended to fade from the public consciousness.

She goes into some depth about four specific LOL murder-sprees: in New York, Chicago, Los Angeles and Tokyo. In each of these cases, the perpetrators were small gangs of disaffected youths who portrayed themselves as vigilantes exacting revenge on members of a society that was indifferent to their problems and had effectively disowned them. Thus, feeling overlooked, alienated and excluded from any meaningful economic activity, they had turned to violence, 'executing' (as they would think of it) largely white, middle-aged citizens who were comfortably off – at least by comparison to themselves.

Fennimore, however, deviates from her social and political analysis by pointing out that many of the perpetrators had previous criminal convictions for acts of violence, and goes on to say that *[t]herefore the veneer of LOL provided these individuals with an excuse for the type of behaviour that they might well have indulged in anyway.*

She further notes that organised crime was also keen to gatecrash the party, and used LOL as a 'flag of convenience' to disguise activities such as smuggling, drug distribution, and even people trafficking. This is one of the paragraphs that Webster has underlined and entered some exclamation marks in the side margin. Though whether that specific section has major significance for him is open to speculation as he marked out lots of the book. His spidery handwriting peppers the pages of Fennimore's work with insightful comments such as, *Really? Not sure I agree with this! Seems unlikely? Too much detail! Not enough detail! Only in America! It's lucky we don't have a gun culture in England!* Etc, etc.

He likes his exclamation marks, does our Ronald.

The learned professor summarises thus.

The League of Loki cannot ultimately be regarded as a political movement, or even a collection of political movements. There has never been any recognised leader of the organisation, and it has no coherent structure per se. In this respect, it is a multi-headed hydra, resembling independent, cell-based terrorist organisations like the original ISIS, but lacking in any underlying or unifying philosophy. It is more akin to an idea: the idea that, if you regard yourself as being a member of a subjugated or persecuted class, it is acceptable to indulge in brutality and carnage as a way of striking back against your perceived oppressors. The end justifies any means, in other words. Though what that 'end' might be is far from clear. The members of the League of Loki, one could say, are not so much Rebels Without a Cause as Rebels Without a Clue.

Why would any of this be of interest to Ronald Webster? And why – judging from all his enigmatic doodles, scrawls and scribbles – did it get him so worked up? Was he, perchance, contemplating a change of career from secretive, railway-obsessed pedophile to champion of downtrodden youth?

Unlikely.

I consider our own disaffected youth of Great Britain. The homelessness among young people that I've witnessed first-hand in recent days. The removal of the comfort of being part of the European family, as some will have seen the pro-Brexit vote. The gradual but insidious erosion of hope about the future. Depressing stuff if you're positioned towards the underclass end of the social spectrum. It's hardly surprising that the number of public demonstrations and protests are on the increase, and that young people are at the forefront of them. From climate change to the implementation of governmental austerity measures, they seem to have the shitty end of the stick.

I have a whisky to cheer myself up before Da and the kids get home.

My phone rings.

It's Chalky telling me that our bass-player has broken his leg falling downstairs, so our gig at *Blue Rhythms* is off tomorrow evening.

"But it's OK because they've already lined up *The Wailing Horns* to stand in for us."

"Ah, right. Good."

"In fact, I fancy listening to the *Horns*, so I'm taking my missus to the club for a night out. Why don't you and Da join us?"

"I can ask her," I say carefully, "but I doubt she'll want to come."

"Well, there's no harm in asking."

XVIII

Goosey Goosey Gander

When I casually mentioned Chalky's suggestion to Da yesterday evening, I was expecting a flat *no, thanks*. My wife is not a great lover of jazz, but it appears that she is making an effort at improving the tense atmosphere between us.

"It's been a while since I've seen Chalky and Maureen, and she's always a laugh," she said. "Besides, it might be good for us to have an evening out together. I'll have a word with Samantha and see if she'll baby-sit."

"We don't need a baby-sitter," the ear-wigging Pratcha had commented grumpily. "Jenny's old enough to be in charge."

"No, she isn't," my wife and I had responded in unison.

So, I have a date for tomorrow night with an attractive Thai woman. And, happily, I'm married to her, which avoids any complications.

And to keep the bonhomie flowing, I volunteer to do our grocery shopping this morning, as today the only item on my agenda is a visit to Goose's address.

Maybe I'll get lucky and find him at home. And if I'm especially lucky, he'll be able to give me all the information I require about Ronald Webster. Maybe I'll even discover the missing railwayman sleeping in his mate's spare room, and I can wrap up the case – thus avoiding the need for me to have dinner with Ursula d'Ambrosi.

As if. Sadly, the world doesn't work that way.

And to confirm the randomness of providence, when I climb into our car to go shopping, and turn the key, the battery is as dead as a circumcision joke at a bar mitzvah. No good deed ever goes unpunished, does it? Cue a call to our local garage mechanic who, on his arrival an hour later, tells me I don't need a jump-start so much as a new battery. Fortunately, he happens to have one with him. Lucky me.

I hand over my credit card. Emergency call-out plus new battery equals a level of extortion the Mafia would be proud of. But I have no choice.

* * * * *

By the time I've finished the shopping and unloaded it, it's gone noon.

I grab a bite of something from the fridge and head off on foot to my local Temple of the Tube. I pass through the Notting Hill Gate propylaeum and descend into the lower intestine of the station. My journey will take me to Angel, doubtless disturbing several burial places of London's dead along the way, as I have two changes of line to make: onto the Piccadilly Line at Holborn, then onto the Northern Line at King's Cross.

And while my deceased wife may no longer be speaking to me, that doesn't stop other internal dialogues taking place.

Like, for instance, the imagined voice of Ronald Webster, inviting me for a cosy chat on the subject of railway trivia.

Ever since I started reading his manuscript, the non-obsessive part of my brain has become increasingly cluttered with irrelevant information. Unused sidings. Deep cuttings. Extraneous engineering works. Incomplete borings (in both senses of the word). And though it might be advantageous to have a profounder understanding of his world-view, I have to ask the question, *Do I want to put myself in this man's head, now that I know what warped thoughts linger in its corners?*

Then there's the matter of Ursula, and what is going on in her head. She'll be at work now; castigating some unfortunate employee for speaking rudely to a passenger, or for dropping chewing gum on the platform. I haven't witnessed first-hand her hard side, but she must have one. She is a Human Resources Manager, when all is said and done.

I have to tread carefully there, and give myself a good talking-to to be on my best behaviour on Saturday. No flirty stuff. No playing footsie under the table. No accidental brushing of hands. If she's anticipating that our dinner date will mutate into a carnal encounter afterwards – and I suspect from our last conversation that she *is* – then I need to disillusion her. Preferably after she's given me whatever further info she has about RW.

Ursula d'Ambrosi is a 'source' and nothing more. Albeit a source with a sensuous mouth and naughty eyes, and one who gives the impression she's dying for a good shag.

Yes, I do realise that sounds both sexist and exploitative, like I'm preying on her female vulnerability and hormonal urges, but what's a PI with only a few leads to do? And when I play back our discussion at the wine bar, of the two of us, she is the one who sounds more like the predator. No, I shall be hard-nosed this weekend, and I will make damn sure that my nose is the only part of me that gets hard.

I wonder what her professional HR association would make of her conduct? Will she actually have any useful material for me on Webster, or was that a ploy? Isn't all the relevant HR info for TfL on computer? Couldn't she just have printed that out for me on Monday when she gave me Goose's address?

By the time I change trains at King's Cross, one of my other obsessions has begun whispering in my ear. *Are you sure you're not being followed?*

Unlike my previous visual hallucinations and conversations with Claire, a professional would describe my current (and hopefully temporary) delusional disorder as being a *non-bizarre* one – something that *could* happen in real life and which doesn't breach the laws of science. Plus, there are two candidates for stalkers this afternoon: a man and a woman who got on the Tube with me at Notting Hill Gate, and who both changed at the same stations that I did. Neither of them looks particularly sinister, but then neither did the Boston Strangler by all accounts.

When I emerge into the daylight at Angel, I hang around outside for a couple of minutes to see if one or both of them appears.

Neither does – at least not through the exit I took.

I tell my paranoia to shut up, and evict the matter from my head.

* * * * *

Islington is generally regarded as one of the better areas of London, comprising as it does some of the best Georgian and Victorian properties that the capital has to offer.

But not all the borough is like that.

Goose's flat is in a modern, five-storey carbuncle off the High Street and which, I imagine, was not a popular addition for the more well-heeled residents.

The front doors to the property are open, but given that there are entrance-buzzers outside, I imagine they are locked after dark.

In the entrance hallway, a rotund old lady of Chinese descent is mopping the floor while a radio plays.

"Excuse me," I say, "are you the concierge, by any chance?"

She removes the cigarette from her mouth and gives me a sour stare.

"Not really," she replies without a trace of foreign accent. "I live here, but I help out the owner by keeping the common areas tidy and sorting out small problems with the tenants when the letting agent can't be bothered to do it."

"Then, I wonder if you can help me."

"That depends," she says gripping her mop.

I hand her a card.

"I'm looking into a missing person who was a work colleague of Gustaw Belka, one of the tenants here. Do you know Mr. Belka?"

"As well as anybody does, I suppose."

She's finished reading my card, and she squints at me.

"Are you that detective who was on the television the other week? That business in Highgate, wasn't it?"

"Yes, that's me."

Her manner immediately becomes less surly.

Ah, the magic of celebrity.

"My name is Yao," she announces with a small Asian bow. "How can I help you, Mr. Braddock?"

"I don't suppose Mr. Belka is in, is he?"

"No. We haven't seen anything of him for a few weeks now. To tell you the truth, the landlord's becoming annoyed about it as Belka's rent hasn't been paid."

"Has anyone else been round asking about him? Friends or the police, for instance?"

The old woman's lined face crinkles further into a mask of concern.

"Why? Has he done something illegal?"

"Not so far as I am aware."

She relaxes.

"No. Nobody's been here. I don't even think Belka has any friends. He's a bit of a strange person. A loner."

"But his things are still here?"

"They were last time I checked."

"Do you have a key to his apartment?"

"I have keys to everybody's apartment," she chuckles. "I realise I'm not supposed to, but —"

"I quite understand," I say. "Sometimes emergencies happen. And tenants do a runner from time to time. The law forgets that."

"That's right. It does."

She drops her cigarette into the mop bucket.

"I don't suppose there's any chance you can let me see Mr. Belka's flat, is there, Mrs. Yao? I appreciate it might be considered irregular, but like I say, I'm trying to find a missing person. I'll only be five minutes, and you can stand over me if you want."

To reinforce my request, I show her one of the photos of Ronald Webster. She peers at it.

"Have you seen this man before?"

"I can't say that I have."

I remove a twenty-pound note from my wallet.

"And I'd be happy to make a contribution to the maintenance of the building, if that will help."

The part-time janitor tucks the banknote into a pocket. The deal is done.

"Wait here a minute, will you?"

She goes into one of the ground-floor flats and re-emerges seconds later with a huge bunch of keys.

"Belka's apartment is on the fifth floor. We'll take the lift. The stairs are too much for my knees."

After a creaky ascent, Mrs. Yao unlocks Goose's door, leans on the jamb and lights another cigarette.

"Five minutes only," she says before following me inside.

Despite the fact that nobody has lived here for a while, I can't see any dust. The apartment might be small, but its Spartan furnishing makes it seem bigger. Unlike Pearl Webster's place, there is no clutter: everything appears functional. In the living room-cum-dining-area, the only items of a personal nature are three framed photographs hanging in strict alignment on one of the walls. Each one depicts an unsmiling Goose standing beside a worn-out Eastern European lady who also wears a serious expression on her face.

"That's Mrs. Belka," my host informs me. "The tenant's mother. Polish. A hard-worker and a nice lady, though her English was limited."

"*Was*, you say?"

"She passed away about two years ago. I thought Belka might move out after that to a cheaper one-bedroom apartment. But he didn't. I don't think he likes change, and this place was familiar for him, I suppose."

The kitchen is spotless and impersonal. The oven is cleaner than ours. As one might expect, however, the milk in the fridge is rancid, and the fruit and vegetables are shrivelled and mouldy.

The first bedroom is empty save for a bed and a mattress. There is nothing in the chest of drawers or the free-standing wardrobe except for a few wire coat-hangers.

This was Mrs. Belka's room, I guess.

Goose's bedroom is the smaller of the two. The single bed is made up with military precision. A large map of the London Underground is stuck with Blu Tack to the wall above the head of the bed. On the bedside cabinet are a digital alarm clock, a pen and a small note-book which has nothing written in it. Several pages have been torn out.

"He uses that to make notes for himself," Mrs. Yao offers. "I know that because I've seen him reading them. Not out loud, but you can see his lips moving. Like I said: odd sort," she adds gratuitously.

My companion is untroubled when I go through the pockets of Goose's clothes which hang – dark-to-light from left-to-right – in his self-assembly wardrobe. Nothing. There is nothing of interest in his drawers either. It's like the abode of a spy, or somewhere that might be used as a safe house.

A bookcase with three shelves holds books on railway history and various works on astronomy, astrology and number theory, including the three-volume *Principia Mathematica* by Whitehead and Russell (a hard read if ever there was one). As with Ronald Webster's library, there's not a novel in sight. But unlike in RW's man-cave, there is no laptop.

I mention this to Mrs. Yao who gives an unconcerned shrug.

"It's possible the landlord decided to sell Belka's computer to offset some of his overdue rent," she comments.

It's more likely that you sold it since you have keys to the flat, I don't say.

"I'm done," I tell her.

When we're back in the lobby, I give the part-time janitor a tenner and ask her to call me if Goose turns up again or if anyone shows up asking for him.

She nods, lights another cigarette and picks up her mop. Our business is ended.

I bid her a good afternoon.

* * * * *

Goosey goosey gander,

Whither shall I wander?

* * * * *

The monk-like lair of Gustaw Belka has yielded up diddly-squat of value to my investigation, and I'm thirty quid down. The one thing I have learned, though, is that Goose has also definitely vanished off the face of the planet. And it was at about the same time that RW did. Perhaps at exactly the same time. But I doubt that anyone has reported the younger man missing, unless TfL has – but that's unlikely.

One presumes that Pearl Webster would have mentioned Goose to the police, but if she did, and Mrs. Yao is correct, they haven't followed up on the connection.

My hopes of avoiding that dinner date with Ursula d'Ambrosi have taken a knock-back. The only lead I have left on Goose is to try my luck with his previous work colleagues at Tower Bridge Beanz. But it's some time since he worked there, and the baristas from his time might well have moved on.

I decide to leave that visit until tomorrow. The afternoon is already long in the tooth, and I've had enough disappointment for one day. Plus, this evening, I want to concentrate on giving my wife some quality time and attention while we're at the jazz club, without the Ronald Webster case intruding on our conjugal joy.

But first, I'm off to a Hatton Garden jeweller's where there's a bracelet that Da wants – because she hinted so last month when we were out shopping.

And this small romantic gesture might be just the ticket to keep me out of our local hospital's A&E unit, at least until the weekend.

XIX

All That Jazz

Our sitter Samantha has come up trumps for us. She arrives early for duty while Da is still dolling herself up.

Although the kids would rather be left on their own this evening, if someone *has* to be here to babysit them, they'd rather it was 'Auntie Sam' than some hormone-crazed teenager who would spend the next few hours texting love messages to her wet boyfriend while raiding our fridge for alcohol. Sam, by contrast, is a sensible retired lady who lives in our street, and whose daughter owns a beauty salon and does Da's nails.

When Mrs. Braddock eventually deigns to join us downstairs, she looks like a million dollars. Black dress, hair piled on top of her head, classy makeup, and come-to-bed eyes. Were it not for the trauma it would inflict on our impressionable children, I'd dismiss the sitter, carry Da straight back upstairs and ravish her.

Sometimes I forget how gorgeous my wife is. But not this evening. That would be impossible.

"Am I underdressed?" I ask her.

"Always," she says. "But I've got used to it over the years."

A black cab whisks us off to Soho.

I take it as a good omen that our driver is not one of the talkative ones. Not that I'd be able to converse coherently with him anyway. Da's perfume is too intoxicating.

* * * * *

From an audience perspective, *Blue Rhythms* is a rather cosy jazz club, with its relaxed atmosphere and small tables that each seat a maximum of four people.

On weekdays, the first performance spot – which lasts an hour – is allocated to a new, relatively unknown group, and the punter numbers can be thin. But during this session, you can order food from the club's limited menu and sometimes the music is surprisingly good.

Chalky and his wife are only coming for the second session, so this gives Da and me some time alone. We order some nibbles and a bottle of white wine; after which I present Da with the bracelet that I bought her this afternoon.

"You're naughty giving me this now," she says, "when it's so close to Christmas. I suppose this is your way of saying sorry about Saturday, is it?"

Her words aren't exactly lovey-dovey, but her eyes are sparkling. She slips the bracelet on and inspects it admiringly before giving me a peck on the cheek.

The first set of musicians mounts the small stage. They go under the name of *Hearty Beats*. They're a relatively new lot but are already making a name for themselves on the circuit. Their female saxophonist/vocalist has a voice like honey.

"That singer's attractive, don't you think, David?" my wife asks.

"I suppose so. If you're into European women. Which I'm not these days."

"Not even European women in managerial jobs?"

I don't give this unsubtle dig the dignity of a response.

Da squeezes my hand to reassure me that she's only teasing.

I pour us some wine, and the next hour passes pleasantly enough; although the food, when it turns up, can hardly be placed in the category of top notch. We eat it anyway.

As soon as *Hearty Beats* are done, and the food has been cleared away, the lights are turned down further and the atmosphere in the club becomes more intimate.

I have ordered a second bottle of wine, and am stroking Da's thigh (and she's not objecting) when Chalky and Maureen appear. Our keyboard player smells like a Victorian chimney and there is cigarette ash down the front of his shirt, but Da kisses him on the cheek anyway.

Then I spot another couple arriving, and I tap my wife on the shoulder.

"Da, can I have a word?"

I apologise to Mr. and Mrs. Nicotine and tell them we'll be back in a minute, before leading my wife to the back of the room.

"*What*, David?" she says without preamble. "I'm sensing drama."

"Pearl Webster is sitting two tables ahead of us, to the right. And she's not alone."

Da cranes her neck.

"She's that lady with the perm, is she?"

"Yes."

"So, who's that with her? Judging from the expression on your face, I'm guessing it's not her supposedly-missing husband."

"No, it's not. It's Fred Eggers, the Chairman of the Clapham Junction Locomotive Club."

"Ah. They seem comfortable with each other," Da observes.

"That's exactly what I was thinking."

Eggers is leaning in close to his companion, and they are both beaming.

My wife turns her attention back to me.

"And I know what else you're thinking," she says. "You don't want them to realise you've seen them together, so you're about to suggest that we leave now and you drop me home. Then you're going to go and stake out Eggers' house to see if they go back there after they've finished here. Am I right?"

"Almost."

"Ah. What have I missed?"

"I was going to propose that you stay here with Chalky and Maureen and keep an eye on them while I slip away. See how intimate it gets. They don't know what you look like so they won't be any the wiser. We can compare notes later."

"David Braddock," she says in a tone laced with danger and disgust in equal measure. "You are supposed to be taking time off from detecting and spending the evening with *me*. Instead of which, you want to leave me here to play gooseberry while you catch a cold standing for hours on a street corner in Battersea in the hope that you might see something untoward."

"Vauxhall, actually."

But just as I worry Da's going to rip me a new bum-hole, she calms down.

"All right. I understand that you don't want to mess up the chance of a lead on the Webster investigation. But *you* have to explain what's happening to Chalky and Maureen. I'm not doing that. And if the two lovebirds catch sight of you in the meantime, that's too bad."

"It's a deal," I say with some relief.

"And no sneaking off to see Ursula d'Ambrosi while you're waiting for the music to end here."

I recognise that Da's upset with me, but even so this feels a bit below the belt. I bristle.

"If you're that worried about where I am, you can always put a tracker on my mobile."

"What makes you think I haven't done that already? And don't expect to have sex with me when you eventually get home. You've blown that for this evening."

"Understood."

* * * * *

During my walk past Soho's sex shops and drunken revilers and revellers, I vacillate between continuing on my mission and chucking it in and returning to *Blue Rhythms* to salvage the evening with Da. But the damage has already been done, so I continue my wistful promenade to Piccadilly Circus (the scene of Pratcha's video game massacre), and take the Tube to Green Park where I change onto the Victoria Line, heading south.

Vauxhall is dead when I surface and make my way to the address on Eggers' business card.

It's in an unremarkable terraced street, at the end of which, fortunately, there is a pub. I check out a suitably shaded vantage spot – a low wall with an overgrown hedge behind it – where I can keep an eye on Eggers' front door.

However, as it will likely be some time before Mrs. W and the Chairman show up, I retire to the pub and sit at a corner table where the November chill won't make my toes and fingers numb.

I order a pint and a whisky chaser and reflect on the fool's errand that I may be running.

It is a reasonable assumption that if my targets are going to indulge in a spot of vertical jogging tonight, they will do it at Eggers' place. I can't see Pearl Webster taking him back to her house. Not with Rebecca Oliphant next door. That would be way too risky.

Though if Eggers also has a nosey neighbour, it's more likely they'll check into a hotel. That could be anywhere in the city, and probably a good way from here. In which case, I'm not going to see a thing, and I've pissed off Da for no good reason.

Nosey neighbours.

It occurs to me that if the likes of Doris Trent, Elsie Schilling, Rebecca Oliphant and Mrs. Yao were put on the government payroll and each given a Taser, there'd be no need for a London police force at all – except perhaps for crowd control at demonstrations and football matches. Plus, the clear-up rate would likely be much improved because, let's face it, the Met's record on solving crimes isn't exactly brilliant. Indeed, if it gets much worse, there'll be no choice for the law-abiding citizens of the capital other than to resort to vigilantism if they want to see justice done.

I order another pint and glass of whisky, and check my watch. *The Horns* will be part-way through their second set now, so there is still some time to go before Eggers and Mrs. W leave the club. Assuming that they haven't decided to leave early because they couldn't keep their hands off each other. But if that had happened, Da would have called me, I'm sure.

Doubts about the usefulness of my foray into Vauxhall continue to assail me.

Supposing Eggers and Pearl Webster are having an affair, what does that prove? It certainly doesn't prove that they've done away with Ronald. Their affair could have been going on for ages, and Mr. W might have been aware of it from the get-go. It could be the price he has to pay for being into child pornography. A quid pro quo understanding between the spouses.

And, then again, what about the business of Ronald Webster's life insurance? His wife might have done away with him just for that and Eggers may or may not be involved.

Or what if the Websters are playing a deep, long game and are both in on some insurance fraud? Then, Pearl's affair would be a smart cover for what is really going on.

But supposing there is no body and no fraud, and that Mr. W is still alive. That he simply took it into his head one day to walk out on his wife and his boring life.

Then, there is no crime, I'm not going to find the missing man, and all my efforts are for nothing.

Da rings me.

"Everyone's leaving now," she says. "The lovebirds will be on their way in a couple of minutes."

"How did they behave?"

"Like two people on a date. And I don't think it was their first one either. *They* had a great time this evening."

"Are you still angry with me?"

"Not as angry as I was. *The Horns* were good and Maureen and Chalky kept me amused. Luckily for you. Also, I've had another half-a-bottle of wine. That helps."

"I'll be home as soon as I can."

"I'll see you later, then. I expect I'll be awake."

I down my whisky, exit the pub and take up my surveillance position.

It's bloody freezing.

I'm going to give it an hour or so. If they aren't here by then, I'll call it a night.

* * * * *

As it turns out, I only have to wait about half-an-hour before a black cab pulls up outside Eggers' place.

The Chairman of the Clapham Junction Locomotive Club and Mrs. W climb out of the taxi, and go straight into the house.

Ten minutes later, the downstairs lights go out and the light in the upstairs front bedroom goes on. Five minutes after that, the whole house is in darkness.

My work is done here.

Since it's nigh impossible to get a cab south of the river – and I can't face another journey on the Underground – I walk across Vauxhall bridge and manage to flag down a taxi at Bessborough Gardens to take me home.

Da is sitting up in bed, reading a bodice-ripper novel.

"Well?" she asks setting the book aside.

"The pair of them went back to Eggers'. As was expected."

"Good. Now get your clothes off and get into bed."

I do as I am told, and Da throws back the duvet and extends her arms to me.

She is wearing nothing but her new bracelet.

Everything is all right again.

XX

Bridges and Arches

Da and I are having a later-than-usual breakfast. The children have already left for school.

Despite our pre-slumber embrace, neither Da nor I slept well but we're each wearing our best brave face. Continuing to rebuild bridges, as it were.

"Talking to Pratcha before we went out yesterday evening, it appears he's grown bored with playing that dreadful *League of Loki* game," says my wife before biting into a slice of toast.

"I guess the challenge must go out of it once you've slaughtered half the population of London," I reply while knocking the top off a boiled egg. "And I've been thinking that as a thank you for the work he's done on my website, I'll try and fix up a visit for the little chap to *Matchatho Games*. Their HQ is in one of those converted factories near King's Cross, and they might welcome the PR. Anyway, I'm going to email their CEO, a guy called Waddle, so we'll see."

"Are they the assholes that came up with LOL?"

"No, that was a bunch of American assholes. These are British *arseholes*. Quite different. Their avatars probably apologise before shooting anyone."

"Ha."

"So, what time shall I drop by your office today to take you out to lunch, my darling one? I assume you haven't already forgotten our lunch date?"

"Since you only told me about it an hour ago, that's not likely. Shall we say, one o'clock? Though I'm not sure we'll be able to get a table at *Carte Blanche* as you haven't booked ahead."

"We'll get a table," I tell her confidently. "I can be good at persuading people, even when they don't want to be persuaded."

"Yes, David, unfortunately that's true," Da says without elaborating further.

* * * * *

Since I only have a few hours before lunch with Da, I defer my bloodhounding activity in relation to the mislaid Gustaw Belka until this afternoon, and instead spend the first part of the morning marshalling my notes on the Webster investigation, and phoning my stepmother to apologise for my non-presence this weekend. I neglect to mention the fact that the contact I'm meeting is a divorced thirtysomething woman. There is such a thing as being too open.

"But you will be coming to us for Christmas, won't you?" I ask keeping my tone light.

"Yes," Nang replies, "provided you're not going to badger me again about coming to live with you permanently, and giving me all that nonsense about my house being too big for me. I'm not in my decrepitude yet, David."

"I never suggested you were. It's just that babysitters are so expensive nowadays, and Da has been dropping hints about having a live-in maid –"

"Oh, shut up, stepson. You're already on thin ice."

"All right. Let's talk about politics instead. What do you think your Tory friends in government should be doing about the homelessness problem, and how are we going to stop all this illegal immigration? Plus, how is Brexit working out for you?"

"Now you're on even thinner ice. If I believed for one second that you were in any way concerned about how our country is being run, I might be inclined to enter into a discussion with you on the subject. But you're not, so I won't. Have you even registered to vote since you got back from Thailand?"

"Now that you mention it, no."

"Then, you don't even deserve to have an opinion," she tells me before going on to talk about some mooted local by-pass which the Leicestershire NIMBYs are opposing. I visualise her lying down in front of the diggers while bemoaning the despoilation of the English countryside and the corruption which is rife in planning departments.

"Our finest cultural traditions are being undermined by thoughtless fools," she concludes.

I love this *our*, though I doubt that Nang can appreciate the irony of an immigrant Thai woman being the last bastion of Britishness. So, we leave it there.

After our conversation has ended, I spend an hour working out at the gym, before returning home to shower and ringing the restaurant to book a table for lunch.

* * * * *

I arrive at Da's office a few minutes early.

"We have a table at *Carte Blanche*," I inform her, "though I had to tell them it's our wedding anniversary, and I'd disremembered the date. Fortunately, it was a man I spoke to and he was suitably understanding. He didn't want a divorce on his conscience. If it had been a woman, it might have been a different story."

We pass a pleasant hour at a window table watching the city's workers drift by, and chatting about everyday things. Da is in a good mood, buoyed by the French cuisine and two glasses of Chablis.

While we're having coffee, she tells me she has some new intel for me on the Webster case.

"Are you playing detective too, wife of mine?"

"I figured you need all the help you can get. Anyway, it might not mean anything, but Pearl Webster has registered an interest with our agency and one or two others in having us find her a property in London."

"She wants to move?"

"Apparently so. But she's not putting her Battersea house on the market yet. Probably because she's not in a position to do so until the matter of her disappearing husband is resolved."

"That's interesting. And where exactly is she looking to buy a place?"

"Well, let's say in one of the better areas of London. And she'll need more than the proceeds of the sale of her Battersea house at the price range she's specified."

"Supplemented by life insurance policy proceeds, perhaps?"

"Could be."

I muse on this news.

"She doesn't hang about, does she, our Pearl? The first time I met her, she seemed the cautious type, but her recent behaviour is nothing short of reckless. Anyway, I appreciate that titbit. It's something else for me to chew on."

"You're welcome. So, what's next for you today?"

"To see if I have any more luck finding Goose than I've had so far tracking down our missing railwayman. I'm going to his previous employer's coffee shop near London Bridge. Maybe there's an old work colleague there who is still in touch with him or who can give me some pointers. If so, I'll take it from there."

"So, you might be late home tonight, then?"

"Honestly, I've no idea. But I'll call you."

"The d'Ambrosi woman might have some useful information about this Goose character too," Da says while assuming an unreadable expression.

"Possibly," I respond. "And I know I'm flailing around with long shots, but I half-hope that if I can locate Gustaw Belka quickly – and without her help – I might be able to cancel my Saturday dinner appointment. Perhaps even come with you and the kids to Nang's."

"I wouldn't bank on that happening, David. You're deluding yourself if you think you can wrap everything up today. But it's a sweet thought," she adds tapping my hand. "And I shan't worry if you're late home tonight. Do what you need to do, and go wherever you need to go. I'm OK with it."

"Thank you."

I raise my coffee cup.

"Happy anniversary, darling," I say.

"Happy anniversary, Sherlock," she replies.

* * * * *

It's misty. Or foggy. I struggle to distinguish between the two. In any event, there is a penetrating afternoon cold, and a denseness about the air. As I make my way to the nearest Tube station – having deposited my wife back at her place of work – I reflect on her disclosure about Pearl Webster.

London might be a big city, but it's also a small town: harder than one might suppose to keep secrets. Particularly when individuals like Da have access to networks that can keep them informed of what's happening. And especially so when a large sum of money is involved.

Along with my fellow dead-eyed Tube travellers, I clutch an overhead bar while we rattle and sway beneath and across the capital. Emerging into the cold afternoon air at London Bridge, I drop a pound coin into a beggar's cup then set off on foot along Tooley Street.

I pull up a mental picture of Janice, the barista at Tower Bridge Beanz whom I hope is going to be able to assist me in my search for Mr. Belka. She was a friend and protector of Goose back in the day – someone who would give his tormentors a mouthful if she decided they were ragging him too much. Good-hearted and ample-chested Janice who was in that porn film I found on Webster's computer (albeit she was fully-clothed).

The partially-recovered image in my head is a trifle fuzzy. I remember her Rubenesque shape and her dirty laugh more than any other specific features. Plus, I recollect that she came onto me rather hard during our encounters, although I *think* most of that was tongue-in-cheek. I was so preoccupied with my daughter's situation then, that I let most of it go over my head. Her prattling provided me with light relief in what was otherwise a depressing time.

Anyway, maybe Janice has a husband by now.

Hell, she could be on her second.

Or perhaps she's given up on men altogether, and decided she's gay.

Stay positive and resolute, Braddock. And do not under any circumstances get drawn into using *double entendres* or anything that smacks of innuendo. Just in case.

By the time I reach Potters Fields Park, the mist has grown thicker, and Tower Bridge is a mere silhouette rising out of the gloom. The traffic sounds muffled as I pass under Tower Bridge Road and enter the cobbled Dickensian streets of Shad Thames.

Here, in the expensively-converted nineteenth-century warehouse of Butlers Wharf was Katie's old apartment which she shared with her brute of a husband. No happy memories there. My promenade takes me past the entrance lobby, but I don't so much glance at it.

This is the first time I've set foot in this part of London since the aftermath of my daughter's trial, though I can still remember where Tower Bridge Beanz was all those years ago – and hopefully still *is*.

Aha!

Yes, there it stands in all its glory. Apart from the fact that the outside signage has been recently repainted, it doesn't look any different. Same grey aluminium window frames embedded in the brick walls, same welcoming smell of coffee as I push open the door and go inside.

They're busy. There are six people ahead of me in the order queue, and every chair is occupied.

While I'm waiting, I scrutinise the harassed baristas. There are three females, but none of them is Janice. Not unless she's got younger or her skin colour has changed in the last few years.

Maybe she's not working this shift, I tell myself. Or maybe she hasn't worked here for ages. But let's be optimistic, and assume it's the former. Regardless, I need a coffee to thaw out.

When I reach the counter, I ask the Japanese-looking girl for a large cappuccino to go. Her badge reads, *Naomi*.

"What's your name, sir?" she says before writing *David* in felt-tip on the cup and passing it along to the barista manning the coffee machine.

"Anything else? Sandwich? Cheese cake?"

"No, thanks. But can you tell me if Janice still works here?"

"Janice Marlowe, you mean?"

I have no idea what Janice's surname is, but I nod anyway.

"Yes, she does. She's had to pop out but she should be back in a few minutes." Naomi eyes the people who have joined the growing queue behind me before adding, "At least, I hope so."

In due course, I collect my cappuccino, and grab a window seat which has become vacant.

I've barely sat down when the street door opens and a familiar figure enters Tower Bridge Beanz.

It's the Janice I remember. The Janice with the fresh country-girl face and the enormous breasts. And, like the coffee shop, she doesn't seem any different except for the fact that her badge now reads *Manager*. I'm in luck.

I call her name and wave at her.

She eyeballs me, as if trying to place me, then a big grin appears.

"*David?* It *is* David, isn't it?"

"It is. You haven't forgotten me then? It's been a while."

"I never forget anyone I've had a crush on," she replies, and to underline her statement she gives me an energetic hug.

"What's it been? Five, six years?"

"More like seven, Janice."

"Oh, my God. Are you on holiday? If I were you, I'd have stayed in Thailand. It's colder than a penguin's pecker here."

"No. I live in London now. Long story."

"Well, it's lovely to see you again."

I take her aside.

"Actually, I'm wondering if you and I can have a chat. It's about a case I'm working on."

"You're still in the private detective business, then?"

"Yes. You have a good memory."

She studies her overwhelmed baristas. Naomi's eyes plead with their manager for help.

"I'm afraid we're having rather a rush, and I need to pitch in," she says. "Will you be around later?"

"What time do you close?"

"Six. But it will be more like seven before we've finished clearing up. I can see you then."

"If it's not too much trouble. I promise I won't take up much of your time."

"It's all right. I'm not in any hurry to get home this evening. We can meet at that cocktail bar at the top of Tower Bridge Road, next door to the Indian restaurant. They'll be quiet at that time and we can have a proper catch-up. If that works for you."

"It does, thank you. What's this place called?"

"*The Cock's Tail.*"

Janice laughs her dirty laugh and tells me it's more up-market than it sounds.

Alcoholic drinks after work with a young woman. Again.

At an establishment with a smutty name.

Da is not going to be happy about this.

I'm beginning to loathe Ronald Webster.

"It's a date," I say.

* * * * *

I have hours to kill before my rendezvous with Janice, and it seems unfair for me to hang around Tower Bridge Beanz doing nothing but stare at the girls who are keeping the coffee flowing. That sort of thing can be misinterpreted, and might even alarm the manager and make her re-evaluate the wisdom of agreeing to meet me.

Plus, this is the wrong time of day to be knocking on the doors of SE1 homeless hostels, even if I were inclined to do so.

If it wasn't the middle of November and the weather wasn't more suited to polar bears, I could stroll around the local parks and feed the ducks. As it is, I don't want to be outside in the cold any longer than necessary.

I am, however, only a short walk from Bermondsey Street, and it might not be a bad idea to locate the French restaurant where I'm supposed to be having dinner with Ursula tomorrow night.

Ursula…

Damn.

I stuff my hands in my pockets, leave the cobbles of Shad Thames behind and cross Tooley Street again. A cut-through I know takes me past locked-up tennis courts in Tanner Street Park. A couple of hardy dog-walkers are doing their best to be as cheerful as their charges, but otherwise it's quiet.

I find the restaurant straightaway. It goes by the unimaginative name of *La Brasserie*, and it is dishearteningly small and intimate: only a dozen tiny tables. It's also currently closed, and doesn't open until six.

This will be my second meal of French cuisine in as many days. Perhaps Brexit will put an end to this foreign nonsense once it gets properly going, and we can all return to eating fish and chips out of a newspaper.

Nang would welcome that.

I wander up and down the street in search of somewhere to hunker down from the cold for a while. There are several pubs, but I can't face alcohol right now, so I settle on a greasy-spoon café called *Mario's* which has outrageously long opening hours. It doesn't close until 11.30 pm, and I suspect many of the clientele are cab-drivers. There are daily newspapers on a display stand for the use of *Mario's* patrons.

I go to the counter and order a mug of tea from a swarthy individual who has filthy fingernails and a wonky left eye. Then I sit down with a well-thumbed copy of today's *Daily Scum* which carries the headline *BENEFIT SCROUNGERS*. After this catchy front page, the tabloid continues in this lowbrow vein with extended moaning about NHS waiting times, (in)human interest stories, a rant about the *Brexit Betrayal* and a potentially libellous article about Prince Harry and his involvement in a mental health awareness campaign. I skim the sports sections, then turn my hand to the crossword puzzle. (1 down, 7 letters: Sold down the river. *Cruised*.)

This Herculean task completed, I order another mug of tea and take out my notebook and the photograph of the railway anoraks group that Pearl Webster gave me. I attempt to re-familiarise myself with the Goose of his Tower Bridge Beanz days. I can only recall him having two facial expressions: that of a meerkat high on drugs, and Nobody at Home. In this picture, he is wearing the former. Even if I do find him, I reflect miserably, I wonder how much help this idiot savant is going to be to my investigation.

I review my notes on the Webster case, and become so engrossed that I realise my tea is now cold and I've hardly drunk any of it.

I carry the mug back to the counter, but before I can speak, Wonky Eye Man asks me aggressively, "Is there something wrong with it?"

"No, no," I reassure him, "I was so engrossed in my reading that I forgot I had any tea."

"Yeah, I noticed you've been sitting there for quite a while without buying anything. This isn't a free library, mate."

To placate him I order some more of his delicious brew and a Belgian bun.

"Is that all?" he asks accusingly.

"All right, I'll have one of your full English all-day breakfasts as well."

"That's more like it," he says. "I'll bring it over when it's ready."

I have no intention of eating his heated-up grease, but at least I can sit for another three-quarters of an hour in the warm without having to worry about being placed in a head-lock and black-balled from this fine dining establishment.

I phone Da to tell her what's happening. She's tied up with a client, so it's a brief call.

At six-thirty, I step out of *Mario's* into the freezing darkness, suffer a brisk walk to Tower Bridge Road, find *The Cock's Tail*, and order a whiskey sour.

* * * * *

Janice appears a few minutes before seven.

She's freshened her make-up and done something with her hair. Don't ask me what, but she is less employee-like. And when she removes her coat, she is wearing a pink sweater stretched over her black Tower Bridge Beanz polo shirt. This makes her boobs appear even bigger, and as she moves, it looks like two basketballs demonstrating the principle of Newton's cradle. I get a waft of a Lancôme fragrance as she greets me with a kiss on both cheeks, European-style, as if we are old friends. Which I suppose we are, in a way.

I ask her what she wants to drink, and she says she'll have the same as me.

"It's *so* nice to see you again, David. And after all this time."

"Yes, people's paths have a funny way of crossing and recrossing, don't they?"

"So, what have you been up to since I last saw you? I read all the stuff in the newspapers about your daughter Katie, by the way, and I'm glad that turned out right in the end. We don't have to talk about that, if you don't want to."

"That's all ancient history, Janice."

"You said that you're living in London now? How long have you been back? Have you left Thailand for good? I remember that when you used to come to our coffee shop, you were a widower. Have you remarried? Is there anyone special in your life at the moment?"

I must look a little stunned at this barrage of queries, because she adds, "Sorry, that's a lot of personal questions. I'm not trying to interrogate you, honestly, I'm just *really* pleased you dropped by to say hello to me. Even if it is because you are on a case, and not because you missed the pleasure of my company."

"Janice, I –"

"It's all right," she laughs. "I'm winding you up. And you can relax. You don't have to worry that I'm trying to get into your trousers, even though you're as sexy as ever. Get a load of this."

She holds out her left hand. On her third finger is a small diamond engagement ring and a wedding band.

"You're married?"

"Three years. And don't sound so surprised about it. That's extremely rude of you."

She says this with a twinkle in her eye, so I don't feel the need to apologise.

"Well, congratulations, Janice."

Her drink has arrived, so we clink glasses.

"My husband Colin works for BT," she continues blithely. "We're trying for a baby, but no luck so far. He won't get tested, but I've had tests on the quiet, so I know that the problem's on his side, the poor dear. But we'll keep at it. He's a good man. And there's always IVF."

"Won't he worry if you're late home tonight?" I interject to forestall further revelations.

"No. He's away in a conference in York for a couple of nights, so I'm all alone."

"Ah."

"I don't suppose you'd like to come back to my place afterwards and impregnate me, would you? It's not far. We can be there in ten minutes. It would save all that waiting around for fertility treatment. And Colin wouldn't mind."

"You're still teasing me, right?"

"Yes, I'm still teasing you, silly. Now, tell me what you've been up to since I last saw you."

I give her a summary of my adventures over the last seven years and she listens intently.

"So, your new wife is Thai?"

"Yes."

"And is it true what they say about Thai women?"

"I dunno. What *do* they say about Thai women?"

"Is she a lot younger than you?"

"Not disgustingly so. I'm not ready for a dirty old man label yet."

"Ah, I'm glad. So, what is it I can help you with, Detective Braddock? Oh, and by the way, I did see you on TV the other week, but they didn't mention that you were living here. I kind of took it for granted that you were on a visit from Thailand. I should have paid more attention, I suppose. Whereabouts in London are you based?"

"Janice, would it be quicker if I give you my mobile number and email address, then you can contact me whenever you think of something you want to know about my private life?"

"Sorry, I'll shut up and keep my curiosity in check. You ask the questions and I'll answer from now on."

"Good. But let's order another cocktail first. Same again?"

"Yes. I'd better not mix my drinks. I can be a flirt when I'm tipsy, and that would never do."

"It certainly wouldn't, Mrs. Marlowe."

I explain that I'm searching for a middle-aged London Underground train driver who has disappeared, but before I can expound further, Janice asks, "And what's this man's name?"

"Ronald Webster."

She frowns.

"That doesn't ring a bell with me."

"I'm not surprised, but here are a couple of pictures of him anyway. Have a look."

She squints at the photographs before shaking her head.

"Nope. You've had to hang around and buy me two cocktails for nothing, David," she says. "But what made you think that I'd know this Webster person?"

"Actually, Janice, it's not Webster that I want to talk to you about. It's Gustaw Belka, your former work colleague at Tower Bridge Beanz."

"*Goose*, you mean?"

"Yes."

Her eyes widen.

"What does he have to do with this guy who's gone missing?"

"They're friends. And they're both members of the same railway appreciation society. Ronald Webster's writing a book about the London Underground, and Goose has been accompanying him on his research outings."

"And you think Goose might have information about the train driver's disappearance?"

"It's possible."

"So why don't you ask Goose about it directly?"

"I would if I could. But he's vanished as well."

Janice's mouth drops open.

"But I only saw him recently," she says.

"How recently?"

"Give me a minute, David, would you? This is a bit of a shock. Goose is an old mate of mine."

"Of course. But while you work that out, maybe you can tell me what you know of his history from when I met him in late 2009 – the time that I met you – up until now."

Janice has a large swig of her second cocktail.

"Let's see. When you first walked into our coffee shop, Goose was going through his *Angel* phase."

"His *what* phase?"

"Don't you remember the 'Angel of Death'? That serial killer who was murdering young women around the Angel Tube station?"

"Vaguely," I reply. "But my mind was on other things at the time. Refresh my memory of events."

"Yes. Sorry. Well, Goose was obsessed with the belief that he could track down the killer by using one of his crackpot numerological systems. He used to go out on night patrols, and I suppose there must have been some method in his madness, because he witnessed one of the murders."

"*He did?* Wow."

"Yes, but nothing came of it in the end, and nobody was ever convicted. Then, when the killings stopped, Goose moved onto some other weird fixation about poison in the drinking water."

"When did he leave Tower Bridge Beanz?"

Janice frowns as she concentrates.

"Our manager Sean quit his job the following year and moved up to Edinburgh. Then the coffee shop changed owners, and I was promoted to the manager's job. That was five years ago. It must have been two years after that that Goose landed a job with Transport for London. So, 2013. Yes, 2013. We were all surprised they'd taken him on because… Well, you've met Goose. But he'd always been interested in railways – all those interconnecting lines and dots and circles.

That sort of stuff. Lots of scope for his imagination and conspiracy theories to run riot."

"What do TfL employ him to do exactly?"

"Even they're not stupid enough to let him drive their trains or to interact with the public," she says with a chuckle. "He works on a team repairing escalators and things like that."

"But you've stayed in touch with him since he left the coffee shop?"

"Not in a formal way, but he drops by Tower Bridge Beanz every now and again. For some company, I suspect. And since his mum died a couple of years ago, he's been showing up more frequently. He found Mrs. Belka's death hard to deal with because they were very close. For a few months he hit rock bottom."

Which, coincidentally, is the name of the porn movie that you were in, I don't say.

Janice goes silent for a while and stares at her cocktail glass.

"Life is tough for somebody like Goose," she says eventually. "I hope he's OK."

I produce the photograph of the Clapham Junction Locomotive Club and hand it to her.

"This is the only photo I have of him," I tell her. "And it's not great. I don't suppose you have a more recent picture of him, do you?"

She picks up her mobile and flicks through the images stored there, then passes it to me. It's a selfie of her and Goose. She is wearing her Tower Bridge Beanz polo shirt, so I'm guessing it was snapped at the coffee shop.

"I took that in January, the first time I saw him after New Year. As a kind of record for the start of 2016."

"Goose doesn't smile much, does he?" I say.

"He never smiles. Do you want me to send this to your phone?"

"Yes, please."

I give her one of my business cards.

"Then you have a picture of me too, haven't you?"

"And you have my phone number."

She suddenly becomes serious.

"October," she says abruptly.

"What?"

"October. It was October when I last saw Goose. Not this month. Last month."

"Beginning, middle or end of the month?"

She shrugs.

"Middle, I think, but it's hard to keep track of what goes on at Tower Bridge Beanz, David. One day merges into another. Same faces, different faces, rush hours, quiet hours. Coffee, spillages and clean-ups. That's our day. Goose's last visit was brief, but then his visits usually are. I'm sorry, that's all I can tell you."

"Did he seem happy to you? Or depressed?"

"He seemed like Goose. Only partially present, as always."

"Can you think of anywhere that he might have gone? His flat's empty and the janitor there can't recall seeing him for nearly a month."

"*A month*, David? He's been missing that long?"

She sounds horrified.

"Afraid so."

"I can't think of anyone he would be staying with. He doesn't *have* anyone. Except perhaps this Ronald Webster. Have you tried asking at the homeless shelters? Or checking the railway arches? There are some places around here where people sleep rough."

"We have a *lot* of shelters in London, Janice, as I've recently learned. And innumerable other places where the displaced and the destitute spend their nights. Frankly, without a firm lead, I'm unlikely to locate either Goose or Ronald Webster."

"If Goose shows up at Tower Bridge Beanz, I'll call you at once. And I won't let him leave until you arrive. Even if I have to pin him to the floor. And if *you* find him first, make sure he comes to see me, OK?"

"I will."

The atmosphere has become sombre. I ask Janice if she wants another drink, but she declines.

"I'd best be off," she says. "I'm sorry that I couldn't be more help."

"You've told me what you can."

"And please come by Tower Bridge Beanz again. Don't be a stranger. Bring your wife with you. I'd like to meet her. See what she's got that I haven't. I bet she's gorgeous, isn't she?"

"She is. Yes, why not? I like to introduce Da to all my female friends so she won't get suspicious that I'm playing around."

"And I promise not to mention our steamy affair or our love-child."

"Thank you, Janice. I take that as a great personal favour."

* * * * *

After Janice has sashayed pneumatically out of the cocktail bar, I order my third whiskey sour and try to decide what to do next.

My chat with her hasn't given me anything particularly useful so far as Goose is concerned, but her suggestion that I check the hostels and places to crash around here, might not be a bad idea. It's gone eight-thirty, so it's the right time of day to find homeless people starting to doss down. Plus, it is possible that a down-and-out Goose might choose a place to hang out that is not far from where his friend Janice spends most of her time. Though the fact that he hasn't been to see her for a while tends to argue against this. But what else am I going to do for the next few hours? And as I'm already in the area, why not?

I toy with my cocktail and try to put myself into Gustaw Belka's head. That's not easy. It's a rather cramped space; not really big enough for an adult human.

Let's reflect.

The fact that Goose went missing round about the same time that Webster did (and I can't say that it was at *exactly* the same time) doesn't necessarily mean they vanished *together* – but there must be a high probability that that's what happened. Which introduces a significant complication. What joint motive could they have had for disappearing together? A gay affair? Nope. Goose is too old to appeal to RW's pedophile tendencies, and I doubt that Goose himself has any sexual tendencies at all: he'd likely have to wear a tin foil hat and recite the Fibonacci sequence to make intercourse tolerable. So, if it was a joint decision, what communal motivation was in play? Always assuming that their respective disappearances were intentional…

My phone pings.

It's Janice sending me the selfie photograph of her with her nutty friend.

There is no accompanying message, so I return a quick thank you (no kisses).

I consult my notebook. There are two hostels within easy walking distance of where I am, and a popular hang-out for those who don't have the money, or inclination, to use a shelter are the railway arches on the south side of the main line into London Bridge, close by Maltby Street Market. I might as well give these a go. But first, I call Da to let her know what I'm up to.

"Have you eaten?" she says.

"Not yet."

"Well, make sure you do."

I grab a bag of chips from a Turkish takeaway to munch while I'm pounding the pavements. They are flaccid and tasteless, but they soak up the whiskey sours, and the warmth keeps the night-chill at bay.

Fingers crossed, I don't bump into Ursula d'Ambrosi, as I must be in the general vicinity of her place. That would be awkward.

At the two hostels, I show the photographs of Webster, Goose and Anneke to the doorkeepers and meet with the same negative, distrusting reaction. Despite my expressed concern for these three missing persons and their frantic families, the response – as I've previously experienced – amounts to, *Off you trot, you don't belong here, Mister Detective.*

Chastened and further dispirited, I weigh up whether to write off the day completely and go home; but decide on one final effort. I'll give the railway arches a try.

And it is fortunate that I do. Because, by way of reward for my persistence, and out of the blue, the Braddock luck finally changes.

* * * * *

A figure stands on a small patch of waste ground beside one of the vacant railway arches, lit only by the quivering flames that rise from a battered oil drum. As I walk towards him, he remains motionless, staring forward, his head tilted slightly to one side.

Gustaw Belka wears an old duffel coat, blue jeans and a pair of scuffed trainers. The top two toggles of the coat are unfastened, and his prominent Adam's apple bulges out from his neck like a tumour. His hair sticks up as if he's connected to the mains. That's Goose all right. And it is almost as if he has been expecting me.

"Mr. Braddock," he says.

"Goose. I'm surprised you remember me."

"I wasn't sure it was you until you got closer and I could see your aura."

"Ah, yes," I reply, reminding myself that I am dealing with a nutjob. It's going to be best to humour him – at least for now. "My purple aura. My gift of insight."

"Yes."

His stare is slightly disconcerting.

"Well, this is cosy."

I indicate the slumbering shapes under the brick arch.

"You've been looking for me," he says in a way that sounds midway between a question and a statement.

"I have. I called at your flat a few days ago, and Mrs. Yao told me you haven't been there for a month."

"A month," he echoes flatly.

"So where *have* you been?"

"I've been trying to find myself."

Oh, God. Goose might be at the extreme end of the autistic spectrum, but that hasn't protected him from the Millennials' disease of self-discovery. Or *narcissistic self-obsession*, as we plain-speaking types call it.

"I mean, where have you been staying? Where have you been sleeping?"

He blinks at me. It's his first blink since we started talking.

"Around here?" I press.

"Mostly," he answers.

"I was speaking to Janice today –" I pause before continuing. "You *do* remember Janice, don't you, Goose? From the coffee shop?"

He jerks slightly as if someone has pressed a button to activate him.

"Janice Marlowe, born Janice Mary Yallop in Bromley, Kent. Married to Colin Bernard Marlowe. She is five feet six inches tall, and is the manager at Tower Bridge Beanz where she has worked since –"

I raise a hand and he becomes immediately silent, clicking back into standby mode.

"Yes, *that* Janice. When I told her you'd gone missing, she was very worried. You should have let her know you're all right."

"You think I ought to go to Tower Bridge Beanz?"

"Absolutely, you should."

He shakes his head decisively.

"They won't see me there," he announces.

"What do you mean? Janice would *love* to see you."

But he's switched off, so I don't pursue the matter. I have bigger fish to fry.

"Listen, Goose," I say, "I've been employed to find Ronald Webster. Your friend Ronald, the TfL train driver and member of the Clapham Junction Locomotive Club. He's disappeared. About a month ago. Around the same time that you quit your apartment."

"Ronald?"

"You used to go out with him in the evening sometimes to help him research his book," I prompt.

"Ronald Webster." He blinks again.

One of the vagrants has stirred in the shadows of the arch. He has sat up and lit a cigarette stub, and is studying me curiously.

It occurs to me that this is not the ideal place to have a deep conversation – assuming Goose is capable of such a thing. I check my watch. *Mario's* will still be open.

"Let's go and have a cup of tea," I suggest. "I know somewhere only five minutes away. We can sit down and get out of the cold for a while."

He doesn't move.

"I'm not going to hurt you, Goose. I only want to talk to you for a few minutes. That's all. You'd like to help me find Ronald, wouldn't you?"

He nods.

"Then, come on."

I lead the way and he follows behind like a clockwork toy. I decide not to engage him in chatter until we are ensconced at a table at the greasy-spoon café.

When we arrive in Bermondsey Street, Goose checks the number above the door of *Mario's*. It's twenty-three. This appears to reassure him, and we go inside. There are no other customers.

I order two teas from the man behind the counter. He is the spitting image of the guy who served me earlier in the day, except that his eyes are not misaligned. Maybe they're twins.

He plonks two mugs of steaming brew in front of me and I slide one across to Goose who stares at me blankly.

"When did you last see Ronald Webster?" I ask in a non-threatening tone.

He does something odd with his fingers before declaring, "The thirty-first of October. A Monday."

Now we're getting somewhere.

"That's the last time his wife saw him too. Was it in the evening?"

He nods again.

"You met up somewhere? To help Ronald research his book?"

Another nod.

"And where did the pair of you go?"

He stares at his fingers for a few seconds, then looks back at me.

"I don't remember."

"You remember the exact date you last met Ronald, but you don't remember where you went?" I ask incredulously.

"Yes."

"Try again. Use your fingers," I suggest, although I have no idea what he uses his fingers *for*.

Goose concentrates hard, then breathes out, defeated.

"No," he says. "My fingers aren't moving."

Maybe a trip to the police station will help jog your memory, I consider saying, but don't. I mustn't spook him now. He's my only firm lead. Plus, perhaps the way his unusual brain works – I'm being kind here – means that he only retains certain numerical-related or essentially systemic material. Where he and Ronald went that night must be locked up *somewhere* in that weird head. It might only require the right trigger to free it up.

"You *do* recall that Ronald was writing a book on the London Underground," I say.

"Yes, and he knew a lot about the history of the tunnels and the stations. Even more than me."

A cog turns inside Goose and he begins reciting like an automaton.

"For instance, many people don't think that Mornington Crescent is a real Tube station. They think the name was made-up for the Radio 4 panel game, *I'm Sorry I Haven't a Clue*, but it is a real station on the Northern Line. Although," he continues relentlessly, "it's not actually *on* Mornington Crescent, but on the corner of Hampstead Road, Camden High Street and Evershalt Street. It was closed temporarily for refurbishment of its staircase in –"

I stop him again. Jesus, but this is hard work. Maybe Ronald Webster hasn't been murdered after all, but has committed suicide. Spending too much time in Goose's company would definitely make me want to self-harm.

"Do you remember what Ronald was researching when you used to go out on your night excursions? I mean, *specifically* researching?"

Goose scrunches up his eyes.

"It was – oh, what's the name of it? It's a geometric term."

"It's a what?"

He gazes at his wiggling fingers.

"An *angle*," he says. "He said he was looking for an angle."

"An angle? Ah. Something novel to make his book appeal to general readers? Is that what you're trying to tell me?"

"Yes. So lots of people would buy his book."

I scroll through the photos on my mobile until I come to the one of the miniature signs on Webster's train set.

"Ronald seems to have been interested in abandoned Tube stations. The so-called 'ghost stations.' Was he looking into those when you were with him?"

Goose frowns, but says nothing.

I pick one of the signs in the photo at random.

"How about South Kentish Town? Did the two of you go there?"

He mulls this over, and stares at his fingers again. Despite the fact that they don't move, he answers confidently.

"Yes, we did."

"So, you know exactly where the old station is?"

"Yes. It's close to Kentish Town station. Too close. That's why they closed it."

This is like pulling teeth, but we're making slow progress. I need to prompt his memory further.

"Would you be prepared to meet me there, Goose?"

"When?"

Tomorrow isn't possible because of Ursula, and I'd better keep Sunday evening free unless I want Da to remove my genitals with extreme prejudice.

"Monday night. Let's say eleven o'clock to keep it simple. We'll rendezvous outside Kentish Town and go on from there. Will you do that for me? To help me find Ronald?"

He gives a reluctant assent.

"And you promise me you won't disappear again? You'll stick around near the Maltby Street Market railway arches, so I know where you are if something comes up?"

He hesitates.

"Just until we find Ronald. Then you can go wherever you like," I add.

A sigh, then, "All right. I promise, Mr. Braddock."

"Good lad."

But then I have a pang of conscience. I lay out three twenty-quid notes on the table.

"On second thoughts, for the next couple of nights, there's some money so that you can book into one of the local hostels. The weather's freezing, and I don't like the idea of you sleeping rough. If I need you before Monday night, I'll ask for you at the hostels. Understand?"

A vacant gaze from my companion. I feel suddenly drained.

I tell him that I need to use the toilet and that he should drink his tea.

I have a pee and splash cold water on my face to liven myself up.

When I return to our table, there is no sign of Gustaw Belka.

His mug of tea is untouched and the three banknotes remain where I had left them.

I scoop up the notes and address the man behind the counter, "Young people, eh? Who can say what goes on in their minds?"

He scowls at me like it's not Goose but me who needs their head examined.

It's twenty minutes to midnight. He's waiting to close. I'm no longer welcome.

When I arrive home, Da wakes up long enough to fetch us both a glass of water and kiss me good night.

Before I switch out the light, I inform her that I've found Goose, but that I won't bore her with the story now.

"Good," she says.

I think we're OK.

XXI

Home Alone 2

It's Saturday. D-Day.

This evening, I'll be sitting down to dinner with Ursula d'Ambrosi unless a miracle happens in the meantime or I cancel out of sheer funk. Based on my meeting with Goose at *Mario's*, I'm not confident that that lunatic's input is going to be of much help to me in finding Webster – and that's assuming he doesn't vanish again in the meantime, and actually shows up on Monday. And that means I *do* need to listen to whatever it is Ursula has to say.

However, based on my bizarre time with Mr. Belka, I am at least sure of one thing. If Ronald Webster has been murdered, his killer wasn't Goose. That would be too incredible: like hearing that Dopey from the seven dwarfs had fathered a child with Snow White while they were both high on cocaine.

I half-wish that I had asked him more questions yesterday and probed more deeply into where he and Ronald had been together. But, in my defence, I was already tired after my day's labours. Plus, I'm not sure it would have got me any further in any event. With Goose, it's probably best to keep things basic and proceed slowly with digestible data chunks. If I overtax his peculiar mind, it could explode and then I'd be covered in ex-barista brain. Which would be messy.

Softly, softly catchee monkey.

I'm not sure I still possess the patience for this type of work, though.

If I'd dragged Goose off to a police station last night, informed the desk sergeant that *this man* is the last person to have seen Ronald Webster alive, and left the Met to do its job, I'd be off the hook. Then I could redeliver RW's laptop to his ungrieving widow and tell her, "You might want to get rid of this, unless you and your new boyfriend want to watch some child pornography," and wash my hands of the whole affair.

But if I were to take the easy route, then I wouldn't be David Braddock, would I? And I *have* to be David Braddock because everyone else is already taken.

Despite Da's reasonable tone of last night, she's rather frosty when it comes time to usher the kids in the car. I can't blame her.

I give her a hug and a kiss before they leave.

I whisper to her, "You have nothing to worry about while you're away."

"I know that," she says. "You're the one who needs to do the worrying. Call me later when your business meeting has finished. No matter how late it is, I'll be up. I want a full report."

"And you shall have one."

* * * * *

I ring Janice to tell her I've found Goose, and we have a brief conversation about her favourite nutter. She is relieved to hear he's OK.

I explain that he has agreed to help me on my missing person case, but that in a few days' time – if he hasn't already dropped by Tower Bridge Beanz – I'll drag him along to the coffee shop to see her.

"I hate the thought of him sleeping rough," she says. "Tell Goose that if he has nowhere else to go, he can sleep on my sofa until he gets himself sorted. Colin will be cool with that."

"So long as you understand that you might have to have your sofa fumigated afterwards. Our Mr. Belka doesn't exactly smell like a rose garden."

"Now you're being mean. Perhaps you should try living on the streets for a while and see how you cope."

"If my wife ever finds out about our love-child, Janice, that's exactly where I will be living."

After our call ends, I again scour the TV channels and the Internet to see if there is any breaking news on Anneke Reid or Ben Quinlan. There isn't. There's no update either on Lee Vance, the supposed-murderer of my orthodontist neighbour. The journalists' latest fad appears to be hounding the Right Honourable Giles Feathercroft while he pursues his one-man crusade against the less fortunate. I suppose the journos and their editors have become bored with the labyrinthine twists and turns of Brexit. Much like the general population.

Thinking about Anneke and Ben makes me wonder whether another phone call might be in order. Although I can't claim to have any warm feelings towards Jamie Sykes, I should check on my former client to make sure he is all right and that the earth hasn't swallowed him too.

I baulk, however, at calling the little git's mobile, and instead ring his parents' land line. Jamie's father answers.

Sykes Senior tells me that Jamie is spending a lot of time out on the town with disreputable friends and co-workers – including, apparently, his boss – and this seems to be making his son's fits of temper and anxiety attacks worse. He asks me whether there is any chance of my seeing his son in a professional capacity again soon, and I tell him *no* in a voice that I hope sounds apologetic rather than exultant. Right, good. I can forget about Jamie with a clear conscience.

I spend some time re-reading my notes on RW in the hope that a lightbulb might come on, but it doesn't. It's the same idle speculations on mariticide, crimes of infidelity, bad writing and insurance scams; plus, some tenuous linkages to closed Tube stations, pedophilia and the League of Loki. A shit stew without seasoning, in other words.

Going forward from here, I muse, amounts to this. First, pump Ursula for information. Next, see what I am able to extract from Goose (maybe breaking and entering into a few abandoned TfL sites along the way). Then, if that all proves fruitless, focus my efforts on discovering as much as I can about Pearl Webster's affair with Fred Eggers.

If and when I hit an evidential wall, the next step would be to hand over everything I've found out to the police and conduct a shameful retreat from the investigation business.

I make a cup of tea and peer out of the window of our front room.

A white van is moving slowly down our road. Perchance it is driven by a kiddie-fiddler searching for prey, but more likely it is driven by a plumber eager to wring as much cash as possible out of some unfortunate pensioner with a dripping tap.

Now, how to while away the rest of the hours until I meet Ursula?

Start reading a new book? Go for a work-out at the gym? Play *LOL* on Pratcha's games console?

No. None of the above. And, as winter has set in, and there's no gardening to do, I do a clean and tidy, and settle down to watch an old movie or two on the box.

The hands of our wall clock move agonisingly slowly towards the appointed hour of my pseudo-romantic date with Ursula d'Ambrosi.

Funny. Time usually moves quickly when something you're dreading is approaching.

Perhaps I'm not dreading it quite so much as I'd like to believe.

Perhaps, on the contrary, I'm looking forward to it.

XXII

Vulnerable

Corpses and decay.

Bodies turning up and bodies not turning up.

Missing half-bodies and missing whole bodies.

These are the sorts of bodies that I need to spend my Saturday night focusing on, and not on the type of body that Ursula d'Ambrosi has. That is to say, a ripe... No, let's *not* say it. Let's not say anything. Let me fill my head with images of putrefying cadavers, in the way that the meditators of old used to, in order to remind themselves of the transience of human life and the perils of attachment to the flesh.

But now, it's time to plant the Braddock body in the shower, give it a good soap and scrub, shave away the day's bristles, then choose some suitable attire before stepping out into the November streets in an appropriately resolute fashion.

Do the right thing. Be straight with Ursula. Consider Da's feelings. And don't buy a box of condoms.

Before I leave the house, I ring my wife.

"Is everything OK at Nang's?" I ask.

"Yes."

She isn't inclined to add anything further, so I say, "Excellent. Well… I'll call you later."

"Right."

The London streets are even colder than the tone of Da's voice. The inky sky above me is swamped with low cloud. The day's heat – such as it was – has rapidly evaporated into the heavens.

I take the Tube to London Bridge and encounter a noisy hen party, presumably doing the rounds of Southwark pubs. None of the women appear to be wearing enough clothes for a November evening. The bride-to-be sports a veil and a bright red sash emblazoned with the words, *VIRGIN, FOR NOW*, which I'm sure isn't fooling anybody. She gabbles loudly in a Midlands accent, and is already unsteady on her feet, which suggests the drinking started early. Before their party leaves the station, one of the bridesmaids throws up beside the windows of WH Smith, which causes much mirth among her companions. She is still retching zealously when I exit onto St. Thomas Street.

I'm way too early for my dinner date, so I meander aimlessly around the streets of Bermondsey. Given the looming assignation, I have become skittish. At one point, I convince myself that I'm being followed by a young white guy, so I duck into a general store run by an Indian gentleman, buy a packet of chewing gum and ask if he wouldn't object if I went out of his back door. He is completely unfazed by this, and nods resignedly – which tells me a lot about his usual clientele. Passing through a back yard piled with empty boxes and overflowing rubbish bins, I find I'm in a small pedestrian alleyway which reeks of dog piss.

If someone was following me, which they likely weren't, I've lost them. I make my circuitous way to the St. Mary Magdalen Churchyard on the corner of Bermondsey Street and Abbey Street, where I sit down on a bench and stare at the old graves while I talk myself into the right frame of mind to meet Ursula.

Time to move before my ears and bum get even colder.

I'm a minute or two early arriving at *La Brasserie*. There is no sign of Ms. d'Ambrosi. The place is already heaving with heterosexual couples, but I give my companion's name and the waitress ushers me to a table under their menu blackboard and removes the 'reserved' card. I take off my coat and ask her to bring me a beer and a wine list.

All the wine is of French origin. I knock back half the beer and order their most expensive bottle of red. It's a *Château Rip-off* from some place I've never heard of.

Ursula is fashionably late, but not excessively so. My beer glass is empty and the wine is breathing when she removes her coat to reveal a smart black dress beneath. She has had her hair done, and is carefully made up; though she seems less confident than she was at our last meeting, nervous even. Some reassuring bonhomie might be in order.

I stand and give her a respectful hug, which settles her a little.

"You look good enough to eat. Better than anything they have on their specials menu, in fact."

"Thank you," she replies, relaxing further.

I pour out two generous glasses of wine, and offer a toast to Transport for London and the successful completion of the Crossrail project.

She throws me a tight smile and sips from her glass before setting it down.

"Is it all right?"

"Yes, very good."

She isn't meeting my eyes, so I ask, "Are *you* all right, Ursula? Has something happened?"

She shakes her head and glances at the couple at the next table. They are engrossed in their mobile phones, and – despite the fact that they are only two feet away – appear unaware of our presence.

"This place might not have been the best choice for a private conversation," she says in a low voice.

"Don't concern yourself," I reply. "We're here now."

"Yes," she sighs. "I suppose so."

"Let's pretend everyone here is deaf. We'll never see any of them again anyway. Unless this is one of your regular haunts?"

"No, it isn't."

"Well, then."

I reach across the table and squeeze her hand briefly. She squeezes my hand back, but her expression remains serious.

"Are you regretting that you agreed to have dinner with me, Ms. D'Ambrosi?"

"It's not that, David."

"Then, what is it?"

"I was thinking today that I've pressured you into this, and I feel bad about it. I wouldn't want you to have the idea that this is how I normally behave when I meet a man I like. Especially one who is married."

"None of that has crossed my mind," I reply in a manner that I hope is convincing.

"Maybe it would be better if I just give you the information you want, then we can finish our glasses of wine, and go home. Separately."

Now, any sensible man in my situation would accept this offer unreservedly. It would mean I have no further hassle from Da, and I won't have to tread a careful path through eggshells for the next couple of hours.

Instead, I say, "Absolutely not. If you'd rather we ate somewhere else, then that's fine. But I *am* going to buy you dinner this evening, and we *are* going to finish this bottle of wine. What is more, you are not going to feel guilty and neither am I. The information you have for me can wait until we are both suitably lubricated."

I realise I could have phrased this better, so I add, "Our throats, I mean. When I talk about lubrication."

Now she gives me a proper smile.

"All right. If you're sure."

"I'm sure."

She raises her glass again and takes a more substantial swig.

I have made my task of avoiding inappropriate physical contact much more difficult. I tell myself that I am merely indulging in some light flirtation to oil the wheels of conversation, but this is not entirely convincing; and it strikes me that the motivation for my loose talk might have more to do with the fact that her presence here is flattering to the Braddock ego.

Now, I will have to proceed with my original plan: get her so drunk that intercourse becomes out of the question. And if it turns out that she can handle her alcohol, then I will go to Plan B: get myself so drunk that intercourse becomes out of the question.

"So, do you want a starter, or shall we go straight to the main event?"

As these words leave my mouth, I note that they hang heavy with innuendo. Ursula picks up on it, but thankfully doesn't comment.

"No starter."

We consult the blackboard and give the waitress our orders.

"So, David, how is your investigation into Mr. Webster's disappearance going?"

"Not brilliantly. Though I did manage to track down Mr. Belka. He's living rough under the railway arches not far from here."

"Ah, interesting. Has he been of any help?"

"Not so far, and I have serious doubts that he ever will be. However, I'm meeting him again on Monday. We'll see how that works out."

I down some wine and Ursula follows suit.

"Did you consider asking at the TfL Lost Property Office to see if Mr. Webster has been handed in? Everything that is found on the Underground passes through there: bags, laptops, wallets, bones, sex aids, prosthetic limbs, the lot."

"If you're going to make jokes, you'd better warn me first."

"Sorry," she giggles.

Clearly, Ursula is no longer worried about the couple on the next table, and is starting to enjoy herself. More disconcertingly, so am I.

"Well," she goes on, "let me see if I can be of more use to you than Mr. Belka."

"I'm sure you can."

"Get out your notebook, then, Mr. Investigator, you might want to write this down."

"You have my full attention."

She tops up our glasses.

"And you need to drink faster if you're going to keep up with me."

"Duly noted. Shall I order us another bottle?"

"In a minute."

I get out my notebook.

"Fire away."

"Well, a couple of weeks before Ronald Webster disappeared, we had a disciplinary issue with him. With him and Mr. Belka, actually. An unusual issue."

"Oh?"

"The pair of them were discovered by the police in the British Museum station at about one o'clock in the morning. That's one of our closed stations. They'd used a bolt cutter on the padlocked street door, and broken in. The reason the police were hanging around is because the previous week, there'd been a break-in at the same location, and graffiti had been sprayed on the walls. The police probably thought it had been kids, but then they find Webster and Belka. Weird, eh?"

"Were they caught spraying graffiti?"

"No, they had no paint with them. Just torches, and, of course, the bolt cutter."

"So, what do you think they were doing down there?"

"When I conducted the disciplinary interviews with them, Webster claimed he was doing research for his book on the London Underground, and Belka was assisting him. Though, I'm not sure I believe him."

"Why?"

"There was something creepy and shifty about the man. I've been in this game long enough to understand he was hiding something. But I don't know what. And as for Belka... Well, if you've met him, you know what he's like."

"Peculiar."

"Yes."

"So, what happened?"

"The police left it to us to decide what to do. We intended to dismiss them both, but then Webster's shop steward got involved. He'd been spoiling for a fight with management over pay and automation, so the matter was dropped in view of Webster's long service and otherwise spotless record. And, because we let Webster off, we couldn't sack Belka. But the pair of them were given a stern reprimand and it went on their service records."

"Hmmn. Intriguing. By the way, I've read Webster's manuscript on the Underground and he mentions British Museum, along with the other ghost stations. But I don't recall him writing anything startling about that particular one."

"Anyway, David, that's all I have for you, I'm afraid. I hope you think it was worth *this*."

Ursula gestures at the table with her left hand. She no longer appears to be self-conscious about her missing fingertip. Perhaps the wine is helping. We've almost finished the bottle.

"It was worth it. *Is* worth it."

Our food arrives and I order us another bottle.

"Are you trying to get me drunk, David?"

"Yes."

"Well, I warn you, in that case we'll have to move onto cocktails later. But we'd have to go somewhere else."

"We can do that."

"Really?"

"Yes. Now, eat your food."

* * * * *

My watch tells me it's gone ten o'clock, which means Ursula and I have been together for three hours.

We're in an underground bar in Bermondsey called *The Cistern*. It has been converted from a Victorian public toilet to a place where people put liquids into themselves rather than letting liquids out. It still has white and black tiles on the floor and walls. The lighting is more subtle than it would have been formerly, and I doubt you got to listen to nineties rock music while you were taking a leak. It's heaving with people who have money to burn and enjoy being overcharged for their drinks in a cellar with no windows. There are no tables or chairs, so everybody has to stand. I guess that constitutes some kind of satirical allusion to this hole-in-the-ground's previous function, an impression which is supported by the urinal positioned behind the bar in the middle of the spirit optics.

Ursula and I have found a space where we can lean against the wall (and each other) while we cradle our cocktails and continue to talk nonsense.

We are both pissed. After downing two bottles of red wine at the restaurant, we are on our fourth cocktail – this one being a Manhattan.

As is usual on such alcohol-fuelled occasions, we have done some baring of souls; of the type which will be recalled with embarrassment the next day. Ursula has disclosed to me the details of her failed marriage, how lonely she is at times, and the awkwardness of conversations with new people about her missing fingertip. For my part, I've given her some dirt about my years in Thailand. I have also (ill-advisedly) reminded her that my wife is away for the night, but that she is aware of our dinner date.

"And was she OK with that?" Ms. D'Ambrosi had inquired, and when I replied *yes*, she had asked, "So, would you say that you have an open marriage?" I at least had the sense to answer *no, definitely not*. Ursula took this on the chin, and chuckled a bit. Then we had a Mojito, and moved on to discussing the differences between men and women.

It's fair to say that, so far, the evening has not gone as I'd planned. We have passed through the various stages of drink-induced befuddlement, during which emotions swing between depression and exultation. I need to make sure this is my last cocktail.

My head is swimming somewhat, and a vague nausea is rising in my throat. So far as I can tell, I am speaking normally, though Ursula's words sound rather slurred to my ears.

At various points over the last hour, I have considered going up the steps into the street and ringing Da to tell her I've deposited my companion at her house, and am about to go home. This, so she wouldn't worry. But I have decided this white lie would be unacceptable. I will call my wife when Ursula is safely at her house, and not before, and take my punishment accordingly.

We've finished our Manhattans.

Ursula looks up at me with bleary eyes. Her cheeks are flushed, and there is a patina of sweat on her forehead.

"I don't want another cocktail," she declares.

"Me neither. Let's get you home."

The night air hits her hard, and she staggers against me. I take her arm.

"Jesus," she says.

"Are you OK? Shall we take this taxi?" I ask, indicating a cab parked nearby.

"No, let's walk, if you don't mind, David. I need to sober up. It's not far. Fifteen minutes from here. Well, maybe twenty in my current state."

She giggles, and we start walking. Slowly, because she is not too steady on her feet. I, on the other hand, appear to have been jerked rudely back into sobriety. Or at least, something close to sobriety. A numbness, perhaps. One engendered by the thought of wifely reprisals.

"I haven't been this drunk in ages," Ursula continues. "I haven't had sex in ages either," she adds. "Not since my divorce. Not unless you count, you know."

She makes a rude motion of her fingers.

"Ah."

"You understand?"

"Yes."

"*Petting the cat.*"

"Yes. I got it."

"I shouldn't be telling you this, should I?"

"Well –"

"But I'm very drunk, David. I'm very, very drunk."

"Don't worry, Ursula. I'll make sure you arrive home safely."

"I know you will. You're lovely."

She hugs in closer to me. It's fine. It makes it easier to steer her. Less meandering.

"You don't think I'm a bad girl, David, do you?"

"No, I don't."

"You're just saying that."

"I'm not."

"Really?"

"Really."

"Good. Because I don't want you to think badly of me, David."

"I don't."

She stops suddenly and stares up at the sky.

"I can't see any stars."

"There's too much cloud."

"But there should be *some* stars."

"They're still there. You just can't see them at the moment."

"Ahhh." She understands. "Right. Carry on."

* * * * *

The conversation continues in this spluttering, nonsensical vein. Happily, sex does not resurface as a topic of discussion. I have the feeling that Ursula has accepted at some level that there will be no hanky-panky tonight – though that might be wishful thinking. She remains coherent enough to answer my queries on directions, and in due course we reach her front door.

Her house is a small end terrace off Jamaica Road, and, I estimate, maybe half-a-mile from Bermondsey station. It's one of those places that probably has a paved yard out the back, just big enough to swing a cat (provided you swing it over the wheelie bins).

"Home," she says, fishing in her handbag for her keys. "Isn't that sad?"

I let this question go unanswered.

"Come in," she says, opening the door.

"It's late, Ursula, I should –"

She grabs my hand.

"Oh, *come on*, David. I'm not going to bite you. One last drink, then you can go home. Nobody's waiting for you at home anyway. Live a little."

She pulls me into the house, switches on a couple of lights, and closes the front door.

"Here's my living room. Take your coat off and grab a seat. The sofa's the most comfortable. I'll be with you in a minute."

I remove my coat reluctantly, choose an armchair, and hope to God that she's not sobering up.

Nobody's waiting for you at home anyway, she'd said. That short sentence hangs heavy with subtext.

But then a thought pops unbidden into my head. *Would it really be such a bad thing if we ended up in bed together?*

This is immediately followed by: *Hell yes. Yes, yes, yes, you stupid bastard. It would. It would be a chuffing disaster.*

However, I am partially reassured by Ursula's staggering gait as she reappears, shoeless, holding a half-full wine bottle and two large glasses. She sets them down on the coffee table, and comments that the ceiling light is too bright. The glow from a standing lamp is now all that illuminates the living room.

She plops herself down on the sofa.

"Sit beside me," she says, her voice still comfortingly slurred. "You're miles away over there."

I move gingerly onto the sofa while Ursula empties the bottle into the two glasses. Christ, those are *big* glasses. Big *full* glasses.

She hands me one and raises her own in a toast.

"To happy days, and happy nights," she says.

I take a small taste of wine and she chugs about a third of hers, before we set both of our glasses down on the coffee table.

"Now give me a great big hug," she orders. "I've wanted one all evening."

I comply. She wraps her arms around me and buries her face in my shoulder. A contented sigh escapes from her, and I fancy she whispers, *That's better.*

After what seems a long while, she takes a deep breath and pulls away. For a second or two, I worry that she's going to kiss me, but then she swivels into a lying position and lays her head in my lap. She turns onto her side, and I feel the weight of her skull pressing on my thighs.

I rest my hand on her shoulder and stroke it gently, hoping that this will encourage sleep rather than erotic stimulation.

The strategy works. Her breathing slows.

I sit completely still for a few minutes until I am sure she is in the Land of Nod, then ease myself from underneath her and substitute a cushion for my lap. She doesn't stir.

I pick up my coat, switch off the light, and close the front door carefully behind me.

Two late-night cyclists go by. An eponymous white van is parked on the street. A woman in a beret is walking a dog. An overhead lamp buzzes. A siren blares in the distance. Life and death continue as normal.

The Necropolis exhales.

And so do I.

XXIII

The Necropolis Exhales

Da answers her phone after three rings.

"Hi, it's me."

"Oh, hello, husband. I was wondering if I was going to hear from you before dawn."

"Yes, sorry, I know it's rather late."

"Where are you?"

"I'm walking along Jamaica Road towards London Bridge."

"And how did your evening go?"

Da's voice sounds terrifying reasonable.

"I got some information about Webster that might be useful. Apparently, a few weeks back, he and Goose were found in one of the disused Tube stations –"

"No, David," she interrupts coldly. "I meant how did your evening go *with Ms. D'Ambrosi*. Did you flirt with her?"

"I was pleasant to her, if that's what you mean."

"That's not what I mean."

"I didn't come on to her."

"And did she come on to you?"

"Well, maybe a bit."

"I see."

"But, listen, Da, everything's fine. Nothing happened. And to make sure nothing happened, I got her good and drunk. That's why I'm so late calling you. She was unsteady on her feet, so I saw her home and had a quick glass of wine with her. That's it. I left her asleep on her sofa a couple of minutes ago. Or, to be more accurate, passed out on her sofa."

"So, you went into her house?"

"Yes, but only into her living room, and only briefly."

"You like to live on the edge, don't you, David Braddock?"

"I had the situation under control, Da. There was never any danger of anything untoward happening. For goodness' sake, give me some credit."

Da gives me an unconvinced, *Hmmn*. I wait for the next question.

"So, you didn't kiss her?"

"No."

"And she didn't kiss you?"

(My wife is a stickler for detail.)

"No. I held her arm on the walk to her house. Mainly so that she wouldn't fall into the road and be run over. And I gave her a friendly hug at the beginning and end of the evening. That was the extent of any physical contact between us."

"You gave her a hug at the end of the evening? I thought you said she passed out."

"It was before that. Go on, ask me anything else you want."

Da considers this.

"What was she wearing?"

"A black dress and a long coat. Oh, yes, and a lacy black bra with matching knickers."

"Very funny."

"Let me ask you this. Do I sound guilty? Do I sound like a man who has just taken advantage of the HR Manager of Transport for London?"

Da relents a little.

"Perhaps not."

"I *have* had quite a lot to drink, though."

"Yes, I did wonder."

"But you can rest assured that I will not be seeing Ursula d'Ambrosi again. All right?"

"You've squeezed all the information out of her that you can, so now you're discarding her like a used rag. Yes, I understand. The poor woman."

"Now you're feeling sorry for her?"

"She must get terribly lonely, being a divorcée and so on. Plus, trying to build a career in a man's world. It can't be easy. I can't blame her for wanting to have dinner with an attentive man."

"I can't keep up with you."

There is a brief silence at the other end of the phone, and I become suspicious.

"You're winding me up, aren't you?"

Da laughs.

"Well, I suppose I deserve that."

"Yes, you do."

"But am I forgiven?"

"According to you, there's nothing I need to forgive you for."

"No, there isn't. Apart from the fact that I'm not there with you and Nang."

"Yes, all right, you're forgiven. Are you headed home?"

"Not straightaway. I'm going to drop by the railway arches first, to see if Goose is around. This might be a good time to catch him."

"Remember you're in London, not on Koh Samui, and there are some dodgy people around after dark. Be careful, David. Don't take unnecessary risks."

"I never take unnecessary risks."

"I beg to differ."

We end the call on an upbeat note. Terrific. By the skin of my teeth, I've managed to navigate the last tricky few hours without becoming an adulterer or having to worry about poison in my tea or an expensive divorce.

I am no longer drunk – not at all – though by rights, I should be. The fact that I am aware of the coldness seeping into my bones is evidence of my prematurely-returned sobriety. I am, however, starting to tire.

If I can have a word with Goose, I will. But it's going to be a quick word.

Jamaica Road has morphed into Tooley Street. I turn left into Tanner Street, and see the railway arches ahead of me.

And there's Goose.

* * * * *

He is standing in exactly the same place that he was last time.

"Hello, Mr. Braddock."

Again, there is that lack of surprise at my showing up out of the blue. It's like *Groundhog Day*, but without the laughs.

"Good evening, Goose. You're still here, then," I add unnecessarily.

"Yes."

"So, you haven't found yourself yet?"

He shakes his head.

"Maybe you need to look harder."

His face remains blank.

I indicate the unmoving human forms under the arch.

"Don't you *ever* sleep?"

"Soon. If I'm lucky."

Mario's will be closed now. Which is a shame, as I could murder a mug of tea. There is no option but to engage Goose in conversation here by the dying, guttering light of the burning oil drum. My world is turning dystopian.

"I want to talk to you about the British Museum Tube station."

His internal clockwork kicks in, and in a dull monotone he starts to regurgitate the history of the place. I interrupt the flow impatiently.

"Yes, yes, we don't need to go into all that."

He falls silent.

"I understand that you and Ronald went there one night about a month ago."

Goose stares at me but says nothing.

I prompt, "And the police found you."

He tilts his head to the side and squints at me.

"Do you remember that?"

His eyes roll around for a few seconds, then he says *yes* in an unusually positive voice.

"What were you doing there?"

"Angles," he replies. "Looking for angles."

I catch on.

"Ah, *angles*. For Ronald's book?"

Goose nods.

"And did you find anything?"

He closes his eyes, attempting (I guess) to visualise the scene.

There is a long silence.

Jeez, it's like trying to talk to an infant. I'd be inclined to throw him over my shoulder and burp him were I not worried there might be nasty, wormy things crawling around under his parka.

Suddenly, he says, "A sign on the wall. A big red circle."

"Yes, Goose, that's what you'd expect to see in an Underground station."

"Then two policemen came and took us away."

I count to ten in my head.

"Did you and Ronald go to British Museum station again the last time you saw him? The night he disappeared?"

"No."

"You're absolutely sure?"

A beat, then, "Yes."

"Have you remembered yet where you *did* go that night?"

A slow headshake.

I'm too fatigued to continue with this for much longer. The alcohol I've consumed might not be impeding my thinking too much, but it's drained my energy.

"Listen, Goose, you recall that we are supposed to be meeting at Kentish Town at eleven o'clock on Monday night?"

A nod.

"Well, I want us to meet outside British Museum station instead. But at midnight, not eleven, as it's likely to be busier round there, more people. Midnight, yes? Is that all right?"

"Yes."

"You'll *definitely* be there, won't you?"

"Yes."

"Then, I'll see you on Monday. Good night."

He makes no reply.

As I walk away, his scraggy figure stands motionless, gazing ahead.

At London Bridge I take the night train to Bond Street where I change onto the Circle Line. Then it's a short, freezing walk home.

* * * * *

I've been lying in bed for ages. It's now past three in the morning.

But despite the fact that I am physically exhausted, there is so much crap buzzing around in my head that sleep is impossible. Maybe if I commit my thoughts to paper, my brain will leave me alone.

I pull on my robe, go downstairs and put the kettle on, cursing the Old Monk as I do so.

The Old Monk.

This is all his fault.

He's the go-to person I blame whenever I suffer from fevered, unceasing mental activity. An image of him floats across my vision now. A bald head with beady eyes perched atop a tent of orange robes.

Ever since I first encountered him on Koh Samui – around fifteen years ago – I've been indoctrinated with the notion of all-pervading *karma*, and I can't escape from it.

"Everything is connected to everything else," he used to tell me. Frequently. When I investigated my first multiple-murder case in Thailand, the Old Monk's 'helpful' education resulted in my drawing up a huge spider web chart of interconnected people and events which may or may not have been relevant to the solving of the crimes. It barely fitted on a page, and it did my head in trying to find a useful pattern to my scribbling. And, despite the fact that the solution to the murders turned out to be fairly straightforward in the end, I have been unable to shake off this way of looking at the world.

Perhaps everything is indeed connected, but what matters is what is connected in a *relevant* way for the problem at hand. Whenever I pointed this out to Ananda – for that was his name – he would simply shrug and come up with some impenetrable Zen saying. *What is the sound of one testicle clapping? Tell me what the moon desires.* Or whatever. Then he'd scrounge cigarettes and tell me off for smoking while he puffed his way through a packet of my Marlboros.

I do miss the old bugger though. The last I heard of him he was in Chiang Mai. He must be about two hundred years old by now, assuming he's still alive.

I think that what has brought back these memories of Ananda is my encountering Goose – who reminds me of him. Not that the Old Monk ever wore a filthy parka or was obsessed with trains or the number 23. It's more that, neither of them is capable of smiling, and when they talk, they sound like autistic stand-up comics whose jokes don't include a punch-line. Also, they both frustrate me beyond reason.

However, unlike Goose, Ananda has/had a spiritual life. Goose wouldn't be able to relate to God unless he could fit him on a chart or assign him a number. And I doubt Ronald

Webster (if he still possesses a pulse) has any time for the Almighty either: so far as I know, He played no part in the construction of the London Underground.

And the idea that Gustaw Belka might replace the fag-stealing Buddhist holy man as my new sidekick is depressing in the extreme.

I stand on my front doorstep with my mug of tea. I stare out into our frigid, deserted street: a fragrant Goose in a dressing gown. Five minutes of that is enough to make my genitalia retract, and I close the door and sit down on the sofa with my notebook.

Now that I have temporarily banished the Old Monk from my thoughts, my imagination replaces him with a representation of Ursula d'Ambrosi. A voice that sounds not unlike Da's scolds me for exploiting a vulnerable woman, and for using her loneliness as a way to get information on RW. The voice may have a point. I shall ring Ursula this afternoon and check she's OK.

Happy now, Da?

I open my notebook and write on a new page:

STUFF THAT'S HAPPENED IN THE LAST 3 WEEKS

1.   My neighbour is murdered, cut in half and his bits left in Highgate. I have my doubts that pedophile Lee Vance is the killer.

2.   Two ghosts from the past show up: Ken Reid (who knew my father) and retired copper Martin Banks (who has an enigmatic conversation with me about my old nemesis Jim Fosse). Am I, like Scrooge, due a third visitation?

3.   *Two of my hypnotherapy clients disappear: Anneke Reid and Ben Quinlan.*

4.   *I go into therapy myself and seem to be cured of hauntings from my dead wife Claire. I cease my own therapy practice.*

5.   *I am engaged to investigate the disappearance of Ronald Webster, an employee of TfL who is a pedophile, obsessed with railways, and whose wife/widow is shagging the Chairman of the Railway Anoraks Society. Weird shit about closed Underground stations, and he has a copy of a book on the League of Loki??? Also, through RW I am reintroduced to Gustaw Belka, former barista, whom I encountered some years back, and who was involved in the 'Angel' murders. I'M SHORT OF LEADS!!!*

6.   *I almost have sex with the HR Manager of Transport for London. By accident.*

I read back what I've written.

Apart from the fact that the word 'pedophile' appears twice, there is nothing that obviously connects any of these disparate facts. In fact, I'd challenge anyone to make them fit together. The only place all these items could possibly appear side-by-side would be in some tacky whodunnit novel where the author was trying to 'write something different.'

Pedophiles? If the media are to be believed, they are so common in the UK these days that my coming across two of them barely warrants a second thought.

In my mind's eye, I conjure up an image of the Old Monk.

So much for your 'method', I tell him. The only way these things are connected is because I've written them down in a list. What do you say to that, eh?

He says, *You are so enmeshed in the net of Samsara that you can't see what stares you in the face.*

Then he asks me if I have any cigarettes.

No. Buy your own.

I take up my pen and cross out items 1 and 3. I write in the margin, *Trust the Metropolitan Police to sort these out.* I can't resist adding, *Hahaha.*

Then I put a line through items 2 and 4, and write in the margin, *NOT EVERYTHING IS ABOUT YOU, BRADDOCK.*

Item 6 I'll cross out tomorrow – sorry, *today* – after I've called Ursula.

That leaves only item 5 – which is what I should be concentrating on anyway. Let's see what British Museum station has in store for me on Monday night.

Thus, my life is simplified once again.

Now I think I can sleep.

Goodnight, Old Monk. And by the way, fuck you.

XXIV

Wearing a Hair Shirt

It's shortly after ten when I finally rise from my pit. It requires a good hour and a large mug of coffee before I feel human again. Fortunately, I've dodged a hangover. I suspect Ursula may not have been so lucky.

During a brief phone conversation, Da informs me that they expect to be home between four and five, traffic permitting. Everyone is OK and Pratcha hasn't suffered any discernible withdrawal symptoms from being off his LOL game for over twenty-four hours, so we shouldn't have to medicate him with horse tranquillisers.

When the family does arrive back, I need to be on my best behaviour. Reparations for my neglecting them this weekend are in order. To that end, I will go shopping and whip up dinner. And, while I'm at it, I'll buy an expensive bottle of wine. Da will like that, hopefully.

While my brain slowly cranks back up to full functioning, I open my laptop and review Webster's notes on British Museum. There's nothing very salutary, so his and Goose's nocturnal visit either didn't throw up anything of interest or whatever they did find stayed in his head – where it remains, assuming he still has a functioning brain.

I skim through his entries on the other ghost stations: Bull & Bush, Highgate, et al. Did they break into any of those too, I wonder? I'll pump Goose on this topic tomorrow night, though I'm not getting my hopes up that that will produce anything useful.

I mull over the miniature signs and the other recently-added paraphernalia on Webster's model train set. Something about them is bugging me, but I can't figure out what.

Highgate. The place where the two halves of my murdered neighbour were found. But it's probably a coincidence, and besides, I've already crossed the Banerjee/Vance puzzler off my list of things to worry about, so I should let sleeping dogs and dentists lie. Otherwise, I'll start making all sorts of unwarranted connections with Karl Marx and other notables who are buried in the cemetery there. Then I won't have any peace.

I must ring Ursula to check on her condition.

But before I do this, I play through in my head possible conversations that we might have, so that I'll be prepared. The scenarios run like this (in order of the best to the worst):

SCENARIO 1:

URSULA: I'm sorry about my behaviour last night, David. And I'm sorry I pressured you into having dinner with me. I should have just given you the information on Webster without all that flirting nonsense. I'm sorry. Please forgive me.

ME: There's nothing to forgive, it's fine.

URSULA: That's kind of you. And I promise you'll never see or hear from me again.

SCENARIO 2:

URSULA: *David, would you have taken me to bed last night if we hadn't been so drunk?*

ME: *Well —*

URSULA: *No, no, wait, don't tell me. It would depress me either way. It's better that I don't know. Let's not see each other again, or even speak on the phone.*

ME: *All right.*

SCENARIO 3:

URSULA: *David, would you have taken me to bed last night if we hadn't been so drunk?*

ME: *Absolutely not.*

URSULA: *So, you were just using me? Messing with my head? You're such a twat. I've a good mind to tell your wife that we DID have sex. Rough sex. And that you forced me to do really disgusting things.*

SCENARIO 4:

URSULA: *I don't care about our getting drunk last night, David, or what anyone thinks. I don't care that you're married. I love you, I love you, I love you, and I need to see you again. Today. Come round to my house now, before your wife gets home. I want you to violate me over and over until I can't take any more. And after that, my darling, we'll work something out. Life won't be worth living for me unless I can hold you and see you. And if I can't do that, I'm going to kill myself.*

ME: *Can we take a step back for a second? [I don't know what I say after that.]*

Maybe my imagination has become a trifle fanciful.

I grit my teeth and ring her.

There's no reply. Either she's not answering my calls – because on reflection she's concluded that I've been a bastard to her – or she's busy doing something more useful. Like having her stomach pumped out or reading *HR Manager Monthly*. I'll try again later, and hope for Scenario 1.

I nibble a chocolate digestive and wolf down a Mini Babybel Cheese (subtle notes of grass with a touch of nut, encased in a fragrant, easy-to-open red wax wrapper). That's better. There's nothing like a spot of dairy for steadying the nerves.

Outside, it's overcast and grey. Wintry London at its suicide-inducing best.

* * * * *

Evening has descended on the Braddock household, and with it an end-of-weekend calm.

Da hasn't mentioned Ms. D'Ambrosi and, so far as I can tell, isn't harbouring any grudge towards me. Once we've got into bed, I'll know for sure. If we have sex, it means she's put yesterday's events behind us. If not, I'm going to have to grovel a while longer.

I made us all breaded chicken breast with gravy, mashed potato and salad for dinner – which was well within my range of culinary expertise – finished off with individual tiramisus from the deli down the road. My wife appreciated the wine. At twenty-five quid a bottle, I'd have been outraged if she hadn't.

Plates were duly cleaned, and Jenny and Pratcha retired to their rooms.

Da and I are on the sofa finishing off the wine. She's regaled me with stories of Nang's latest political manoeuvrings at her local Conservative Association. It appears that if current Tory Prime Minister Theresa May doesn't honour the spirit of the Brexit vote, Nang and her neofascist allies will descend on Westminster and raze it to the ground. Purely in the name of democracy, of course.

I recount my progress, or lack of it, on the Webster investigation, and conclude by telling Da of my plan to visit British Museum with Goose tomorrow night.

"So, your strategy is breaking and entering public premises during the hours of darkness?"

"Er, yes."

"Investigating one possible crime by committing a definite one?"

"Well, when you put it like *that* –"

"How else should I put it?"

"Don't worry. I'll be careful."

She makes an *I'm unconvinced* noise.

"And this is based on the information that Mrs. Ambrosia gave you?"

"*Ms. d'Ambrosi.* And, yes."

"Have you called her today? To check she didn't choke on her own vomit while she was lying on her sofa?"

"Yes, I did, but she didn't answer. And, by the way, that's an awful image. It's not like I don't feel guilty enough."

"Perhaps she's pissed off with you leading her up the garden path."

"That had occurred to me."

"You should try calling her again. To make sure she's all right."

I squint at my wife.

"You're very concerned for her welfare all of a sudden. It's not like I owe her anything for her information. I *did* buy her dinner."

"You should call her anyway. It's only polite."

Da picks up my phone and hands it to me.

"Go on. Ring her now."

I grudgingly pull up Ursula's number and press the dial button.

It rings and rings, then times out.

"Nope. I'll try her again in the morning. I'll ring her at work."

My wife decides to let the subject drop. Instead, she says, "Why are you taking this guy Goose with you tomorrow night? It's not like he's been helpful so far. He sounds like a waste of space."

"More like a waste of oxygen," I reply. "He's one of those blokes who's *trying to find himself*. But then again, maybe revisiting the closed station might trigger something in him. Even if it's an anxiety attack. If nothing else, that might be amusing."

"Well, if you want my opinion –"

"Which I always do, my darling."

She ignores the interruption.

"You should concentrate your efforts on Mrs. Webster and this guy she's hanging around with. She's your most likely suspect, I'd say, if it turns out to be a murder case."

"Yes, but that's still an *if.*"

We have finished the wine.

"Shall we go to bed?" Da asks.

We turn in and have sex. Rather a long session actually, if you must know.

Today might have started out unpromisingly, but at least it's ended well. Plus, I don't have to worry about engaging a divorce lawyer.

Result.

XXV

Intimations of Mortality

A bright, clear Monday dawns. Summer skies and November temperatures, as the weathermen would say.

The kids toddle off to school, and Da totters off to work in her high heels. She looks smug, but I'm not complaining. The boat is steady and there's nothing to be achieved by rocking it.

Conscious of my wife's advice of the previous evening, I telephone Pearl Webster.

"How are you coping, Mrs. Webster?" I ask.

"Well enough, thank you, Mr. Braddock. Everyone is being kind."

Especially Fred Eggers, I don't say.

"Do you have any news for me?"

"Some. I'll drop by your place later in the week and give you a full report, but I wanted to tell you that I've found Gustaw Belka."

"You have?"

"Yes. He's living rough in Southwark. Under the railway arches."

"My goodness, he must have been difficult to track down."

"Well, he wasn't easy, that's for sure."

"And has he been of any help? Has he given you any pointers as to where Ronald might be?"

"Not yet. He's a rather cagey and difficult character. But I'm meeting him again tonight, and I'm keeping my fingers crossed that we might make some progress."

"That's most encouraging, Mr. Braddock. See, I was right about your insightful aura."

I don't want to be drawn into this witchy drivel, so I tell Mrs. W a small white lie in the interest of protecting Ursula d'Ambrosi's integrity.

"Goose did say something interesting, though."

"Oh?"

"Apparently, in October, he and Ronald were caught breaking into one of the disused Underground stations late at night. TfL took disciplinary action against them both. Official warnings. It sounds like they were lucky not to be sacked. Did you know about that?"

"I certainly did not," she replies.

Her surprise sounds genuine enough, but I will probe her more thoroughly on the topic the next time I meet her.

"Goose said they were doing it for research for your husband's book, but it seems like an inappropriate way of going about things."

"Yes," she replies with some annoyance in her voice. "It certainly does. And I can't believe Ronald didn't tell me about it."

No, I find that hard to believe too.

"Are you aware of any other instances where Ronald might have gained access to TfL premises illegally?"

"Not at all." Then she adds, "The stupid man."

"Well, Mrs. Webster, it might be something or nothing. It's not necessarily relevant to his disappearance, but I'm going to follow it up anyway."

We chat for a little longer, and pencil in the diary for me to see her on Friday afternoon.

And it's interesting, I reflect afterwards, that Mrs. W didn't ask *which* Tube station Ronald had broken into.

If that had been Da, she would have wanted all the details, including how I had gained access, the exact time of the offense, and what colour boxer shorts I was wearing.

My next call is to Ursula's mobile. Again, there is no answer, so I ring her office.

A woman's voice greets me with, "Good morning. TfL HR Department. How may I help you?"

"Hello. Can you put me through to Mrs. d'Ambrosi, please?"

"I'm afraid she isn't in this morning," she replies brightly. "Is there someone else who can assist you?"

"No. It was Mrs. d'Ambrosi that I wanted to speak to. Is she on leave today, and if so, can you tell me when she'll be back at work?"

"She's not on leave, and she hasn't phoned in ill – at least, not yet – so I'm afraid I can't tell you when she'll be back. I suggest you try again tomorrow."

"Right. I'll do that."

"May I ask who's calling?"

"Oh, it doesn't matter, no need for me to leave a message or anything. I'll catch up with her soon enough. Thank you."

"All right."

I cut the line.

There is a sinking sensation in my stomach. And it has nothing to do with what I had for breakfast.

I decide to head over to Bermondsey.

When I reach the platform at Notting Hill Gate, it is crowded with exasperated people.

"We apologise to passengers for the delay on the Central Line. This is due to an earlier incident," the announcer says helpfully.

* * * * *

After a sweaty journey crammed up against fellow disgruntled travellers, I make my way from London Bridge to a hardware store on Southwark Street. This detour is for the purpose of buying a large set of bolt cutters and a sturdy flashlight – both of which I expect I'll need for my sortie to British Museum later. I stuff them into the outsized rucksack that I've had the foresight to bring with me. From there it takes me half-an-hour on foot to get to Ursula's house.

An ugly surprise awaits my arrival.

* * * * *

Two police cars and a police van are parked in the street.

Ursula's property is cordoned off with tape, and a couple of constables are making sure the crowd of spectators is kept at a distance.

I pick an alert elderly lady who looks to be the Bermondsey equivalent of Doris Trent – that is to say, she carries that busybody air about her – and politely enquire what is going on.

"Terrible business," she replies.

"An accident?" I ask hopefully.

"No. A murder. And a particularly nasty murder at that."

"A – murder?"

She points at one of the constables.

"That's my nephew," she says.

I flinch.

"Of course, he's not supposed to say anything, but – well, I am his auntie."

"I guess they haven't brought the body out yet."

"There is no body," she announces casually.

"Then, um, how do you know it's a murder?"

"Because of all the blood on the sofa, and on the carpets. That poor young woman. Mrs. d'Ambrosi. Divorced. Lives on her own. Well, *lived.*"

"How – awful."

My innards are contracting into a knot.

I need more details, but how to ask without sounding too interested? Or ghoulish?

However, I don't need to say anything, because my new friend continues blithely. She's only too happy to have an audience.

"My friend Frances was in the alley out the back of this row of houses this morning. It's not used that much, but she goes out there periodically to sort the rubbish that piles up there. Frances is good like that. Neighbourly and socially responsible, if you understand what I mean.

"Anyway, she noticed Mrs. d'Ambrosi's gate was open, and when she peeked inside, she saw the back door was smashed and there was a trail of blood out of the house and into the garden. And when she looked down, she saw she was *standing in it*. Can you imagine? Poor Frances."

"So, she called the police?"

"You bet she did. Straightaway."

I try to take this in. I'm not worried that I appear shocked. Because all the faces around me are equally stunned.

"The police think some men broke in, killed this d'Ambrosi lady and dragged her away into the back alley? Then what? Took her away in some vehicle?"

"*Stabbed her.*"

"What?"

"Stabbed her. Multiple times. My nephew says it's like a slaughterhouse in her living room." This is stated as if she's commenting on the decorating.

She continues, "The forensics folks are in there now. My nephew says it's likely that they'll find lots of evidence. You know, *forensic* evidence. I should bloody well think so too. I hope they lock up the man who did this and throw away the key."

"Man?" I reply. "Surely it must be more than one man?"

"Well, I don't know about *that*," she responds. "All I know is, that Frances saw Mrs. d'Ambrosi bring a man home with her late on Saturday night, and they went into the house together. What do you make of that?"

"And did your friend see the man leave? Assuming he did leave," I add quickly.

She shakes her head.

"Frances isn't the sort of woman to spy on her neighbours."

Oh, really?

"But if this man was already in the house, why would he have to break the back door?"

A shrug.

"Maybe he did awful sexual things to her, and left. Then later he panicked that she would report him, so changed his mind about leaving her, came back and… Did what he did. Who can say what goes on in the head of a man like that?"

She stops to draw breath, and I jump in with, "Did Frances get a good look at this man? Would she be able to identify him?"

"You can ask her yourself. She's around here somewhere."

She glances around while I cringe.

"No, it seems you're out of luck. She must have gone back indoors to make lunch."

I breathe a silent sigh of relief.

"So, the police think this woman was killed on Saturday night? Not yesterday?"

Mrs. Nosey considers this.

"That, I can't say. That's for the medical boys to sort out with their blood tests and what-have-you. But so far as I know, nobody saw Mrs. d'Ambrosi yesterday."

I suddenly have an urgent need to get away.

"Well, thank you for your time. I'm sorry, I don't know your name."

"Agatha. And you are?"

"Edward," I reply without pausing. "Just passing through. I'm only in London for a few days. Well, thank you again, Agatha. Awful thing to happen. I'm sure everybody round here must be upset about it."

"Can you imagine what it would be like having an intruder in your house? It makes me shiver. At least I have my Stan in bed with me. Though, if we did have burglars, I expect he'd be hopeless. He'd probably help them carry out the TV set."

I keep my head down and slip away.

* * * * *

The pub is quiet, its interior gloomy. Which is how I want it. Outside, it remains sunny and cloudless – which is out-of-synch with the events of the day thus far. Given the discussion

I've had with one of Ursula's neighbours, the sky should be heavy with threatening black cloud portending the rage of some vengeful storm god. Lightning should be striking church steeples; ferocious winds should be uprooting trees and toppling buildings.

But none of this is happening, except in my head.

My hand trembles slightly as I raise the pint glass to my mouth. My throat is so tight that it's an effort to swallow. The enormity of what has happened only a few streets away from this public house refuge is difficult to absorb.

If old Agatha's account of the break-in is even half accurate, then I've been dropped without warning into the middle of a horror movie.

Ursula is dead. Ursula d'Ambrosi is dead.

But wait. Perhaps she isn't dead after all. Perhaps she's been injured and kidnapped, but is still alive somewhere. Otherwise, why would the perpetrators of this crime have taken her away? Why take the risk – not to mention the difficulty – of dragging off a blood-soaked corpse when they could have simply left her in the house and made a discreet getaway?

This comforting thought doesn't hold up to scrutiny, and swiftly evaporates. I'm clutching at straws. The chances of Ursula being anything other than deceased are miniscule at best. For whatever obscure or perverse reason she has been removed from her home, she can't have been breathing at the time.

I realise how little I know of the HR Manager. She could have been in all sorts of trouble with unsavoury characters, but not told me. And what about her Italian ex-husband, for example?

Might he have mafia or other underworld connections? Might his account of their break-up differ from hers? Did she have dirt on him? Is he the jealous type? Was he having her watched, and her evening out with me tipped him over the edge into violence?

All good questions maybe, but I doubt I'm going to be the one to find the answers. I'm simultaneously too close and too distant from the victim.

Poor Ursula. Christ. Christ Almighty. The nature of her death haunts me. A multiple stabbing. Unspeakable.

Did she put up a fight or was she still drunk (thanks to me)? Did she realise what was happening to her?

It's like a slaughterhouse in her living room, Agatha had said.

I feel sick. Another gulp of beer to take away the dryness in my mouth doesn't help. I go to the toilet and retch.

Back in my chair, I wonder what the hell to do next.

One thing, however, is crystal clear.

I am in trouble. Deep, deep trouble.

I take out my mobile and call Da.

She picks up on the tone of my voice immediately.

"Something's happened, hasn't it?" she asks, concerned.

"Yes."

"Something bad?"

"Yes, but I can't talk about it over the phone. Is there any chance you can get home earlier than usual tonight? I need to run some stuff past you."

"I'll reschedule some appointments. Are you at home now?"

"No, but I'm heading back shortly."

"I'll get away as quickly as I can."

"Thank you."

I leave the rest of my pint and pick up the rucksack containing my tools for tonight's British Museum burglary – which now seems like a trivial piece of lawbreaking by comparison with what has occurred half-a-mile away.

Suddenly, the Ronald Webster investigation feels unimportant.

It's not the railwayman's disappearance but my own well-being which is uppermost in my mind.

* * * * *

Da steps through our front door a few minutes before three.

Since I've been home, I've been pacing the carpet in our living room, brooding and trying to make sense of everything. So far, I've failed.

"What is it, David? What's wrong?" asks my anxious wife as she throws off her coat.

"You might want to sit down first."

She takes me up on my suggestion.

"Well?"

There is no easy introduction to what I have to tell her, so I just come out with it.

"Ursula d'Ambrosi is dead."

"*Dead*? She's dead?"

Da stares at me uncomprehendingly.

"Yes. And not just dead. Murdered."

* * * * *

My wife is both practical and uncommonly unflappable.

After I've blurted out a summary of what happened in Bermondsey, she raises a hand.

"Right," she says. "First, we're going to have a cup of tea and calm down."

"You seem amazingly calm already."

"I'm a good actress. I've been faking my orgasms for years, and you've never noticed.

"Now, listen. The children will be home soon, and there's no reason to burden them with any of this. We're not going to be able to talk about Ms. d'Ambrosi while they're around because they are bound to pick up on the atmosphere. And that would not be good. So, we have to behave as normal as possible. I'll make them something to eat, then you and I will go to that wine bar down the road and talk this through."

"You mean, we leave them on their own? We never do that. They'll be suspicious."

"We'll say that you have a meeting with a key female informer on the Webster case, and that you need me along because she won't talk to you without another woman being present."

"You're one heck of a liar, Da. Impressive."

"I'll give Jenny and Pratcha strict instructions on what they're allowed and not allowed to do while we're out. Just this once. I don't want this to be used by them as a precedent. Agreed?"

"Agreed."

"Good. So, stop moping and slap on your best smile. Right?"

I nod.

"I do have one question, though," I say.

"Oh? What's that?"

"Is it true that you fake orgasms?"

"Practically every time. Now hide that rucksack in case Pratcha gets curious about what's in it. You know how nosey he is."

"I do. And I can't think who he gets it from."

"Shut up, David."

* * * * *

"Do you have a theory about why Ms. d'Ambrosi was killed?" my wife asks.

"To grace my ideas with the title *theory* would be to overstate matters, Da. *A few vague hypotheses* would be a more accurate description of where I'm currently at."

We are in the *Green Bottle* wine bar, tucked away at a corner table. In her usual thorough way, Da has confirmed with me what I actually know about the events in Bermondsey before she allows me to move onto any speculation. I don't know, for instance, what Ursula's time of death was, but I can be certain it occurred after I'd left her on Saturday night, and it almost certainly happened before dawn. The scenario that she was killed while still lying on her sofa during daylight hours on Sunday is barely credible – particularly given the removal of her body.

"Go on, then. Throw your hypotheses at me, and I'll see what I can do to demolish them and give you better ones."

"Well, maybe her ex-husband was behind it."

"You alluded to that earlier, but frankly, my dear, you're not going to get far with that line of inquiry. Next."

"It could be the work of a stalker. Someone who had identified her and knew she lived alone. The fact that I'd been with her that evening might be entirely coincidental, or perhaps he was watching her house and saw us arrive there, realised she was drunk, and took his chance after I'd left."

"That wouldn't explain how he managed to remove the body on his own. Unless he phoned a friend to help him. Which, let's face it, is unlikely."

"Yep, it is. I do have a third notion." I hesitate. "But you might think it's a trifle…" I flail around for the right word before settling on *egocentric*.

Da raises a curious eyebrow. I plunge in regardless.

"Maybe she was killed not because of who she was, but as a way of somebody getting at *me*."

"Yes, you're right, that does sound egocentric, David. But you're going to have to explain. Other than your obvious assumption that the world revolves around you. But there's nothing new there."

"All right, then, reflect on this. In the last few weeks, two of my therapy clients have disappeared without a trace. Statistically speaking, that is extremely unlikely to happen, wouldn't you agree?"

"I suppose so."

"And recently I've had a sense of being followed."

Da gives a start.

"You haven't mentioned that before."

"No, well, considering you packed me off to see a psychiatrist, I didn't want to give you any more ammunition for thinking I was going off my rocker. Plus, I'd largely managed to convince myself that it was paranoia. Though on Saturday evening, I did have that feeling again."

"And have you noticed anyone specific who keeps showing up? Have you been seeing the same face in different parts of London."

"No, I can't honestly say that I have."

"So, this is more of a general feeling that someone might be tailing you? Or that different people are tailing you?"

"Yes, I realise it sounds a bit rubbish, but when you put it together with Anneke Reid and Ben Quinlan going missing – and now Ursula's murder – the connecting factor is *me*."

"Hang on a minute. I need another drink before you go on."

Da waves at a flunkey, and asks him for two more glasses of wine. I'm beginning to wish we'd ordered a bottle to start with; and that we'd had something to eat. It could be a long evening.

We sit in silence while Da mulls over what I've said. Once the new drinks appear, she leans forward.

"Let's assume for a moment that the Anneke and Ben vanishings are a statistical quirk, and that your suspicions about someone following you are the product of a disturbed mind."

"All right. And, by the way, thanks for the vote of confidence in my mental state."

"Be quiet and listen. Could what happened to the d'Ambrosi woman be related to the Webster investigation rather than some vendetta against you?"

"How do you mean?"

"She had information about Webster and Belka breaking into that Tube station, didn't she? Perhaps she had other information on them too, and was saving that for your next date."

"No, I'm pretty sure she told me all there was to tell. And anyway, are you suggesting that RW and Goose did away with her? I can't speak about Webster – who certainly has or had his own dark secrets – but I cannot imagine Goose taking part in a murder and carting away a body."

"Even though he had some involvement with the Angel of Death serial killings some years back?"

"*Some involvement* is exaggerating things, Da. He witnessed one of the murders and had some crackpot notion about how he could find the killer, but that was it."

"So far as you know."

"And what would be gained by their silencing Ursula given that we'd already spoken? No, that won't fly."

"But it doesn't rule out her death being connected to the Webster case."

"But how?"

Da shrugs.

"That I can't tell you. Though it's no more insane than your idea that this is all about *you*."

I drink some wine, and become more entrenched.

"Well, let's view this from the perspective of the Metropolitan Police, shall we? And, specifically, from DCI Zachary's point of view.

"Here's this guy, David Braddock, who has a checkered history and who, in the past, has had various run-ins with the police. He identifies half the dead body of his neighbour, then miraculously discovers the other half in Highgate. Two of his therapy clients disappear, and he starts seeing a shrink because of his mental state. Then, while working on an investigation, he takes the HR Manager of TfL to dinner, plies her with too much alcohol and sees her home. He goes into her house. She is butchered and her corpse removed from the premises.

"It looks like a pattern, wouldn't you say? A man traumatised by various violent experiences while living in Thailand, returns to England, then suddenly snaps. If I were DCI Zachary, I think I could make a case out of that. And, let's face it, I'm not exactly on her list of best friends."

Da is still unimpressed.

"How would the Met even *start* to go about placing you at the centre of all this? Plus, it's all circumstantial evidence."

I snort.

"It's hardly that, my dear. If they've done their job, the forensics team at Ursula's house will have found non-Ursula DNA and fingerprints on my wine glass, the light switch in the living room and on her front door. If and when a public request for information goes out asking for sightings of her on Saturday night, there are plenty of people in the French restaurant and at *The Cistern* bar in Bermondsey who saw her with a man. *And they both looked the worse for drink, officer.*

"Ursula's neighbour Frances might even be able to identify me in a line-up. Then there's my visit to Ursula's office, and phone calls to her mobile which are traceable to my mobile. Her PA also spoke to me. I'm not going to be able to deny my connections to Ursula. And, so far as anyone will be able to tell, I was the last person to see her alive."

Now Da is shocked.

"I – I hadn't thought –"

"No, but I have."

My wife pulls herself together. She's made of stern stuff is our Da.

"But pause a second, David. For your hypothesis to be correct – and not simply mania and coincidence – that would mean that some individual is setting you up. And for someone to go to these lengths would require not merely a dislike of you, but a deep hatred of you. Is there anybody you've pissed off that much? And, if so, then why not just kill you instead of entering into this elaborate scheme of having you locked away for murders you didn't commit? Such a person would have to be psychopathic in the extreme."

"I realise that."

"Then – who?"

I scratch my chin, and say quietly, "There is something that points to a certain individual. Do you recall my telling you that I'd had a visit from a retired copper by the name of Martin Banks?"

"Yes."

"Well, he wouldn't say why he'd come to see me, though he was fishing around for information on my former acquaintance Jim Fosse. You remember Fosse?"

"It's difficult not to."

"I have a feeling in my gut that Fosse, after dropping out of sight, might be active again. Hence the reason for Banks' house call. Fosse would certainly be happy to see something unpleasant happen to me. I did put a bullet in him the last time I saw him in Bangkok. Plus, he has the sort of twisted intelligence to come up with a scheme like this."

"But why would Banks still be interested in Fosse after all these years?"

"That's something I need to get out of him. That, and whatever else he knows about Fosse's current whereabouts and activities. So, after you and I have finished here, I'm going to ring Banks and set up a meeting. And this time, I will extract some info from him. One way or another."

Da takes a large drink from her glass.

"In the meantime, what are you going to do about the police, David? Are you going to report to them what you know about Ursula the night she was killed? That you were with her?"

"It will certainly look better if I step forward voluntarily than if I wait for them to come knocking on our door. But I think I have a bit of time. The plods aren't going to move that fast. And I can plausibly deny that I didn't see the reports of Ursula's death immediately. Between now and then, I need to get my story straight."

"Provided nobody at the crime scene this morning – like that woman Agatha – says she told you what had happened. If the police uncover that lie, they'll start digging for others."

"Yeah, but that's only a small risk."

Da drains her glass, and I drain mine.

"We'd better go home. The kids have been on their own for long enough. I assume that with all this going on, you won't be breaking into the British Museum station later."

"Oh, I'll still be doing that," I reply casually.

"Why?" She asks, appalled. "Forget about Ronald Webster, David. You have more than enough on your plate."

"It will give me something different to mull over. Besides, I doubt I'll be able to sleep tonight, so I might as well push on."

"You're crazy."

"Yes, I think we've already established that. But perhaps I'll make myself a sandwich at home first. That would be sane and sensible, wouldn't it? You should have one too. Soak up that wine."

"It's not a sandwich I want."

"Sorry, Da, but I'm afraid coitus is out of the question. Unless you're awake when I get back."

"You're such a dickhead sometimes."

XXVI

Into the Darkness

When Da and I arrive home, the children are watching a news programme on the TV. Politician Giles Feathercroft still appears to be flavour of the week. He is standing at a podium while his moustache flamboyantly denounces the fecklessness of modern youth. I suppose he's good for ratings, if nothing else. And he does appear to be good for nothing else.

"This guy's a moron," says Pratcha. "If his character featured in my League of Loki game, I'd make sure he was the first one I killed and dragged off to the Underworld."

"Have you two finished your homework?" asks an undeflected Da.

"Yes," they chorus wearily.

I dig out Banks' business card, go upstairs and phone him from our bedroom. I tell him I need to speak to him urgently but remain tight-lipped about why. He grudgingly agrees to see me tomorrow.

Once back downstairs, I make a sandwich and throw together a salad for my wife. She chases the children off to their rooms. They don't seem to have picked up on the underlying tension in the house, which shows what convincingly duplicitous swine Da and I can be when we set our minds to it. We are indeed well matched.

We sit on the sofa while we eat, and I switch the channel to one showing a David Attenborough documentary about endangered monkeys. Neither of us is concentrating on it, however. It's simply a background of moving wallpaper while our thoughts are elsewhere. When that finishes, we find an action movie that we've seen before, and therefore don't have to concentrate too much. We make some unconvincing small-talk, and I put the kettle on for tea, which we consume with rather more enthusiasm than the film.

At quarter-to-eleven, I check the children are asleep before slipping on my coat, scarf and a black woollen bobble-hat, and heaving my rucksack onto my shoulder. I hope I appear suitably anonymous and unmemorable.

"You're still determined to go through with this break-in, then, are you?" says Da in her scolding voice.

"I am."

"Well, don't get caught. You're already in enough trouble."

Then she relents and kisses me.

"I'll be careful," I say. "Don't wait up."

"Do you seriously think I'm going to be able to sleep with everything that's going on?"

To this, I have no answer.

I close the front door quietly behind me.

The night is cloudless. The moon is only a sliver, yet the stars present as muted and remote. Space appears frozen, and the air is chilled, but at least I'm not one of London's homeless unfortunates. There will be quite a few shivering bodies on the streets tonight.

I pull on my gloves and set out for Notting Hill Gate at a brisk stride.

* * * * *

The Central Line is surprisingly busy: a bad omen. If the area around Holborn is still crawling with people when I meet Goose at midnight – assuming he turns up – then we're going to have to amuse ourselves somewhere until it quietens down. And amusing myself in the company of Goose with his manic, joyless energy, isn't a prospect I relish.

Nevertheless, I remain hopeful that that won't be the case. It isn't exactly a night spot, so there's not much for workers to hang around for after their daily toil is done.

I climb the steps at Holborn and surface to the roar of traffic and the snort of double-decker buses carting off passengers to and from Oxford Street and up to King's Cross. Comfort is to be had, however, from the fact that there aren't too many people on the street apart from a few hardy souls hunkered down in doorways in their sleeping bags.

I take the short walk to what remains of British Museum station, and run through in my head what I remember of Webster's history of the place. After its closure in the 1930s, its above-ground building was used as military offices before being converted into retail units. Underground, its eastbound tunnel is reportedly still visible from the Central Line, although you'd be lucky to catch sight of it as you whiz along in the dark. I've certainly not seen it, and that isn't a method of access that I'd be up for trying.

I'm at the site in a couple of minutes.

And there it is, our only way in: large, metal double doors fastened with a substantial padlock. A worn sign reads, *THIS PASSAGE IS FOR LT ACCESS ONLY*. It's on the intersection of two roads: High Holborn and, I guess, Bloomsbury Court. I'm sad to see that the street lighting is in full working order. Why can you never find a vandal when you need one?

Shuttered retail units sit either side of the doors. The windows on the higher floors are all unlit. It doesn't look as if any of the floors have been converted into flats. That makes it a dead zone outside of working hours, but it doesn't stop people passing in cars or on foot. We're going to be rather exposed when we attempt to gain entry. Timing will be crucial.

I check my watch. It's ten-to-midnight. I retire to a nearby shop doorway to wait for Goose, and to force out of my head thoughts of Ursula d'Ambrosi which have crept in over the last few minutes. I set my rucksack down on the ground.

Just breathe.

* * * * *

Midnight comes and goes. Five past twelve. Ten past twelve.

I'm about to give up on Goose when I notice his shambling form heading towards me from the direction of Chancery Lane.

"You're late," I say. "Maybe I should start calling you *the Late Gustaw Belka.*"

"Huh?"

He stares at me as if I've said something extraordinary.

In truth, I'm not that annoyed. It's provided some extra time for the pedestrians to thin out. I'm half-tempted to suggest we walk around the block a few times, and go about our business around one o'clock to reduce the risk further. But it's cold and I've had a long and trying day.

"What do you remember about the time you and Ronald came here?" I ask him.

"It was later," he replies. "Less cars, more deserted."

"That's not what I meant. I meant, what do you remember of your time down in the station? Surely, you've thought about it since our last chat. You must have done."

He furrows his brow.

"No lighting. It was pitch black. We didn't go very far in," he replies.

"But you did go right down into the station, because that's where the policemen found you. That's a fact."

"Ah, right."

I judge that a change of tack might be appropriate. I'll go and root around, then tell him what I've seen and ask him to comment on it. That might be more productive. Plus, I've already decided that he's staying outside to keep watch and alert me if we need to scarper quick. I don't want to be trapped in there with policemen chasing me. Were that to happen, my only escape route would be through the British Museum tunnel onto the Central Line – where I'd likely either be electrocuted or run down by a train before I'd made it to the platform at Holborn.

I pick up my rucksack and indicate for him to follow me.

I watch Goose's expression as we stop in front of the metal doors. There is some apprehension in his eyes, but he remains silent. I tell him I'm going in alone and I want him to shout down the stairs if he is challenged by anyone or if the police show up.

"Understand?"

"Yes."

"Once I've cut through the lock, I'm going to position my rucksack against the door here so that it looks like it's closed and hasn't been interfered with. All you have to do is stand in front of the door and try not to be too suspicious. In fact, don't even stand. Sit on the pavement and pretend you're drunk or trying to figure out where to sleep for the night. Can you do that?"

"Are you sure we have to do this?" he asks.

"Hey, I'm the one who's doing all the work," I blurt out. "And, yes, we *do* have to do this since you can't tell me anything useful."

Goose doesn't reply. He stares at me with that irritating, nobody's-at-home expression.

"You want to help me find Ronald, don't you?" I say as if I'm talking to a five-year-old.

He nods dumbly.

"Then, do as I ask, OK?"

I scan the streets around us. Now is as good a time as any to get cracking. No going back.

I remove the bolt cutters and the flashlight from my rucksack.

A final glance around and I apply the cutters to the padlock.

Damn, this is hard. But the lock falls away. I'm in.

I stuff the cutters back in the rucksack and position it so that it rests against one of the doors. I slip inside, through the squealing rusted gate, into the darkness. Only after I've pulled the second door shut behind me, do I switch on my flashlight.

* * * * *

I'm standing on a rough concrete floor. The structures around me have been divested of anything that might indicate this was once part of a public transport hub. The ceiling is pitted and stained. Dead electrical cables are evident, and any visible metal is eaten with rust: a silent festival of the ferruginous to which no humans have been invited.

To my left and right are unrendered walls separating the ends of the former station lobby from the shops on either side. Ahead of me are stairs which fall away beyond the limit of my torch beam into the inky bowels of the earthworks. I move down the steps gingerly since the last thing I need is a twisted ankle or broken bones.

As I descend, the traffic noise of the street behind me fades, and is replaced by the distant rumble of a Central Line train plying its trade between Holborn and Tottenham Court Road.

I reach the bottom of the stairs and keep going.

Now it's like being in a cave. Ancient spider webs hang between the coarse, grey pillars, like the remnants of some insect apocalypse. If I called out, my voice would echo; but I have no intention of making any noise that I don't need to. I recall reading reports of the spectre of the so-called 'unlucky

377

mummy' from the nearby British Museum. Yes, this is the sort of place to attract hauntings and tales of the supernatural. But I'm no longer concerned about ghosts. I'm way past that.

Another train rumbles by.

I keep moving, and inspecting. Anything which could have been of use here has been stripped and removed. The stone platforms are long gone. The air is stale and noxious. It smells like death down here. I wrap my scarf across my mouth and nose.

I hear a noise to my right, and turn to see a large rat scuttling along by the wall. Rodent droppings lie everywhere in the dust.

I am, in fact, using the dust to navigate my way around. Wherever it has been disturbed, it means that people have been walking through it recently. Wherever it lies thick is of no interest to me. I only want to visit the areas where Webster, Goose and their arresting officers trod. I am following in their footsteps, like the Page in a gothic, unedifying version of Good King Wenceslas.

My flashlight picks out lots of stacked wooden crates. I'm in the unused railway tunnel proper now, and I recall from Webster's notes that TfL uses this area for the storage of spare parts and equipment – presumably metallic, non-perishable stuff. The crates carry numbers on peeling labels, probably logged in an engineering register somewhere. I must be near the adjoining Central Line tunnel. If a train goes by, it's going to sound really loud from here, and I can expect to be met with a blast of displaced air infused with electrical discharge and particulates.

One of the crates – a large one – sits in splendid isolation on the left side of the arching wall. Above it, on the stone carapace is a large splash of whitewash which looks recent, and I remember Ursula telling me that there'd been an issue with graffiti prior to Webster's nocturnal visit. Some lazy employee has used a minimum of effort to obliterate it, and he hasn't done much of a job. I move closer.

Beneath the white, I can make out the trace of a large red circle, and something in the middle of it that I can't identify – dark smudges. Goose had mentioned this circle. Perhaps it's relevant, perhaps it's not.

But – *crates?* I visualise RW's train set. The model crates he'd made. The miniature signs for the ghost stations…

I examine the large crate sitting under the splash of paint. I try to move it. No chance. It's too heavy.

I'd like to peek inside, but it has a padlock on it. I'm going to need the bolt cutters. And that means I'll have to retrace my steps to the door, then trudge all the way back to the tunnel again. Why on Earth didn't I bring the cutters with me in the first place? Stupid, stupid.

And I realise something else. I've come a long way from the door. If Goose were to call a warning to me, I wouldn't hear him from here. My exit might already be blocked by a curious and vigilant policeman.

Bollocks.

I head back the way I came and ascend the stairs cautiously.

The doors are still closed. I open one of them a crack and whisper Goose's name.

There is no reply.

I try again, a little louder. Still nothing.

I poke my head out.

There is no sign of Gustaw Belka.

Then I spot two police officers on foot patrol heading straight towards the building. They're going to notice the rucksack and wonder what it's doing there. They might worry that it's a bomb.

I don't think they've seen me yet, but they will as soon as I break cover. But maybe if I play it cool, it'll be OK.

I open the door and pick up my rucksack as nonchalantly as I can.

The ploy doesn't work.

"Hey, you!" shouts one of the coppers.

I leg it.

* * * * *

My panicked flight takes me in the direction of Russell Square, before I zig-zag left and pass Bloomsbury Square Garden. The edifice of the British Museum looms up to my right, and I stop for a breather. There is no sign of any pursuit behind me. My back hurts from the metal in my rucksack bouncing against it. I open the zipper and stuff the flashlight inside. Then I squat down on the cold pavement while keeping a wary eye open for passers-by. But there aren't any. Nobody in their right mind is going to be viewing the exterior of the British Museum at this time of night.

And, speaking of people who are not in their right mind, there's Goose. He's standing by the pedestrian crossing at the museum's entrance gates, and looking as if he doesn't have a care in the world. I beckon him over, and haul myself to my feet.

A couple of cars drive by, one in each direction. Their drivers pay us no heed.

"Where the hell were you?" I say.

"There were two policemen," he replies.

"I *know* there were two policemen, Goose. You were supposed to warn me."

"But the doors were closed."

This street is too exposed for my liking to have a conversation. More cars have appeared, and so have a few pedestrians. I tell him to follow me, and I lead him around the back of the museum and into a side road bordering Malet Street Gardens, where I take off my rucksack again. My back is definitely bruised and I expect I shall be stiff in the morning.

If I'd thought this through properly, instead of dressing up like a burglar, I should have gone to the station in broad daylight wearing a hard hat and a high-visibility jacket, and carrying a box of tools. That way, nobody would have batted an eyelid. Everyone would have assumed I was a TfL maintenance worker. Oh well, we live and learn. Next time.

"Did you find anything?" Goose asks.

"Well, I certainly didn't find *you*," I reply sullenly.

"I was there for a while."

I ignore this.

"I found crates. And one especially large one. Underneath that graffiti on the wall of the tunnel. That's where you and Ronald went, right?"

A light goes on behind Goose's eyes. It's a tiny light, but a light nonetheless.

"Yes. In the tunnel."

I am no longer in the mood to pussyfoot around with this idiot. Enough is enough. It's time to take off the metaphorical gloves. And to emphasise the point, I take off my actual gloves.

"Tell me about the painting on the wall above the crate. It was a red circle, yes?"

"Yes."

"And was there any image or writing inside the circle? *Think*."

He thinks. Or at least, I think he thinks. Descartes might have a different opinion.

"Black lines," he says eventually. "Spray-painted."

"Like what? A lightning flash or a swastika or letters?"

My prompt to Goose agitates a memory in me, but I don't reveal it to him.

"Like capital letters."

"And the big crate. Did Ronald open it?"

He shakes his head in a definitive *no*.

"There wasn't time before the police found us. Ronald was interested in it, though."

"Was he?"

"Yes. But not as interested in it as he was later. After he'd read the book."

My ears prick up.

"What book?"

"I remember it was red. He showed it to me."

It was red. For fuck's sake.

The book.

"Was the book about the League of Loki?"

"The – what?"

"The League of Loki. LOL. And were they the letters you saw in the middle of the red circle?"

He nods enthusiastically.

"Yes, yes. They were."

At last. We're getting somewhere.

But maybe this prevarication is not Goose's fault. Perhaps some trauma is hindering his recall. It's not that he's being deliberately difficult. He doesn't *want* to remember, it's too painful. The information has to be dragged out of him bit by bit.

I adopt a less aggressive tone.

"What did Ronald tell you about LOL?"

"He said it might be a good twist for his history of the Underground. What he'd been searching for, he said. *To spice it up.*"

I recall Webster's scribbled notes and the excited underlining in Felicity Fennimore's academic tome on the anarchistic group.

What did RW think he'd discovered in the bowels of the abandoned station?

As if reading my thoughts, Goose says, "Drugs."

"Drugs? Are you telling me that Ronald thought some League of Loki cell was using the tunnels in British Museum for storing illegal drugs? Heroin or cocaine? That sort of thing."

A nod.

I rack my over-tired brain. What was it that Professor Fennimore had written in her exposition? That the LOL brand name had been used as a cover by criminal gangs for various nefarious purposes? Words to that effect. And I'm sure she specifically mentioned the distribution of illegal drugs.

"Did you and Ronald ever go back to British Museum station?"

"No. After we got caught there, Ronald said it wasn't a good idea."

"Ah. Disappointing."

"But I do remember him saying that maybe other closed stations were being used for the same thing. He got worked up about that," he adds, as the trickle of memories turns into a flood. "Happy. He was happy."

"Is that why he made those signs for his model train set? Platform signs of some of the ghost stations? And the model crates? And the double tunnel?"

"I don't know about those," Goose replies.

The double tunnel.

"Did you visit any of the other abandoned stations? After you'd been to British Museum?"

The double tunnel. The grassed-over double tunnel.

My companion is suddenly frightened.

"Yes." The word sounds as if it has been dragged out of him.

The above-ground double tunnel. I recall one of the photographs in Webster's research notes. A black and white photograph. I can picture it. And I can picture the label under the photograph.

"*Highgate*," I say. "Was it Highgate?"

Goose's lip quivers.

"Did something bad happen at Highgate? Did something bad happen there to Ronald?"

"We never made it inside."

"You didn't go into the station?"

"It's where I lost myself," he replies.

"What do you mean?"

Silence.

"We have to go to Highgate," I press.

"I can't."

"Look, I can see you're scared, but –"

"Use your gift, Mr. Braddock," he intones solemnly. "You don't need to visit Highgate if you use your gift."

"My –?"

He's talking about my ruddy woo-woo 'aura.' Jeez, just as we were making progress, he goes wonky on me again and starts sounding like Pearl Webster.

"Perhaps I *am* using my gift. How can you be sure the spirits aren't telling me we should go to Highgate?" I reason patiently.

But he won't say any more.

"Goose, listen –"

He turns from me and walks away.

"Goose!"

I see his shoulders hunch and he shakes his head vehemently.

"Goose, wait!"

He starts to run.

I grab my rucksack and chase after him, but he's too quick.

In seconds, he's gone, swallowed by the London streets and the freezing night.

* * * * *

I follow a circuitous route to Tottenham Court Road on the off chance that the police officers who spotted me are in the vicinity.

This, and the remainder of my journey home, gives me time to consider the last two hours.

Could Ronald Webster have been murdered because he uncovered a drug operation? Or *might* have uncovered a drug operation? But how would any criminal gang even know he'd been into British Museum station in the first place?

The only people aside from Goose who were aware of his break-in there would have been the arresting officers and TfL's HR Department.

TfL's HR Department.

Where Ursula d'Ambrosi worked.

Ursula…

Might her death and disappearance be somehow linked to RW's disappearance? And therefore, nothing to do with my notion that the detestable Jim Fosse might be involved?

Are the two cases actually one?

* * * * *

I enter our bedroom as quietly as I can, but Da is awake anyway.

She demands an account of my adventures, which I give her and add in my speculations.

"That's head-spinning, David," she says. "If anything, matters are even more complicated now than they were a few hours ago. Have you decided what you're going to do about the police and your evening with the d'Ambrosi woman?"

"Yes. Tomorrow – today, rather – I'll talk to Banks, see if I can get booked on one of the afternoon guided tours of Highgate Station, and after dark I'll make another visit there."

"You mean you're going breaking in again."

"If I feel the situation warrants it."

Da sighs.

"And on Wednesday, I'll present myself to the police and tell them about Ursula and Saturday night."

"So, you're basically giving yourself a day to crack the Webster and d'Ambrosi cases. Or single case, as it might be."

"Yes. Pretty much. After that, I'm out of ideas, and it's going to have to be somebody else's problem. Or problems. I'll hand over everything I've found out and everything I suspect to the Met. Let them earn their money."

"That sounds like a tall order, considering you don't have a shred of firm evidence on anything."

"Yep, it does, doesn't it?"

"Enough. Come to bed now."

"I thought you'd never ask."

"But have a shower first. You smell like you've been digging in a graveyard."

"Well, metaphorically speaking, I suppose I have."

XXVII

Up the Hill

The kids are hunched over the dining table vigorously attacking breakfast.

Da intercepts me before I reach them.

"Just so you are aware, you woke Jenny when you arrived home last night. She asked me why you were out so late, so I told her you've taken up burglary as a new hobby."

"That's cool," says Pratcha who has been earwigging on the conversation. "Can I come out with you next time, Papa David?"

"No."

"Mama Da wouldn't tell me who you were robbing though," chips in Jenny.

"I wasn't robbing anybody," I reply. "I was gathering evidence."

"Through an illegal break-in," my daughter says.

"I prefer to think of it as an unauthorised access carried out for the common good. But, if you must know, I went down into one of London Underground's ghost stations."

"Ghosts have their own Tube stations?" This from my stepson.

"They're not literally for dead people, no."

"Are you going out again tonight, Dad?"

I turn to Da.

"Do you see what you've started, wife?" I say.

Da shrugs.

"Yes, I am," I continue. "But don't ask me where. Satisfied now?"

But Jenny is not ready to let the topic go.

"Do you have proper burgling equipment?"

"I have a set of bolt cutters, a flashlight, gloves and a scarf which I can wrap around my face for disguise. Oh, yes, and a large sack with the word *SWAG* on it in bold letters."

"Bolt cutters?" says Jenny wrinkling her nose. "That's rather crude and last-century, isn't it?"

"An acetylene torch and gas cylinder wouldn't fit in my rucksack."

"You should have lock-picks," she continues. "Much more elegant and practical. You can keep them in your jacket pocket."

"Lock-picks?"

"Yes. You can borrow mine, if you like." She rummages in her school bag.

"Why do you have lock-picks?"

"In case I lose the key to my bicycle padlock."

"And you know how to use them?"

"I do."

"Did you find that out on YouTube?"

"No, I taught her," chimes in Da. "I've taught Pratcha too."

"And how do *you* know how to unpick a lock, may I ask?"

"Oh, David," she replies with a dismissive wave. "In the property business, my clients often lose keys to sheds or doors or whatever. I've found it useful to be able to get past a lock when that happens. For my job, it's almost an essential skill."

"How come nobody ever told me I was living under the same roof as three professional criminals?"

"Maybe we did and you weren't listening."

My daughter is proffering two thin, curved metal sticks that look like dentist's tools.

Da opens a drawer and throws Jenny a Yale padlock.

"Show him how to do it," my wife says.

Jenny wedges the lock against the table and inserts one of the sticks. She informs me the second stick is called a *Peterson Short Hook*. After some ingenious wiggling, the lock opens.

"Now you try, Dad."

With some coaxing and tuition, I manage to get the thing open. I am nowhere near as expert as my teenage offspring.

"Hang onto my picks for now. You can try them out tonight. Perhaps we can buy you a set of your own for Christmas."

"That would be a fitting present. Though whether they'll allow me to keep them in my prison cell, I rather doubt. And, by the way," I add darkly, "I don't want either of you two gossiping with your school friends about what your father does in his spare time."

They roll their eyes at me as if to say, *Perish the thought.*

Following this exchange, Da shoos the children out of the front door and places a plate of scrambled eggs in front of me.

"Whatever happened to your deep-rooted belief in protecting our kids' innocence for as long as possible, wife of mine? Until yesterday, you were reluctant to leave them unattended in the house for more than five minutes. Are there any other unlawful activities you've been schooling them in?"

"They need to be equipped for living in the real world, David."

"I'm glad we don't live in the US, then," I remark. "Otherwise, you'd have them out in the back garden practicing with semi-automatic rifles."

"Now you're being silly. Will you be here when I get back after work or won't I see you again until the night is half over?"

"I'll probably come home after my tour of Highgate Station. We can all have dinner together before I head off out again."

"Good. That will give the pair of us the chance to run through how your hypotheses have progressed in the meantime. You remember the saying that two heads are better than one."

"Unless you happen to have a conjoined twin who suffers from halitosis."

"Eat your eggs."

* * * * *

Once my Thai nymph has departed for her daily real estate huckstering, I settle down with my notebook to try and arrange my thoughts and to distract me from the twinges in my bruised back.

The page I wrote the other day with the heading *STUFF THAT'S HAPPENED IN THE LAST 3 WEEKS* is already hopelessly out of date. I tear it out of the book and toss it away.

Now a blank page stares at me discouragingly. I close the notebook and set it aside. Let's reflect before we write, shall we?

I consider how I feel about the hypothesis that my old enemy Jim Fosse is behind the disappearance of two of my therapy clients and the death of Ursula d'Ambrosi; and all this has been done to incriminate me, David Braddock. What's my hard evidence for that? An irrational sense that some person or persons might have been following me, and the visit I had from Martin Banks where Fosse was mentioned. When I boil it down, it's pretty flimsy. But I tell myself, perhaps something will coalesce when I've spoken to Banks today. *Perhaps*. And the consequences of this almighty guess being confirmed would be that the Ronald Webster case is entirely unconnected to these events.

Now, how about the notion that the League of Loki or some other criminal organisation is behind the vanishing of Ronald Webster – and then later of Ursula d'Ambrosi?

For this to hold water, RW's declaration to Goose that the crate in the British Museum tunnel was storing illegal drugs would have to be correct. But Ronald, like me, never opened the crate. That was therefore speculation on his part. While desperately seeking a twist for his history of the Underground by rummaging around in ruined stations, he might have seen the (entirely random) LOL graffiti, purchased and read Felicity Fennimore's book, and made an entirely unwarranted leap of logic. If there are no drugs, there is no reason for him to be murdered. And no reason for Ursula to be murdered either.

But supposing his guess was correct. The gang (if they exist) would have to know that Webster knew about the drugs – even though the crate holding the merchandise hadn't been opened. How could that happen? Webster said nothing about the matter to Ursula at his disciplinary interview, and I doubt Goose would have been the cause of any leaked information, even assuming anyone could understand what he burbles about.

And even if the (likely fictitious) gang heard about the British Museum break-in, the simplest thing for them to do would be to quietly remove the drugs to a different location. Job done. No need to kill anybody.

The other implication of this reasoning is that whatever the truth of the matter is, I wasted my time last night. The crate either never had drugs in it, or if it did, they are no longer there. The weight of the damn thing when I tried to move it suggests that it is full of engineering ironmongery, and nothing else.

So, if I want to keep the League of Loki hypothesis running, then I have to assume that Webster and Goose – energised by the potential of their British Museum 'discovery' – took it into their heads to see if there were further stashes of narcotics hidden in other abandoned stations. There *were*, and RW was unlucky enough to be caught by the gang in situ. They then killed him and creatively disposed of his body. How Goose would have managed to escape is a mystery, though it's possible Webster was acting alone on that occasion.

I'm stretching things pretty far now. I'm well into the who-could-have-known-what-about-who-and-when part of the equation. And how would Ursula's death tie into this labyrinthine series of events? Could she have been one of the criminal gang or associated with one of them? Could what she knew about Webster have been pertinent and she talked to the wrong person? And what would have driven the timing of her death, and why was it necessary to remove her body?

Even on my fleeting association with Ursula d'Ambrosi, it is difficult to imagine her being involved in any criminal enterprise. Is the TfL HR Department awash with felons and smugglers?

I have the sneaking suspicion that Ronald Webster, excited by the possibility of a sensational element for his tedious book, joined the dots wrongly. Made two and two equal five. Wanted to believe that something sensational was going on, because that fantasy gave him purpose.

Am I following unwittingly in his erroneous footsteps because it makes my investigation more interesting?

Drugs. Shady criminal gangs. Derelict railway stations at night. The sickening death of an attractive woman in her own home. The plucky private detective (with his idiot sidekick) cutting through the lies and obfuscations…

It's all too melodramatic to be credible, isn't it? Well, *isn't it?* In the cold, harsh light of this bright November morning, my overriding sense is that I have been seduced by a conspiracy tale of my own devising, and that the League of Loki narrative is nothing more than a fantastical, anfractuous path that will ultimately lead to a dead end.

And, like the Jim Fosse hypothesis, it is built on speculation and random events, but on nothing of any substance.

The only pertinent facts I have at my disposal on the Ronald Webster investigation are that Pearl Webster is shagging one of her husband's fellow railway enthusiasts, and that the life insurance claim she is submitting is the second such claim in a suspiciously short period. A betting man, I'm sure, would place his money on Pearl being Ronald's killer, maybe with her fancy man's help.

Always assuming, that is, that RW is actually dead.

I have no evidence that the disappearance of two of my clients, the murder of Ursula, my preoccupation with stalkers, or Martin Banks coming to see me have anything to do with each other, or the missing railwayman.

Is it even going to be worth my while talking to Banks today or visiting Highgate Station?

Regardless, I open my laptop, search for the *Hidden London* website and book a ticket for this afternoon's Highgate tour. I've left it late, but there are still spaces.

Ah, if only real life were like an Agatha Christie story where the detective gathers all the suspects in a book-lined room, and announces the name of the murderer based on nothing more than the virtuosity of his little grey cells. The guilty party bursts into tears, confesses his guilt, and is led away by a couple of dumb policemen. No need for hard proof. No awkward defence barrister pointing out all the evidence against his client is circumstantial. No xenophobic slurs about Belgians with weird moustaches. No delay in the triumph of justice. Let the music swell and roll the credits. (And, by the way, there will be a sequel out next year at all good movie theatres.)

It is at this depressing stage of my cogitations that our front door bell rings.

* * * * *

You know how sometimes when you're almost at the end of your rope, Fate throws you a conciliatory bone? It pats you on the head and says, "There, there, now, things aren't so bad after all, are they?"

Well, that's just happened to me.

For standing on my doorstep is Anneke Reid.

She's lost weight, and isn't wearing goth makeup. She's a bit dazed and drawn, but she's *alive* – and that's the important thing.

"Hello, David."

Her greeting is shy and winsome, and none of her former bravado is evident. I'm at a loss as to how I should react to this unforeseen development. I register that my mouth is hanging open, and promptly close it.

"I suppose you didn't expect to see me this morning," she adds.

I find my voice.

"You could say that, yes. Well, you'd better come in."

I stand aside for her to step into the hall, then close the front door.

We both hover awkwardly.

"I suppose a joint in your garden is out of the question?"

"It most certainly is. Go through to the living room. I'll offer you some tea in a minute, but first I want to give you a bollocking."

"Yeah, I guess I deserve that."

She sits self-consciously on the sofa, and I sit pompous and straight-backed in an armchair. I don't want her to realise how relieved I am to see her. Not yet.

"Are you *very* angry with me?"

"You mean am I annoyed that I've had the police round here virtually accusing me of raping you and then murdering you afterwards? Yes, that did miff me at the time. But I'm over it now, and my family is speaking to me again."

"I'm sorry, David. I didn't intend to cause you any trouble. I didn't think, I —"

"So, who was it that you *did* intend to cause trouble for? Your parents, perhaps?"

I have interrupted her brutally, and am about to launch into a tirade on selfishness, but her crestfallen expression makes me pause. Give the kid a chance, Braddock.

I lean forward and touch her hand. Therapists aren't supposed to do this sort of thing, but luckily, I'm no longer a therapist.

"Anyway," I say in a more conciliatory tone, "you're back now."

This brings tears into her eyes, and when I try to withdraw my hand, she grips it. I detach myself gently, and tell her to take a breath while I put the kettle on.

When I return from the kitchen with a pot of tea, a jug of milk and two mugs, we are both less emotional. I've even brought a plate of digestive biscuits. They always lessen the sting of a difficult situation. Provided you're English, that is.

As I pour, I say, "Tell me what happened, Anneke, in your own words and in your own time."

I pass her a mug.

"I didn't intend to disappear for long. Only a couple of weeks. I wanted my parents to worry a little, and make them reflect on how they were treating me. Unfortunately, it made my grandpa frantic, and obviously resulted in you getting a lot of aggravation too. I'm really, really sorry. I wasn't thinking clearly."

She spoons some sugar into her tea and gives it a stir.

"When did you get back?"

"Yesterday evening. After I'd apologised to my family, I wanted to see you straight after and grovel to you too. That's why I'm here."

"Right."

"My grandpa gave me a right old ear-bashing. There was lots of crying. But we've made up now. At least, I think we have. And though they all tell me they've forgiven me, I expect it's going to be some time before they trust me again. Maybe they never will. Not in the same way as before."

"Where have you been staying?"

"I've been shacked up with a thirty-six-year-old Brazilian DJ called Luiz, whom I met a couple of months ago at a party. We've been living in a squat in Hammersmith. A pretty dingy squat, if I'm being frank. Chaotic. Group shagging sessions and stuff. And most of the people in the house were drug users."

"And you?"

"Only weed. And I only slept with Luiz, in case you were wondering."

"I wasn't."

"Oh."

"And how did Luiz feel about your leaving him and going back to live with your parents?"

"He wasn't in a position to feel anything about it. He died from an accidental heroin overdose two days ago."

This puts a stop to my flippancy.

"Shit. I'm sorry. That must have been awful for you."

"It was. Worse for him, though."

Anneke drinks some of her tea before peeking at me bashfully.

"You know, David, I half-hoped that you might come looking for me. As you're a private detective, and all. I'm sure you'd have checked out that part of London, you being so street-savvy."

I shake my head.

"No, because that would have required me to take a train on the Hammersmith & City Line. And I only ever travel that line if I'm going to Shepherd's Bush Market – which is once in a blue moon. Plus, I'd *never* go to Hammersmith. It's a dump and it's full of dead Brazilian DJs."

Anneke takes this on the chin and peers at me.

"Do you think I might have Daddy issues?"

"I'm certain you have Daddy issues."

"Yeah. Grandpa says I need therapy more than ever now." She hesitates before continuing. "I don't suppose there's any chance of you giving me therapy again, is there?"

"Not a cat in Hell's chance."

She shrugs.

"Well, I thought I'd ask. But if you ever decide to set up a proper office for your PI business, would you consider having me working for you?"

"*What?* Surely, you're going back to school, aren't you?" I say in an attempt to dodge this unanticipated question.

"Only until the summer. I guess I owe my family that. But then I'm keen to go out and find a job. Studying's not for me."

"You might feel differently by next summer. Besides, you're a bright girl. It would be a waste if you jack in your education."

"But *would* you? Consider taking me on, I mean?"

I reach for a safe answer.

"*If* I ever decide to open an office – which is hugely unlikely, given what a heap of steaming crap my current case is – then, I'll consider it. But I'm not promising anything."

"Do you want to talk about your case? I'm a good listener."

"No, I don't. I want you to get out of here. I have work to do."

"OK," she responds cheerily. "But do you forgive me, David? For all the inconvenience I've put you through?"

"Yes, Anneke, I forgive you. Now bugger off."

"Can I at least have a hug before I go?"

"You cannot. I realise I'm an incredibly attractive older man, but it would only give you false hope."

* * * * *

I've barely got Anneke out of the door when my phone rings.

It's Jamie Sykes' dad. He tells me that he's concerned about his son's anxiety levels, and wonders whether there is any possibility that I might agree to see him again as a therapy client.

"I don't like to bother you with this, Mr. Braddock, but Jamie's a complete mess these days," the poor man informs me. "And I don't think his job at *Ackerman's* is doing him any favours. They're all a bunch of wasters and ne'er-do-wells so far as I can make out. I've told him to hand in his notice but he won't. He's worried he won't get another job."

He probably won't, the obnoxious toe rag. But I'm not going to express this opinion to his father. The guy sounds like he's the one who should be seeing a shrink for high anxiety levels. And no wonder: he almost certainly believes that he's the one responsible for his fiasco of a son.

I let him down as apologetically as I can, reflecting that, had I been so inclined this morning, I could have taken on two of my former therapy clients in the space of a few minutes.

And, *Ackerman? Ackerman?* How does that name ring a bell?

No. *NO.* I'm not going to let my monkey mind pull me back into the quicksand of conjecture. I have to refocus on my programme for the day, which shows every sign of being blown off course already.

It is unquestionably good news that Anneke Reid is safe and well, and (I suppose) it's reassuring to be told that Sykes is still hyperventilating. But it does leave my Jim Fosse hypothesis somewhat in tatters – and it wasn't that sturdy to begin with. Now only *one* of my therapy clients is missing, not two of them.

Unless my discussion with Martin Banks delivers something, I'll have to bin the Fosse line of inquiry.

That seems to be how things are going for me at the moment: come up with an idea, become excited, then dump it the next day.

I'm beginning to wish I had Da's structured brain.

Well, any brain other than my own, actually.

* * * * *

I look up at Highgate Hill mournfully.

My back is tight and stiff, and I could do with a good Thai massage. Instead of which I have an uphill walk to the dental premises of my former neighbour, which is where I've arranged my rendezvous with Martin Banks. I turned down his offer of meeting at his house in Belsize Park or at his offices near Euston because I'm keen to have a gander at his orthodontist missus to see what sort of a woman would be foolish enough to marry this dour ex-copper. Also, the rest of my business today is in this part of town, and if I can avoid dragging myself backwards and forwards across London, so much the better. Plus, the fact that Banks was reluctant to meet me at the surgery, made me even more determined to insist on that venue. Bloody-mindedness is a deep character trait of mine.

However, I'm paying for that now with back twinges as I make my slow way up the main street. Maybe I should have borrowed one of Da's corsets. Why not, after all, add transvestitism to my growing charge sheet?

During my Tube journey to Archway, I tried to block out thoughts of the League of Loki, and of Ursula d'Ambrosi, so that I could better concentrate on my waning Jim Fosse hypothesis. But this met with limited success. It's only three days ago that I was dreading my dinner date with Ursula. Now – if it could bring her back – I would happily sign up for another meal.

I'm about fifteen minutes early when I cross the threshold of Devesh Banerjee's former premises.

Behind the reception desk is a bleach-blonde admin girl, whom I'd put at about Anneke Reid's age. Conversing with her is a striking Filipina in a white coat, probably in her mid-forties. She wears glasses which serve to accentuate her Asian cheekbones, and she speaks in the agreeable sing-song voice that I associate with individuals from that part of the world. She is carefully made-up, and her eyes sparkle with intelligence, and perhaps something else. Banks is definitely punching above his weight with this one.

He is also in the reception area, standing guard. He has anticipated that I'd show up ahead of time, and doubtless wants to make sure that any interaction I have with his other half is managed within whatever boundaries he deems appropriate. My reputation, as ever, has preceded me.

He gives me a gruff greeting and introduces me to Mrs. Banks – *Estela*.

She smiles and extends a hand. I take it.

"Ah, the famous Mr. Braddock. Martin has told me a lot about you."

"Nothing good, I expect."

"No, nothing good." She smiles again and Banks twitches uncomfortably. "But thank you anyway for what you did for Devesh. Identifying him, and everything. That must have been unpleasant. I'm sorry I wasn't here. I could have spared you that."

"It's quite all right," I interject smoothly. "And I gather you had your own loss to deal with. A relative's funeral in the Philippines, wasn't it?"

"Yes," she says, letting her smile drop. "My brother."

"Ah, my commiserations."

"Well, Braddock, now that you've met my wife, let's go somewhere more private," Banks says firmly. "Besides, Estela has customers to attend to." He indicates two miserable-looking specimens sitting on chairs at the side of me.

His wife flashes him a hard glance, and I have a glimpse of who wears the trousers in their marriage.

"Don't be so rude, Martin. It's not every day that I meet an old friend of yours. You don't have to drag Mr. Braddock away immediately."

An old friend is hardly an apt description of our relationship, but I let the comment pass. Then to annoy Banks, I say, "Please. Call me *David*."

"David. First name terms already. Good."

She appears to be happy to let her pain-wracked customers suffer for a little longer. She removes her glasses and inspects me intently. Rather too intently for comfort.

"So have you managed to get things back to normal here, Estela?" I ask to end the silence. "I gather there was a lot of vandalism done."

My new best buddy heaves a sigh.

"Unfortunately, Mr. Banerjee considered that investing in computer equipment was a waste of money, so all his client records were in manual folders."

"In this day and age? Really?"

"So, you can imagine how time-consuming it's been to try and make sure all the records were returned to the right folders. In fact, it's been impossible. And some of them were burned. I've largely had to start from scratch." She taps her receptionist's computer screen. "Now, we're doing it the right way. Devesh was a wonderful dentist, but he was lacking in organisational skills."

"Ah. He wasn't terribly meticulous about sorting out his bins either."

Estela Banks slips her glasses back on, and glances at her customers. Her charm has suddenly evaporated, and there is something unsympathetic and calculating about her expression.

"Well, I must return to my work. It's been nice to meet you, David."

"You too."

I am dismissed. She's seen all she needs to see.

Banks shepherds me outside. He seems relieved.

"There's a pub I know not far from here, up the road. We'll go there."

He notices something unnatural in my posture.

"Are you in pain?"

"I hurt my back yesterday."

He mutters something under his breath. It sounds like, *Good*.

* * * * *

Banks and I are installed in a pub near the top of Highgate Hill.

It's one of those places where they have live music in the evenings, only serve craft beer, and don't employ a cleaner.

I'm braced in a wooden-backed chair, and my lumbar region feels the better for it. Two pint glasses sit on the table in front of us. They are filled with what looks like water out of one of London's more rancid canals.

"So, what's all this about?" says Banks coming straight to the point. "And why were you so insistent on our meeting at the surgery?"

"I was interested in seeing your wife."

"Why?"

I steeple my fingers.

"You should understand what it's like when you're in the middle of an investigation. You don't know what's relevant and what isn't until you check it out."

He makes a huffing sound.

"Your wife is an exceedingly attractive lady, by the way. What she's doing with you, I can't imagine."

Banks looks at his watch.

"You said this was important. So, make it quick, Braddock. I have things to do."

The false bonhomie of his visit to my house has dissolved. I'm not *David* any more, but *Braddock*. We're down to brass tacks now.

"All right, then. Here it is. I think I'm being fitted up for two murders. Correction: *at least* two murders."

This momentarily throws him.

"What murders?"

"One of my therapy clients and a manager I've met who works for the London Underground."

"Names?"

"Never mind about their names. Oh, and for your information, the bodies haven't been found."

He snorts.

"So, what makes you think they're even dead? Unless you did it."

"I'm hardly likely to be sitting here with you if I had."

"So, what does any of this have to do with me? Why would I know anything about it – even assuming someone is trying to put you in the frame? You do remember that I'm retired, don't you?" he adds condescendingly.

"Not completely retired," I say.

"What do you mean by that?"

"Well, for instance, you're still interested in Jim Fosse, aren't you? That's the only reason you showed up at my house. It was nothing to do with Banerjee's death. You wanted to see if I knew anything about Fosse that you didn't."

"I was just making conversation, that's all."

"Bullshit."

Banks isn't inclined to say any more. He downs some beer, then folds his arms.

"All right. Cards on the table. I think it's Jim Fosse who's trying to get me stitched up for these murders," I tell him.

My companion maintains his poker face.

"You're going to have to lay more cards on the table than that."

"Oh, am I?"

"As I recall, Braddock, you pretty much refused to say anything about Fosse the last time we spoke. Is there anything you'd like to say regarding him now?"

"*Quid pro quo?* I tell you something and you tell me something?"

"Maybe."

He has me over a barrel and he knows it. Oh, well, here we go. In for a penny, in for a pound.

"After Fosse fled England following the murder of his wife, he faked his own death in Bangkok."

Not a flicker of surprise from Banks.

"Continue."

"And about six years ago, I bumped into him again purely by chance. That was in Manila. For reasons that I'd rather not go into, I persuaded him to assist me in a disagreeable assignment in Bangkok involving some Russian mafiosi."

"You *persuaded* him?"

"Something like that."

Banks stares at me.

"You must have been in a pretty desperate state if you needed to ask Fosse for help. Especially with all the grief he'd given you in England. Talk about making a pact with Lucifer. I presume this project you enlisted him for involved something illegal."

"Highly illegal, yes."

"Which you don't want to talk about."

"Correct."

My companion clicks his tongue.

"And you've had no contact with Fosse since then?"

"No."

"And you have no information as to his whereabouts?"

"No. None."

Banks takes another pull on his beer and weighs up what I've told him. I leave my own glass of swamp water untouched. Since none of my intel on Fosse is recent, it's unlikely any of it is of much use to him.

"What makes you think that Jim Fosse might be behind some attempt to frame you? I realise that you two have a history, but if you haven't seen him for years, why would he want to go after you now?"

"As to the timing, I have no answer. I was rather hoping that you could shed some light on that. But he's the only person I know who hates me enough to come up with such a twisted scheme. Plus, Fosse has a long memory for grudges, and the last time I saw him I put a bullet in his back. But not a fatal one, unfortunately. People don't tend to forgive such a thing lightly."

Banks raises his eyebrows.

"Your last interaction in Bangkok didn't exactly end on a happy note, then?"

"No. But I got a bullet hole of my own. In the chest."

"Show me."

I unbutton my shirt self-consciously and show him. He nods, apparently satisfied.

"Your turn," I say.

"If someone is trying to frame you, it's not Jim Fosse," he announces.

"You seem very sure."

"I am."

"Is that because you're keeping tabs on him? Any why are you so interested in him anyhow? It's not as if you're a police officer any more."

"It's better that you don't know why I'm interested in him."

This ruffles my feathers.

"Better for who? For you or me?"

"For both of us. But Fosse's not your man. You can rest assured that he currently has his hands more than full with his own problems. He won't have the time to get involved in some fantastical scheme of revenge against you."

"And how do you know this, may I ask?"

Banks mimes zipping his lips, and I have to resist the urge to punch him in his smug mouth.

"At least tell me *where* he is. Is he here in the UK?"

A shake of the head.

"Then, where is he?"

Banks stands up and fastens his coat.

"I have to go."

"Surely, you can at least tell me *that*."

He regards me pityingly.

"If you must know, he's in the Philippines."

"Where your wife comes from?"

"We're done here, Braddock."

"But –"

"Forget about Fosse. He's not your concern. And he's not behind those murders either. You're just going to have to take my word for it."

With that, Banks is gone.

I hazard a sip of beer, then spit the revolting stuff back into the glass.

My mobile pings a message to tell me that, due to unforeseen circumstances, the Highgate Station tour will not go ahead this afternoon. I can have a full refund or I can be booked on another tour or whatever.

My world has become full of disappointments and dead ends.

Plus, my back hurts.

XXVIII

End of the Line

I am not discouraged. I refuse to be discouraged.

Indeed, the cancellation of the Highgate Station tour has its bright side.

I had intended to use it to imprint the layout of the site into my head, and to check out the place's buildings by peering through the windows to see if I could spot any crates or boxes, and by examining the walls for LOL graffiti. And these activities are best done during the day: no suspicious torchlight flicking around at night on the open ground where it might be spotted from an upstairs window of a nearby building. Then, I could focus solely on the tunnels when I return later. Thus, was my reasoning.

But I can still do all this without the presence of a tour guide.

All I have to do is find a way in that doesn't require the use of my burgling tools, since I don't have them with me.

I head over to the station, and skirt its perimeter.

It lies on roughly a north-west to south-east axis. The ground level is highest at the end point of each axis (where the tunnels run), so that it appears sunken in the central area by comparison with the surrounding land. The back gardens of houses and two pubs butt against the plot for much of its boundary.

To the approximate north-east, there is a steep footpath separated from the station land by a two-metre-high chain-link fence and a dense bank of trees, untended undergrowth, and bushes in profusion. Towards the bottom of the footpath is a padlocked gate, through which is it possible to get a glimpse of a brick building nestled between the plentiful foliage.

A right turn at the bottom of the footpath leads down into the still-functioning Underground station which lies beneath the abandoned one. It has an unloved, cramped feel to it. I walk straight through, and emerge up some steps at the other side.

Here is a worn road – a cul-de-sac – which time has largely forgotten, and which is officially known as the Highgate Station Car Park. This explains the ticket machine, and the pale blue sign reminding people to *pay*. There is only one battered, stationary car, and no moving ones. Not a popular place to leave your motor, evidently. An arboreally-infested embankment screens this area from the buildings on the higher road beyond. There is not much by way of street lighting, and no CCTV cameras that I can see.

Here, for a length of maybe a hundred metres, the boundary of the car park with the old station comprises pillars with concrete slats interleaved into them. Some of the slats have slipped down. It's not much of a barrier. It's not even enough to discourage a middle-aged man with a bad back from breaking in.

I stand on tiptoe and peer over the wall. My view of the buildings is blocked, but I can just about make out the dark curves of the entrances to the two eastern railway tunnels.

I glance about me. There's nobody around.

I scramble up the barrier, check I won't land on something sharp or otherwise injurious, then drop over. The ground is firm, and crunchy with dead leaves and fallen branches.

I make my way down the embankment of the deep cutting, using the tree trunks as handholds. The grass is long, but flattened in places. It's not going to be much fun coming this way again tonight. I'll have to go slowly.

I reach the bottom of the incline, and have a good look at the tunnels. The stonework surrounding them has been liberally, if inartistically, spray-painted by the bored youth of Highgate. It seems that individuals going by the name of Arnold and Ken like this spot, and there's a phone number for Debbie for anybody who wants a good time. But there's nothing to suggest the League of Loki has ever been here.

Access to each of the tunnels is blocked by high metal railings which have padlocked gates. There is enough space between the bars that the protected bats who have taken up residence here, can fly freely in and out. But humans can't get in. The interiors of the tunnels have further rusted grills, corrugated iron sheeting, peeling doors and lumpy brickwork. The area beyond is pitch black.

If only TfL had told me earlier that they were going to scrub today's sightseeing, I could have brought my equipment with me and avoided a repeat visit, but hey ho.

Well, let's see the rest of the site.

The station buildings are a huge disappointment – not even a sniff of a crate – and there is nothing of note on the abandoned platforms. A shuttered, closed-off set of stairs leads down to the Northern Line beneath. On a board, there's a big, old photograph of the surface station; presumably used by tour guides as a starting point for visitors. The railway tracks have all gone, and the trackbeds are covered with cement. At the end of the platform sits a ventilation shaft. Some graffiti is in evidence, but not much.

Beyond, there is an abundance of luxuriant green growth blocking the west tunnels and no sign of anyone making a pathway through. If there is any illegal activity going on, it must be taking place in the east tunnels.

OK, I've ridden my luck long enough. It's time to get out.

I climb the wall at the same place that I entered. The ground is lower on this side, so it's a bit of a scramble, but I make it up. Some bloke is walking through the car park talking into his mobile phone. He isn't interested in me. I use one of my keys to carve an 'X' on the nearest cement post, to mark the spot for later.

* * * * *

I'm lying in a hot bath on the recommendation of my wife. She's sitting on the bathroom floor beside me. I have draped a flannel over my naughty parts for the sake of modesty, mainly in case one of the children comes in, but also to discourage Da from making any cruel comments on the state of my manhood. My back feels much better.

My partner has been brought up-to-date with the day's happenings.

"Do you believe what Banks said about Jim Fosse?"

"I'm inclined to. I have no idea how or why he's involved with the man, and I'm curious as to what's going on there – but I guess I'm going to be left unenlightened as far as all that is concerned. It's annoying. But Banks is not a bad fellow really, despite being an ex-policeman. If he suspected that Fosse might be the cause of my troubles, I think he'd tell me."

"You're taking a lot on trust, David."

"I'm well aware of that, but I have no choice. Banks is not going to say anything more."

"So that theory is out of the window, then?"

"*Hypothesis*. And, yes, it is."

Da considers.

"You still have nothing concrete on Pearl Webster."

"Nope. Her affair with the Chairman of the Railway Anoraks Society doesn't prove anything."

"And neither do you have anything firm on Ursula d'Ambrosi's murder or Ben Quinlan's disappearance."

"True."

"Except for some vague lead on drug-smuggling which might not be happening."

"Also true."

"And which may or may not have anything to do with Ronald Webster's going missing."

"You've got it. Well played."

"Yet you remain determined to return to Highgate Station tonight, break into the railway tunnels, and have a load of bats shit on your head. Not to mention being attacked by other wildlife, and probably falling over in the dark and breaking an ankle or something."

"Everyone needs a hobby, Da."

"Do you want me to come with you?"

"No. Apart from the question of who would look after the children, it's better if only one of us is savaged by a TB-carrying badger, or some parasite-ridden fox."

She appears dubious.

"I doubt there are badgers."

"With this case, nothing would surprise me. Not even the presence of a mutant crocodile wearing a bow tie."

"Are you going to take a nap before you go out? It's still early."

"Yes, I will. But I'll sleep on the sofa so I don't disturb you when I leave. What have you told the kids about what I'm doing tonight?"

"I told them to mind their own business."

"You're an amazing mother."

* * * * *

I sleep for longer than intended.

It's gone eleven-thirty when I open my eyes. The house is quiet. No matter. It's not like I have to be in Highgate at any particular time. No goggle-eyed Goose is waiting for me. And arguably the later I arrive, the better. Less people around.

Thank goodness that TfL, in their wisdom, started running night trains on the Northern Line a couple of weeks ago. Taking our car or a taxi would make me way too identifiable if things go pear-shaped.

I slip on my shoes, a jumper and a thick jacket – less likely than my long coat to get snagged on branches, thorns, etcetera. I check my rucksack: flashlight and bolt cutters (wrapped in a towel and cushioned with another towel to protect my back). My phone is in my inside jacket pocket, along with Jenny's lock-picks. Wallet and keys. Right. Gloves, scarf and woollen hat. That's all I need.

I'm ready for what will be the last throw of the dice so far as my investigations are concerned.

If nothing useful comes of tonight, all that remains is for me to talk to the Metropolitan Police tomorrow and dump everything I know on them.

Highgate Station really is the end of the line. In every sense.

* * * * *

No alighting at Archway and having to walk all the way up Highgate Hill for me this time.

Tonight – after waiting nearly fifteen minutes for a connecting train at Tottenham Court Road – I disembark my near-empty carriage at Highgate Tube station. The functioning one. Well, functioning after a fashion. Without the presence of people to decorate its platforms and narrow corridors, the place's dinginess presents its unadorned self in its full ingloriousness.

I follow two listless passengers up into the entrance area, and we pass, unspeaking, through the ticket barrier. They turn left, and I turn right. There are no TfL staff in evidence. So far, so good.

I ascend the steps into the car park. It's empty. Even the lone car I saw this afternoon has gone. As anticipated, the exterior lighting is dim and hopelessly inadequate for any purpose except a criminal one. The hum of London is unusually muted, even for this witching time. A solitary vehicle passes unhurried along the top road.

The sky is clear and there's a new moon. Which is to say, no moon. A spot of moonlight washing the ground would have been handy tonight, and would have made my job of navigating through the Highgate wilderness easier. But it's not to be.

I switch off my mobile phone. I doubt that anyone patrols the abandoned station during the hours of darkness, but I'm not taking any risks. For the same reason, I've decided not to use my torch until I'm in the tunnels lest some meddlesome local inhabitant spots a flash of light through the nocturnal vegetation and chooses to phone the cops.

I locate the 'X' on the concrete post, take a final scan of my surroundings, and climb the wall. I remove my rucksack and let the strap dangle from my foot before allowing the bag make the short descent to the ground.

I drop to the earth, and make a good landing.

It's murky under the tree cover. I pick my way carefully through the foliage and down the grassy slope. The occasional brittle branch cracks underfoot, and at one point I hear something scampering away ahead of me.

I reach the tunnels.

There is not much growth overhanging them, so I give my eyes a while to accustom themselves to the slightly-less-gloominess. Now, I can see what I'm doing, more or less. I'll try the right tunnel first.

I set down my rucksack, and take out Jenny's magic sticks. I brace the padlock against the bars of the iron palisade and work the first lock-pick inside the keyhole, then the second. It's more difficult to manage the action wearing gloves, and I'm not so well-practiced as my daughter – in fact, I'm rather ham-fisted. I drop the second pick and have to rummage around on the ground for it. I wipe it on my sleeve and insert it again. More wiggles, but the bloody thing doesn't want to give. I swear under my breath.

Then, just as I'm about to abandon the attempt and reach for my bolt cutters, the lock clicks open. I'm in.

Now, I have a different dilemma.

After my experience at British Museum, I feel I should close the lock again behind me, in the event that some (likely fictitious) patrolling guard finds the gate unsecured and decides to investigate. But what if I can't get the padlock open again? I'll be trapped.

But, wait, I won't necessarily, will I? If the worst comes to the worst, I can use the bolt cutters. Unsubtle, but hey, by that time I'll be past caring about finesse.

Thus reassured, I step into the tunnel and close the lock by slipping my hands through the bars. Only now do I switch on my torch.

Such barriers as exist ahead of me are not problematical. By moving one of the large corrugated sheets slightly, I can slip through into the interior.

I let the flashlight play over the brickwork. The tunnel has a slightly oval shape, and is higher than that of a modern Tube line excavation. This would have been to accommodate the line's old steam-powered trains, I guess, and to give the choking smoke plumes somewhere to go other than into the carriages.

Parts of the arch above me are water-stained, and calcification or some other chemical process has occurred. The train tracks have been removed, but the sleepers remain, as do the clips that would have held the rails in place. These represent a significant tripping hazard, and I keep my flashlight beam pointed down as I try a few tentative steps forward.

My nostrils are immediately assailed by the ammonia-like reek of guano and bat piss.

I stop, fasten my scarf around my face, and direct the torch beam forward. To the left and right, are 'bat bricks' for the various species of flying mammal that roost here. Unused, and possibly broken, bricks sit on the floor. But there is nothing that resembles the crates I saw at British Museum. Nothing substantial that would be suitable for storing an illegal cache of narcotics.

The light disturbs a few of the winged vermin, who flutter around for a while. I stand still until they settle again, then move past the boxes and deeper into the tunnel. It stretches ahead of me, endlessly. Here and there is the odd section of rail which someone couldn't be bothered to remove.

I spot something several yards forward of me, to the left. It looks like sacking or coverings.

As I draw nearer, it becomes apparent that they are tarpaulins, six of them, laid out in a row. And there is something large beneath each one. Something *lumpy*. Something with a vaguely caustic odour.

I raise the corner of the first canvas.

It's a body. It is positioned face-down on a ground-sheet, and the smell I detected is that of quicklime. This has been liberally shovelled over the corpse to disguise the stink of decomposition and to accelerate that process. Judging from the footwear and what I can make out of its attire, it's a man's body.

I take a moment to steady myself before replacing the tarpaulin, and moving on to the next one.

It's another male corpse. So is number three, and number four, and number five.

Number six is a woman. For some reason best known to the perpetrators of this atrocity, not much quicklime has been thrown over her. She has no shoes, and wears what appears to be a smart dress. And then I see something that makes my heart miss a beat. The tip of the index finger on the woman's left hand is missing.

Christ, no.

This lump of rotting meat used to be Ursula d'Ambrosi.

I drop the corner of the tarpaulin, turn away, and dry retch.

As I do so, the torch slips from my grasp. Its bulb smashes on one of the metal rail clips, and I am straightaway plunged into utter darkness.

Leaving aside the bats, I am alone in the black with six cadavers. The alarm that this realisation invokes makes me dizzy, unsteady on my feet. I stumble before reaching into my jacket for my phone.

But, hold on. I am not alone.

Emanating from the tunnel entrance, a murmur of voices reaches me. Now there is a flickering light, and I hear the screech of the metal gate opening. People are coming. How many, I can't tell, but I don't think they are security staff.

I scrabble on the floor but can't locate the now-useless flashlight. It must have rolled away. I'll have to leave it.

Holding my arms in front of me like the blind man that I am, and stepping carefully, I make it to the wall, and start to inch along it to escape from the voices.

But where can I escape to? There is nowhere to hide, and a light beam could pick me out easily. But I keep moving, in the hope that there might be some barrier behind which I can conceal myself.

The sound of a discussion echoes down the tunnel. I count at least three voices, maybe four. They are men's voices, some out-of-breath as if they have been running or are lugging something heavy. East London accents. There is only a single torch beam, however, playing on the uneven floor. I guess that one of the party is leading the way for the others, shining a light at their feet so they don't trip.

Then suddenly, in the Stygian black, I feel out a hiding place. It's a curved recess in the tunnel wall, a niche, one of those places where small pieces of equipment could be left or into which a man might squeeze himself as a last resort if a train were passing through the tunnel and he had no time to get out.

The alcove is shallow, but it's all I've got. I slip off my rucksack the better to press myself into the space against the bricks.

I estimate that I've moved no more than twenty yards from Ursula d'Ambrosi's body; which is where the visitors come to a halt.

Something heavy hits the floor, and more torches are switched on. Their beams flicker over the tunnel ceiling and walls, but my recess remains unilluminated, aphotic, out of the line of fire, at least for now. I make a deliberate effort to slow and quieten my breathing, to keep at bay the rising tide of panic.

This is where my cockiness, my arrogance, my devil-may-care attitude, and my lack of respect for the rules, have brought me. To a secret crypt in the spectral centre of Highgate. To the bowels of the earth. To a place where I might die.

Sometimes you go looking for trouble, and sometimes trouble comes looking for you.

Could one of those quicklime-covered carcasses be the residuum of Ronald Webster? Did he stumble inadvertently across this serial killer theme park, and was this where he met his end – as I might do? Or was he, like Ursula, killed elsewhere and dumped here, to occupy one of the spots in this ghoulish line-up?

But reasoning is for later, assuming there is a later. For now, I must concentrate on survival, or at least making a fight of it. I quietly open my rucksack, take out the bolt cutters, and hold them to my chest.

The killers – for I'm sure that's who they are – are chatting. And I'm certain the *whoomph* I heard a few seconds ago was the sound of a new corpse being dumped on the tunnel floor.

"Right, boys, let's get him lined up. Nice and neat now. Get the wrapping off. Face up for a proper show."

It's the husky voice of someone who smokes too much. And it's commanding, demanding obedience. This must be the leader of the group.

"Give us a minute, Ackers," one of the others replies. "It's all right for you. You haven't had to lug this fat bastard over that wall and all the way down here. I think I've put my back out."

"Oh, stop yer moaning. If runty Sykesy here can manage it, you should be able to. Otherwise, your gym membership's bin wasted."

"Less of the 'runty' if yer don't mind, boss," responds another group member. "But, yeah, I'd like to get this job finished and done with. It's late and I'm sick of havin' to make up stories for my dad about where I've bin and what I've bin doin'."

"Aww, Sykesy, you're worried your old man's gonna give you a hard time, are yer? You are such a pussy."

Sykesy. Ackers. Boss.

Shit. The runty one. I recognise that voice. That irritating, unforgettable whine. That repetitive articulation of the hard-done-by. The sound of disaffected youth. The bleating of

427

someone who believes all their faults can be laid at the door of others.

My former therapy client: Jamie Sykes.

Ackers. That must be his boss at *Ackerman's.* God knows who the other arseholes are.

What was it Sykes' father said to me on the phone the other day? That his son was hanging around with wasters and ne'er-do-wells? Well, he certainly got that right. No wonder his little darling has anxiety: being involved in mass murder must play havoc with the nervous system.

I hear the sounds of activity. They must be moving the body into position.

I risk peeking around the wall of my niche.

There are five of them.

It's not easy to identify Sykes in the inadequate illumination. Lit from below, they are like extras from a low-budget vampire movie. I guess he's the smallest of the group. The other four seem alarmingly bulky.

Ackers is satisfied with the cadaver's positioning. Whatever their unfortunate prey was wrapped in is being stripped away.

"Hey, what's this?" someone says.

A light beam tracks in my direction, and I press myself back into the alcove.

"What?"

Scuffing footsteps.

"It's a torch." A beat. "An' it's broken. I don't remember seein' this before."

"So what?" says an unconcerned Ackers.

"It looks new."

"Don't be a jumpy dick, Boyley. If somebody had been 'ere, and seen these stiffs, don't yer think this place would be crawling with coppers?"

"Maybe Boyley thinks one of the stiffs has been up havin' a walk around and dropped 'is flashlight," another chimes in. "You seein' spirits are yer, Boyley?"

Guffaws of ridicule.

"Hey, maybe we should call Ghostbusters."

'Boyley' – whoever he is – can be no more than a few metres away from my hiding place. If his curiosity persists, and if it brings him forward only a few steps, I'm screwed.

I sense him considering what to do.

If I am discovered, I'm going down swinging. And I'll start by taking Boyley's face off with the bolt cutters. I feel a spurt of adrenaline, and ready myself.

A chorus of ludicrous ghost noises echoes down the tunnel. Boyley's companions are voicing their scorn at his timidity.

This decides him. His torch beam swivels away and he rejoins the group.

"We didn't bring any quicklime," comments Sykes.

"Weren't you listenin', Jamie? We don't need it for this one. No point."

"Ah, yeah."

"Right, who's got the paint bag?" asks Ackers.

I hear the sound of ball bearings being shaken in aerosols, and then the hiss that announces the creation of graffiti. Long bursts, then short bursts.

"Lovely job, boss."

"I haven't finished yet."

More spraying, followed by laughter.

"OK, team," the leader announces. "We're done. Tomorrow, we're all gonna be famous. Though, of course, nobody's gonna know it's *us* who is famous."

"*We'll* know."

"Yeah, we will. Then, we'll have a bit of a break while we work out what our next project's gonna be."

"Our *next project?* What do yer mean, boss?" The voice is that of my former client, and he sounds uneasy.

"Well, we ain't stopping now, Jamie. Surely, you didn't think this was *it*, did yer? No, there's more fun ter be had, me boy. We just gotta put our thinkin' caps on, is all. But it'll have ter be somethin' special ter top this."

"Ah, right."

Slaps of high-fiving.

The group heads back the way it came. The sound of their conversation grows fainter, and the tunnel turns black.

Nausea floods me. My legs begin to shake.

I slide down the wall.

* * * * *

The darkness is absolute, impenetrable. It makes no difference whether my eyelids are open or closed. I am sightless.

And it seems that my other senses are failing me too. Without visual data to provide me with spacial awareness and context, my body's feedback loops are in confusion. Sitting in this shallow vertical grave, I can feel the brickwork at my back and the tunnel floor beneath me, but not much else. The hands that clutch my bolt cutters are numb, the fingers locked into position. I can't move them. I have no control over them. My funk has disabled some of my motor responses.

Is that an insect crawling over my neck or am I imagining it? The void pulls at me silently.

I can't hear my own breathing, though I can detect an elusive, high-pitched resonance in my ears; like the onset of tinnitus.

I fancy I can smell dust, but dust has no aroma, does it?

And now my brain, desperate for input, is creating strange, moving shapes on my retina. Hallucinations, mind-phantoms. But I'm not actually *seeing* anything.

Is this what the state of non-being is like? The Nirvana, the extinction, the annihilation of the self of which the Buddha spoke? Is this how it is to be possessed by death?

I want to scream, but if I do, I fear I will be unable to stop.

Counting in my head gives me something to focus on: the passage of time. *1, 2, 3, 4, 5…*

Each number, I hope, equates to a second. But it could be longer, or shorter, such is the distortion in my racing mind.

Think. Just think.

I need to give the gang enough time to be gone before I stir. They could still be sitting in their vehicle in the car park, smoking and having a can of beer, celebrating a job well done. Or they could have driven straight off. In a van, perhaps?

They must have come in a van: something roomy in which to transport their latest kill. I'll bet it's a white Transit. Why wouldn't it be? Like those unmarked, windowless vehicles they use in Dubai to move bodies around without upsetting the city-dwellers. Anonymous, ubiquitous, something you wouldn't look at twice.

Or maybe they simply stuffed their victim in the boot of a car.

Right at this moment, it doesn't matter. What matters is to stay alert. Not to give in to claustrophobia, to the terror of the abyss.

My count reaches three hundred. That's five minutes, more or less.

It feels as if I've been entombed here for hours, for days.

I can't move yet. Let's give it another sixty seconds, or perhaps a hundred or a hundred and twenty. How long for them to walk back up to the wall and climb over it? Have they had to wait until any late-night Tube passengers have cleared the car park? How long does it take to smoke a cigarette? Five minutes?

My count reaches six hundred. I can't bear to sit here any longer.

With difficulty, I unfasten my fingers from their hold on the cutters and put the implement into the rucksack at my hip.

I remove my mobile from my pocket and switch it on.

At last: light.

I select the torch app. The beam is not terribly strong, but it's strong enough. I can see. I can make out the arch of brick, the sleepers and the grimy floor of the tunnel. I am alive again. I am Lazarus.

I haul myself to my feet, swing the rucksack over my back, and force my legs to move.

As the leader of the group had ordered, the latest victim has been deposited on his back. The plastic wrapping in which they brought him here has been ripped away so that his corpse is on full display. The man's throat has been cut, and his clothes are soaked through with blood. And even though his features are drained of colour and the eyes barely human, the handlebar moustache is unmistakable.

The Right Honourable Giles Feathercroft has met his end; butchered, fittingly enough, by representatives of the very youth he so vigorously insulted.

Some of his blood and other body fluids have leaked through the torn plastic onto the floor, and I notice that I have some of Giles on my boots. I scrape off the muck as best I can onto a sleeper.

Slightly to the side of the corpse, sprayed on the wall of the tunnel, is a large League of Loki symbol in its now-familiar red, white and black. And, next to it, are the words, *FUCK THE SYSTEM*.

I make my way past the other bodies and the bat bricks, through the guano and the dust, to the corrugated iron sheeting at the tunnel mouth. I peer out and listen for the slightest rustling. There is none. All is quiet.

With trembling, inefficient hands, I unpick the lock, and step out into the night air. I leave the gate open behind me and walk slowly up the incline, through the thick grass, towards the boundary wall.

It takes me three attempts before I manage to clamber over it.

The car park is empty.

I phone DCI Zachary.

"What the hell are you doing calling me at this hour of the night, Braddock?"

"You'd better get over to Highgate Station quick," I tell her. "I've found some more dead bodies."

"*Some?* How many?"

"Seven. And I suspect there are others in an engineering crate at British Museum station. Plus, I have a few additional ghost locations you might want to check out."

"Where are you now?"

"In the Highgate Station car park, freezing my nuts off."

While I wait for Zachary and her team to arrive, I call Da.

Because…

Because I have to hear her voice.

Because I need my wife to remind me that there still exists a world that is not all violence and horror.

XXIX

In Limbo

I feel a hand shaking my shoulder, and I open my eyes.

It's Da. I'm at home, in bed.

"I've brought you some tea."

"What time is it?"

"One o'clock. You've been out for about ten hours."

She helps me to sit up.

"How do you feel?"

"Like I've crawled out of a pit, but otherwise OK. Shouldn't you be at work?"

"Never mind about that."

She hands me a mug of tea. I taste it and gag.

"How much sugar did you put in this?"

"Just drink it. Sugar's good for treating shock."

"It's disgusting. It'll give me diabetes."

"I don't care. Drink it, all of it. Then we'll talk."

"It's too hot."

"I can wait."

I do as I'm told. Da holds my free hand and watches me. Concern is etched on her face. When I'm done, I hand her the mug and she sets it down on the bedside table.

"What do you remember of last night, David?" she asks.

"Everything I saw and heard in the tunnel." An involuntary shudder runs through me. "I don't suppose I'm ever going to be able to forget that. Do you know –?"

She nods.

"Seven bodies. What can you recall after that?"

"Calling DCI Zachary from the car park, then ringing you. Then it's a bit of a blur."

Da bites her lip.

"You were gabbling to me over the phone. Virtually incoherent. It was all I could do to get you to tell me where you were. I got into the car and drove over to Highgate straightaway."

"You left the kids in the house on their own?"

I sit bolt upright.

"There wasn't time to mess about with sitters, David," she says crossly. "Don't worry, they're fine. They don't even know anything happened. I told them you were having a lie-in this morning, as you got home late. They're both at school now."

I relax again while Da continues.

"When I arrived at the Highgate Station car park, there were three police cars and an ambulance. You were sitting on the back steps of the ambulance wrapped in one of those silver blankets and holding a cup of coffee. You didn't seem to recognise me, or even be aware of what was happening. One of the paramedics said you were in shock – as if I couldn't see that for myself. You don't remember any of this?"

"No. I have a vague recollection of Zachary's face, and of her lips moving, but I couldn't tell you what she was saying."

Da makes a noise of disgust.

"Yes, I spoke to DCI Zachary. She's a cold-hearted bitch, isn't she?" my wife says savagely.

"I'm glad I'm not the only one who thinks so."

"She told me that when she got there, you were sitting cross-legged on the ground. You kept repeating the same thing over and over again; and you wouldn't – or couldn't – engage her in conversation. *East tunnel, gang of five, Jamie Sykes, Jamie Sykes, Jamie Sykes.* Over and over. *Catatonic*, I believe, was the word she used to describe you. I must say, she could do with some lessons in empathy, the frigid cow. Anyway, that's when she called for an ambulance. Before she sent a couple of her men into the tunnel."

"What else?"

"Zachary asked me why you were at Highgate and I said you were following up a lead on the Ronald Webster disappearance, but that I didn't know any more than that. Then she asked me who Jamie Sykes was, and I told her. I got his number from your phone and she wrote it down."

"I don't recall any of that. And you brought me home?"

"Yes. I wasn't going to leave you with the ambulance crew, and I told them so in no uncertain terms. There may have been some swearing."

"And you undressed me and put me to bed?"

"Yes."

I consider these revelations.

"Well, I don't feel too much the worse for wear now, all things considered."

"See, that sugar's helping your recovery already."

My wife's relief is palpable. I'm functioning, even if I can't currently remember the events in the car park or our drive home. But I'm sure she'll be keeping a close eye on me for the next few days in case I relapse. There might be nightmares and flashbacks to deal with.

"Oh, Zachary gave me her card, by the way," Da adds. "She wants to talk to you when you feel up to it. She even offered to send a car. I told her that *I* would decide when you were ready to answer her questions."

"OK. I'll have a shower, tidy myself up and eat something, then I'll go and talk to Zachary."

"*Today,* David? Are you sure –?"

"Yes. This is urgent stuff, Da, and I'd rather get it over with. I'm fine, don't worry. Or I will be when I'm cleaned up and have some food in my stomach."

"Then, I'll come with you."

"No, you won't. You've done enough."

"But –"

"No *buts*. I'll tell Zachary everything I know and then it'll be over."

"Everything?"

"Well, I'll leave out the irrelevancies. But I've got nothing to hide."

"That sounds dangerously naïve. Whatever happened to my cynical husband? The one who mistrusts authority, especially the police? Are you sure you're not still in shock?"

"I'm fine, I tell you. Then I'd better ring Nang and Katie and fill them in on what's been going on."

"I've already done that this morning. They both send their love."

"Good. What should we say to Jenny and Pratcha?"

"We'll cross that bridge later."

"Right. Would you call Zachary and tell her to send a car for me in an hour? Somehow, I don't fancy travelling to her by Tube today. I'm not eager to set foot in a railway tunnel again just yet."

* * * * *

A police car duly pulls up outside our house.

I climb into the back seat and wish the two uniformed officers in the front a good afternoon.

I'm bringing Ronald Webster's copy of the League of Loki book with me. The notes that RW made in it might be of interest to Zachary. Then again, they might not, since the row of corpses in the Highgate tunnel don't necessarily include our missing railwayman. And until such time as his body is found or he shows up alive, Webster is like a human version of Schrödinger's boxed cat: simultaneously alive and dead.

What I am not carrying is his laptop. I see nothing useful in Pearl Webster's humiliation should the police discover the pornographic material her husband stored there. If the Met asks for it, then I'll hand it over. If not, I won't.

As we drive through the London streets, there is silence in the car. The two officers show no sign of being interested in conversation, not even with each other.

I gaze out of the window and think about Da; about what an amazing person I'm married to. Not many women would put up with the nonsense that I foist on her. She's tough.

Unlike Ursula d'Ambrosi, who appeared tough on the outside, but inside was soft and starved of affection. And now she's dead.

She's dead, and I'm alive.

That's enough of that.

* * * * *

I'm in an interview room sitting opposite Zachary and a muscular police officer of Indian descent. He doesn't look the talkative type. Either that or he's made the mistake previously of interrupting his DCI, and is now worried about doing it again.

Since the interview is being recorded, Zachary is being unusually restrained and polite with me. Protocol requires this behaviour of her, but I know that all the while she is wrestling internally with an unprofessional craving to utter expletives at me and slap me around the face. This serves to cheer me up, and adds a certain poignancy to proceedings.

"How are you feeling, Mr. Braddock?" she asks. "Last night was difficult for you, emotionally upsetting. Traumatising, even. It's very good of you to come in today, but are you sure you are up to having this discussion?"

"Let's get on with it, while it's still fresh in my mind. Plus, I have a few questions for you."

She ignores my last remark.

"I would like you to tell me how you came to be at Highgate Station last night."

"Do you want the long version or the short version?"

"In as much detail as you can. If you're giving me too much, I'll let you know."

I recount at length how I came to be employed as a private investigator by Pearl Webster to find her missing husband, the inquiries I carried out, and the people I spoke to along the way. I explain Webster's passion for trains and how he was assembling a work on the history of the London Underground. I talk for a while about his model railway set, and how some of its recent additions caught my attention.

Then I hand over RW's copy of the League of Loki book and draw Zachary's attention to the comments he had written in it. The DCI has a cursory flick through, then passes it to her colleague.

"We'll hang onto this and read it later, if you don't mind," she says.

"I don't mind. It's not mine."

Zachary flicks through the notes she's made.

"So, if I may summarise, Mr. Braddock, you formed the view that the small station signs that Mr. Webster had made – coupled with his interest in the book you've just given us – were significant in some way to his disappearance."

"Yes. Plus, all the signs were the names of abandoned Tube stations. And I learned from Ms. d'Ambrosi that Webster and a friend of his called Gustaw Belka had been apprehended by the police having broken into one of these stations – British Museum – supposedly while carrying out research for Webster's book."

"Who is this Ms. d'Ambrosi? You haven't mentioned her before."

"She's the HR Manager at TfL, Ronald Webster's employer. I spoke to her with Pearl Webster's permission to see if she might have some pertinent information on the missing man."

"And she told you about this break-in?"

"She did."

"I'm surprised Ms. d'Ambrosi was prepared to disclose that to you. That's confidential employee information."

I don't respond. The whole Ursula thing is tricky for me, and the less I say about her, the better. I am not going to mention that I recognised her body in the tunnel either. That would open up a whole new can of worms.

Zachary looks like she wants to say something else about the TfL Manager, but instead she moves on.

"Tell me about this Gustaw Belka person."

I launch off. And unlike my abbreviated account of Ursula, I hold nothing back.

When I've done, my interrogator says, "So, in pursuit of clues as to Ronald Webster's disappearance, you are telling me that you and Belka broke into British Museum, and that you used a bolt cutter on the padlock to effect an illegal entry."

"I am, yes."

She is unable to hide her satisfaction at this admission.

"And when did you last see Mr. Belka?"

"That night. Monday night."

"He didn't accompany you to Highgate yesterday?"

"No. We didn't part on the best of terms. He was jittery about visiting any more ghost stations. And, to be frank, he was of no real use to me in my investigation. I doubt he'd be of much use in yours."

"Nevertheless, I'd like to talk to him."

I describe to Zachary the exact location of the railway arch where Goose has been sleeping rough, and suggest that she also speak to Janice Marlowe at Tower Bridge Beanz. Janice won't thank me for this, but hopefully it will only put her to a minor inconvenience.

"Let's move on to Highgate. I presume that your going there was in furtherance of your theory about Webster and these ghost stations?"

"Yes."

"You went there alone last night?"

"I did."

"And how did you get into the site?"

"I climbed over the wall."

"No, I mean how did you get into the tunnel?"

"I used a lock-pick."

Another gleam of gratification in the DCI's eyes.

"Not a bolt cutter this time, then? You've become rather skilled at this work very quickly, Mr. Braddock."

It's not a question. My heart sinks. And it's not simply at the thought of my break-in activities being recorded for a possible prosecution later. There is more here at stake than that. No, it's that I'm shortly going to have to relive what happened in the east tunnel.

Zachary seems to sense this, and asks, "Do you need to take a break?"

"No, but I'd like a coffee. Black."

She stops the recording and sends her colleague to fetch me a coffee. She's not completely heartless, I suppose.

"Have you identified any of the bodies yet, Zachary? Aside from Giles Feathercroft, that is."

No reply.

"Have you checked any of the other stations? British Museum, for example?"

"I'm not at liberty to discuss this with you, Braddock."

"At least tell me you've arrested Jamie Sykes."

She looks me in the eye.

"We're talking to him," she says.

The other officer reappears, the recording is restarted, and we continue the interview.

"Mr. Braddock, I have to ask you to tell me what you saw and heard in the tunnel at Highgate. I understand that this will not be a pleasant experience for you, but I am sure you appreciate how important it is."

I take a sip of coffee.

The DCI is right. It's not a pleasant experience.

* * * * *

We're done. Except that we're not done.

"I'm afraid that you're going to have to stay a little longer," Zachary says. "Some of my colleagues from SO15, the Counter Terrorism Command, want to talk to you. If these people you saw in the tunnel were indeed members of a League of Loki cell, it is imperative that we gather as much information as we can. As you're probably aware, there has been an increase in anarchistic and other subversive activity in recent years, and our national security needs to be protected."

"Huh."

"I'm sure they won't keep you any longer than necessary."

Two stony-eyed goons then proceed to go through the whole rigmarole again from scratch. Same questions, same recording, same note-taking, same humourless official tomfoolery.

They don't even offer me a thank you, or an apology that it's taken so long, when they close the door behind them and leave me alone in the room again.

After a few minutes, DCI Zachary reappears.

"You can go now."

"Thanks a lot," I say gruffly.

"We'd appreciate it if you make no mention of what you've seen and heard, and what we've spoken about today. Not to anyone. And especially don't mention the League of Loki. We don't want any copycat behaviour. There are plenty of unhinged minds out there who would love the publicity."

"There are plenty of unhinged minds in *here*, when it comes to that," I grumble.

"I'm serious, Braddock."

"You're always serious, Zachary. And secretive. But you're going to have to release something to the press about Giles Feathercroft. You can't hush up the death of a Member of Parliament."

"That's already been done. There was a live news conference while you were having your discussion with SO15."

"How convenient."

"We'll be in touch if we need to talk to you again."

I ring Da to tell her I'm on my way home.

She sounds relieved.

* * * * *

I've travelled home by Tube. I figured, what the heck, kill or cure. Fortunately, I was too mentally drained to be unduly apprehensive about the experience. Plus, I wasn't up to listening to some cockney cabbie drone on about his latest obsession.

I feel like collapsing in a heap once I'm through the front door. But there is some cheer to be had.

"Hello, stepson."

Nang gives me a rib-crushing hug. She might be old but she's strong.

"I took the train down here this afternoon. I wanted to make sure my family was all right. Are *you* all right, David?"

"I'm always all right. Though encountering killers who turn out to be white and English has been a bit of a shock. I suppose we can expect more of this sort of thing once we leave the European Union. At least you know where you are with the Poles and the Irish."

"You're not going to wind me up about Brexit tonight," Nang replies coolly. "Now, come and let's eat. We've waited for you."

"And just so you are aware, David," chips in my wife, "I've spoken to Jenny and Pratcha about last night. Not all the gory details, but they know you found some dead people in Highgate. They have a million questions."

"Unfortunately, Da, so do I. Zachary wouldn't tell anything, so I have no idea how all this fits together. If anything, I'm more confused than I was yesterday."

"Enough talking shop," says Nang. "Our food's getting cold."

Da forbids the children to quiz me during our meal, deeming the subject inappropriate for a dining table conversation. She also makes it clear to them, that whatever I say is not to leave the room.

"If word gets out, your father will be in a lot of trouble with the authorities. Do you understand? This has to be kept in the family."

They cross their hearts.

As soon as the eating is done, they wade in.

"Were the dead people all men?"

"How were they laid out?"

"Had they all been killed with knives?"

"What was the smell like?"

"Did the murderers take trophies?"

"How many people do you have to bump off to be a serial killer?"

"Was that politician's moustache a *real* one? Because I always thought it was stuck on."

"Where else do you think they've hidden bodies? And how many?"

"Were you scared?"

And (this from Jenny), "How long did it take you to pick the lock?"

Etcetera. The curiosity of the naïve and unafraid.

I sanitise my responses as best I can, and make light of how frightened I was. I do not mention the League of Loki. That's too sensational a revelation for Pratcha to keep from his school friends – whatever he might have promised. After a few minutes, Da calls a halt to the interrogation.

"One more question," our daughter pleads.

"Go on, then."

"Why did they do it, and how did they choose their victims?"

"That's two questions," my wife observes.

"And *I don't know* is the answer to both of them," I say.

Jenny looks dissatisfied with this response.

"Then, you haven't really *solved* the case, have you, Dad? Not properly."

"That's true. Now, it's up to the police to sort out the rest."

"Will the police will use rubber hoses on the suspects or will they waterboard them?" says Pratcha.

"That's enough," my wife cautions. "And the police don't use torture in this country."

"That's the European Union you're thinking of," Nang adds helpfully.

The children are dismissed to their rooms while the grown-ups settle on the sofa to watch the TV news. There's a recording of the press conference which was held while I was being interviewed by SO15.

A high-ranking official – way above Zachary's pay grade – stands at a lectern. He announces in a regretful voice that the body of Sir Giles Feathercroft MP was discovered late last night in Highgate, and that initial inquiries have revealed that there are other bodies at the site.

"It is too early in the investigation to say more at present," he adds, "but we will keep the public informed of progress. In the meantime, our thoughts and prayers are with Sir Giles' family and friends, and we would ask everyone to respect their privacy at this difficult time."

He refuses to take questions. His performance for the cameras has been mealy-mouthed and a not a little disingenuous. He hasn't mentioned the League of Loki – which is only to be expected – but he implied that *the highly efficient police* had found the murder victims, rather than David Braddock Esquire. Not that I want the publicity, quite the reverse. But something rankles about the police taking the credit for my hard work.

The TV screen cuts back to the news anchor who shows us her shocked face and reports that only hours before his body was discovered, Sir Giles gave a speech to a group of prominent industrialists on labour productivity and the cutting of red tape for new businesses.

Some wild-haired, spectacled 'political expert' is wheeled out and asked his views about what has happened and what it might signify.

"It's too soon to speculate as to whether this incident concerns Sir Giles as a private citizen, or whether it might be politically-motivated, *but*…"

He then goes on to speculate regardless, citing the MP's views on Europe, free markets and "his sometimes-controversial statements about the young, the poor and the unfortunate in our society."

The expert concludes by reiterating that this is, "still early, and no doubt more will come out over the next few days."

"All very concerning," says the news anchor vacuously. "And what about the fact that the police have discovered other bodies?"

"Well, we'll have to wait and see how things unfold," declares the wise man.

The TV is turned off.

Before we turn in, I ring Katie to reassure her about my unusual situation.

"You mean your *usual* situation, Dad," she replies. "It would only be unusual for a normal person."

* * * * *

Predictably, I have trouble falling asleep.

Narratives of death swirl around in my unquiet mind. I should be spending more time with Nang: to make the most of her while she's still with us. Perhaps I shouldn't cancel that life insurance policy I've taken out through Titus Kettle: not because Da would need the proceeds, but because the direct debit going through my bank account will serve as a regular reminder to me of life's fragility. Maybe I should review the wording of my will, have a medical check-up, and stop fussing over things that don't matter. Then, there's the issue of Ursula d'Ambrosi's life being cut tragically short – which leads me on to an extended, unresolved meditation on the fundamental loneliness of human existence.

At least I'm no longer talking to Claire. My shrink has well and truly rid me of that habit. I never even thought about her once while I was crouching, petrified in the tunnel. Perhaps I should bring forward my next session with Ogilvy.

What pesters me most of all, however, is that I can't tie up the ends of the Highgate tunnel conundrum. I know what I saw and heard but what does it mean? How do all the pieces fit together? What has been done to whom and why? Is Ronald Webster to be numbered among the dead?

I try to convince myself that it's going to require the considerable resources of the Met to cut through that Gordian knot, and that it is well beyond the capability of a solo PI, working in the dark, to resolve the mystery. *It's still too soon*, as the political sage of the TV news would say.

This line of reasoning unfortunately doesn't provide me with much comfort. If I believed that Zachary would give me any information, I'd call her. But I'm certain she won't. She'll only give me grief.

I decide there's no point in lying in bed staring at the ceiling any longer. I might as well get up. I ease myself carefully out of bed so as not to disturb Da, but it turns out she's awake too. She sits up and puts on the bedside lamp.

"I can't switch my brain off," she tells me.

"Me neither. I'm going downstairs to pour myself a whisky. Do you want one?"

"Yes. Make it a double, no ice."

"Right. I'll be back in a jiffy."

I pull on my robe.

"David."

"Yes?"

"I could have lost you last night," she says in a quiet voice.

"I know, Da."

"You're a very stupid and stubborn man. I don't understand why I love you so much."

* * * * *

The morning brings an unwelcome blow for the Braddock household.

There's been a leak, and my face is back in the news.

The *Daily Fail* leads with *LONDON'S SHERLOCK IS ON THE CASE AGAIN*. It goes on. *It was ace private detective David Braddock who discovered Giles Feathercroft's body, according to a source.*

Wow, that was fast. To make the deadline for this morning's edition, the 'source' must have blabbed yesterday evening, no doubt for a tidy roll of cash in return. Could it have been one of Zachary's officers, or maybe one of the paramedics who attended the scene recognised me from the Banerjee case and decided to make a quick buck? My favourite DCI must be livid.

And naturally, all the online media outlets have picked up on the story. Tomorrow, it will be in all the newspapers.

Once again, the pavement outside our house is packed with journos. Don't these people ever sleep?

After breakfast, Da escorts the children through the crush of newshounds, having first repeated to our offspring that they are to say nothing to anyone.

"No comment," she declares loudly three or four times as she departs for work.

By eleven o'clock, Nang has had enough of being besieged, and suggests we go out for a coffee. I offer to wear a false beard, but she considers this excessive. We run the gauntlet of the mob, who abandon their pursuit when we reach the end of the street.

After we've each downed a cappuccino and a chocolate muffin, I tell my stepmother that I'd like to take a couple of Tube journeys for therapeutic purposes, and she volunteers to accompany me in case I freak out. Fortunately, I don't.

When we get home, we again sadden the hacks with our silence.

Some envelopes addressed to me have been pushed through our letterbox. I leave them on the hall table.

And when I open my laptop, I find that the emails have started too. There are a few from trolls, but most are from would-be-clients imploring me to help them with their problem. There's even a message from Anneke Reid saying that *surely* I have to open a proper detective agency now, and repeating the mantra that she'd like a job if I do. I close the laptop, make a pot of tea for Nang and me, and switch on the television.

There is a live broadcast from the House of Commons. The Home Secretary is on her feet, telling the assembled benches that she has been briefed by the Commissioner of Police of the Metropolis on the situation regarding Sir Giles Feathercroft.

"The Commissioner has assured me that no stone will be left unturned in bringing to justice the perpetrators of this *outrage*," she says to loud cries of support and shouts of, "Hear, hear."

The MPs are clearly wound up by what has happened to one of their own.

I turn off the sound so I won't hear if some politician decides to ask a question about the private investigator whom the media have named as being involved in the discovery of Feathercroft's body. I don't want to hear that.

Nang makes a comment about most elected officials being baying arseholes and we might be better off under a benevolent dictatorship.

I reflect that, unfortunate as the MP's death might be, this will give Theresa May's government some respite from the Tory infighting over Brexit implementation and the ceaseless attacks of the opposition. For a while at least, Parliament has a common cause. The Commissioner of Police, on the other hand, is going to be under considerable pressure. And that means Zachary will be too. What a shame.

* * * * *

Chalky phones me.

"I hope all this publicity hasn't turned your head," he says, "and that you haven't forgotten we're playing at the jazz club tonight. In fact, we've been bumped up to top spot."

"I had forgotten."

"Well, shape up. *Blue Rhythms* think there'll be a big turnout with you being famous and all. So, we can't disappoint the punters, David. Even Noel's up for it, and his leg's still in plaster."

Nang has been eavesdropping. She taps me on the shoulder.

"Hang on a second, Chalky. Yes?"

"You should go," she tells me. "It will take your mind off things."

"I really don't feel like it, Nang."

"You mustn't let your friends down. If you don't go, it will reflect badly on them too. Don't be such a baby."

I turn my attention back to Chalky.

"Apparently, I'm coming," I sigh. "What time is our set?"

* * * * *

Before I leave for my later-than-usual gig, we have a family conference. Jenny and Pratcha have been very popular at school today. They assure me that they've only talked in general terms (whatever that means) about what went on at Highgate. Even some of Da's clients have been badgering her for the inside story of Giles Feathercroft's fate.

The Early Evening News reports that Feathercroft was almost certainly abducted from the location where he was giving his speech. His driver was beaten unconscious in the venue's car park by a gang of men in balaclavas, who proceeded to tie him up and lock him in the boot of his car. Five men in their teens and twenties are understood to be helping the police with their enquiries. Information is dripping out slowly.

"The Met want to make sure they have everything sewn up tight before they make any definitive announcement," I say. "They can't afford any screw-ups. The stakes are too high."

There are interviews with some of Feathercroft's constituents, and a feature on the MP's undistinguished career in politics. Still no mention of LOL.

A separate, more low-key, section of the news states that police officers have been cordoning off some of the abandoned TfL Underground stations, but as yet the Met has made no public announcement on why this is happening. No link to the events in Highgate is suggested.

While I'm in the bedroom changing my clothes for the jazz club, Da joins me and closes the door.

"How are you?" she asks.

"Processing," I reply.

She kisses me on the cheek.

"Be brilliant tonight," she says.

There are still a few journos hanging round outside. I ignore them.

* * * * *

Blue Rhythms is heaving, and we receive an excellent reception for our set. I've hardly picked up my sax recently, but we're doing the same old stuff, so I don't make any glaring mistakes. I am asked for my autograph by several punters, one of whom requests I write *London's Sherlock* in brackets after my name.

It's all rather surreal, but it has driven Ursula d'Ambrosi from my head for a couple of hours. That's something.

On my Tube journey home, I reflect guiltily that, in all my mental turmoil of last night, I didn't once think about Goose. I wonder where he is and whether the police have spoken to him yet. If it weren't for the fact that Zachary might do me for witness tampering or some such, I'd go looking for him tomorrow at the railway arches.

Da is awake when I get upstairs.

"How did it go?"

"It seems that you're married to a rock star," I tell her.

* * * * *

During the night, I wake up sweating from a dream in which I was trapped in a Tube carriage filled with rotting cadavers.

The shine has definitely gone off that particular mode of transport for me. I suspect that I will never again be able to descend into an Underground station without the accompanying thought that the subterranean aspects of the capital conceal death and inhuman crimes; that the walls so plentifully decorated with advertisements and maps of the system also hold back the corpses of London's disremembered dead. I am acutely aware of the darkness that lurks in the tunnels, the transits and the grimy corners. I notice the dust in the air more, and have to fend off a growing sense of claustrophobia. Every time a train comes roaring into the station, my nerves jangle, and my heart sinks at the notion of boarding it. What inconsiderate zombies and malodorous lowlife will accompany me on this journey? The seeping background smell of electrical discharge, piss, sweat and neglect are becoming increasingly difficult to ignore. But I'll have to go on tolerating all this crap since above-ground travel is frustrating, time-consuming and noxious in its own way.

Mind the sodding gap.

* * * * *

Friday morning.

The press corps has left. They must be harassing someone else. I'm no longer making the front pages.

There is a message on my mobile from Pearl Webster. She is cancelling this afternoon's meeting, and says she will be in touch to rearrange. No explanation is offered. I try ringing her back, but there is no answer.

Have the police identified one of the bodies as Ronald's and been round to see her? Or even asked her to identify it? That would be a grisly task considering how long his corpse would have been in the Highgate tunnel and what damage the quicklime would have done to it.

Once again, I have the sensation of being on the outside of events, gazing in.

I receive a call from an unknown number and ignore it. There have been several of these over the last couple of days, and I've declined to take any of them. But this is followed a few minutes later by an SMS from the same number.

It's from Iain Waddle, the CEO of Matchatho Games. He's responding to my email of ages ago to invite Pratcha and me to visit their offices tomorrow morning. I wonder if this sudden urgency has anything to do with the fact that I'm in the news, and he wants to use me for some free publicity before public interest wanes.

I phone him and confirm our attendance at ten o'clock. The CEO has a strong Birmingham accent and sounds like a slimy git.

In the afternoon, I accompany Nang to St. Pancras Station and put her on the train. She is reassured that her family isn't falling apart, so she can return to the Midlands. And, anyway, she'll be back in three weeks to spend the Yuletide with us.

Once I'm home, I go through my inbox of unsolicited emails and send off replies politely refusing whatever it is the senders want. I respond to Anneke Reid by emailing her that I have made no decision about taking premises for my detective agency, but that I'll tell her as and when I do.

Two DHL envelopes arrive, and I add those to the growing pile of unopened correspondence on the hall table. Then I reorganise the fridge to keep me in touch with reality.

In the evening, the news channels have nothing fresh to report on the Feathercroft murder. So-called experts continue to conjecture, but they're flailing around, merely filling screen time.

I inform a delighted Pratcha that he and I are going to Matchatho Games tomorrow. Neither Jenny nor Da feel slighted that they will not be accompanying us on this geeky excursion.

When I casually mention to Da my reply to Anneke Reid's email, she wants to pursue the topic further.

"You should at least consider re-establishing your detective agency business," she says to my astonishment.

"After everything that's happened in the last few weeks? After Highgate? Why in God's name would I want to do that, Da? Do you want me to get murdered?"

"No, of course I don't," she chides. "And the whole Highgate episode upset me a lot, in case you hadn't noticed."

"Then, why?"

"Because at least you've been *engaged* recently, David. Not sitting around the house moping and being bored. Your brain has been working, you've had a project. You've been more alive. We've had more interesting conversations in the last few weeks than we've had in ages. It's been like the old days on Samui."

I don't know how to respond to this. But I don't have to because my wife continues.

"Don't misunderstand me. You need to be selective about which jobs you accept, and don't agree to any that will place you in any physical danger. But I can help you with screening them. I'd probably enjoy that."

"Yes, you probably would," I say. "However, I'd like to remind you that the Ronald Webster investigation didn't look hazardous at the start. It was supposed to be a simple missing person assignment. All legwork and research with little expectation of a positive result. Look how that turned out. Hiding from serial killers."

"That was your own fault."

"*Excuse me?* My own fault?"

"Yes, if you'd behaved like a sane person, you wouldn't have been in that position. You got carried away and took ridiculous risks. Breaking into derelict stations at dead of night indeed."

"Wow."

"I've given this a lot of thought."

"Yes, I can see you have," I grumble none-too-pleasantly.

"But it's my fault too. I should have reined you in, been firmer with you. I shan't make that mistake again."

"Again, *wow*."

Da takes my hand. It's a conciliatory gesture. My indignation withers.

"To be honest with you, wife-of-mine, I'm not sure I'm cut out to be a detective. Not here. Not in England."

"Oh? And why is that?"

"Because it's different to Thailand. Here, it's all forensics and databases. We have a *proper* police force – even if I do give them a hard time. On Samui, when I look back, the police were floundering around as much as I was. Under-resourced, not properly trained, more interested in, shall we say, 'spot fines' than in serious detective work. And most of the cases I investigated were pretty uncomplicated. Straightforward. I wasn't exactly dealing with criminal masterminds, was I?"

"Now you're being unfair to yourself."

"But, am I? You see, I've been thinking too. I've been thinking about what DCI Zachary told me a couple of weeks back, when I was involved in the Devesh Banerjee business. I'm paraphrasing here, but she said that I'm playing at being a detective; that I have no serious method in my work; that I'm sloppy and slapdash; and that, if I do achieve a result, it's because I've tripped over something accidentally. Now, I'm inclined to agree with her. Because that's what actually happened at Highgate: I stumbled over seven corpses."

"You're missing the point, my darling. What sets you apart, what makes you successful as a private investigator, is that you have something that years of police training and experience can never provide."

"Oh, and what's that?"

"Luck."

* * * * *

Saturday.

I escort Pratcha to the games company. The offices are flash, and there are screens everywhere. Some of the workers appear normal while others are decidedly feral and have no idea how to dress. I wonder if they even know it's Saturday.

Waddle is a short, pricky man with a Napoleon complex, though he's pleasant enough to my wide-eyed stepson. After the tour, Pratcha is presented with a complimentary copy of the company's latest product offering which is entitled *Field of Targets*. As expected, I have to pose for publicity photographs.

What sort of a ridiculous name is Matchatho Games anyway?

A burger lunch, then home.

* * * * *

I've just completed a purge of my emails when Da appears in our living room bearing paperwork. She had volunteered to go through the heap of unopened letters that were cluttering up the hall. It's taken her a while.

"Anything interesting, or can we feed the whole lot into the shredder?"

"Most of the cases you've been offered are pretty mundane, but this one appears promising."

She waves a sheet at me which has a heraldic crest at the top.

"Give me a summary."

"You can read it yourself later. But, as a taster, I'd call it *The Case of the Impossible Pen Pal*. I'll leave it in the desk drawer."

I sigh.

"You know, Da, rather than wasting our time on this detective nonsense, maybe we should be doing something more constructive with all the money we have tied up in stocks and shares and funds and stuff. It's not like we're on our uppers."

"What did you have in mind?"

"How about setting you up with your own property agency business? I'm sure most of your clients would come with you."

"Hmmn. Well, I'll have to think about that. It might be too early. Perhaps in a year or two when I'm more established."

"Plus, I could help out."

Da shakes her head.

"Absolutely not, David. No way. You'd be useless. You'd have no empathy with the sort of people I deal with."

* * * * *

Giles Feathercroft has been pushed out of the headlines.

Explosions are today's big news. Two bombs have gone off in Istanbul, and a suicide bomber has killed dozens of soldiers at a barracks in Yemen.

One interesting snippet follows the sensational coverage of the carnage, however.

The charge against Lee Vance for the murder of Devesh Banerjee has been dropped.

"So, you were right about Vance all along," Da says. "See, I told you that you were a good detective."

"No, you said I was a *lucky* detective."

"Same thing."

I'm more flummoxed than ever, but my wife tells me not to worry about it.

After lights out, Da and I make love for the first time since the Highgate incident.

Afterwards she rates my performance as adequate, and tells me not to worry about that either.

* * * * *

Sunday.

The dam of police silence finally breaks, and the evening news is nothing short of sensational.

"Today's top story. Five men have been charged with the murder of Sir Giles Feathercroft," announces the serious-faced news anchorman. "The Deputy Commissioner of London's Metropolitan Police Service announced at a news conference a few minutes ago that, following an exhaustive investigation, five men in their teens and twenties will be prosecuted for the death of the Member of Parliament for Upminster Central."

Five mug shots flash up on the screen.

"William Ackerman, Joseph Boyle, Francis Hare, John Lycett, and Jamie Sykes are all residents of London. Ackerman is understood to be the leader of the group. Four of the men have been charged with a further twelve counts of murder, and the fifth man – Sykes – has been charged with a further three counts."

"Holy shit," says Pratcha.

"Shush," says Jenny.

The anchorman continues.

"The bodies of all but one of the gang's victims were concealed in three abandoned railway stations in the Transport for London network: these being, South Kentish Town, British Museum and Highgate. They have been cordoned off in recent days while the police search was carried out.

"The remains of the other victim, Mr. Devesh Banerjee, were discovered in Highgate itself.

"Charges against Mr. Lee Vance for the murder of Mr. Banerjee were formally dropped yesterday, as was previously reported; although Mr. Vance remains in police custody on charges of possessing child pornography.

"The Deputy Commissioner stated that the bodies of all but one of the gang's victims have been identified, and their families notified accordingly. Details of the victims now follow."

More photographs come up and their names are read out one-at-a-time. I guess the images would have been too small if all thirteen were shown together.

Feathercroft is the first one.

I only recognise three of the others.

Ronald Webster is there. So is Ben Quinlan. And finally, a picture of Ursula d'Ambrosi.

The report cuts to footage of the Deputy Commissioner's press conference. But I can scarcely absorb what is being said. I'm dazed. Da puts her arm around me.

The news anchor quotes the Home Secretary praising the swift, efficient action of the Metropolitan Police.

A couple of MPs are interviewed outside the House of Commons. They seem relieved that now they can return to the business of ripping each other's throats out over how to implement Brexit.

I haven't heard the words 'League of Loki' although the term 'terrorist' was bandied about rather loosely.

Then it's over, and we're onto an update of the casualty figures from yesterday's bombings in Istanbul and Yemen.

Da switches off the television.

"At least we know now," she says.

"Do we, though? And what, exactly, do we know?" I reply.

Four of the dead are connected to me in one way or another. That's one heck of a coincidence. Have I discounted the possible Jim Fosse connection too soon? Was I right to accept Martin Bank's reassurance that Fosse was too engaged in other matters to be interested in me? The news report contained a lot, but not everything. There are still too many unanswered questions for my liking.

"I'm going to phone Pearl Webster."

"David —"

"I shan't be long. She probably won't answer anyway."

I take my mobile into the back garden.

Amazingly, Mrs. W does answer.

"Hello, Mr. Braddock."

She sounds frighteningly calm.

"Mrs. Webster, I don't mean to intrude, but I've just watched the news and —"

"It's all right."

"I'm so sorry for your loss."

"Thank you." There is a brief silence. "Actually, I was expecting you to ring. I apologise for not taking your call on Friday but, well, I'd had the police at the house telling me about what had happened to Ronald, and I wasn't up to talking to anyone. Thank you, by the way, for your help in finding him."

"I, um, right." I struggle to think of what to say next. "I have Ronald's laptop, by the way, which I need to get back to you."

"Are you free tomorrow morning?"

"Well, yes. If you're sure it's not too soon —"

"Life goes on," she says flatly, and I wonder if she's still in shock.

"Yes, I suppose it does."

"Right. I shall expect you tomorrow. Shall we say ten-thirty?"

"Ten-thirty will be fine."

"Good night, then, Mr. Braddock."

"Good night, Mrs. Webster."

XXX

The Living and the Dead

The following morning, I am about to leave the house carrying Ronald Webster' laptop, when my mobile trills. The display tells me the call is from DCI Zachary.

"Hello."

"Braddock? Are you available to see me this afternoon?"

"Straight to the point, as ever. Whatever happened to small talk? A simple 'How are you?' would be sufficient."

"Yes or no?"

"Yes. May I ask what this is about?"

"We'll discuss that later."

She tells me where and when to meet, then hangs up. Her choice of venue is somewhat troubling.

During my walk to the Tube station, I phone Da.

"Do you have a minute?"

"No. Be quick."

"DCI Zachary phoned. She wants to see me this afternoon."

"Did she say why?"

"She didn't. But the fact that we're not meeting at a police station suggests that it's not about charging me."

"Whatever it's about, David, be nice. Don't antagonise Zachary."

* * * * *

I'm sitting in Pearl Webster's lounge. Her husband's laptop is on the sofa beside me.

I've already accepted her offer of tea – provided it's not herbal – and now she reappears bearing a tray.

She is attired entirely in black, and seems to have aged considerably in the short time since I last saw her. Grief can pull you down rapidly, as I remember only too well from when I lost Claire. There is suddenly a gap in the world where a person used to be; a hole torn in the fabric of reality; a space that will hereafter remain forever empty. The Websters may not have been close in recent years, but they must have been once.

She pours out the tea and sits down in an armchair. Her movements appear stiff and slightly uncoordinated.

"Let me say again how sorry I am for your loss, Mrs. Webster."

She acknowledges my sympathy.

"I had read in the newspaper that you were there when Ronald's body was discovered, Mr. Braddock. And the two police officers who came to see me confirmed that you were the person who found the – *site* – and that you identified at least one of the culprits."

"I'm a little surprised they said that to you."

"Well, they knew you were working for me, so they figured they weren't telling me anything I didn't already know, or would soon find out."

"I can't claim too much credit, I'm afraid. I wasn't even aware that one of the bodies was Ronald's until I saw the news yesterday. The police have not been terribly forthcoming."

"That doesn't matter. Your intuition led you to the right place, just as I thought it would the very first time we met."

"Ah, yes. My aura."

To steer her away from this thorny subject, I hand over her husband's laptop.

"You might want to think carefully about what you do with this," I say. "There is certain material on the hard drive that you wouldn't want anyone to see. In fact, the mere possession of this might constitute a criminal offence. Forgive my being so blunt, Mrs. Webster, but I'd advise you to destroy it. After you've copied the folders containing Ronald's manuscript and the accompanying notes, that is."

She regards me steadily. There is no astonishment or denial in her eyes. She *knew* about the child pornography. At the very least she guessed what her husband was up to.

"You're a discreet man, Mr. Braddock."

"I'm not about to add to your troubles."

"Would you wait a minute, please?"

She rises and leaves the room. When she returns, she is holding a cheque made out to me for five thousand pounds.

I can't decide whether I'm more astonished by the gesture, or by the fact that some people are still using cheque books.

"This isn't necessary," I say. "I explained right at the beginning that you would not be charged –"

"Please take it," she insists, and places it in my hand. "It's for your *discretion*. And, besides, I have a large payout coming soon from Ronald's life insurance policy. *Manchester and Edinburgh Assurance* won't be able to prevaricate any longer now that my husband is officially dead. This is my way of saying thank you."

"Well, if you're sure."

I pocket the cheque.

Now that I've done what I needed to do, it's time to leave. I finish my tea and put on my coat.

"By the way, I held a séance here on Saturday," Mrs. W announces. "Only a few close friends. And I spoke to Ronald. He's at peace, and he's happy. I was sure you'd like to know that."

She smiles at my embarrassed silence.

"I realise that you don't believe in the spirits, Mr. Braddock," she says kindly. "But, for your information, the spirits believe in you."

I hope that she and Fred Eggers make a go of it once the dust has settled. I don't think too many people would begrudge her that.

* * * * *

I give a fiver to a homeless woman at Pimlico.

She looks stunned.

I wonder what my shrink Ogilvy is going to make of my new-found compassion for the destitute.

* * * * *

A light drizzle is beginning to fall as I approach the appointed location for my meeting with Zachary. I'm a few minutes late because of an incident at Victoria. And no, it wasn't me having an anxiety attack on the Underground; although an anxiety attack may well occur shortly.

For the place that the good DCI has chosen for our encounter is *The Grapes of Ralph,* the wine bar where I had my first drink with Ursula d'Ambrosi.

I push open the door and step inside.

The place is about half full. Zachary's not here yet. I eye the table where Ursula and I sat, then choose another one.

When the police officer does appear, she doesn't look like a police officer. She is wearing one of those buttonless beige camel coats, a dusty pink blouse, a long brown skirt, and high boots. I can even detect a hint of makeup. Anyone who didn't know better could easily mistake her for a human.

She sits down opposite me, lets her coat fall from her shoulders, and places her clutch bag on the table. She doesn't smile.

"Are you on duty?" I ask.

"It's my day off," she replies curtly.

"Well, I *am* honoured. Seeing me on your day off and getting dressed up for me too. That's awfully flattering."

"I'm not dressed up for you," she says. "And I'm here under protest. My boss ordered me to talk to you, and that's the only reason I'm here. If it was up to me, I'd have you down the station charging you with criminal damage for what you did at British Museum. Plus anything else I could think of."

"I take it, then, that it's not up to you?"

"No, unfortunately not. Higher powers consider it would be petty of us to prosecute you for relatively minor offences in view of the help you've given us." She pronounces the word 'help' with undisguised distaste.

"Is your boss a man?"

"Yes."

"That must rankle. So, is this an official discussion or is it off-the-record? If it's official, I must warn you that it's going to be hard for me to remember you're a copper when you're dressed like that. Are you recording our conversation?"

"No, I'm not. And it's unofficial. I've told you, I'm not on duty. Although I do have a couple of questions to ask you."

"You need some more of my help, then, DCI Zachary?"

This is fun so far. I hope it lasts.

"Can we order some wine, Braddock? Alcohol is the only thing that's going to make my time with you anything like bearable."

I order us two glasses of a reasonable red.

We sit in silence until the wine arrives.

She tastes it and gives an approving nod.

"So, why are we here?" I ask.

"Here?" she says innocently.

"Yes, I mean *here*, in this specific wine bar."

"I'll come onto that in a while," she replies airily. "But first, I want to ask you about crates."

"Crates?"

"Yes. When you rang me from the car park at Highgate Station you said there might be bodies in a crate at British Museum. How did you know that was the case? The particular crate where we found additional bodies hadn't been opened. What made you think there were bodies in it? Did you smell something off when you were there? And, if so, why didn't you report it straightaway?"

I shrug.

"No, none of that. It was merely a hunch based on what I'd witnessed in the Highgate tunnel. And I wasn't being particularly rational at the time, if you recall. Anyway, I was following Webster's clues. And as I told you when you interviewed me, he didn't think there were bodies in the crate at British Museum. He thought there were illegal drugs. And he suspected there might be drugs at Highgate and elsewhere too."

"And you learned this from whom? Pearl Webster?"

"No, it was Goose – Gustaw Belka – who said that Ronald had mentioned the possibility of there being drugs. Have you spoken to Goose, by the way?"

My companion leans forward.

"Now," she says, "I want to ask you about Belka –"

"*No*," I interrupt firmly. "It's about time you told *me* something. Like what is going on and how all this stuff is connected."

Zachary raises an eyebrow.

"You mean that your mega-detective brain hasn't figured it all out yet?" she remarks with heavy sarcasm.

"No, it hasn't. Spit it out. Go on. Your boss told you to talk to me, so talk."

I sit back, take a gulp of wine, and wait.

Zachary, however, isn't to be drawn so easily.

"Tell me what you *think* you know first," she purrs unpleasantly. "Even you must have picked up something from the TV news."

Cat and mouse. The damn woman.

"All right, if you insist.

"I think this group of five young thugs killed people for kicks; because they wanted to be famous as the mass killers who were never caught. I think they used the League of Loki logo at their grave sites not because they had any political beliefs, but because it would help to sensationalise the whole thing. Murdering Giles Feathercroft was to be the icing on the cake. That would make LOL appear to be a real terrorist organisation, and it would create fear that there may be other anarchist cells who were up to the same thing – or who were about to do the same thing."

I look into Zachary's eyes. She is studying me closely.

"How am I doing so far?"

"Not bad. Continue."

"I'm puzzled about the Devesh Banerjee killing, though. You've dropped the murder charge against Lee Vance, and four of the group are being done for that murder too. But the method by which the dentist was dispatched doesn't tie in with the LOL gang's usual modus operandi. Why wasn't his body left in a deserted station, and why was he tortured and cut in half?"

"You don't know?" Zachary grins evilly.

"I know that I was right about Vance not killing Banerjee, and that you were wrong," I say.

This ruffles her a tad.

"Statistically speaking, even an idiot will be right some of the time," she mutters.

"Plus, how did the gang choose their victims?" I press. "It's understandable that they topped Feathercroft, but what about the others? Was it entirely random? And where did they get the idea to use the ghost stations? That requires some insider knowledge, I'd say."

"All right, let me put you out of your misery — or rather out of *my* misery."

She indicates to the waiter that she wants a top-up, and he obliges. I've hardly touched my wine.

"This conversation hasn't taken place, Braddock, understand?"

"I understand."

"We especially want to keep any references to the League of Loki out of the public eye for as long as possible. You can guess why. Though it's inevitable that it will come out at the trial."

"Yes, yes. Get on with it."

"As to how they chose their victims, it was random to begin with. But that changed.

"I should explain at this point that Sykes joined the group later, after Banerjee's death. The initial gang comprised the leader Ackerman and three of his former school friends Boyle, Hare and Lycett: a right bunch of delinquents, all of whom had criminal records. Sykes was only involved in the last three murders.

"Lycett's cousin works for Transport for London, by the way, and it was he who drew his relative's attention to the existence of the abandoned railway stations. Innocently, I might add. He has nothing to do with any of these killings."

"I don't suppose this cousin is a member of the Clapham Junction Locomotive Club, by any chance? If so, I might have met him."

"I have no idea. It that relevant?"

"Probably not."

"Well, this is where we come on to how Banerjee fits in. And the first thing you need to understand is that William Ackerman is the nephew of Lee Vance."

I rummage around in my memory box.

"Yes. Ackerman, *Ackerman*. Didn't he give an interview to one of the papers about Vance having a violent temper at the time his uncle was charged? Runs a building firm out of Walthamstow?"

"Correct. And Sykes works for him. Now stop interrupting, or we'll lose the thread."

"Sorry."

"Anyway, Ackerman hates his uncle. Absolutely loathes him. He claims that Vance sexually abused him when he was a child, and that he's been stewing about it for years.

"Once Ackerman had a few LOL killings under his belt, and had grown in confidence as to his slaughtering abilities, he decided it was time to pay back Vance for what he'd done to him. But he was worried that topping Vance and treating him like the other LOL victims might have led a trail back to Ackerman himself, so he decided instead to fit up his uncle for murder.

"Devesh Banerjee's running over Vance's dog had made the local paper, which gave Ackerman a different route to revenge. If Banerjee were to be murdered, Vance would be an obvious suspect, especially if the dentist was killed in a frenzied attack to make the incident look personal. The victim's lower half was left on Jessop's allotment in an attempt to tie Vance to his pedophile friend and supposed helper. Unfortunately for Ackerman, Jessop had an alibi for the night of the murder."

"And as I told you at the time, DCI, Banerjee's killing couldn't possibly have been carried out by a person acting alone. Though that didn't stop you from going ahead and charging Vance."

Zachary ignores this, and continues.

"Ackerman and his group broke into Vance's white Transit van and left traces of Banerjee's blood there, which they knew would be picked up by police forensics once the finger had been pointed. Incidentally, Ackerman also owns an unmarked white Transit, and whenever the LOL gang were out on their deadly business, they'd switch the numberplates. The fake numberplates they used were the same letters and numbers as on Vance's van. Ackerman seems to think this was funny."

"And you learned all this from confessions? I'd guess that Jamie Sykes broke pretty quickly under questioning, and dumped his friends in it in the hope of more lenient treatment for himself?"

"Yes. He really is a gutless little shit, isn't he? I bet you enjoyed giving him therapy sessions."

"Not so much."

"In fact, every one of the gang caved in as soon as they realised that Sykes had shopped them. Ackerman was quite proud of what they'd done, boastful even. We have a full set of confessions in gut-wrenching detail. It's pretty watertight now, I'd say."

I take a moment to process this.

"You said that the victims were chosen randomly *to begin with*. What did you mean by that?"

"Webster's death wasn't random. The group discovered him nosing around in the tunnel at Highgate. He'd seen too much and they killed him then and there."

Zachary pauses dramatically.

"And this is where you come into the story, Braddock."

"*Me?* How?"

"I told you that Sykes officially joined the gang after Banerjee's murder."

"Yes. What of it?"

"Well, once he was made aware of what had gone on, it was important to Ackerman that Sykes 'get his hands dirty' like the rest of them. So, part of the price of his admission was that Sykes was to be made responsible for selecting their next couple of victims – and, unsurprisingly, taking part in the butchery itself.

"Sykes decided it would be fun to pick people associated with *you*. Apparently, he didn't enjoy having you as a therapist. He considered you arrogant and patronising. I can see where he was coming from."

I say nothing.

"His initial idea was to kill you or a member of your family. But then he thought that choosing a couple of your clients might be less risky and more interesting. It might even result in your being arrested at some stage, or at a minimum it would make your life uncomfortable.

"Anneke Reid was his first choice, but then she ran away from home, so that spoiled that."

"She was saved from death by shacking up with a Brazilian DJ in Hammersmith, then?"

"Evidently. So, they moved on to Ben Quinlan."

I remember my suspicions of recent weeks about being tailed.

"Were they following me?"

"Off-and-on, yes. To see who you were associating with. Once you'd shut down your therapy practice, they needed to find someone else you were talking to. And that's how Ursula d'Ambrosi came to die."

What if I hadn't met Ursula that night or one of them hadn't followed me? Would they then have murdered Da? Or Jenny? Or Pratcha?

Zachary gives me a minute.

I down my wine and order another.

There was no Jim Fosse Grand Master Plan for my ruination. But there was a minor plan drawn up by homicidal gorillas. I wasn't entirely off the mark.

The DCI plays with her glass.

"Braddock, I know that you were in Bermondsey the night that Ursula d'Ambrosi was killed. One of the LOL gang was following you and told us. One of our men was also tailing you before you managed to lose him. And I'm pretty sure the fingerprints we found at Ms. d'Ambrosi's house are yours."

"The Met has been following me too?" I cry. "Why?"

"Because your behaviour over the last month has been highly suspicious, not to say erratic. First, your finding Banerjee's legs, and pestering me about Vance's supposed innocence. Then the disappearance of your therapy clients. Oh, yes, we talk to each other in the Metropolitan Police. We're not so dumb as you might suppose. You'd be amazed how often your name crops up in conversation."

The penny drops.

"So that's why you wanted to meet here, in this wine bar. One of your goons followed me here when I met with Ursula d'Ambrosi."

A smug smile from my companion.

"That's right."

"You've been trying to come up with a reason to arrest me."

She doesn't deny it.

"However, that's all history now. Though I did want to warn you that, despite the confessions from the League of Loki lot, it might still be necessary to call you as a witness at their trial. And, I'm afraid, it might all have to come out that you wined and dined Ms. d'Ambrosi – which, I'm sure, may be distressing for your wife to hear –"

"Nice try, Zachary," I interject. "But for your information, my wife knows about my seeing Ursula d'Ambrosi. When and where, what we talked about, what we did, everything, in detail. We happen to have an honest and transparent marriage, which is something you probably can't imagine. So, my giving evidence will not be a problem for me or for my wife."

She looks disappointed, and is at a momentary loss for words. Her attempt to make me wriggle with discomfort has been unsuccessful. Too bad.

"You said you wanted to ask me about Gustaw Belka," I prompt. "Have you spoken to him?"

"No. As a matter of fact, we haven't been able to find him. We checked with that woman at the coffee shop, but he hadn't been in. Then we visited the railway arches and quizzed the men that were living rough there, but they all denied knowing Belka or even having seen him."

"I assume you sent uniformed policeman?"

"Yes."

"Then, it's hardly surprising they weren't helpful. The Met are not exactly their best friends."

"When two of our officers went to notify Pearl Webster that her husband's body had been found, they asked her whether she could shed any lights on Belka's whereabouts, but she couldn't."

"Well, I could have told you Mrs. W wouldn't be able to help you there. She knows bugger all about Goose."

"She did say, however, that Belka and her husband had the same dentist: Devesh Banerjee. Did you know that?"

I shrug.

"I didn't, but so what? Is it relevant?"

"No, but it's a strange coincidence, don't you think?"

"Coincidences do happen, Zachary. Not everything is the workings of karma. And anyway, do you really need to talk to Goose? It sounds like – with the gang's confessions – you already have all you need. Why not leave the homeless madman alone?"

The DCI chooses her next words carefully.

"It's to do with the body we haven't been able to identify. We thought Belka might be able to shed some light on who he is."

"Why would Belka of all people be able to do that? Didn't you say that the victims before Ronald Webster were selected at random?"

"This was the person that was killed *with* Ronald Webster."

"Now I'm confused. Webster was murdered because he stumbled on the Highgate tunnel while the thugs were there, right?"

"Yes. But according to the gang members, he had a young man with him. They killed him too. *He* is the unidentified corpse."

"So, you want to speak to Goose to see if he can tell you who else Ronald Webster might have been taking with him on his nighttime sorties?"

"Correct. Pearl Webster couldn't suggest anyone."

Zachary hesitates.

"I don't suppose –" she begins.

"What?"

"I don't suppose that during your investigation into Webster's disappearance, you came across a name? Anyone that might have befriended Webster, shared the same interest in the London Underground or whatever? Anyone at all?"

"Are you asking for my *help*, Zachary?" I ask, amused. "The assistance of a – how did you put it? – bumbling amateur sleuth?"

She replies through gritted teeth.

"Yes."

"You've got some brass balls; I'll give you that. Especially after pulling this stunt by meeting me here and trying to land me in trouble with my wife."

I consider her question.

Nobody springs to mind. None of the railway anoraks. Webster was a loner. Arguably, Goose was his only friend. Unless, of course, RW's unhealthy obsession with children led him into communication with other pedophiles. But I found no evidence of that on his laptop. And if the unidentified cadaver *is* a dead pedo, so much the better. Whatever the case, I'm not going to mention this aspect of my investigation to the Met. Pearl Webster deserves my discretion. After all, she's paid me for it.

"No," I reply. "I didn't come across anyone who would fit that bill. I don't have a name for you. Can't you identify the John Doe the way you identified the others?"

My companion snorts.

"You make it sound easy, Braddock. It's not. It's taken a large dedicated team, and a variety of methods, to be able to work out who the remains were. Some had been dead for a while, remember. The use of quicklime had accelerated decay. Some had ID or partial ID still on them. We've had to work with police records, medical records, dental records, anything we could use. Given the state of the corpses, we didn't want family members to have to see them – even assuming they would have been able to recognise what was left of their loved one. Only Giles Feathercroft's wife took part in a formal identification."

"I suppose it helped that Feathercroft was one of the victims. The Commissioner must have been throwing resources at this like confetti to keep the politicos and media off his back."

Zachary pulls a face.

"Don't flatter yourself, by the way, Braddock, that we only found the bodies because of you. All you did was accelerate their discovery by a few hours – a day, at most."

"Oh, and how's that?"

"Because in the morning, an envelope was delivered anonymously to New Scotland Yard, addressed to the Commissioner. It contained a manifesto for the League of Loki, listing the grievances of the 'ignored majority,' railing against the establishment, and saying that the death of Sir Giles Feathercroft was 'only the beginning.' It disclosed the locations of the dead, and proclaimed that 'anarchy is the only true way,' and that society had first to be destroyed before anything useful could be achieved. The usual ideological ranting to justify murder, in other words.

"This document had been produced by Ackerman and was dropped off before he knew that we'd picked up Sykes.

"So, you see, your little jaunt to Highgate wasn't as important as you might suppose."

I'm not having this.

"That's all as maybe," I tell her. "But without me pointing you in the direction of Jamie Sykes, all you'd have at this stage is a pile of bodies, the Commissioner breathing down your neck, and a whole lot of plods on overtime. The Met owes me big time."

"You are such a pompous prick, Braddock," the DCI responds with undisguised contempt. "Don't ever kid yourself that you're a detective."

I smile at her benignly.

"You know, Zachary, if you weren't so obsessed with being more macho than your male colleagues; and if you could discover your femininity on occasion; then you might be able to have a relationship with a fellow human, instead of having to rely on your cat for affection."

"What makes you think I have a cat?" she growls back.

"Well, I couldn't help but notice the cat hairs on the front of your skirt when you came in. Something furry had been sitting on your lap. And if I were to hazard a guess, I'd say it was a long-haired Persian. Am I close?"

Zachary doesn't trust herself to answer. She's only just controlling her temper.

I continue with, "You see, I might not wear a police uniform, but I do have certain intuitive and observational skills which some of your lot could learn from."

"One of these days, Braddock, you'll step so far over the line that you won't be able to go back. And I'll be there to nab you when you do."

As she declaims this, she stands, pulls her coat over her shoulders, and picks up her clutch bag. I, meanwhile, have taken out her card and am studying it.

"Oh, I don't think so," I say with equanimity. "You're smart, but you're not *that* smart, Zachary." I indicate what is written on her card. "Or perhaps, as we're such old friends now, I should call you *Amelia? A-m-e-l-i-a.* Such a pretty name."

Finally, Zachary snaps.

"Don't you ever call me *Amelia*," she shouts angrily. "Don't you fucking well dare."

She turns on her heel and stomps angrily out of the wine bar.

The heads of curious patrons are turned in my direction.

I spread my arms in resignation, and tell them, "I guess that's the end of that romance."

In the last few hours, I've received a cheque for five grand from Pearl Webster, learned the full story of the LOL murders, and managed to piss off DCI Zachary.

All in all, it's been a pretty good day.

* * * * *

Now that the events leading up to my grievous experience at Highgate Station have been clarified, my brain settles down, as does life in the Braddock household. Case closed.

I don't expect ever to see the elusive Gustaw Belka again, but in fact I do, and in the most unexpected of circumstances.

On the foggy Saturday following my meeting with Zachary, the kids and I find ourselves in Highgate. They have developed an unhealthy fascination with my work, and want to visit the place where the top half of our former neighbour's body was discovered. They have also expressed a desire to experience the gothic horrors of Highgate Cemetery first hand – though I envisage it will lead to a few sleepless nights for them once they've processed the sobering nature of mortality.

Da is not keen on this kind of macabre outing, so she has gone Christmas shopping instead and left us to it.

As Jenny, Pratcha and I are walking up Highgate Hill, I am surprised to see Goose standing on the pavement outside Estela Banks' dental surgery. He is engrossed in something, but as we get nearer, he starts off up the slope and I lose sight of him.

I show the children the place where Banerjee's torso was found, then buy tickets for us to enter the eastern section of the cemetery.

But while we are strolling near Karl Marx's grave, I catch sight of Goose again through the trees. He's on one of the narrow, minor paths, and seems oblivious to everything around him. I call out, but he doesn't hear me.

I tell Jenny and Pratcha to stay where they are, and hurry on a parallel course, expecting to intercept Goose at the point where his walkway intersects one of the main thoroughfares.

But when I reach the junction, there is no sign of him. The path is deserted.

Gustaw Belka has melted away like mist into the December air.

Postscript: DCI Zachary's Day Off

Officer Irving looked up from his desk as the door to the incident room swung open.

The new arrival was his superior, DCI Amelia Zachary, and she did not appear to be in the best of moods. She was dressed in a beige coat and, as she entered the room, was plucking something from the front of her brown skirt and muttering under her breath.

"I didn't expect to see you today, boss," Irving said. "I thought it was your day off."

"It is," Zachary replied tersely.

She moved to the coffee pot, and poured herself a mug of hot dark slop.

"Disgusting," she pronounced.

"Oh, you were meeting that Braddock guy this afternoon, weren't you?" Irving persisted. "I remember now. How did that go?"

The DCI's response was a grunt.

"He couldn't help us with finding Belka then? Or shed any light on who the unidentified body might be?"

She shook her head.

"He was useless. What about you? Have you made any progress on that front?"

"Not really. I figured that following the information from Pearl Webster about her husband and Belka sharing the same dentist, we should check the dental records for Belka. But no luck. His records were destroyed when Banerjee's surgery was torched."

"What was the fucking point of that?" Zachary snarled at him.

"Well, I, um," Irving stammered. *"In the absence of any other leads, I thought that maybe Braddock might have been mistaken about meeting Belka, or that it was somebody passing themself off as Belka. And, if that was somebody else, then the John Doe who was killed with Webster might well be Belka…"*

His explanation fizzled out, and Zachary fixed him with a hard stare.

"You're a bloody idiot, Irving. If you'd been paying proper attention, you'd have known that Braddock knew Gustaw Belka from years back. So, he wouldn't have been mistaken about that. Unless you think that he imagined meeting him?" she added sarcastically.

"No, boss."

"No, indeed. Let's not get too fanciful here. David Braddock might be many things, but he's not the sort of person who talks to ghosts. Of that, I'm sure."

AUTHOR'S AFTERWORD

Virtually all the information in this novel on the London Underground is based on detailed research, recorded interviews and site visits. But in the interests of accuracy, I should point out that – for dramatic purposes – I have taken a few liberties, most notably with British Museum station. Underground elements of the station still exist but it is not accessible in the way that I have described, since the overground building was demolished before the action in *Possessed by Death* took place. A commercial premises now stands on the spot.

So, should you be set on accessing the closed station to verify my description of what remains below ground, the only route into it is a hazardous and illegal one – which I would not recommend.

And, yes, I could have used one of the other derelict stations as a setting, but there was something irresistible about murder victims being hidden in Central London, only a stone's throw from the historic British Museum, that I couldn't resist.

John Dolan, October 2023

RELATED BOOKS

If you have enjoyed *Possessed by Death,* there are seven other David Braddock novels for you to dip into:

Everyone Burns
Hungry Ghosts
A Poison Tree
Running on Emptiness
Restless Earth
Two Rivers, One Stream
Everyone Dies

In addition, *Land of Red Mist* is the story of David's father Edward, and his adventures in Malaya in the 1950s.

These are all available from Amazon in paperback and Kindle formats.

ABOUT THE AUTHOR

"Makes a living by travelling, talking a lot and sometimes writing stuff down. Galericulate author, polymath and occasional smarty-pants."

John Dolan hails from a small town in the North-East of England. Before turning to writing, his career encompassed law and finance. He has run businesses in Europe, South and Central America, Africa and Asia. He and his wife Fiona currently divide their time between Thailand and the UK.

He is probably best known for his mystery series *Time, Blood and Karma* and *Children of Karma.*

All John's books are available on Amazon worldwide in Kindle and paperback formats.

You can find all these books on his Author Page on Amazon or Goodreads or follow John's ramblings on X (formerly Twitter) @JohnDolanAuthor or see his latest writing news and sign up for his free Newsletter on his website https://www.johndolanauthor.com/